The Flight

The Flight

Ruth Stephan

ALFRED A. KNOPF · NEW YORK · 1956

This is a Borzoi Book published by Alfred A. Knopf, Inc.

FIRST EDITION

 Published simultaneously in Canada by McClelland and Stewart Limited.

Manufactured in the United States of America

L. C. catalog card number: 56-8913

To Christina's unhesitating friends,

particularly Marguerite Young

and John Stephan

The Flight

I

I SHALL burn these papers, of course. Being a Queen, all that I say and do is magnified to common minds, and, to them, my thoughts are as mysterious as the expanses of the Frozen Ocean. They do not dare to approach them. How can they understand, then, the inward dimensions of the reasons for my abdication of the throne? After I have settled in Rome and have time for such literary purposes, I may select the parts of these memoirs that everyone may read and digest, but now, as I examine my heart and the peregrinations of a spirit that astonishes me although it is my own, I can have no confidants. A secret is more rare than one thinks. Men have confidants, these confidants have others, and the chain eventually winds back to oneself. I will have no one, that is, except God. There is one's self to ask, one's self to answer on the pulsating problems of life, but the human heart is an abyss unknown to itself; the One who made it is the only one penetrating its fathoms.

A year and a half has passed since I, Christina, the last of the Vasas and sole offspring of the great Gustav Adolf, voluntarily surrendered the throne of Sweden in my twenty-eighth year, in the year of our Christian civilization 1654, so that I could enter a new life where I would be a new kind of Queen. How relieved I was! The fullness of leisure I had prepared for myself was ready, I could correct the errors of my past life without repentance, having joyfully done good to humanity and punished those who deserved punishment, having sacrificed myself cheerfully to the interests of the State above all other considerations, having resigned without apparent difficulty. The personal era opening before me sparkled like the heavens on a summer night with crowds of stars, warm and close, ready to fall into my hand. At last I could go to Rome, my spiritual home, the city golden with sun and art, the city of palaces that are palaces and not cold tombs, the city of Michelangelos and plump Veroneses, not scrawny Dürers, the city of music and cardinals, of manuscripts and savants, the city of Bernini who is alive, not of Descartes who lies dead. It would be good to be far away from Sweden, from the North of the frigid ground where the culture, too, stiffens from lack of warmth and is sluggish in awakening to a proper springtime. I am free of it, I thought, even if it is at the expense of my crown.

A strange thing, however, has happened to me. Until recently I was certain of controlling my destiny by my will and cleverness, having succeeded in doing so beyond the realization of those around me. Not long ago, in April to be exact, the week before Easter, the news reached me in Brussels of the death of my mother, Maria Eleonora. I had seen her last in the castle at Nyköping, after my abdication, when I stopped to bid her farewell on my journey out of Sweden. She had been in tears, as usual, not for any sympathy or loss of me, but because I was doing something she did not want me to do. We never had had a deep affection for one another. That is why it is strange, the effect of her death on me. At first I thought it a momentary blindness, self-imposed by my putting on mourning in my mind as well as in my dress, the kind that is apt to come with a sudden change of habits when the new lacks the definiteness and spice of the old. Months have passed, summer lapsed into autumn, my carriages have begun to roll, slowly, toward Rome, yet the melancholy mood has refused to depart. It has attached itself closer than my shadow, interfering with my thoughts and dulling my conversation, and I begin to fear I am growing to be like the interlocked trees of the palace park with evening always lying on their branches.

When I abdicated, my reasons seemed as clear to me as the framed pictures on the walls of my apartment. I could trace their lines and colors, then, as easily as if I had composed them myself. Now the lines begin to blur, the colors to melt and change, and I do not know whether the fault lies in the pictures or in my vision. Perhaps I did not abdicate for the reasons I thought I did. I am not free of Sweden as I had hoped to be. At any moment the new King and Councillors may cut off my income and turn me into a pauper. When they hear I have become a Catholic, will they not do just that, hating Catholicism as they do? How could they permit the daughter of Gustav Adolf, the champion of Lutheranism who fought to erase Catholicism from the North, who turned the tide of the Thirty Years' War, to be a black scar on his victory? How could they permit me to mar his glory in the eyes of the world, to question the right of his cause? Would they not rather see me dead? I wish I could stop worrying.

When I awoke this morning, for instance, I could not remember where I was. Blinking against the entombing darkness, the stillness, the unworldliness, I rubbed my hand on a strange silkiness. Was it reindeer skin matted with bygone icicles? No! I had left Sweden, hadn't I? Christina, I told myself, you must shed the dark, you must know you have escaped. You are only in an unfamiliar bed, covered with old velvet. The stuff is wreathed in age, recumbent from slight usage. This cannot be a palace. I shook the fringe of the bedcurtain to let in the light. It shivered, gold and silver, in its own dull glow, no other. Pushing it aside, I stepped onto the cold floor, into the gray slumber of the chamber. Better to face the swords of the day than the ghosts of the mind.

Near me a ceramic stove shone in the gloom, colored like spring grass, miniature blue-winged angels fluttering on it, its pillars cold, sleeping, wrapped in stony verdant vines and bubbles of blue grape clusters. It had no hint of welcome, no warmth. I looked around at shadowy chests and heavy chairs, at a room long, not broad, with carved beams bearing its ceiling. Ah, there in the dimness at the other end was my throne, hardly nicked from its travels. From the beam above, a bearded wooden face jeered down at it. I nodded at the stillness. I was in the Tyrol, in—what was the name of the village? Zirl?—a few miles from Innsbruck. We had arrived the day before. It was, it is, the last day of October.

Drawing a thick coat around me, I opened a window at the back of the room. There, waiting outside, was Dawn, the rosy-fingered, love of Ulysses and all travelers, beckoning to me that the moment had come for us to journey together. She leaned her pink arms on the mountaintops, a mist in the valley lay a silver cloth in her lap, the village houses huddled like toads at her feet. In the distance, on mountains where autumn had splashed red, brown, and ocher down the slopes, her breath blew caps of pale blue on the peaks. Up the sides of the near mountains stretched the dark blue of pine forests, yellow larch trees waving cool flames among them, here and there stark groups of birches. Higher, Dawn touched the snow spots with her dazzling fingers, idly, playfully, then, sighing until one leaf and another turned its back and trembled, she opened her hand wide and from her palm floated a whole wide golden sky.

She had given the signal. The overture began. From the inn-yard beneath rose the first strains of the country man's fugue, roosters crowing, geese protesting, sparrows gossiping, horses wheezing for their oats. Doors creaked open, banged shut. Boots stamped on the dirt. Voices, speaking German, had the sound of water bumping over rocks.

"The old sow is out again."

"Fetch her, brother, fetch her."

"The Count calls for his gruel."

"He'll curl his mustache while he waits."

"Good life to you, here is the Poisoner."

"Poissonnet, wife, Poissonnet."

"Ho. Tell me, is it true your Queen is half bird?"

"Your tongue is awake, but your head is not, brother."

"They say she perches at night on the bedpost, that she needs no coverlet, her feathers being cozy enough."

"It would be best to perch on a bedpost here. The straw you gave me bristled at me all the night."

"Otto, Otto, where do you go now?"

"To the plowing. It is a fair day."

"Stupid! The horses cannot plow today. They pull the post chariot to Innsbruck. The master himself drives the Queen. Quick, to their brushing! My Lord says the horses must shine brighter than the Emperor's buckle."

A servant fellow moved into my view, yawning, scratching in his rumpled hair. I leaned from my window and called to him.

"What o'clock is it?"

He looked up and, seeing me, his face seemed to freeze, his mouth hanging open. Not a word did he say, but turned and ran out of sight as if he were nipped by demons and had to find his godfather to ask him the name of the hour, be it evil or godly. Well, I thought, I am not as ugly as Medusa. At least he was able to run away.

A tap at my door and Poissonnet, his cheeks and sharp nose reddened by the freshness of the morning, came in, Poissonnet, Clairet Poissonnet, my valet, my ghost-chaser, my friend, my secret minister. He remains his taciturn self, as little disturbed by our change in situation as if abdication took place every Tuesday, caring no more whether I am Catholic or Lutheran, although the rest of the world may crack and scream at the difference, than if religion were a label on a jar of his famous jelly, never letting anything disturb his valet duties and the dozens of commissions, big and little, that no one else seems able to do. It is remarkable that this illiterate man, this French innkeeper's son who cannot speak even French properly, mixing it with Swedish, Italian, and Spanish until he sounds like two crows competing in a duet, and who cannot write a word of any language, is the most capable man I know. He becomes the exception to make me wonder about the value of books. When I am speaking to him he stands in front of me awkwardly, his thick boots on such big feet that his thin sprightly body is poised on them as on a branch. I cannot believe he grasps what I am saying, yet he understands perfectly the meaning of the words and all the echoes behind them. His sleepy eyes observe everything, he tells my secrets to no one, and brings everyone else's secrets to me. When he drinks at a tavern I am sure he opens his puckered mouth only to drink beer. If I had stayed in Sweden I could not have resisted making him one of my Councillors.

Disdainfully he set the stove to a glowing warmth, clucking at Tyroleans who did not know how to keep a Queen comfortable, no better than wild mountain goats they were, sleeping on straw the most of them, eating old crusts of bread, they had best go to France to take lessons from his father, there was an innkeeper for you, an ancient, but oh the sauce he could make for a fowl!

"Clairet," I cut off his soliloquy. "You and your friends were drinking beer last night. You rivaled the owls with your hoots. Where were you, in the kitchen? The planks of this *Gasthof* are not thick enough."

Poissonnet pursed his lips. "There is plenty to listen to, Your Majesty."

"Politics?"

"Not justly. There is the Archduke, you know."

Yes, the Archduke, I knew, the Emperor's cousin, Ferdinand Carl, who rules the Tyrol, a sensuous-mouthed elegant fool, grown from his mother's blue-eyed darling to be the murderer of his mother's lover. What can you expect of a pretty specimen nurtured on Marino rather than Cicero or Plato? He had ridden to Zirl to welcome me, had paced the floor of my chamber for three quarters of an hour, stepping slowly so as not to distress his red curls, constantly clasping and unclasping his tiny hands as if to keep from applauding his own words, rippling courtier's words, the same the world over.

"It was his embarrassment at your visit," Poissonnet said.

"Embarrassment!" Damn me, a worse fool than I had thought.

"The honor, Your Majesty, the honor of it! Where was his money? Not in his coffers. They were so light he could lift them and hear the lonely pieces rattling together for company. How he groaned! Christina, the Pallas of the North, the most spectacular Queen in the living world, comes to the palace of a Habsburg. Cleopatra on an elephant, Helen of Troy on a white charger, Venus herself on a cloud of pearls—who could compare with the Snow Queen riding to Rome on the Pope's blessing? And he, the famous Archduke of the Tyrol, miserably poor, with nothing for her welcome but a gray glory!"

"Famous?" I questioned it. He must have started the rumor himself.

"The poor man had to do what he hated, attend to money. His salt mines were the thing. He could get a loan on them. And then he borrowed whatever else he needed, wagonloads of silver cutlery and gold plates, from the Archbishop of Salzburg, and they arrived in such numbers they still sit on the kitchen floor in the castle, for nobody knows where to put them, the cooks and stewards making paths through silver and gold to carry their cabbages and leeks. He borrowed servants from whatever neighboring court could boast of them with combed hair and indoor habits, and carpenters, masons, painters, woodworkers, all such. Special wine he brought from South Tyrol, fresh roes from Füssen, from Kitzbühel, crayfish—two thousand, Your Majesty!—salmon, trout, all manner of fresh, salted, and smoked fish from Brigenz, and special cooks to cook them with their special helpers. The fish pasties—"

"Clairet!"

"This you will like, Your Majesty. The Archduke has brought singers and actors, lute-players and musicians of the viola da gamba, all that you like, from Italy, for you, Your Majesty. They say The Golden Rose in Innsbruck overflows from one night into another, that the owner has no sleep for his old bones, that it is such a center of brawls, sudden romances, and unlaced tales as you never have seen. And no, it was not enough for the Archduke, the theater he already had built, the one so big it had to be turned into a riding school, and, now, set again as a royal theater, no, he must have another theater, a Court Theater, for you, built by the biggest machines ever seen in the Tyrol. Oh and the cleaning of cannons, the polishing of halberds, the practicing on trumpets, the stacking for bonfires! The town is in a turmoil of preparation, your entertainment, Your Majesty, the sole industry left to it. Even the coffinmaker hammers on stage scenery, for no one dares to die while you can be seen and talked about."

"This is a farce!" I stormed, torn between anger and laughter. "Do they think my public confession of faith is a farce, too?" Dear God, I prayed, You know I have loved comedies and balls, but never have I confused them with Your worship. This revelry is not of my making. Please do not let it be my ruin. Is it not enough that the Pope insists I make public that which I begged to keep secret, my conversion to the Catholic faith? Is it not enough that the Swedish Councillors may divest me of my income once the intelligence of my act has reached them?

"No, no, Your Majesty," Poissonnet's tone rose in surprise. "The Archduke had word no sooner than Your Majesty of the holy honor to befall him. About the time that Father Malines arrived to inform Your Majesty of His Holiness's pleasure—two days ago, that is—the Archduke received in audience the Papal Nuncio sent to him, the famous Lucas Holstenius. When he heard the motive of his coming and the function to be performed in the city of his residence, he was filled, some say, with wonder and unspeakable joy at the conspicuous glory for his court. Others say he was unspeakable for other reasons. It is certain he came from the audience wringing his hands like a wet towel and was speechless for an hour or more, although his wife, the Archduchess, pestered him with questions. How, he finally sputtered, could he clear the town of singers and dancers and cannonball-makers and boisterous farmers come for the fun, how could he stop the workmen urged to race to a finish on his theaters, how could he calm the street crowds to a pious gait and saintly looks while the beer was still warming their hearts, how could he make the town turn a flip-flop to this supreme religious occasion?

"His wife, being Italian, was at no loss for words. 'No balls? No comedies?' she cried. 'What shall I do with my new scarves, fringes, fans, and embroideries, my colored ribbons, ruffs, and spangles? What of the gowns I have ordered in haste, my silks, damasks, and cloths of gold and lace, my red velvet dress with the lovely flounce? Oh! To waste those thin tiffanies, those tissues in pale blue and pink that my sewing man complained so to find! And when, again, can I wear my coronets, bracelets, and combs, my earrings, my beads of pearl, and my precious rings?'

"Thus she wailed while her husband moaned to miss the pleasures he loved, yet must he do so, being an Archduke subject to the divine guidance of the Pope. Then his wife, her Italian practical ways coming through, tendered advice with her own divine spark.

" 'My love,' she said, 'we are being foolish to act as if all the festivities we have prepared must be at an end. This is a momentous function, but it is not like Lent, when the bells are tied and worldly display restricted. And even then, my love, when Easter Day arrives, do not the bells ring out while we all rejoice in the affirmation of faith? A confession of faith is solemn, how solemn! My soul bows in reverence. Ah, it is glorious, too, it is a triumph to have won another soul for the Church, and the more eminent the person, the greater the triumph. It would be wrong, wrong, my love, not to celebrate the conversion of the great Queen of the North with all the means at our disposal.'

"Now you would believe, Your Majesty, that the Archduke would be pleased to have such a clever wife. Not in this world! He stamped his foot in his satin slipper.

" 'You would ruin me! The Pope would demand penance for such worldliness, more than I could pay. Where can I borrow more? Are you a fool?' And the Archduke paced back and forth as his wife calmed her tongue and lowered her head.

" 'What a pity,' she said at last, 'to waste everything we have done! You are right, of course. We cannot offend His Holiness when the eyes of Europe are upon us.' She paused. 'They say His Holiness is fond of plays, as is all Rome, so you are doubly right, my love. It would not do to outshine Rome, as you would do in your new theater. Who in Rome would spend fifteen tons of gold on one occasion? What palace there has a theater as magnificent as yours? When have such glittering costumes been fashioned? Are there finer musicians in Rome than Boni and Conci, who have traveled to Innsbruck for you? For whom else would Anna Renzini leave Venice? What prince in Rome has machines to bring Venus from the sky, her heavenly car drawn by pigeons, as in dreams and legends? Who, there, would dare have a chariot drawn by lions race across the stage? And the Moors, the men from Mars, the ballets of sword-flashing soldiers in Cyprus, the ghosts that vanish into the air? Ah, you are right, my love. It would not be pleasant to have the princes in Rome jealous and whisper against you to His Holiness. Your devoutness will be proved by your rejection of the wonders you have prepared.'

" 'My devoutness does not need to be proved. You see you are wrong again.'

" 'Yes, my love.'

" 'In truth, there is nothing sacrilegious about the comedies. Their music is quite enchanting and stirs noble feelings in one.'

" 'Do you believe so?'

" 'If I had had more time, if I had been notified of the religious character of the Queen's visit, I would have chosen plays of a sacred nature. Appolonio could have written one just as easily on the life of St. Birgitta.'

" 'Yes, my dear, how truly you speak.'

" 'What do they think I can change in two days? We have been preparing for a month for the Queen's visit, and we thought that undue hurry. I believe it is quite enough to omit the balls and dancing. The plays may be light, but there is no harm in them.'

"'And you will stop all the dancing?'

"'Not the ballets, for what would the play be without ballet? Do not be so hasty to change everything!'

"Thus, Your Majesty, the matter was decided. There will be fireworks and bonfires, music and comedies, banquets, of course, as before. Now the carpenters are hammering in the court chapel to erect a special platform for the public ceremony, the court seamstress is plying her needle on a red velvet cushion for you to kneel upon, the court preacher is studying the history of your life to choose the right theme for his sermon, and the Jesuits are arguing with the Franciscans that to them and to their chapel belongs the honor of the ceremony, they being the ones who waged for your conversion."

"They do not have much time to argue," I was saying when a tapping on the door turned from a soft politeness to a sharp insistence. Poissonnet, a man who does not like his eloquence disturbed, had ignored it. At my nod he smoothed his face to its usual immobile expression and answered the summons. It was the Archduke's chamberlain to wish me a good morning and ask, in the name of his master, if my night's rest had been pleasant. The official day had begun.

By afternoon the bustle in the innyard was immense, the horses stomping, grooms steadying them and fastening harnesses, servants running out with trunks and boxes and dusting the cushions of the carriages. The owner of the inn, Lord von Steinmetz, in a fine green coat, strode in and through the activity, his eye on each detail, his voice quiet, his hand quick, directing, adjusting. The hundreds of persons in my suite swarmed the streets of the village in the sharp sunlight, their chatter, laughter, and orders to one another marking them as a migrating flock. It is a good-spirited day, I thought, as I moved to the door of the inn. There was General Montecuccoli pulling at his mustache, maintaining his dignity as the Ambassador of the Emperor in a fine posture at the side of the disorder. My secretaries were buzzing about unnecessarily, as usual. The ladies of the suite, holding their gowns from the dust, were stepping among the curious villagers on the arms of their cavaliers to reach their carriages.

The local postilion arrived in his coach coat, his ruff, and his high-steepled hat and began to climb on his horse, which was to lead the procession. Just as he threw his leg over the rump, Poissonnet ran out, almost under the horse's nose, chasing a red feathered cap, which I could swear he had thrown himself, and the horse fell to kicking and dancing as prettily as in a show. Down went the steepled hat into the feathering dust, almost the ruff, cloak, and man, the cries rising: "Hans! Hans! Have a care! That horse will throw you to the Devil!" The Devil had hold of his nose, I'll say, and was pulling him down, when out ran Von Steinmetz and grasped the bridle. Too bad, I considered, as the horse heaved a last wild sigh and Hans reasserted his gravity, there has not been much gaiety here.

Where was Don Pimentel? Poissonnet had not been able to find him this morning. I was to ride in the post carriage as a favor to Lord von Steinmetz, who would hold the reins himself, not wishing to trust the charge of so valuable a personage, he said, to anyone else. His carriage stood before the door, bright in new paint, with four muscular horses harnessed to it. Otto, I noticed, had done his work well. The beasts shone like polished bronze. Their strong necks arched, their nostrils extended in impatience to be away, their ears twitching, alert for the signal to start. How could I leave without seeing Pimentel? The wretch! Where was he? Then I saw him hurrying to me through the crowd, resplendent in his French clothes and plumed hat, smiling so to see me that I could not resist smiling in return.

"Christina," he said when he was beside me, "you look wonderful. How the day becomes you!"

I laughed without wishing to. One of Pimentel's charms is his ability to find something about one to compliment. Nothing had changed in or on me since the day before, I wore again my fur-trimmed gray skirt and jerkin, and, not having had time to comb my hair, I had wrapped my head in a piece of black taffeta. It is Pimentel who is the peacock, but, although I abhor the habit in women, I do not mind it in him, for he is neither arrogant nor idle, his gorgeousness being in his distinguished bearing and in his extravagant clothes, his brocades and colored satins, his plumes, his ribbons and laces, cut and draped in the latest fashion permitted the French court. And he is careless of being a peacock, tall and dark, appearing far younger than his fifty years, his mustache a curling black, his eyes deceptively somber in his olive-toned skin, not a trace of stiffness in his manner or his movements. He tenders a genuine courtliness that never is jarred into an ungracious moment. We had formed a close friendship when he was in Sweden as the Ambassador of Spain while I was on the throne, and he had been one of the few persons who had accompanied me from the old life into the new. I like the ardor of his interests, the skill in his persuasions. I like his intelligent attention for me.

"Everything is arranged," he continued, "the reception at the Tiergarten outside Innsbruck while the light holds, no further formalities today, as you wished. Your evening is yours alone. Everything has been arranged." His tone lowered. "Is your heart arranged? Are there shadows on it?"

His is the voice in the crowd, the chord of privacy chiming through the babble, his the assurance to make the leap in the dark a natural flight, to make the search for Virtue in an untamed universe a less lonely one. His is the voice I hear as I sit, now, at this ebony desk in the palace in Innsbruck. We have had the reception at the Tiergarten, the formal entrance into this Tyrolean city with mountains for its neighbors. The welcoming trumpets have died away, the Archduke's twittered phrases and the soft answers of the Archduchess have faded from the room. Poissonnet has lit the tapers and gone. Outside, the mountains lean over the town, their peaks blacking out the stars. The wind, in rising, whistling through the chimneytops, creaking the grilles over doorways, twists a lonely sound around the tower: *Everything is arranged. Is your heart arranged? Are there shadows on it?* Shadows! Pimentel, my dear Antonio, the shadows of centuries lie across my heart. How can I disperse them?

November 1. The Devil is here. He has followed me to Innsbruck. Today he snatched the life of a man, almost before my eyes. Was it in pique because he was deprived of my life? Was it not I he meant to take, I from whom he was pushed aside by some divine interceptor?

It happened shortly after the noon hour during the first meal of state. The table had been laid in my antechamber, an immense room, its walls exquisite with tapestries. The nobles of my suite and the favored ones of the Tyrolean court were eating and talking in a high mood. I presided, on my right the Archduke and his serious young brother, their feathered hats low on their brows, on my left Anna di Medici, the Archduchess, rustling in silk and jewels, just below us Don Pimentel, the most splendid of all. The food was delicious, dish after dish of it borne in on the borrowed gold plate by pages. At the door stood the Archduke's high chamberlain, surveying the food as it passed, occasionally tasting a dish. Continuous music lifted our senses, vivacious silver trumpets, then a mass of stringed instruments, bows singing Carissimi, Monteverdi, oh, these Italians, I was thinking, their singing souls! I found my head moving in time to the melodies, the world around me colored in harmony. I threw my arms to heaven in delight.

"God! My thanks! What music!" Then, to the Archduke: "Who is the fantastic fellow with the little violin?"

I can see, now, the Archduke leaning toward me, framing a name with round, pink lips. I never heard what he said, a frantic kind of call, a heaviness dropped on the floor, a sibilant commotion in the next room, and one of the Austrian barons hurried in to whisper in the Archduke's ear. The news of the whisper went around as instantaneously as if it had been beat on a kettledrum. The high chamberlain, the food-taster, he at the door, was writhing in a fit of unknown origin. Poison? Everyone looked the word, no one spoke it. In a moment he was dead. I felt a crackling within me, whether of excitement, of nervousness, of exultation, I do not know. The man might have deserved to die. I was alive! I raised my goblet of ice-cooled water to my lips, drank, and picked up a piece of wild fowl. Next to me I overheard the Archduke's pressured words to his baron:

"A post-mortem. Immediately."

It was Pimentel who broke the uneasy hush, lifting his glass of wine. "To the long life of Her Majesty, Christina, Queen of Sweden!"

"To Her Majesty," echoed the husky voices, "a long life!"

The viola da gamba started to play a solo, conversation went on, the banquet went on, life went on. That is eternity, I thought, the going on. A long life! What is a long life? It is eternity going on longer than long that is hard to catch, to hold, even for a little while, eternity the golden medal always rolling out of sight. Do I fear death, my death, the explosion of my private world, the vanishing of a thousand dreams, the leap away of the lion? I am wedded to the present, in life, in death, the present and I are one. And does not the present carry eternity as a passenger in its coach, the passenger who never reaches his destination? I shook my head at the paradox. What of another's death, of the man, for instance, who lay freshly dead in the next room? Can I distinguish any feeling for him that is not feeling for myself in disguise? Can I say I feel sorrow for him when it is for myself I wince, I to whom a skull has been served on a gilded platter? What perception have I of his dreams, his lion? They say some lions are glad to escape a cage.

When the crowd had gone and Pimentel and I were alone in my apartment, I threw myself on a chair, sighing relief.

"It must have been apoplexy," he began.

"The Devil took him, poor soul."

In detail we went over the event, the persons in my suite, the Archduke's court and his politics, the possibilities of treachery and its advantages. I suppose everyone in the palace was talking the same subject. Pimentel did not favor poisoning as the cause of the death. I was not sure. It was, he said, completely the wrong atmosphere, the wrong time for a poisoning. I replied any time would be right to a poisoner. It was the opportunity that counted. The part that troubled Pimentel was the poor man's dying without receiving the holy sacraments. He grieved with him for the quick passing without a priest. Who knows what the wretch had done, how he had sinned, to be so burdened?

"You believe he will go to hell for that, that God will have no mercy?" I asked.

"Who wishes to take the chance? I will be glad, I tell you, when you are safely in the Church. Thank God we have not much longer to wait."

"Antonio." He was leaning comfortably in his chair in an embroidered silk coat, lace cuffs falling gracefully onto his strong soldier hands. "When you were on the battlefield did you fear death? And if you did, was it for its own sake or that you might die without a priest?"

"A soldier's thoughts are of fighting, not of death."

"Never?"

The serious line of his mouth did not change, nor the light in his still, dark eyes, but the lace cuff moved, a finger was tracing a thought, remembering. "A soldier who says he never is afraid is a liar. And who would not want the familiar hand to lead one into the unfamiliar when the hand is God's?" This he said, then he would speak no more of it. Never can I press him into a long discussion on death or eternity. A quip, a polished observation, and he shifts the subject. "Your blue eyes will grow dim trying to gaze such distances," he would banter. His worldliness becomes a shield, his brocaded clothes, plumes, and fripperies a positive armor against the unknown. Now his evasion was a notice for action.

"You must not forget Holstenius," he said. "He waits for you to appoint the day of the ceremony, and he tells me he bears a personal letter from the Pope for you."

"A letter from the Pope! Have him come this instant! Where are you hiding this jewel of a Nuncio?"

I jumped up and began pacing the room in excitement. It is true I had forgotten Holstenius, Lucas Holstenius whom I had waited so long to meet. In thinking of death I had overlooked life. With Holstenius, the famed Keeper of the Vatican Library and the Canon of St. Peter's in Rome, I had carried on a secret correspondence for years. His letters, in script as beautiful as a sixteenth-century drawing, had found their way to me in Stockholm, and his descriptions of Rome, its myths and monuments, its line of popes and philosophers, its passions of art, had inflamed the desire I already had to make this fabled city my home. Who, better than he, who had written an impressive number of books on those subjects, could tell me? I do enjoy, yes, I respect, authority.

How could I prepare myself for a favorable impression while Pimentel was on his way to fetch him? He comes, I reminded myself, on a holy mission, the chosen instrument of His Holiness. I must quiet my wild heart with prayer. In my chamber there are three silver statues, the Virgin, the Christ, and St. Anne. Before the Son of God I knelt, close, so I almost could whisper into His ear, thanking Him, promising. "This heart was Thine since it first beat in my breast. Nothing can content me, nothing satisfy me but Thou alone. Thou art all and I am nothing. Thou knowest how often in a language unknown to common persons have I prayed to be enlightened by Thy Grace, how I made a vow to obey Thee at the expense of my life and my fortune."

On I prayed until I heard footsteps approaching. Had I been listening for them all the time, I asked myself, can it be that my prayer is not deep and true, that my ear, turned inward, upward, cannot be made oblivious of its surroundings?

"Thou alone understand," I whispered to God, "how the rivers of my mind seem to flow in many directions, yet, in Thy vastness, they all reach Thee."

I rose, hurried into the antechamber, warm with expectation, to find no Nuncio, only Poissonnet shutting the door. I almost screamed in my exasperation, forgetting my vow not to use oaths aloud.

"Damn me, you aren't the Nuncio!"

He cocked his head, "No, Your Majesty. It is Clairet."

"What are you doing here?"

He bowed. "My Lord Holstenius changes his purple robe for his black to present himself to Your Majesty."

Proper, proper. My hot wind subsided.

"The post-mortem, Your Majesty." Poissonnet was eager.

Not now, I told him, picking up my little brown copy of Vergil. Let that river follow its own course.

When, a quarter of an hour later, Pimentel ushered Holstenius into my apartment, my first reaction was surprise that such a significant scholar could appear so insignificant. Pimentel was a magic giant beside him. Grayed, slight, so slight it seemed he could slip between the covers of an old folio, he spoke to me in a hoarse, low voice, expressing his pleasure at having been chosen by His Holiness for such an auspicious mission, and requesting that I name the glorious day for the ceremony. The Church waited to embrace its cherished daughter. Let there be no more waiting.

"The ceremony may be in two days' time," I said.

The Nuncio's thin cheeks wrinkled with delight. "The third of November. A good day. The day of St. Winifred, patroness of virgins. The poor dear girl was beheaded for keeping her virginity. She refused to marry a prince." He shook his head in sympathy. "Seventh century. Yes, yes, His Holiness will be pleased."

I had chosen, unaware. I, too, as everyone knows, have refused to marry. But I am a Queen. Now, I thought, he will give me the Pope's letter. I smiled expectantly, and he smiled and nodded in return. Pimentel twirled his mustache. I could not ask for the letter. I began to question Holstenius on his scholarly studies, on Rome, speaking very quietly, kindly, else, I feared, his thin form would break or blow off or bend at my feet. What would he do,

I wondered, if I let out my manly boom of a laugh, the laugh no one can believe comes from a woman, a little woman at that?

For an hour or more he basked in history, the suns of the past lighting his face, spending his tongue on the treasures of the Vatican, on the obelisks from Egypt older than Rome itself, on Cleopatra's pearl and the pure marble grace of the Grecian Venus, on Michelangelo's "Last Judgment" and Dante's poems in his own hand.

"Dante!" I had to exclaim. "The prince of poets!"

Even more rare, he went on, writings from the sainted hand of Thomas Aquinas, letters from the bedeviled, like Luther and Henry VIII, books written on the leaves of trees, books in Hebrew, Syriac, Arabic, every language, books with pages garlanded in brilliant flowers, in birds and purple dragons, in saints illuminated in thick gold, books proving the humble adoration of God through dark stretches of years. When the treasures come to be numbered, he said, there will be no place in the world found as rich as the Vatican. And why not? Since the beginning of counted time, perhaps before, the Vatican has been the site of holy mysteries, even before it was realized to be God who made it holy. Did not those early people, the Etruscans, enthrone their oracles in that very spot, knowing it to be a place of divination? There, later, Roman Emperors promenaded by torchlight in the Vatican circus, Caligula, Nero, murderers of Truth, crazed worshippers of themselves, pallbearers of a false glory. "So the new grows out of the old, Your Majesty, so Truth rises a phœnix from its own ashes."

He ceased, rested a moment. "Your Majesty must excuse my verbosity. To such a scholar as yourself these repetitions will seem tiresome."

"I consider you do yourself more wrong than me when you endeavor to pass me off as a scholar, My Lord Holstenius. My ignorance will continually contradict you. When I am in Rome I hope you will be my guide to these wonders."

"Could there be a more honored pleasure than to be the guide of the great Queen of Sweden? The flame of your learning shines as far as Rome, Your Majesty, and farther, I would believe, did I know the world farther. There is not an Academy in Rome that does not anticipate your arrival with the liveliest joy that such a star should be added to our firmament."

"I shall be sorry to see you punished for your high opinion of me! You only can excuse yourself by admitting that you have flattered me. What advantage is it for you to have studied the ancient philosophers so carefully unless you learn from their writings to instruct princes rather than to flatter them?"

He demurred, his form trembling in a silent laugh. Then, with a surprising gesture of pomp, he presented to me the letter from His Holiness. With what gladness I read it!

"To our most dear Daughter in Christ, Greeting," I read, and on through a poetically embroidered welcome to the Roman Catholic faith and to Rome, "the city of true and heavenly learning," on to the delegating of the Canon of St. Peter's to assist me in my public profession and an admonition that "Your Majesty will be wanting in nothing that may shew you not unworthy of this most ample benefit, and that by your ready obsequiousness and hearty obedience you will testify to all that you have earnestly sought and most ardently received the Catholic faith." The letter was expressed in the most affectionate terms. Still, I blushed. It is one thing to speak humility, another to feel it in every bone in the body. I am being readied, I decided, for the authority I must bow to.

To Holstenius I said: "I shall show His Holiness my joy in the letters I shall write to him as soon as I am able," and signified that the audience was at an end. Gravely he bowed and left, Pimentel accompanying him, the black-robed and the silk-coated passing through the wide door together.

I supped alone and now, again, I am with my friend, the ebony desk. My emotions toss and are mixed like the waves of two currents meeting in a storm. I, unworthy? I, who sacrificed a throne, who refused to give in to the past, who am not afraid to face the Devil himself for the sake of my faith? Is it my fault I was not born a Catholic? I see I shall be condemned by the Protestants and despised by the Catholics, a migrant bird denied rest. Dear God, why are not those who are truly guilty punished for their sins? But who can find their guilt, who can unwind the thistles from their minds, who can uncover the poisonous seeds blown into the forest? How clever the Devil is! How he must smile to watch the guilty, unaware of their guilt, walking in the bliss of belief in their own righteousness!

How many times the world has asked, and will ask, why I have acted as I have, why I have abdicated the throne and left Sweden. I have made no answer, for the world wants a short answer, a clearly cut, simple reason, and my answer is long and blurred, I am not sure I see it myself, wound in, as it is, in my past and in Sweden's past. Here in Innsbruck, cradled by mountains, in a town not my own, a borrowed town, I shall write out my long answer. Here I shall have many hours alone, alone, that is, except for the ghosts of the past and the presence of my mother.

The presence of my mother! How naturally I write that! It is true. Now that she is dead, Maria Eleonora is more real to me than ever she was in life, her slender figure moving into whatever room I sit in, her nervous brown eyes questioning my motives, my flight, my correctness of behavior, her hair turned white, although not with age, an eternal query lurking behind her tight lips: *What of me?* Her pursuit floats around me like her sweet perfume. I rarely thought of her in Sweden, and I thought even less of what her opinion of me must be. She, too, disliked Sweden, but she had neither the wit nor the fiber to escape successfully. If she comes to me now as a misplaced soul, what can I do? It is too late to change her lonely, jeweled career, too late to suggest solutions, to provide comfort, yet her dark eyes carry an accusation, as if I could have helped her, as if I should not have sheltered my secrets from her, as if she would prevent my going further until I explained myself, as if, with her cold delicate hands, she would pull together curtains shutting out a vision of my future. Where has she found the energy to demand an explanation? From death? Is my mother a fugitive from her grave, a Walpurgis Night wanderer who will not return? These ghosts must return! Who can bear them waiting, watching, day and night, for answers denied them in life?

Perhaps when I have written what I feel I must write, Maria Eleonora, Oxenstierna, and how many others will cease disturbing me. I would like to leave them all behind with the snow and iced lakes, the shabby towns and Lutheran gloom of the country I have left.

II

I HAVE decided to go back to the very beginning, not only of my life, but of what caused my being Christina. There is nothing more strange than life, nothing more absolute than its path, nothing more natural than its direction. In our ignorance and conceit of power we cannot see, always, at the time of a decision, that life is inevitable, that the past boils up within us and sweeps us on. We seem to be directing our destinies when we are, in truth, holding firmly to the course of our deepest beliefs.

My past was impressed on me in early childhood. I had a lineage of Kings to account for, I was told, and a strong country. *My* country, Sweden. It is a country of vast forests and cold distances, where the hills, stretching into the North beyond what the eye can see, lie prostrate under a thick blanket of pine and spruce. The rivers radiating into almost every part of the land are the best roads, far better than the rough, infrequent, ill-kept highways, and through the long winter they are the only ones, ribbons of ice over which the sleds glide in a swift passage. Few travelers discover the need to visit the North, thus few realize that the Kingdom of Sweden and Gothland with its dominion the Dukedom of Finland sprawls across the frozen tip of the world, more than twice as large as the Kingdom of France, having the Baltic Sea on the south, Muscovy to the east, the mysteries of Lapland to the north, and the unpassable snow-capped mountains we call The Keel to keep Norway from us on the west.

It was the notable activity of the sun, they say, that first brought men to the North. After the Universal Deluge, when the propagators of mankind descended from Mount Ararat, as Noah's ark came to rest, they dispersed in various directions. Those who traveled toward the North, curious about the phenomena of the celestial bodies, found that the farther they went the longer the summer sun stayed in the heavens, and, contrariwise, the shorter the winter sun gave its light, circling lower than in the lands they knew. A number of men resolved to discover where the different heights of the sun and the inequality of the days and nights might terminate and pursued the answer to its cold conclusion. They were remarkably fascinated with the North Star, which seemed to continue fixed and unmoved while the other stars underwent perpetual revolutions. "Surely," they said to one another, "where such a magnificent star has found a home must be a region of extraordinary happenings. It has left the eternal search of stars through the heavens. We shall make its land the end of our search, too." They found, of course, that the North was a better home for a star than for a man, but they stayed, having traveled so far. Noah's grandson Magog, chief of those who came, reigned several years, then, having formed a kingdom, returned to Cæol-Syria, leaving one of his five sons in his place. This son, Suenon, the first King of Sweden, is my divine ancestor, so it can be seen that I am of a lineage as old as or older than any in Europe, dating back to eighty-eight years after the Deluge.

Most of the country, still, is of birds, lakes, and beasts, more tempting to wild things than to culture-loving men. Not long ago a hawk, caught in his Northern paradise, showed the length of his pilgrimage in the banding on his legs. From France he was, *Je suis au Roy* inscribed on the gold band of one leg, *Duc de Chevereuse me garde* on the silver one of the other. What were kings and dukes to him, himself an aerial lord? Who can blame him his flight to freedom, or what he felt to be freedom, soaring toward a widening sky from his French castle to seek his own pigeons, partridges, and yerpers, to watch from his own fragrant treetops for a shuttle of life in greenery, to listen for bears or elk, to be part of the great woods, his heritage? What strong spirit can resist freedom for long or be held back from discovering what his kind of freedom is? The hawk sensed it, took it. What of the heron who summers with us, then flies to the lands of Southern Europe, to food and civilization's nearness, for a more temperate winter? What of the wild swans in spring and autumn, passing in moving communities, or of the dancing red-necked crane breeding in our moors and fens, then flying on to a more favored place? What do they know of freedom, being immersed in it?

And the people? Over fifteen hundred years ago Tacitus in his *Germania* commented that the Suiones "likewise honor wealth, and so a single ruler holds sway with no restrictions and with no uncertain claim to obedience." From early times the people found more advantage in law than in lawlessness, our *Saga of Burnt Njal* counseling: "With law shall our land be built and settled, with lawlessness wasted and spoilt," a prudence they tried to uphold as best they could. Their chief ambition has been to subsist, their nature, like wild birds, being to bear a family, to eat and live together on a land that could support them. They till the oats and barley in their fields, fields in most places so rich they can be done with one maid and one ox, they raise their cattle and sheep, they build their wooden cottages and barns around their family living, they gather in villages for church and holidays. This is their simple freedom.

Many times when hunting or riding I have stopped to rest in a bonde's cottage, each one of these, ever since, being called Christina's Cottage, and a few more, as well, whose owners figured I would have stopped there if I had been in the neighborhood. In some a crude drawing of me, named my portrait, was added to the colorful designs covering the walls and low ceiling, to the angels, columns, and homemade patterns in red, brown, and blue decorating the boards. I liked to visit these cottages. After the first surprise had subsided, my bonde host would relax with me, for I am a dumpy kind of woman loving familiar manners, and he would show me his workbench with its clock-making intricacies. His wife would bring out the linens she wove in bright patterns, while their baby bounced in a little swing hung from the ceiling and their aged parents sat smiling on rude chairs near the fire. The open brick hearth kept the room warmer than any castle room could be, its flames throwing the painted wall figures into gentle dances, grimacing the faces of the angels. Usually there was a pot hugging the fire and from it the smell of venison cooking, of berries being stewed to a sauce, or of the baking of a barley and birchbark bread. The talk would be of the farm, of the family, occasionally of God and Odin, and of Sweden's problems. In this way I learned much of my country, of the taxes feared as unjust, the benefits valued as blessings, which ravages were attributed to God and which to the nobles, such things as are not found in books nor in the conversations at court.

How different are the nobles, the robust, hard-drinking lords who govern their ample estates on horseback, who believe themselves born to command in battles, who prefer fighting to sitting at home, whose idea of culture is to build a large, ugly house and call it a castle! And what fills the castles? Chilly air. A few boast cabinets of inlaid wood from Holland in the stark white rooms, perhaps a chest from Germany, a Flemish tapestry, or an iron clock. Not a book, not a painting. To speak of art is not to speak of Sweden. When I ascended the throne, one painting by a Swedish artist hung in Stockholm Castle, a poor one at that! And the learning! How can a magistrate write a report when he cannot write his own name? How can a scientist develop when he is persecuted as a magician of the Devil? Sweden sleeps in its own Dark Ages. True, there is a university at Uppsala, but learning does not rule. Let a professor be too serious, too insistent on trying to dose the young nobles with education, let him, worst of all, be an honored, imported sage, and the outraged young men will throw their books at his head, smash the windows of his house, laugh at him, jeer his pedagogy. Their erudition is in drinking, in gaudy clothes and petticoat-ruffling, in fighting. Luckily for the fields and forests of Sweden, the nobles prefer fighting foreigners, the bringing back of looted wealth, adventurous tales, and a soldier's halo. Sometimes I think they fight, too, just to keep warm. Only in the curtailed summer does the sun stay long enough to heat the body and soothe the mind. In winter it slips over the rim of the world and cannot be tempted to more than an indolent look at Sweden for many months.

The Vasas have been one of the rare families with a passion for knowledge. At an early age I decided Odin must have been a Vasas, Odin the greatest of all our Kings, whose one eye glowed like the sun, his other having been traded for his drink from the fountain of wisdom, Odin, called a god, still worshipped, still whipping his wish across the earth in stubborn defiance. They say he could check the winds, become a wild beast, appear in remote places in a moment's journey, that his two ravens, Mind and Memory, flew out to the world every morning and returned at night with the world's news. It was Odin who ordered the mounds of earth raised over the tombs of Kings in the meadow of old Uppsala. There, now, lie the bones of the great Kings, Aun, Egil, and Adils, of King Ingel, who grew wild from eating the hearts of wolves, King Haquin, who slit the throats of his sons, of many King Eriks, King Ingoes, King Björns. There they molder, beneath the meadow where they were crowned, the meadow which belonged to the people, for it was they who chose the Kings, who gathered in festivity on the meadow when all went well, who gathered to kill the King when it did not, who fed the roots of the grass with blood.

Except for Odin, of the many Kings who reigned during the thousands of years until my great-grandfather Gustav Vasa came to power, of the lists of battles, marriages and divorces, murders, and treacheries, I have had little concern, although I had to learn them all by my father's orders. Two things, however, interested me: one, that it seemed the easiest way to rid oneself of a rival was to coax him into trustfulness, then, when he was without a guard, to burn him in his house, or, even more popular, to poison him;

the other, the closeness of the Kings to their gods, and, later, to God.

It was on the highest of the bare mounds at old Uppsala that Gustav Vasa used to stand when he addressed the bönder. Now, he was a man the people adored, and rightly, for he had, almost with his own two hands, lifted his country from the Danish rule, returned it from a black defeat to a proud sovereignty, and laid the foundation of modern Sweden. He was their hero, their King, their father, the St. Göran who had rescued them from the dragon. I used to study his portrait and wonder at the breadth of his shoulders and chest, which, it seemed, hardly could be squeezed into the picture. His high forehead was covered partially by a fringe of hair, snipped straight across, straight brown hair that fell on the sides as low as the middle of his ears and met the beginnings of his voluminous beard. His eyes looked as if he were contemplating a tragedy and could not be fooled about it, his strong mouth closed with a downward pull as if it were useless to try words where deeds were needed. His voice, I thought, must have been like the North Wind, his friend and ally, the North Wind that had proclaimed him King. As a child I loved that wind, howling across the glossy snow lakes, clapping the branches of trees together, hitting at the castle walls, prying at the windows. "Gustav Vasa and his friend," I would say, "are chasing away Sweden's oppressors." And I would remember how the North Wind had helped my great-grandfather to win his leadership and save his country from sinking into vassalage. Listen.

It happened in 1520 on the day before Christmas in Mora, a village in the wooded hills of Dalarna in the north of Sweden, where the bönder had gathered for the holidays. They had come down from the settlements, from their farms on the edges of forests and on the banks of rivers and lakes, to start their celebrating on St. Thomas's Day. The feasting, parties, and masked processions would last until St. Canute's Day, seven days after Twelfth-day, and everyone was relaxing in the jovial atmosphere, in the sense of being together and free from work. At twelve o'clock noon on that Christmas Eve, as the people were coming out from the church's morning service, the brass band mounted the balcony of the town hall to blow in Christmas. The bönder assembled in the square beneath, waiting to hear the usual free concert, but after the first piece the music stopped and Gustav Vasa stepped forth in an embroidered coat with a collar of gold, a dazzling figure in the crowd of brown homespun.

Until that day Gustav Vasa had worn the same brown homespun among these people, working as a laborer in the copper mines, his rich clothes hidden in the church of the curate who sheltered him, and with good reason. There was a high reward for his capture, for he was the last Swedish noble of spirit left to challenge the Danish rule. King Christian had been thorough when he conquered Sweden. He had beheaded the chief of every noble family, also the bishops, councillors, and leading burghers, he had strung up their servants beside them, hanged in their boots, he had dug up the body of our last great Administrator, Sten Sture, hacked it to pieces, and sent the parts as his meaningful message to the towns throughout the country. This pretty massacre was carried out during the program of his coronation in Stockholm, an event unprecedented in magnificence and in butchery, an event Gustav Vasa fortunately missed. At the time he was a prisoner in Denmark, one of six young nobles sent as hostages and clamped into chains. Not until he escaped back to Sweden to his family estate, beautiful Rävsnäs, near Stockholm, did he learn of the beheading of his father, the senator, and his brother, of the imprisonment of his mother and sister, of the complete capitulation of the remaining nobles. Not a one would stir to protect him or to protest any Danish measure for Sweden's sake. The sword of Denmark ruled supreme. Over the nobles, yes, but what of the common people? He fled in disguise to the North, to the hills of Dalarna where the royal troops did not dare to penetrate, where the bönder govern themselves, no one being more rich or powerful than his neighbor, respect being for a man's proved strength and judgment. He had lived among them, working as one of them until this day before Christmas when he laid aside his miner's coat and spoke as a Vasa.

His face reflected a mixture of fierceness and sorrow, his voice rang sonorously clear and deep, as if the tragedy of his soul reached out to the soul of each man in the square of Mora. Oh, deplorable state of our country! Oh, grief, that fathers, brothers, friends should be barbarously murdered and the world be silent! Oh, disaster of treachery, that men should kneel before a King who forgives no one for being brave! What of liberty, which the men of Dalarna look on as their most precious birthright? Would liberty die, too, be trampled underfoot like the dung of oxen? What were men without liberty? Who wanted to be made into a cartwheel to carry a load of stinking foreign boots? Not he. He was willing to sacrifice his life in defense of the liberty loved by the Dalkarlarna and all true Swedish men. He, Gustav Vasa, chose to die with a sword in his hand rather than face years of groveling submission, but he knew he was powerless against this enemy as a lone man. He knew, just as certainly, the power of a united, a determined people, a people beloved by God, aroused in a righteous cause. They must not be deceived by King Christian's easing of the salt tax. It was a bribe for servitude that he would more than make up for in new taxes he would impose. His was a cruel nature, his aims were selfish aims. Why should an outsider be the one to benefit from the hard work of the great honest family that was Sweden?

And as Gustav Vasa talked, the bönder before him saw that his splendid coat was no more than an ornament for the greater splendor of his mind and his courage, that his golden collar shone on him like a sun-sparkle on an oak, that his roots grew deep in an earth he cherished, and no tempest could change his proud stance. And the North Wind blew incessantly, insisting on his words, stinging the cheeks of the listeners to wakefulness.

When he had finished, several of the ancient inhabitants rose. The continued blowing of the North Wind, they said, was an infallible sign of continuous success. The Orders of Heaven were declaring for Gustav Vasa and should not be opposed. The younger men laughed. The only message the North Wind brought, they said, was that the day would be cold. Gustav Vasa was a fine man, but it was a hard thing for a young man to leave his hearth and family to fight for an uncertain result. Conditions were not so bad as they were. All they knew of King Christian, other than hearsay, was the relief from the salt tax, and God knew that was a blessing. How could they be sure how the rest of Sweden felt? Who were they, a handful of Dalkarlarna, to throw themselves against the royal troops of Denmark and, perhaps, their own countrymen? Gustav Vasa turned away in despair. The last spark of hope for Sweden seemed to have died away, its patriotism a bed of cold ashes.

Again he fled to the North, this time in no disguise, tracking across the white wastes on his skis toward Norway, where he hoped to find a haven, bending his head against the whistling North Wind. But the wind had not ceased its blowing when a messenger arrived in Mora with the news that King Christian was beginning a journey through his newly won territory to greet his subjects and impress upon them their duty to the crown of Denmark with the prompt extraction of the new taxes levied on them. A special message was given to the chief lawmaker in each village, that he as the representative of the King was to erect a gallows on his land for the punishment of any who protested the King's measures. Gallows in Mora! New taxes! The young men's complaisance flamed into anger. The two swiftest skiers were sent to overtake Gustav Vasa, to bring him back that he might know the men of Mora needed to deliberate no longer. They declared themselves free citizens of Sweden, and four hundred men were ready to go with him to insist on their liberty the length and breadth of their country. The ancient inhabitants smiled. You cannot deny the North Wind, they said.

The rest of the story is familiar to everyone. As Gustav Vasa threw aside his homespun coat, so the people threw off their fear, and leader and people as one overwhelmed their captors. Within a year Sweden was a free country, Gustav Vasa the elected Regent. Within three years he was elected King by the Riksdag. By the end of the twenty-third year the people, convinced of the divine authority of Gustav Vasa and the sons who sprang from his seed, abandoned their ancient custom of an elective monarchy for his sake and decreed that from that time on the Swedish crown was to be hereditary in the Vasa family.

"It was a long time ago," I complained to my tutor when he set me to studying the details of Sweden's development under Gustav Vasa.

"Long ago! A hundred years is not a long time!" Johannes Matthiæ exclaimed. "Count the years since Cæsar stood in the Senate in Rome!" And he would expound on my great-grandfather's extraordinary energy in converting his country of forests and rivers, birds, and bönder, into the beginnings of a civilized State. For forty years he worked with his people, loved them, swore at them, pushed them into motion. "You dumb swine," he would bellow, "give me reports that are not shadows in moonlight!" The settlement that was Stockholm, my tutor pointed out, a town of three or four hundred souls huddled between the bridges of what is now City Island, was shaken into order, pressed into the progress that made it the busy center it is today. "You can see the value of an education," Matthiæ would say. "Gustav Vasa knew what to do."

Yes, Gustav Vasa, almost an Odin, a man to prove the reality of legends, had known what to do with his knowledge. But how much there was still to do! When he flew the blue and yellow banner for the first time on his triumphal entry into Stockholm, parading among the few shamefaced houses over which rose the gray tower of the fort and the spike of Great Church, only bare land across The Stream, and an occasional windmill, think of the centuries of culture needed to have this miserable town approach the grandeur of Rome, Rome that had known more about us for over a thousand years than we had known of ourselves! Tacitus wrote his *Germania* before we learned the art of writing, Pliny the Elder and Alexander Ptolemy the geographer plotted our existence, Procopius noted our joyful celebration for the return of the sun at yuletide. Even in Tacitus' time word of us was not completely novel, as Pytheas of Massilia had borne news of us to the Greeks three hundred years before Christ. While Rome built villas, gardens, temples, decorated them with it flowering art, while it matured in sciences and learning, enduring the fluctuations of war and politics, of Consuls and Emperors, of dukes and Popes, leaving an articulate history in its wake, the North Wind blew across the empty island that was to be Stockholm, a city unthought of, undreamed of by the crude people or their ancient Kings.

One King, it is true, King Agreus, noticed the spot, selecting it for a night's camp on his way home from a war in Finland. There, he decided, would be a good place to pitch his tent to marry the Finnish princess he had brought with him as a hostage. The Princess Schialvia, however, did not share his passion for marriage, and she was, as histories relate, most ungrateful for the honor. As soon as King Agreus had become unmanageable to himself with hard drinking, putting his lips to the kind bottle when his bride was sick of him, she roped his neck and hanged him on the tree the tent stood under, and left him dangling while she with wise expedition fled back to her own country. By this dismal anecdote the site of Stockholm was first marked.

It was clear to me that I was to be the Vasa to spread learning in Sweden, to plant the culture of Rome and the Hellenic world in the North, to bring about a quickened flowering. The Vasas following Gustav Vasa had inherited his feverish intelligence and his capacity for miraculous development, each had hardened the strength and modernity of the country in a different way, according to his particular talents. As Johannes Matthiæ used to say, Sweden can thank God for the Vasas.

For all but one, that is, I would add to myself. Who would want to thank God for Erik as a ruler, an insane murderer? Erik, the eldest of Gustav Vasa's three sons, lone child of an early despondent marriage, who automatically became King when Gustav Vasa ceased his hearty life, was wild and haunted, tortured by demons of an invisible life of his own. He was a Swedish Caligula, who stabbed men to death after weeping on their shoulders in desperate friendship, who tried to sell his brother's wife to the Grand Duke of Muscovy to solve a political problem, and who wrote love letters to all the eligible Queens and princesses of Europe while dallying on which one to choose for his bride. In the end he had none of these, although he barely escaped the fame of a marriage to the marvelous Queen Elizabeth of England, since his love letters became mixed and reached the wrong ladies, so he took as his wife his mistress, Karen Mansdotter, the corporal's daughter. There were gossips to say it was by a love potion she won him, but I say he was no prize for any woman.

He made his decisions by the stars, and when the stars foretold his life would not be secure while his half-brother Johan was at liberty, he imprisoned Johan and his wife. And the stars were right. When Johan was released, he immediately plotted against his older brother. Erik was seized, in his turn imprisoned, and, eventually, poisoned. Then Johan ascended the throne. "It is good," the bishops explained to the country in giving their blessing to King Johan, "for one man to die for the people." Sweden thus kept to its ancient principle: if a King does not suit the times, he is murdered, not deposed.

Johan was a builder. Under his guidance rocks and timber became churches and castles all over Sweden, villages grew into fledgling cities, the fort at Stockholm underwent the massive change into a Polish renaissance palace. More than that, long-bearded King Johan was a dreamer. It is his dream that is vivid to me, that, from its inception to its fulfillment, has taught me the vitality of all dreams, their worth, their disregard of the dreamer. Johan dreamed of gathering together all the Swedish people under the canopy of one religion, those who worshipped Odin and the ancient gods of old Uppsala, those in the bosom of the Holy Catholic Church, those who adhered to the dissenters

Martin Luther or John Calvin. For them all to join as participants in one splendid ceremony of immortal belief, for the dividing jealous tempers to blend in one peace, one harmony, for Sweden, a country growing in power, to show itself to the other members of the world as an undivided soul, was a glorious purpose. This dream Johan bore as his child, he gave it his voice for its speaking, but, like a parent, he did not understand there were prisms in its life beyond his vision. He saw only the side he faced.

A dream diffuses an entity of its own, no sooner is it conceived than it goes beyond the dreamer. It is of heaven and earth combined, the mingling of burning birds and angels singing, it is of languishing virgins scattering Greek coins before a crescent moon, of lions leaping from the dirt of a grave, tossing golden manes, it is the warrior's crimson flag undimmed in battle, it is the stallion bearing the past on his back galloping to his mating with the future. Its forms, endless and uncringing, defy captivity. What net can hold its song, what judge impose a sentence on its obscure laughter, what musket win a mile of its prophetic landscape? What mind can own it, force it to stand still? And who can demand that it be beautiful? What have dreams to do with beauty?

Yet Johan wished to shape his dream, to make it beautiful, impressive, definite. Worst of all, he tried to force its direction. To his dream of a united worship, he added his intention that the worship be in the Roman Catholic Church. On the other side of the dream were the Swedish people, the dreamed-about, not the dreamers of this dream. They were awake and practical. There were those who remembered that King Christian was a Catholic, that his massacre in Stockholm had been sanctioned by the representatives of the Church, that the Catholic bishops had assisted him in planning his bloody dominance. Gustav Vasa was one of the early Lutherans, as were most of the nobles who began to be powerful. Religion, they said, was subject to the State, it could not be the other way around. Why should hard-earned Swedish money support a Roman splendor they never saw? Luther had sent word of what went on in Rome. They would have none of it. Johan, however, lived in the aura of his pious wife, Katarina Jagellonica, a Polish princess renowned for her goodness and faith. Their son Sigismund was raised a Catholic. If, Johan thought, the people could know the radiant peace, the security of being enfolded in the true faith, they would relent. Doubtless, in the years he and Katarina had been imprisoned by his wild brother Erik, they had prayed together for release. God had answered their prayers, had anointed him King. Were not their prayers Catholic? Johan corresponded with the Pope, brought Catholic ecclesiastics to Stockholm in disguise, planted them in the Academy as Lutherans to spread a vine of Catholic thought among the students. But the long noses of the Lutheran nobles and bishops were not fooled, and the Catholics were ousted. "What does this mean," was the cry, "except foreigners, Italian bishops in Sweden, Church ownership of land, and Swedish wealth drained for the Court in Rome! Why?" Lutheranism, they said, offered the same holy blessings, as well as Swedish bishops and Swedish control. Every noble, burgher, and bonde would have a vote with God and the State, too.

In the end, the dream expanded like the sky around the dreamer. His beloved wife dead, his son on the throne of Poland and not permitted to visit his father in Sweden, Johan succumbed to the pressure of his own court and ostensibly turned back to the Lutheran religion. What occurred in his heart no one knows. His dream was fulfilled by his younger brother Carl, my grandfather, who became King after Johan's death, the country having no taste for Sigismund, the legal heir, an unchangeable Catholic, who would be no better than a visiting ruler since he had become King of Poland. Yes, Johan's dream was realized. Sweden became a country of one dominant religion, but it was a religion of its own choice, the Lutheran.

Carl IX, who tacked the dream onto reality, who threw it like a blanket over the country, was not a dreamer at all. Righteous, legal-minded, cautious, and at the same time courageous in whatever step he took, he suffered the violent temper and suspicious nature of all Vasas, but compensated for them by being a remarkable administrator. His temper he used in explosions at dishonesty, his suspicions he directed at the nobles as well as, probably much more than, the less privileged classes, frustrating selfish interests whenever they stood in the way of the common welfare. By popular acclamation he was the greatest of the sons of Gustav Vasa. The bönder idealized him, named him the bonde King.

As in Johan's heart, the expansion of religion ached in the heart of my grandfather, tugged at his mind, a God wind, not to be stilled, not to be locked within private walls. Johan called his God wind a dream, Carl IX called his a mission. After he had spread Lutheranism across Sweden, he was impelled to march his cause beyond the borders, to sweep the world he knew clean of papacy. My first memory of him, since he died before I was born or even intended, came from a portrait which hung on a castle wall. When my eyes fell on his face and figure I shrieked with surprise.

"Look! Look! He has the cross on his head! Why is it there?"

Across the dome of his partially bald head, King Carl had combed two long slender bands of hair, one from the back to the front, the other from the right to the left side, so that one passing the other they appeared in the form of a cross. To me, as a child, it was as frightening as a mark of the Devil. It was too plain, too challenging, too threatening of Judgment Day. It suited well enough the banners and armies he sent out that achieved certain successes for Protestantism, but his own head! I shuddered.

King Carl's misson—"mission," I later decided, being a more polite, a nobler term for what it really was, ambition—became the string with which he bent the bow of his very being. Toward the end nothing else mattered, only his God wind blew through him. When he sensed his life growing limp within him, his thoughts still burned for his mission, left unfinished, not for himself, his family, his country, not for the wonder of immortality unrolling before him. On his deathbed he turned from his good wife, Christina, devoutly beside him, motioned a hand toward his son across the chamber, whispered his last words to the world in Latin: "He will do it." That son, Gustav Adolf, my father, surely would "do it." Then a youth of seventeen, his qualities were apparent. He was glorious, always.

When it came to be my turn to enter the world, these Kings were waiting for me. The flesh dies, not the ghosts inhabiting it, not the ideas pulsing through it. A fresh mind, a fresh body, a fresh instrument of royal power was being born into their realm. Would Odin hold back his ravens, would Gustav Vasa and the North Wind cease their howling for patriotism, would Johan drop his dream, Carl his cross? Never. And how many others pressed to inherit a spark of life, haunted Erik, ancient Kings wise, impetuous, poisoned, unnamed saints, Queens with unrealized fury? I had to have courage to be born. Two infant daughters before me had not had sufficient spirit, one living a few hours, the second almost a year. I, the third event, was prepared for with the utmost care. My father returned from a campaign in Poland, sick and exhausted as he was from it, to be present.

The astrologers, having been ordered to be explicit in their predictions, were zealous in their activity. They measured the stars, the planets, the sun, and, on the day of my birth, noted that the sun, Venus, Mars, and Mercury had reached the same design they had had at my father's birth, thirty-two years before. I would therefore, they prophesied, be born a son, become King of Sweden, and achieve a career as illustrious as that of Gustav Adolf. Furthermore, they announced, one of three deaths was scheduled to occur immediately after my birth: mine, my mother's, or my father's. Since the stars were propitious for my success as King, it would not, it was obvious, be I. If the seers had turned to gaze at the unalterable past, at the shadows cast across my hands by the gathered ghosts, at the stars fallen to earth, they might have divined more of the truth. That was too close, too difficult to see. They shook their heads, examined their books and instruments, looked reproachfully at Venus and Mars when I was proved to be a girl, and no one died. I must admit I had the will to be a boy.

Stockholm was radiant for my arrival. New snow had fallen in the filth of the streets, on the low roofs and rising towers, transforming the city into a silvery garden. Inside the castle the stoves were kept at their hottest. Nobles and ladies-in-waiting hovered excitedly while my father paced outside the chamber where my mother labored. At last I was born, at eight o'clock in the evening of December 8, 1626. I came into the world all over hair, my voice, even then, strong and harsh in its first yell. The women attendants, prepared as they were by the astrologer's forecast, had no doubt that the strident hairy infant was a boy, and gave vent to their joy in loud exclamations that reached the King's ears. He, too, ready for an heir, easily believed what he wished to hear. When the mistake was discovered, the women were afraid to undeceive him, to break into his exultation. His sister, Princess Katarina, for whom he had a warm affection, offered to undertake the task, took me in her arms, carried me to him, and exposed me so he could see for himself what she did not dare to tell him. He appraised me with no surprise, spoke with composure.

"Let us thank God, sister. I hope this girl will be as good as a boy to me. May God preserve her now that He has sent her."

"You are young," Katarina reminded him. "You still have hope for an heir."

His retort was immediate. "My sister, I am quite satisfied. May God preserve her to me." And he issued orders that the event was to be celebrated by the customary rejoicings for male heirs. From that moment on he treated me like a prince, in my education, in physical sports, in his affection. To his friends he even joked about the misconception. "She will be clever!" he said. "She has fooled us all!"

The Queen, my mother, lived for a little while in the bliss she had borne a son, her attendants fearing to worry her in her delicate condition of health. When she was told the truth she was inconsolable. She could not bear to look at me, she wept because I was a girl and ugly to boot. She was right enough. I was ugly, as tawny as a little Moor, scrawny, graceless. And I did not improve. As the weeks wore on, my mother continued to fret, the meanness of her disappointment deepening rather than drifting away, until her dislike of me became so sharp my nurses came to believe it would not displease the Queen if they assisted the astrologer's reading of a death and allowed me to die by accident. Beams fell on me, I was dropped on purpose, allowed to roll off beds, but I insisted on living. One of the "accidents" resulted in the deformity I have carried the rest of my life. That is why my right shoulder is hunched higher than my left.

While my mother's aversion to me mounted, my father's affection more than kept pace as I grew from infancy to childhood. We loved one another dearly. His immense golden arms tossed me in the air, caught me, held me, taught me to be fearless. He teased me, questioned me, joked with me, spent with me the wealth of his spacious mind, roared in delight at my pert answers, encouraged the quickness of my intelligence, started me, in my earliest years, toward a lively natural judgment of the world we were in. Whenever he could he kept me as his companion on his journeys, taking me once as far as Kalmar Castle, where I gratified him by clapping my hands at the booming of the welcoming cannons, never crying or whimpering at whatever conditions were hard during our traveling, for I wanted to be a great soldier like him. When he went to his battles and could not take me, he protected me from my mother's hate by leaving me with my gentle aunt, the Princess Katarina, selecting three men to supervise my education, two senators and his own chaplain, Johannes Matthiæ. He further protected me by ordering that in case of his death the five highest officers of the realm, not my mother, would be my guardians.

And when that death approached, I felt it. As he lifted me to say good-by, leaving me for the blood of the battlefield, leaving to carry the Protestant cross bequeathed him by King Carl, I burst into tears. He tried to brush away my tears, to laugh a little. I could not be stopped. His golden face blurred, I was numb to the comfort of his arms. He was leaving me, deserting the round of our days together, walking away into eternity. For three days I cried while the country whispered that the weeping of the four-year-old princess was a bad omen. I wept, almost crying my eyes into uselessness, but what need had I of sight when I had lost my god? I never saw him again.

Whether present or not, alive or dead, my father dominated my childhood. As a young girl learning my lessons, reading Greek philosophy and religion, I saw how like a Greek god he was and my studies became easy for me, for I felt, then, the gods were my friends, my helpers. I found an intimate pleasure in deciphering their characters, their loves, their rages, their victories. Perhaps, I thought, Gustav Adolf was a Greek god in disguise. He looked like one, tall of stature with an eagle nose that was better than a crown in asserting a majestic aspect, his flesh light and well colored, his hair yellow, his jaw glowing with a yellow beard, altogether giving an appearance of such bountiful fairness he was called the Golden King.

He acted like a god without pause. Nations, armies, princes, generals, he subjected everyone and everything, hurling down whatever stood in his way, victorious everywhere. He flew like lightning, always triumphant, from the Baltic coast to almost the opposite frontier of Germany, the Protestant champion who rescued countries from the Catholic monster as easily as if they were maidens fainting into his arms. He was the marvel of Europe. His ambition was even greater than his strength, but no greater than his good fortune. Not since Cæsar had there been such a military genius, and it was from Cæsar that Gustav Adolf took his lessons. During his campaigns the lamp in his tent burned late into the night as he studied Cæsar's *Commentaries* while his army slept. Wherever he was he persevered in his learning, reading books on the art of fortification, books on mathematics, the Bible, or Grotius and international law.

He loved his books almost as much as he loved people, all sorts of people, all ranges of character. He spoke to his subjects and his soldiers without formality, frequently asking them as he passed how they were, what they did, what they had left to desire. When he was in the field he admitted all gentlemen and private commanders to his table, saying a table is the torment of a secret and a net to catch friendship and affection. Being sincere himself, he could not abide flatteries, nor could he forget any service done him, no matter how great or how small, but he must reward it. He was, on the other hand, as careful to repay offenses, severe with his own soldiers in punishing them for misdemeanors. His beautiful discipline stood in sharp contrast to the other armies, whose soldiers defied, denied, straggled away from or to their commanders. My father's men adored him. He sweat with them, starved with them, froze and thirsted with them, sat the saddle as long as the strongest of them. His recklessness, as some called his riding, fighting, yelling through the worst dust and blood of a battle, was legendary. He had no time for fear.

Much as he loved his country and devoted his life to its service, Gustav Adolf was not to be persuaded to submit his heart to it where his amorous affairs were concerned. He maintained a steadfast aversion to marriage for years, regardless of the pressure of his stern mother, Christina from Holstein, perhaps because she insisted on her notion of royal breeding, that he marry a title and kiss it, while he, charmed by all the ladies and they by him, was more inclined to kiss a pretty face; or perhaps because the sting of an early defeat in love left a raw scar on his pride. He had fallen passionately in love with red-haired Ebba Brahe, a young countess attending the Queen Mother as a lady-in-waiting, a Swedish beauty if ever there was one, and, in spite of his mother's disapproval, he had pursued her with the ardor of an Apollo about to capture his Daphne. That he lost her was his own fault, for he had been kissing in other corners of Sweden, and Ebba could not tolerate the Dutch girl in Göteborg who gave me a bastard brother. His pleas, his prayers, his repentance, his vow he would love no one other than Ebba, that he would give his life for her, did not change her mind. She quickly married one of his generals, Jacob de la Gardie, while Gustav, shocked that a King should be refused forgiveness for allowing himself the pleasure of all young men, walled in his heart that it should not be touched again, that no woman should see it nor learn how to rule it. Neither would he chill his manliness by taking to bed an indifferent princess to please his mother.

The perfect answer seemed to appear in my mother, an intense and beautiful woman, with no capacity to rule anyone or anything, quite suitable politically as a Princess of Brandenburg. He first saw her in Berlin, the Princess Maria Eleonora, and was caught by her wide brown eyes, her sweet pointed chin, her long black hair. Since he was traveling in disguise to widen his education, posing as a Captain Gars, a name any shrewd person could have decoded as standing for Gustavus Adolphus Rex Suecia, he could not immediately present himself as a suitor, but Maria Eleonora surely knew who he was, for she has said she could not for a single instant take her eyes from this marvelous man, this King of Snow, whenever he was near her. Yes, she was ready to be his Queen, particularly when he wrote her the words he had once discovered for Ebba Brahe, that he would love no other, that he was willing to give his life for her. He never had to do either. They were married, then wars and state affairs claimed him where a woman could not. He was reconciled to marriage by her beauty, but his heart was his own, his mind was his own, and his body, as he lent himself more and more to the activities of greatness wherein he was exercised and pleasured beyond the powers of femininity. I must say he always showed himself a tender husband, and the union prospered, on the whole.

Maria Eleonora, however, was a transplanted princess. When she came from Brandenburg, a slender girl with raven tresses and melancholy eyes, to be the bride of her Snow King, she hardly had expected Sweden to be so different from her home. No one had told her of the empty expanses of snow meadows, the empty castle rooms, the empty hours, week after week, when the King was on a campaign or busy with state affairs. She had planned on being with her golden giant, her beloved King, her husband, but where was he? He slipped away from her daily, yearly.

Through the moonlit passages of her mind, disordered by questions she had not the wit to form into speech, moved her demand, her silent monster, unable to emerge. Gustav Adolf was immune to possession, yet she would possess him, she, the fragile, would be his tyrant. Let him be the conqueror of the whole world, she would be his tyrant in love. What else was there for her to be tyrant of? What else was there for her to win and own? She took for granted her jewels and her gowns and her feathered fans. It meant little to her that she wore petticoats of satin and embroidered slippers unknown to a burgher's wife, nor that the drawers of her chest glittered with gold necklaces, pearls, amethysts, and ruby enamels. Those were hers as a Queen, not as a woman.

Besides, she complained, there were finer ones in Germany, everything was better in Germany, not only the jewels. There silver goblets, chased silver platters, and decent napkins made a meal civilized. There they made entire little sailing vessels of silver with silver sails blowing and tiny silver men climbing the rigging or firing muskets on the silver deck at imaginary enemies, with space left in the bow to be laden with sweets for the table. In Germany there were tapestries marvelous in color, paintings of racing, snorting horses that looked alive, not like the sticks of wood the Swedish artists painted, and there, she said, they knew what a comfortable chair was, not like the ones here that were so hard and stiff she couldn't sit in one long enough to finish a piece of needlework. Germany had well-printed books that put those in Sweden to shame, and why not, for who in Sweden knew how to write a book anyone would want to print? Even our most prized national sculpture in the Great Church had been carved by a foreign artist, she said. Sweden was crude, was cruelly cold, was vulgar and unfriendly, and if it were not for my wonderful father whom she adored she would not stay there for a minute. He was the one cultured man in Sweden. He could speak German as well as her own brother—why, he could go to any country in Europe and trade in the language. He knew the works of Grotius as well as the author himself, sleeping with them under his pillow as he did, and he had the taste to bring back presents from the regions he conquered, not just military stories.

My poor mother! How could she speak of learning whose brain could not fathom the studies I had as a child? Only in her chatter could she pretend to understand the education of my father. She was always nervous and undecided, favoring the choosing of a gown with as much intentness as the choosing of a Councillor of State, her homeless thoughts fluttering from interest to interest, never settling on one. How could she hope to own the brilliant Gustav Adolf? When he was not busy with the government or his continual reading, he liked to drink and joke with his friends, to laugh until his cheeks were red and shining in merriment, and if Maria Eleonora came to him with some of her dainty ideas he was apt to forget he was not on the battlefield, shouting his questions at her with such gusto the ideas were blown right out of her head.

Yet she kept thinking the day or night would come when he would capitulate, when he would retire to her boudoir in preference to the Council chamber, when he would stretch his golden form on the brocade of her bed and turn the sky of his blue eyes on her in a summer timelessness. She would enthrall him with tales she herself invented, tales far more engrossing than his Roman history, she would amaze him with teachings he never had imagined existed, the perfect language of a rose, the colors of the hours, which ones were blue or silver or edged with crimson, or how silence is built on ladders. She would take him to swing on the secret gates of her dreams, she would enchant him with the fantasies of her flesh, and he would not be able to tear himself away from her perfumed presence.

She believed that all she could keep of his person or whatever he touched would make Gustav more her own. Carefully she laid away the enameled roses of his childish slippers, the muff with English flowered embroidery and a hareskin lining that had kept his little hands warm, and the small white doublet with two golden-thread lions to guard his chest, one watching over each shoulder.

"Look," she told me, "it is no wonder your father became brave when he had two keepers to frighten away unholy fears and night dragons."

I was sure he would have been brave regardless and retorted that Vasas ever had been braver than lions.

"Oh, don't you see," she cried, "the lions' eyes were the eyes of his heart, direct, unfailing, true, the golden light of the sun shining through their strength. Have you not noticed how his voice is the voice of the lion? When he speaks, the walls of a room echo like mountain rocks and any who dare not to love him are turned into fleeing deer." And she wept because I pretended not to understand.

She laid away, too, his white satin coronation suit, embroidered in silver, and, most especially, his wedding suit, ordered from Hamburg of royal purple wool festooned with gold flowers, and the purple baldric to match, emblazoned with the gold-braid animal whose tail became a flower. To these, when he died, she added the shirt he was wearing when the bullet found him, the lace collar and cuffs still stained with sweat, his blood still an uneven line of brownish red on the soft white linen, and she put it beside his buckskin jacket with the horrid hole in the back.

Everyone at court thought Maria Eleonora would kill herself with grief when the sad news reached Sweden of the Battle of Lützen, the news that the Swedish army had been victorious against Wallenstein, but that Gustav Adolf was dead, shot in the head and in the back. Everyone whispered that her thin spirit would abandon the world to be with him, that she could not exist without him. How little they knew her! This was her moment of triumph, her day to claim ownership. No one could challenge her tears, not even he, no one would deny that she was the one who loved him the most, that she possessed him through her grief. The senators might wail and lament when his name was spoken in the Assembly, the people might line the long weary way of the funeral procession from Nyköping to Stockholm, their faces wet with tears, stunned and hushed, as if something priceless had been stolen from them, the court ladies might hide their streaked cheeks and puffy eyes behind curtained windows as the coffin bore off their hopes, their country's love, their vanity's mirror, the Councillors might burden their hearts wondering what would happen to Sweden without its genius King, she was the single figure in black, his wife, who could claim private possession.

And I? It had been over two years since I had said farewell to my father, since I had exhausted my sorrow in tears for the loss of my beloved companion. A child's memory is short, the thought of his person had become as removed as a story to me. As I watched his coffin being laid beside the other dead Kings in Riddarholm Church, I was not overly troubled. I felt like a spectator at another necessary ceremony, I could not connect the vital father I had known with this waxen image. Death seemed to me just a larger, darker region than America or Muscovy or any other little-explored region. If Gustav Adolf had to journey there, that was his affair, not mine.

After the funeral and the mourning period the country folded its grief into its heart and returned to business and distractions. Not Maria Eleonora. For three years she wept, night and day, for her lost husband. She begged the Councillors to give her his body, not to inter it, to allow her to keep in death what had been denied her in life. Now that her consort was home from the wars separating them for those pale lonely years, let him stay, let him rest where he would wish to be and she would wish to have him, near her, at the side of her devotion, her love unflagging through death. Fate had been cruel in keeping them apart. Let her now behold his body as her own, indisputably, forever.

To her horror, the Councillors refused her request, interred his body, closed their ears to her sobs of eternal love. Hysterically she fled into the world of her shadows and incessant weeping, grasping and appropriating the only two remnants of Gustav Adolf's private love, taking them with her as treasures to be hoarded, to be hidden from all sight but her own. Thus she would triumph, thus she would possess him. These two objects were the King's heart, encased in a box of gold, and his daughter, Christina.

III

NYKÖPING CASTLE sits quite prettily on the banks of a small river, its town and churches settled comfortably behind it, rolling hills dotted with estates around it. It is a day's journey south of Stockholm, at the tip of an inlet from the Baltic Sea, sufficiently secure from invasion that its towers seem more for pleasure than war. Like most Vasa castles, it originally was a fortress, but in the conversion the high stone walls were given a variety of cuts and turns so they are not as formidable as most, and turrets were added here and there, irresponsible and feminine. The two largest towers, fat and square, on the side facing the river, are crowned with turreted curved roofs under which run slender columned loggias, an admirable place, I thought as a child, to survey the happenings of the countryside. This I was not permitted to do, nor to climb into the towers at all, not even to satisfy my curiosity about any remaining bones of King Birger's two brothers, left there to pine to death in the fourteenth century.

Nyköping was my mother's favorite castle, the castle to which she fled after the King's death, taking me, to shut herself up with sorrow, to create a grayed silken world with weeping its only music. That I was an energetic girl of six, not desirous of sorrow, meant nothing to her. Suddenly she was aware that I was her child, the bud of her union with Gustav Adolf, almost a little replica of the man whose body she could not have. The abhorrence she had felt for me veered into a terrifying passion she called mother love. She could not bear to lose me from sight. I could not stay in my own apartments, I had to live in hers, to sleep and waken in her dreadful chamber of mourning, hung, from ceiling to floor, walls and windows alike, in black velvet drapes. The wax tapers were kept burning, no ray of sunlight allowed to penetrate into this room where day and night merged into one dark bridge, endlessly crossed, leading nowhere.

On a table beside her bed Maria Eleonora placed the carved gold box holding the heart of Gustav Adolf. There she prayed, lamented, guarded him, jealously possessed him. I was commanded to revere, not to touch, the glittering little casket. The light of the tapers, not under orders, brushed it with yellowed fingers, tapped on it, called it to life. I gathered courage to put my ear against the box to listen for a beating within, but all I could hear was the tremendous noise of my own heart.

I lived in my mother's chamber, I slept in her bed. I was the image of my father, she would say, touching my eyes, my nose, my chin, running her hand through my tangled hair. My voice was not that of a little girl, sweet and trebled as hers had been, mine, she moaned, was the voice of Gustav, low and resonant, echoing from the tomb. All the embraces she had denied me were mine, then, and more. I was hugged and kissed to excess. I would waken in the night finding myself buried in her arms, her tinkling voice sobbing, murmuring again and again: "Oh, my poor dear, my own, my own!" The caress of her wet cheeks evoked no sweet love in me. No! No! She had hated me. Why this strange agony, why this embrace? Weeping, she would press me to her until I was eclipsed by her shoulder, by the profusion of her dark curls, and I would scream, believing I was being pulled beneath the wing of an unholy nightingale, that I must fight for my breath, fight for myself, against the smothering softness of thousands of blinding feathers. Her tears would fall on me like tiny damp leaves raining down on an early grave, autumn leaves threatening to seal the buried spirit from the freedom of the stars. And when I jerked and pulled away from such sickening dejection, her eyes followed me in the flickering candlelight, brown moons adrift from the true sky.

Jesters, dwarfs, ladies in satin, these were my mother's companions, the ornaments of her royalty. Two Councillors of State she demanded, too, to serve me at table, a demand the Council solemnly rejected, hinting they served me better attending the government in Stockholm. Money, then, she said, give her more money, for servants, for silver spoons, for velvet cushions and pearl-inlaid chests, for black feather fans, for elegant gardens to stroll in, tulips and roses, fragrant green hedges, singing fountains. She would rebuild a part of the castle, she said, waving a slim hand at the high stone walls, to suit better the delicate taste of a Queen, she herself had a plan, look, how much more gracious for her daughter to grow up among arches and columns, gilded cornices and parquetry. Cautiously the Councillors suggested I could be removed to another castle, to Stegeborg, to be under my Aunt Katarina's care, the Queen Mother need not put herself to such trouble, the Princess Katarina being accustomed to the training of children, having three of her own. Maria Eleonora answered them with such a cloudburst of weeping, such a borrowing of linen to blow her pretty nose, her large dark eyes brimming with widow's tears, such an appealing to their obligation to Gustav Adolf, begging her need of me as consolation, as all that was left to her in the world of her beloved husband, begging that the child be not cleft from the mother as well as the father, that the poor gentlemen, confounded and quite helpless before her flowing tears, were not able to refuse her. She alone, she wept, had the right to raise her daughter.

Whatever right she assumed she had, she had no notion how to use. We disagreed on everything, and I was impervious to persuasion. She wanted me indoors, sitting in a quiet, ladylike manner, while I wanted to be outdoors, riding, running. She would have me learning needlework, while I would be studying books. She insisted I drink wine or small beer, which I detested, while I held out for what she called "that unwholesome water."

This last quarrel turned into a feud, for, with water kept from me, I drank nothing. For three days I subsisted without liquids, then, on the morning of the fourth day, I awoke late and alone in my mother's morose chamber, my tongue dry as a board with thirst. What had been the click to hasten me from my dreams, to lift me from my racing after the crystal mountain stream whose water spurted just ahead of my grasp? I looked around the room, at the candlelight's silent visitors dancing against the black draperies, at the heavy damask chairs, dull with emptiness, at the immobile box hiding my father's heart, waiting on the table beside me, waiting for I knew not what. My glance came to my mother's vanity table, to its creams and bottles, and I smiled, for I knew what had wakened me.

The clicking had been the shutting of the door, one of my mother's ladies-in-waiting had brought in her bottle of morning dew, the dew gathered to pat the freshness of each morning onto her complexion. The woman had gone, I was unwatched. Happily I climbed from the bed, ran to the vanity, drank every bit of the dew, every cool delicious drop. No more thirst for me! All I had to do was contrive a few moments alone in the chamber every morning before my mother used her dew, a ritual I arranged, you may be sure. And my mother? She scolded her lady-in-waiting for not gathering the dew, for spilling it, for letting someone else have it, for lying. No one suspected the young Queen-elect, although I was the wonder of the castle for going without water or wine.

Then came the day when Maria Eleonora chanced to enter the room when I was in the act of lifting the bottle to my lips.

"Christina!"

Her shock and fury whipped at me from the door. I jumped, almost dropping the precious liquid. She rushed at me, snatched the bottle with one hand, gripped my shoulder with the other and shook me violently, screaming.

"Christina, you fox, you thief, you vulgar grit! Oh, my dew, my dew! You little thief, where have you learned such things? You have the Devil in you!"

She slapped me, she beat me, my face, my back, my arms. Would I steal her beauty from her, she screamed, wipe the roses from her cheeks, the creamy softness from her neck, that she should be rough as a spotted apple like these Swedes? Who did I think I was? Did I ever remember she was my parent, my ruler, the sole wife and love of the great Gustav Adolf, whom I shamed by my wicked ways, while she, the possessor of his heart, kept his faith? Did I ever pause to consider she was a Queen, born in a civilized country, while I was an obstinate, ugly child, a princess of a wilderness? My ears rang, my flesh smarted, the room and candles were spinning around me. She could beat me into blue bruises, never would I apologize, never would I give in, never could she force me to a belief in her authority. She could not fool me. I would be Queen, I was the Vasa, born to a divine authority, not she. Never, by my own choice, would I drink anything but water, delicious as morning dew. To this day I do not touch wine or small beer. I hate it, as I hated her, then.

During the years my mother strove to wind me into the pattern of her passions, I not only resisted her feminine notions, I pocketed a human knowledge I never lost. Even as a gawky little girl I wasted no love, no false admiration, on what is too often called beauty, the imitation Greek profile, the smooth ivory skin, the clinging curls, for I discovered how it can be the nest of weakness, of insidious selfishness, of deceit. I saw that clear eyes do not denote a clear heart nor tearful eyes a compassionate one, that dainty fingers pushing a needle may have more desire to kill than the muscular hand with the sword, that a title today, whatever its origin of sincere bestowal, does not provide a clue to worthiness, since "noble" and "nobles" may have vastly different meanings.

The countesses around my mother followed her whims, sighed with her in elongated woe, giggled, when she did, at her grotesque jesters and dwarfs, gave no gesture of understanding to me. How

I despised them! My bulwark was my teacher, Johannes Matthiæ, a mild, learned man whom I still cherish. He know how to treat me, he alone, how to sympathize with my childish troubles without stooping to the degradation of pity, how to guide my mind to a healthy enthusiasm for the royal education my father had planned for me. He had been chosen personally by my father, the most fortunate choice that could have been made, restricted, as the King was, to men of Swedish nationality, and, after the King's death, my mother had found nothing to object to in my teacher's kind manner. She could not guess that with him I learned to build a wall high enough to shut her out, a wall of reading, of study, of books wherein panoramas unrolled of foreign lands, where time became a pageant to mark, where ancient people spoke, where old magics were explained, new ones suggested. I was fascinated. I wanted to learn every tongue, every history, every science. Whenever I could evade Maria Eleonora I slipped away to my apartment and my teacher, out of sight of her white pointed face, out of hearing of her prattle and sniffling, to pursue the wonders in books. Twelve hours might pass unnoticed if she did not find me and drag me away. Some days, however, there were no lessons at all for me if it did not suit her sentiments and if she watched me so closely I could not escape.

On the days I spent kicking my heels against the chair in her chamber, warned to attend to her, or to my prayers, I set my lips and told myself that some day I would do as I wished. The interval in Stockholm before she had whisked me away to Nyköping Castle was vivid in my memory. I remembered having my portrait painted with my little gold crown on my head, I remembered my entrance into the Riksdag the day I had been elected Queen. One of the Councillors, Gabriel Gustav Oxenstierna, had led me into the immense hall where the representatives of the Four Estates were assembled to determine the successor to Gustav Adolf. Holding his hand, I walked to the center of the space, looked, as much as I could without turning and spoiling my dignity, at the array of dark-coated men, some whispering, most silent, solemn, all of their eyes on me. I found it interesting to be the centerpiece. The Councillor had told me the reason for my being there, that there were members of the Riksdag who did not believe the late King really had a daughter.

I had stared at him in astonishment. "Gustav Adolf is my father! Don't they know that?" It seemed incredible to me anyone in the world would not know this important fact.

"They never have seen you," he had replied kindly.

And the presentation was made. I stood, a very little girl, before the men whose votes decided the course of Sweden, and one of them came forward, a great hulk of a man with a weather-beaten face. He bent over me, his wintry eyes moving closely on my features. I gazed back at him, at his rough whiskers, at the hairs growing out of his nostrils. In a moment he straightened to his full height and announced his decision in a booming voice.

"It is true! I see the nose, the eyes, the forehead of King Gustav. It is herself! Let her be our Queen!"

He, the spokesman of the bönder, erased the last doubt. I was unanimously elected Queen, to ascend the throne as soon as I attained my majority.

I remembered, too, the court functions at which I was honored as Queen-elect, especially the audience I gave to the emissaries from the Crimea who brought a gift from the Khan. The Grand Constable, Jacob de la Gardie, had prepared me, somewhat nervously, for the occasion, cautioning me not to be afraid of the strange men from the distant foreign land, that I was a royal personage and could not show any fear of their long black beards. I laughed at him, contemptuous that he should think I, although young, would be so foolish.

"You have beards in Sweden, too!" I had retorted.

I had wriggled to try to find comfort in my stiff dress. I had wished to wear my salmon-colored satin bodice, a comfortable outfit, saying it would shine a royal welcome, but I had been overruled, of course, and put into one of my new mourning gowns, a heavy black, embroidered in gold metal threads, its ruff and cuffs of gray lace. It prickled, yet I had to hold myself still and straight so my necklace of pearls with its drops of black beads would not be twisted, nor my crown be tilted on my head. I had to accustom myself to a royal pose.

They say the audience passed off well, that for my age I spoke my lines with éclat. I remember that after the shaggy, booted, black-bearded Crimeans had given a rackety speech in their native tongue that sounded like branches splitting over and over, they placed the gift of the Khan before me, and I had eyes for nothing else. How beautiful, how beautiful!

It was a richly ornamented quiver holding eight gold-tipped arrows, their tiny hind wings bound in red thread, their bodies, long and slender, of a light wood, smoothed for the flight from the painted bow. The quiver, fashioned of blood-red velvet, was crusted in gold flowers and vines wherein jewels nestled, of a soft green brilliance, so thick the rosy background scarcely could be seen. When had I seen such colors, such design? I could wander in it, I could see the green eyes of bodiless cats, the gold eyes of unknown gods, glittering in a profuse garden, watching in an enameled paradise, among unbreakable flowers and twisting scarlet paths, watching for what? For the great bear in the sky to kick down chips of stars in an incautious gambol? For the running feet of forgotten music, the flight of a dove's heart into love and time? Were they watching for promises or dangers? Were they pygmy monsters, hunting and hunted, or dwarfs with lanterns sprinkling a secret light? What eyes were behind the eyes I saw? Oh, that jeweled watching, that never sleeping in gilded hedges, the waiting, the breathlessness behind metal petals! Were they protecting the power of the arrow, the silent power of death, slim and gold-tipped, of death, too soon, too sudden? I could see an arrow splintering a heart's alphabet, the bleeding letters tossed irrelevantly to a fading sky, while the living bow sang. Yes, the silent power was something to watch, to hold. When I ruled I would stay the flight of death, keep it within its quiver.

Death. Death lay like an animal in my mother's chamber, her

velvet cave. I felt it, although I hardly knew what it was. Once I asked my mother: "What is death?"

"You will know when the time comes," she replied. "The White Lady will warn you."

"The White Lady?"

"She appears to each one of the House of Brandenburg when the time comes to die."

"Did my father see her?"

"Stupid! How could he, being a Vasa? If she had tried to warn him, for my sake, he would not have been able to see her. My family has a mystic sight."

I didn't know what "mystic sight" meant. I wondered if a White Lady, made of mists, was waiting outside the door, if she would enter without knocking, whish out the tapers, lay icicle fingers on the one she wanted. I shivered, but it was useless to ask my mother for reassurance. She had a fondness for ghosts. She might even open the door to introduce me to her White Lady.

Death. I was seven years old when the Lutheran idea of death was laid before me, to my absolute terror, to desolate my nights. My mother took me to church on a crisp Easter morning, a day my spirits were sparkling. I was conscious of growing older, eager to learn everything there was to know. In my seat, my little leather Bible in my hand, I gave my most earnest attention to the preacher, listened spellbound to his Easter sermon about the Day of the Last Judgment. As he talked, his voice seeming on edge with restrained excitement, of this last catastrophe on earth when the dead would be summoned from the grave and the living from life, as he described the final ruin of the past, the hopelessness of change, calling out a picture of the horrible depths of hell, the sublime paths of Paradise, emphasizing the meaning of the last utter revelation, my sparkling spirits were eaten away, fear began to grow in my bones. Everything, oh, everything, is lost, I thought, for heaven and earth will collapse and bury me! I began to cry bitterly, afraid to look up at the ceiling where cracks surely were beginning to show, convinced that the catastrophe might happen at any moment. My mother's whispered admonitions to "be good so God would forgive my sins when the final day came" were not salve for my nervousness. As soon as the sermon ended I hurried to find Johannes Matthiæ and question him.

"What does all this mean?" I demanded. "Why have you never told me about this horrible day? When will it come? At night?"

He laughed at my naïveté. "You will go to Paradise. But you must be obedient to your teacher all the time, pray to God daily, and study diligently," was his unruffled response.

This answer caused me thoughts that were beyond my age and abilities. What was Paradise, and why? How could there be a no-earth, where would I be, and how? Would it hurt? Would the castle crumble in one blasting shock, or slowly like falling snowflakes? What did my lessons, my obedience have to do with it? Where was God that He collected my prayers and counted them like coins to pay for my safety, was He above, on a cloud, on the moon, on a pink star? Was he man-like, a King with a white beard even longer than my Great-uncle Johan's flowing over his feet, like a picture I had seen of Zeus? Why did he want to destroy heaven and earth, to have a Last Judgment?

I was frightened the next Easter, when I was taken again to hear the same sermon, but not as much as before, and I did not cry. Again I asked my teacher: "When will the Last Day come which is so much talked about?"

"It will come one day," he said, "but do not worry about it, my child. We must be prepared anyhow."

I was not at all satisfied with his reply. It solved nothing for me, so, since there was no help to be had, I began to reason things out for myself. In spite of the preacher's agitation and warnings, life in the castle and the countryside, as far as I could see, had gone on as usual. None of the ceilings had cracked, nor the sky. Each thunderstorm had resolved in sunshine instead of a final catastrophe. By the third time I heard the sermon, the Easter when I was nine years old, I did not believe a word of it. I sat unperturbed through the preacher's descriptions of horror, admiring his acting, secure in my new spirit of doubt.

"Tell me," I said to Johannes Matthiæ a few days later when we were studying, "is all that is said to us about religion a fable like the Judgment Day?"

He glanced at me sharply, spoke crossly. "The very thought of such a thing is a mortal sin! If ever you utter such words again, I will have you thrashed!"

He, too! I sighed my disparagement. His threat, however, irritated me greatly and I answered with haughtiness.

"I promise you not to say any more things like that, but the real reason I do not care to be thrashed is because you would repent of it if it did happen."

I had come to the truth of the matter, I decided. It was not God's idea to create this horror, it was their idea, my mother's, the preacher's, my teacher's, all those in the castle who wished to frighten me into obedience. I further decided it would be wiser not to tell them of my discovery. They might think of something else to try. Perhaps I need not be afraid in my mother's dark chamber nor in the echoing twilight halls. Perhaps danger was not sly, uncatchable, greedy, waiting in shadowy corners. Perhaps God and I could be friends, after all.

It seems that when we finally have succeeded in lifting ourselves out of a great morass of the spirit, as I had lifted myself out of fear, then the rescuer arrives, resplendent and confident. Why does he not come before? I cannot tell, but it always seems to happen this way. We must rescue ourselves, first. My rescuer came to Nyköping Castle in the person of Axel Oxenstierna, the Chancellor of Sweden, and the most distinguished of the five dignitaries who composed the Regency of the Kingdom after my father's death. As he had been out of the country since the year of my birth, taking charge of the governments of the lands my father conquered, I never had seen him. I knew, of course, that he had been my father's closest friend, that Gustav had claimed he would rather lay down his crown than to go on ruling without the help of his Chancellor, that, when the King died, his experience and judgment had continued to be recognized by the Council and the Riksdag and he had guided the country by correspondence. He was the leading statesman, the true head, of Sweden at that time. When he returned from abroad in July of 1636, one of his first acts was to visit my mother and me.

My initial impression on entering the room where the Chancellor waited with Maria Eleonora to meet me was of my mother's tremulous disquiet. She twitched her fan against her black silk gown, her pointed chin raised in weak defiance, her eyelids fluttering, not prettily, but with anger she hesitated in phrasing. She was not having her own way, she was vexed, paled, apprehensive of whatever little victory she sought. An interesting sight. A tall man in black cloth rose from a chair, bowed, not taking his sober eyes from me.

"Your Majesty."

Oxenstierna, I was pleased to note, had a handsome countenance, and, although his light-brown hair and broad beard were salted with gray, no creak of age about him. He stood straight as a soldier, a commander in the field of government, gray-eyed, decision marking his features. I did not look for signs of kindness, I was concerned with his strength, his control, his attentiveness. He bent his large frame and took my hand in his.

"Christina. Gustav Adolf's daughter!"

I waited for him to say how like to the King I was, for the picture of recognition was on his face, but before the Chancellor or I could speak further my mother burst into her chatter, evidently pursuing the press of her whim.

"You see, Axel, how thin she is! It is as I have been telling you. Six hours of study in the morning and six in the afternoon is too much. Why shouldn't I keep her from doing it? And all theology and Latin and Swedish history and such indigestible subjects! She complains of her stomach constantly."

"She must learn these things to be Queen. She cannot be treated as an ordinary child," Oxenstierna answered gravely.

"She should be taught some of the gentler arts. What kind of woman will she become with her head stuffed with dull knowledge and her complexion pimply with no care? See what a mess it is now! She will not wash her face, she will not comb her hair. She will do nothing for her looks, and her manners are cruelly bad. Her teacher gives her nothing but books, books, books. She must spend more time with me."

"Madame, it was the stated wish of King Gustav that his daughter receive the education of a prince. He himself chose Johannes Matthiæ, and wisely. There is not a better professor in Sweden for theology, philosophy, and the classics. And an excellent character, excellent."

"She is my daughter, too, Axel, and only a baby. Oh, my poor little darling, my dear Tina! You are all I have left! Axel, why do you want to rob me of my child? Why do you want to rob her of her childhood?"

She attempted to pull me toward her, but I slipped away to a chair on the other side of the room. Her mouth quivered, a crystal tear rolled down her cheeks. I wrinkled up my nose. The same old trick. Oxenstierna went on talking, disregarding her plea.

"And as you have been informed, Madame, the Estates are concerned about the education of the young Queen-elect who will one day be their ruler. After their conference with the Regents they issued certain directions which cannot be laid aside because of personal considerations. They say it is necessary that, as her subjects are bound to observe toward Her Majesty an entire devotion and fidelity, even to the sacrifice of their lives and property, so, in return, she should feel for them the utmost solicitude and affection. She should be accustomed to speak well of her country and of the Regents, to pay proper respect to her tutors and the Senate, and to protect everyone in the enjoyment of his rights and liberties, according to law. Madame, the Queen-elect must learn what those rights and liberties are."

"My baby! She is only nine years old!"

"The Estates also desire their Queen-elect to be instructed in the manners and languages of other countries, while carefully preserving her own. For such a program twelve hours a day is not too much. Many would consider such an education the pursuit of a lifetime."

"Truly, it is a terrible program! What a monster she will be! Who will love her? Oh, my poor baby!" A wealth of crystal tears filled her eyes.

The Chancellor turned to me. "How do you like your studies, Christina?"

I was pleased to issue my opinion, to expand on points of history that interested me, to flaunt examples of mathematics, of Latin, of French, to confound my mother, to expose my love of books, many books. Johannes Matthiæ, I said, was a teacher dear to my heart, especially when he talked about ancient Greece and Rome. For good measure in my effect, I felt I must comment on my father's favorite, Julius Cæsar, and exclaimed a curiosity as to what he would have been like, what he would have written, if he had known about God.

"I believe he would have opposed the knowledge of God," Oxenstierna replied seriously, "as the later Cæsars did, since it was not compatible with his Roman politics. There would have been a longer list of unfortunate Christians who suffered for adhering to the truth."

"How did they suffer?" I had not been told of this, that anyone suffered for being true to God, rather, the reverse.

"Caligula had them lit as human torches for his entertainment, and for many sad years the Emperors used the Christians as a sport to amuse the populace in the great Colosseum at Rome, letting loose lions into the arena with them to chase and tear them to pieces. And there were other punishments—"

"Axel!" Maria Eleonora could no longer keep quiet. She had been fidgeting in her chair, pinching and pulling at her lace cuff, tapping her toes in a delicate-sounding impatience. She hated not to participate in a conversation, not to be, in fact, its chief songster. I hurried to keep talking.

"But why didn't God save the Christians and give the Emperors to the lions when they were so wicked?"

"You see, Axel, she asks impossible questions. It is no good to teach her history, for she always will ask why it was not different. Why, why, why! How, how, how! If I would allow it, her tongue would waggle all day and nighttimes as well with silly questions. She has no wish to repeat her lessons, she tries to get out of finding the regular answers by asking something odd no one cares about. And why must you tell her these horrible stories? How shall she learn gentleness with such tales roaring in her ears? If she cannot be pretty, she should, at least, be sweet and gentle. Now she shall have wild dreams of lions devouring her and I shall be the one to pay for it, not you. I shall have the task of catching her in the blackness of night when she slips out of bed, screaming, running after her through the chilled halls when everyone else is peacefully sleeping."

The Chancellor turned a calm face to her, like a benign horse contemplating a fluffy dog barking at his heels. "Madame, it appears that Her Majesty is inquisitive of the truth. Such a quality in a child must be encouraged. It occurs to me it would be beneficial to speak to Her Majesty alone to inquire into her studies in detail. Would you be so kind as to permit me to do so?"

She hesitated before replying, not accustomed to being dismissed, even courteously. Then she stood up, one hand holding on to her silken skirt as if for support. He rose, too, slowly.

"Why have you requested my attendance at all, Chancellor, if you only wish to make an examination of Christina's book exercises? Truly, I believed we would hear important news of Germany from you."

"It will be my pleasure to present the news of your family and the German situation to you, Madame. My first duty, however, is to Gustav Adolf's daughter."

"Good day, Chancellor."

He bowed, in a fine manner, I thought, as my mother hastened from the room, her gown rustling around her footsteps. I felt a lovely tingling in my bones. Maria Eleonora could not fool this man, this friend of my father's who realized what was needed to be a real Queen, who treated me as a royal personage, not as a troublesome child. I leaned forward. There was something I was eager to know.

"Chancellor Oxenstierna, did you bring me a present from Germany? My father always did."

"I have brought you a Bible, Your Majesty. We will look at it later. The Bible was your father's closest friend. He kept it at his side wherever he was, and you will do well to copy him."

A Bible! I already owned two, one in Swedish, one in Latin. I had been hoping for a silver boat, a colorful chest, any one of the beautiful things my mother used to describe. I supposed I would have to win them myself, riding at the head of an army on an ebony horse, swinging a jeweled sword. After thanking the Chancellor, there seemed nothing further to say about gifts. His clothes were so plain, his deportment so disciplined, I didn't think he would understand. The intellectual plane was better.

"I can speak German very well," I chatted happily. "Did you see the letters in German I wrote to my father before he died? I was very young, but I penned them myself with no help from my tutor. It will be a splendid thing to speak to people in their own tongue when I travel to France and Germany, will it not?"

Oxenstierna sat down in a chair near me. Even with the light on his face, his eyes seemed colorless, absorbed in a gray stream of thinking. My father's eyes had sparkled a gold-and-blueness, flashing life and vigor into everything he looked at.

"You may never travel to those countries. Why be a fool and run around in foreign lands? Sweden is your country. When God gives you the right to rule and the mind to stand by your land, you must serve His Word with all your will and power and let the well-being of the State be your highest law and highest privilege. The foreign languages you learn are for the protection of the State. You will be able to speak to ambassadors in their native phrases, to read their reports and correspond with them, thereby improving your own understanding and lessening the chances for deception. King Gustav used to tell me I was an instrument given him by God to accomplish difficult things. You, too, are an instrument of God, and it will not be easy to achieve a peaceful welfare in Sweden in the years that lie ahead. I pray for your success. I pray that the poverty I have seen in Germany will not come to Sweden through any weakness or misfortune. There were days there, all too frequently, when I did not know what I would have to give the people to eat the next day or what they were going to live on in a month's time. And the enemy waited every day before the door."

"My mother says I should be taught more about Germany. She told Johannes Matthiæ he spends too much time teaching me Swedish history, that if I did not learn more about Europe I would not know the true meaning of a civilized land."

"I fear your mother does not love Sweden as we do. The Swedish character is the finest in the world. Unhappily, we are engaged now in a war, but it is a necessary war. We cannot be swallowed by the Catholic empire, our freedom taken away. Everyone should give his life's blood, if needed, and forget all personal interests for the good of our fatherland. There is nothing else for me and other good men to do but to fight with honor, even if it is with despair, until death, to win. Some day the war will be at an end, and, with God's help, we will be able to sit under our trees, our linden and oak, and look after our business in peace. We will win a name like the mighty ones in the world and not be an object of scorn, a very footstool, to them, as we unfortunately have been hitherto. King Gustav has hewn a way for us to follow. He raised Sweden to greatness, and we must support that greatness and not let it fall. His brilliance and his courage have struck a bell that sounds in the ears of all Europe. There cannot be another Gustav Adolf, but you, Christina, are his own daughter, the successor to his mind, his vision, his throne. It is for you to continue along his path, to make Sweden glorious. You will need to study hard for this. There is more for you to learn than you can, at this moment, imagine. Now that I am back, I can guide you. We will work together."

I thought I never had heard such inspiring words. I, Christina, would make Sweden glorious! I jumped and ran to him, taking hold of his black sleeve.

"Oh, yes! I will learn it all! Let us start right away. I will show you the books I am reading in my apartment."

The Chancellor patted my hand, smiling for the first time, saying we would begin soon enough, that on this summer's afternoon he would be content for me to tell him, without my books, how far I had progressed. For over an hour he questioned me carefully while I sat, stood, or paced in front of him. When he had satisfied himself as to the quality of my education and the degree I had reached in it, he gave me a curious compliment.

"You have done well, Christina, in consideration of your situation."

My situation? What did he mean? My weak eyesight?

"It is my belief you could progress even more quickly in a stable routine with a guardian more sympathetic to the education your father, the King, desired for you. The King stated that for your guardian he preferred his sister above all others. How would you like to live with the Princess Katarina?"

I thought of my Aunt Katarina, her serene face, cast in a smaller mold of my father's, but with eyes brown as acorns, her rare manner of seeming to understand a person without cumbersome explanations, her quick gestures, at variance with her low, unhurried voice. And she was a Vasa! My mother disliked her, criticized her constantly, which may have been why her visits to Nyköping Castle were infrequent.

"That would suit me very well."

Neither of us flicked an eyelid at disposing of Maria Eleonora and her tearful wishes. Oxenstierna nodded his assent and made as if to go, but there was something more that had to be said.

"And what of my father's heart?"

"Your father's heart?"

"It is in the gold box by my mother's bed."

There was a moment's beating silence.

"Yes. That, too, must go where it belongs. It shall be placed with the King's body in the vault at Riddarholm Church."

I sighed with relief. It had been a remarkably grateful meeting. This austere man, I decided, was clever. He was worthy of having been my father's friend and I would have him for mine.

IV

THERE was no doubt about my Aunt Katarina's welcome being genuine. When I arrived at Stegeborg Castle she hugged me warmly, kissed me emphatically, then, after looking me over, took me to the cheerful apartment that was to be mine and proceeded to comb my hair "in a more becoming way," talking all the while in her pleasant low voice. My Uncle Johan, she said, had a new horse I must see, a handsome bay, strong, yet with a gentle mouth so a good rider should have no trouble with him. If I liked him well enough perhaps I could persuade my uncle to let me have him. It might be too warm still for long rides, but cooler days would be here soon. The boys liked to ride, particularly Carl Gustav, did I remember him, her oldest son? He was thirteen years old now, and what an appetite he had! His father threatened to turn the lawn into a cabbage yard to keep him satisfied.

Then there were Adolf Johan, the second son, and their daughter, Maria Euphrosina, a year older than I. Maria Euphrosina had helped her paint the doll that had been put in my chamber to welcome me. Now where was it! They had had trouble getting the right shade of pink for the cheeks, so it looked a little pale, but Maria Euphrosina had made the dress all herself, of bits of lace and scraps of silk, and she thought it quite pretty. Here it was, whoever had put it inside this chest, the lovely little paper crown was dented! She pulled it out, handed it to me, a flounced piece of frippery with bead eyes and a stupid staring face, just like my mother's ladies-in-waiting, all imitation, its crown jeweled with ordinary garden pebbles. I beheld it in distaste, went to the chest, put it back in where I could not see it.

Aunt Katarina made no comment. She continued talking, saying that at Stegeborg Castle a regular routine was followed, it being easier to accomplish whatever one had to do, that every morning the entire household assembled in the large reception room for a simple devotional, from my Uncle Johan to the least kitchen maid, so each could go to the day's duties with a pious heart. She would be pleased if I would assist her by attending, by setting a shining example to everyone so early in the morning. Yes, I thought, I would enjoy being a shining example, and I assured her no hour in the morning would be too early for me to be there.

If I had remembered my Cousin Carl Gustav, it was as a pudgy little boy with staring blue eyes. He still had the blue eyes and was inclined to stare, happily, at me, but where had his pudginess gone? On the occasion when I first saw him again, when Aunt Katarina presented her children to me, she had taken us into the garden, where the charm of a summer's afternoon lay about us. She had had benches and chairs brought out and arranged beneath the thick rows of small trees so we sat in a little world of green and spattered sunlight, the leafiness hiding everything else, the castle, the outer wall, the bay and ship masts beyond. The air, washed with sea salt, caught the green smell of the trees, the warm odor of sun and dirt, settled contentedly, listened, waited, hummed in companionable languor.

I selected a seat where a spot of gold light fell through the branches onto my shoulders, and contemplated my cousins. Carl Gustav's bow had been practiced, efficient, his voice, oh, how deep, how manly it had sounded, the singsong of childhood lost, dropped into a soft nowhere. He had accepted young manhood, standing straight, disdaining a chair, his chin raised, his shoulders thrust back in a soldierly fashion, his legs planted slightly apart, solidly stanced, and his blue eyes, so kindly, so almost reverently upon me. Locks of brown hair dripped over his brow in a most appealing way, giving him a strong, careless appearance, as if more noble things filled his mind than being neat. Beside him Adolf Johan fidgeted, looking everywhere and at everything to keep from looking at me, edging away after his crooked bow, obviously not caring to show himself other than as what he was, a restless boy.

And Maria Euphrosina. She seemed to carry a dainty satisfaction in herself, a cherry-cheeked little girl with spruce brown curls and green eyes—eyes, fringed in long brown lashes, that should have been wild as the forest depths they resembled, but were not, were tame as a sleepy kitten's. Well fed, well rounded, not overly tall, she moved in confidence, a placid little satellite, folding her hands in her lap, glancing at her mother to note that all was as it should be. Aunt Katarina plied a needle in and out of a skirt for some poor worthy, talked of summer affairs. Maria Euphrosina regarded me steadily, expectantly.

"Christina," she finally ventured, "do you like the doll?"

At this age I saw no reason to decorate the truth. Heaven forbid she tell me the story of how clever she had been in making it.

"No," I said firmly.

She blinked. Her little upturned nose quivered. Was she going to cry? I would give her another chance, if conversation was what was wanted.

"What books are you reading?" I asked.

She calmed. "We are reading the Bible. In Latin, I mean. Isn't Latin awful? Carl Gustav can figure it out for himself. I can't."

Her older brother smiled. Why not, his expression seemed to say, am I not the oldest, the growing man, the one from whom childlishness has been washed away? Of course I can read Latin. He watched me to see if I realized his feeling, if I guessed his concealed power. Why should I let him know? I spoke crisply.

"Latin just needs to have the words moved around. I find it as interesting as chess."

"You must have a game with your Uncle Johan," came in Aunt

Katarina's quiet voice, her look following Adolf Johan, who had stretched himself on the ground, teasing bugs, his feet kicking dirt against her skirt. A lady without nonsense, she was of a humor to tolerate the pranks of her sons, having no vanities they could annoy, her clothes made for practical country wear, almost as plain as theirs.

Not Maria Euphrosina. She pursed her pink lips, began a protest, stilled her tongue as I went into a monologue on the books in Latin I was studying. Clearly, Latin did not interest her. Clothes did. As soon as I paused she started to chatter on gowns, on what her dolls wore, on what fashionable countesses wore, on their elegance, their beauty, their manners. It did not seem to impress her that I was the Queen-elect. I was another little girl, one, moreover, with anonymous qualities. One thing she saw, that I was not beautiful, that I never would be. She did not say it, but I felt it. Her enthusiasm bubbled for the brocades, the fine laces, the azure velvets she, one day, would wear, and no one, she mentioned severely, would dare kick dirt against her gorgeous gowns in her garden.

Aunt Katarina interfered. "Silks and velvets are for court occasions, my dear, and are a joy only for those who look pretty in them. I myself find the wearing of silk not to my advantage. Silk is too delicate for me. It makes my skin look more than ever like leather. And my nose, well, look at it! Did anyone ever see such a beak on a woman's face? If I were in Rome they would make me Queen of the Romans, for surely I would have the biggest Roman nose of all!" And she laughed, her brown eyes brightly amused at pretending to be a hag. To me she was the loveliest figure of a woman I ever knew, withal I could not describe the exact reasons.

"Some day I shall go to Rome by sea," said Carl Gustav.

"I shall go, too," persisted Maria Euphrosina, "and I shall wear a gown the color of our red roses."

Adolf Johan rolled over. "Ha! You never will go to Rome! You cannot even learn the first conjugation."

"When I am in Rome I will speak Italian to everyone," I boasted.

Adolf Johan eyed me. "Speak some now."

"*Fortes fortuna adjuvat.*"

"That sounds like Latin."

"All the elegant Italians speak Latin. Where do you suppose it came from?"

"It is not Italian."

Carl Gustav translated slowly, "The brave, fortune, it favors."

"Yes." I smiled. I was sure he was brave.

Maria Euphrosina jumped up. "Shall I show you the red roses, Christina?"

I hesitated, wondering why I should leave the pleasant bower, its green summer enchantment, to walk to another corner of the garden with a talkative girl, surely a lady-in-waiting-to-be. Did I care about roses, red, orange, purple, whatever? There was one solution.

"Carl Gustav may show me the roses," I countered.

Aunt Katarina rose, folding her sewing. "Let us all go. Truly, the roses bloom well this year, more beautiful than ever before. Perhaps it is for your sake, Christina."

So we walked together. How tall Carl Gustav seemed beside me! His shadow quite enfolded me, whenever I looked down I found I was stepping in and out of it. Behind us came Adolf Johan and Maria Euphrosina, Aunt Katarina preceding us, praising the sweetness of the almost cloudless sky, the white flash of a gull's wing wheeling above the bay, a rising curl of smoke, from some house in the hills, holding itself a question mark in the high, still air. How red were the roses? I do not remember. I suppose we sniffed their perfume, counted the perfect blooms, estimated the buds, giggled in pretended fright at the visiting bees. It is the solid presence of Carl Gustav I remember, his silent protective presence, his sweaty young-man smell near me, his smiling watchfulness of my movements. The sense of the afternoon drifted away on a cloud puff, let it go, let it go. Time has a rosy chariot for youth, we want to climb in like Noah's animals, two by two, thoughtless to ride the amorphous, believing our twoness to be the gem of an uncrystallized future.

In the weeks and months that followed, my oldest cousin and I were not so quiet together. We learned to converse, to exchange confidences, to play games. Best of all were the rides we took around Slätbacken Bay, its waters alive, sunlit, open, rippling with the breeze from the Baltic, and off through the pine woods in the hills, outstripping our attendants, urging our horses to a race with madness, leaping across fallen logs and streams as if they were our only obstacles to freedom. We laughed as the wind burned our eyes, tugged at our hair, called to each other that the wind had stolen Pegasus and rode with us. Could we gallop after him into the stars?

Carl Gustav was an excellent shot, so I became one, too, able to shoot a hare with a single ball at a full gallop. Ah, but the hare! I could not bear his dying, his wild eyes darting ahead to the bush he could not reach, the blood, the helplessness, the fatality of ending.

"Come on," Carl Gustav would call. "Don't act like a sentimental girl!"

And I would ride on, burying my pity as well as I could.

As the twilight and ice of winter closed in on us, we spent more and more time indoors. Then is when I came to appreciate my uncle, Johan Casimir, the German Count Palatine, his honesty, his clarity, his dispassionate judgment. Aunt Katarina never tired of singing his praises, of telling how he had taken her to live in his family territory in Germany when they first were married, of how the uncertainties and horrors of the war had surrounded them there, how they had fled back to Sweden. Gustav Adolf had been glad to have them, had given them Stegeborg Castle and appointed his brother-in-law High Treasurer of the Kingdom, an office he had fulfilled brilliantly. The remarkable fiscal system he had initiated still was used, Aunt Katarina said, although he had been relieved of his office after Gustav's death, a fine bit of gratitude for all he had done, everyone knew he had the best head for finance in the country. Why, then? I had asked. Dear, dear Christina, the Swedish nobles hate foreigners, and a man never stops being a foreigner to them if he was not born here, she said. Do you think Chancellor Oxenstierna would allow a foreigner to hold the purse strings of Sweden? Now it is his brother Gabriel who is High Treasurer.

How, I wondered, had the Chancellor taken me to this castle to live, having such sentiments? He, evidently, held the true power, and, just as evidently, he and my uncle wasted no love between them. I resolved to ask Uncle Johan, and chose an afternoon when he had invited me into his study for roasted nuts. He, Carl Gustav, and I had pulled our chairs close to his blue-and-white stove. There was a comradely feeling, a cozy friendliness, as if I were not a young girl. I decided to be direct, like a man.

"Uncle Johan, you do not like Chancellor Oxenstierna!"

"No?" He stroked his short beard.

"Why did he bring me here if he does not trust you?"

So that's it, his expression seemed to say. He waited a moment, his head bent, in a way he had as if he were gathering his answer from the corners of his mind, sifting it, testing it for understanding.

"Well—" he looked up, solemn yet pleasant—"let us give the Devil his due. Axel Oxenstierna's devotion to your father exceeds his personal ambition, which I admit, nay, I charge, is very strong. Gustav Adolf's word was law to him, still is. When the King died, many believed the power of the country would die with him, that the Emperor's armies would sweep across the Baltic into Sweden, that the government would collapse without its great guide and protector. Everyone had a different idea on what to do. The bönder were persuaded that Gustav's cousin, King Ladislau of Poland, should be permitted to claim our throne, to be our immediate leader. You, you will recall, were a tiny girl, unknown, except by name, outside your family. Any authority you had had to be represented for you. Some of the nobles were enthusiastic about setting you aside in favor of a republic, thinking, probably, to increase their own importance. Doubtless Oxenstierna would have been the head of it. Not only is he an able man, but he comes of an ancient powerful family that once rivaled the Vasas, and, for all their talk of a 'republic,' it is family background that counts with the nobles.

"Well, old Oxenstierna proved to be a rock of good faith. He was in Frankfurt, as you know, and he wrote back that everything had to proceed exactly as Gustav Adolf had planned, that you should be legalized as the hereditary princess, that the Regency the King had chosen, composed of the five highest dignitaries of the State, of whom he, of course, was the highest, was to rule until you attained your majority, that the war was to continue unabated under a new commander. Now, he was safe in advising this, he must have had a say in selecting the five Regents, Gustav always listened to him, else why would there be three Oxenstiernas among the five and no Count Palatine? However, he would not dream of defying the King's wish to have your Aunt Katarina as your guardian. He could not touch Gustav's affection and admiration for his sister, who could? Or who could hint that she is not a paragon of virtue? No, he will protect her right, whatever he thinks of me. Alive or dead, Gustav is King to him, the greatest King Sweden ever had. And he will be loyal to you, my child, never fear that he shall desist for a moment. But do not doubt that he does not rule Sweden as Chancellor. He does not need to be King. He is the oracle of the Riksdag, or of the nobles, at least, which is sufficient."

"He need not take all the credit for supporting Christina as Queen-elect," grumbled Carl Gustav. "Why don't you tell her what you did?"

I remembered that Aunt Katarina had told me my uncle ever had been my stanchest supporter, in good times and bad, that his heart was whole in my cause. I remembered, too, my mother, in the early days, weeping: "They would not dare! They would not dare put a Polish King on the throne of Sweden—not a Catholic, after Gustav!" Yes, I remembered the words, but the meaning had not been borne in to me before. I had taken for granted I would be Queen. Who else was there? Now, Uncle Johan assuring me Oxenstierna would be loyal to me expressed, more than any negative warning statement that there were those who believed he might not be loyal, that there were people who did not want me on the throne, who were my enemies.

"What would they do to me?" I asked.

Uncle Johan raised his eyebrows. "Who?"

"The people who don't want me to be Queen."

He reached over and patted my hand. "The danger is past, but those were dangerous days for the monarchy. It was the throne that was in danger, not you, Christina. Who would wish to harm the daughter of the beloved Gustav Adolf?"

Who! Whoever wanted the throne, I supposed. Who poisoned King Erik? Who tied his little son in a sack and hauled him off to dispose of him in the forest? That the boy was saved, by the grace of God and the quickness of a friendly squire's eye who noticed the bulge in the sack and rescued him, to smuggle him off to Muscovy, might not happen again. Next time no one might be on the road. Did Uncle Johan think I had not been taught history? Now, for me, the enemy was abstract. Or was it?

Carl Gustav was stubborn. "Tell her what you did!"

Uncle Johan gestured, depreciating his role. "It was natural for me to lead the support in your favor. It was the only thing to do. With panic facing the country, a number of us at home banded together, swearing we would defend Sweden, come what may. The next step was to have the Estates convene to decide on the continuing form of government and to choose a King. It was a blessed honor for me to speak for you, my child, to have you to defend, whom I love and trust. I am not a fighting man if you think of fighting as armies and battlefields, but never have I retreated when victory could be won in a battle of minds."

These were words to ponder, and ponder them I did, although,

I must admit, not to the exclusion of my pleasure. The substitution of possible human enemies for the grandiose but vague punishment of God did not disturb me as much as it would have if I had not been surrounded by an affectionate family and engaged in a wealth of activities. Nevertheless, the meaning adhered, and was etched more deeply in subsequent talks with Uncle Johan. He, one of the kindest persons in the world, alleged that some might think I was too young to be told unpleasant facts, but since I was to be Queen and would have to make serious decisions, even, perhaps, have it in my own power to choose between peace and war, it would be better for me and for Sweden to learn that the world was not a pretty place to live in except as we tried to make it so, that politics was a complicated tangle of many spheres of interest, that the truth could be discovered and pursued by those not waylaid by the flattery of the ambitious or blinded by naïveté and wishfulness. He expanded, too, on the black destructiveness of war, on terrible sights he had seen with his own eyes, on tales he heard that would tear your heart apart, brought to him as the war in Germany stumbled on, year after year.

His theory of winning victories with the mind appealed immensely to me. Carl Gustav and I argued its value day after day. Nothing would take the place of a gun, he would say, had I ever heard of an important country without a busy army? When he was a man he wasn't going to fuss around making speeches in the Riksdag, he would be out in the field where decisions were made in a clear, clean, unmuddled way, he would be a general.

It was dreadful to think of him, of his dear tousled head, in danger of bullets and hostile swords.

"Why not stay home and be King beside me?" I asked.

Well, that would be all right, to be King, Carl thought, but he couldn't stay home, look at my father, how concerned he had been for Sweden's glory and for rescuing the poor people in other countries.

"I would as soon ride at the head of an army myself, I'm not afraid, I'm as sharp a shot as you are!" I would snap.

It seemed natural to plan to be together, afield or in a Swedish castle. Thus, innocently, we played at being man and wife. How easy it was to say "wife" and "husband," to plan "Queen" and "King," titles glowing with happiness in our youthful imagination, terms not yet harnessed to reality!

Yes, I felt secure and happy at Stegeborg Castle. Princess Katarina managed her family and home with such skill and kindness that her household stood out as a model of amiable correctness to all who knew her. Her own virtues were so many, her quiet strength seemingly so inexhaustible, as to have made her into a saint if she had not been in rapport with her time and surroundings. She saw and accepted the good in everything, letting the rest, the not good, wither away from lack of attention. If a problem persisted, she set herself to its cure as best she could, not with any exaggerated notion of reform, wrapping her resolute Vasa will in familiar sympathy and patience. Poverty, for example, and sickness were problems wherever they were, she told me, and it was wise to remember that because we had been blessed by God in wealth and condition He expected us to work harder than others in His way, to share what we knew and had as widely as possible to tether Sweden to His authority, His scheme. None in her neighborhood could be ill but she must attend and comfort them, setting out on the coldest days in her furs and boots, her painted sled stocked with special foods and, of course, a Bible. Nor did she leave the poor to struggle alone with their miserable lot, her beliefs being more than a topic for conversation, but she arranged a system of aid for them whereby they could be helped even though they were too proud or too shy to ask, calling on them herself with gifts and friendly words. Most important for my stay, however, was the love, expansive, intelligent, unremitting, she showed for me. My apprehension may be guessed when she came to my apartment, one day, to ask me to prepare for a journey to Stockholm to see my mother.

"No." I rejected the prospect.

"It is only for a short visit. She is moving to Gripsholm Castle."

Gripsholm, seat of dowager Queens, castle of prisons! I could picture Maria Eleonora beneath its red towers, barring herself within its stronghold walls, thirteen feet in thickness, fluttering her authority and morose fantasies through all of the ninety rooms. How splendid it had looked to me when my father had taken me there to visit my grandmother! Set on an islet in Lake Mälaren, its apple-red towers were festive in summer above the bright green of clustering trees and the blue water of the lake, rippling almost to its base, while in winter they had appeared to be gigantic rubies left on a scarf of white velvet. Inside it was not so gay, or I, at least, could not feel it so. On the second floor of one of the towers was the room where King Johan had waited five years while King Erik wavered weakly on whether to free him, to kill him, or to keep him imprisoned. My grandfather, King Carl, had had the room frescoed, the walls and vaulted ceiling, in a design of leaves, cherries, and fruit, to make it one of the prettiest rooms in the castle, but he could not decorate its past history, and I could not go in there without thinking of King Johan, wondering how many times he had paced from wall to alcove to window in those years, how, held to a limit in his vision of the outer world, he had let his inner vision grow and grow into his enveloping dream. Then there was the secret prison room, a rough cold old cannon room with double iron doors opening off the secret stairs behind the throne room, where two colonels from Finland scratched on the wall on April 3, 1600, that they had been there for two years. What happened to them? Still, how much better off they had been than the thousands of nameless prisoners left to rot in the regular prison under the castle, to stoop or lie on the brown earth, to moan like cattle. Who noted when they came or if they left? There were too many prisons in Gripsholm Castle for my taste, but my mother, who never meditated on the fortunes of others, particularly the nameless, the poor, and the dead, wore a silken armor against such vain thoughts. The prisoners would be no more than last summer's flies to her. Why should they? She was her own prisoner, wherever she moved she could not reach beyond the bars of her grief and her fancies. But I did not want to be caught, again, in her nebulous prison.

"Are you going with me?" I asked my aunt.

"Yes, of course." She stooped to put her arms around my shoulders, telling me what we should take with us, how we would proceed, letting me know she understood my emotion. It had been all she could do, she said, to keep from carrying me away with her on her visits to Nyköping Castle on observing my life there, but one didn't kidnap a princess, even when she was your own niece, even when she had been set to a task beyond her years, to console her mother's consuming sorrow for a beloved husband. Not that she blamed Maria Eleonora. Maria Eleonora always had been like that, beautiful and impractical, loving to hang on to things, to baby dresses, old broken rings, unfinished embroideries, to memories, to melodies, and, now, to grief. But that was over for me. When I saw her on these occasional visits I must forget I had been an unwilling part of it, I must speak nicely to her, be considerate of her health, tell her how I had progressed in my studies. I must remember one always honors one's father and mother.

"No matter what?" I asked.

"No matter what," she answered with her serious smile.

So we went to Stockholm Castle, and, as Aunt Katarina had prophesied, it was not as bad as I had expected. My mother made no gesture to recapture me. She was disgusted with the Councillors for arranging her retirement to Gripsholm, indignant that they would not listen to her architectural schemes. Imagine, she had offered to contribute to the culture of Sweden, a country that certainly needed someone to attend to the finer things of life, and they had shut their ears to her. She was studying architecture, she knew what it was about, she knew a pilaster from a pillar, Ionic from Doric, a plane from a plan. Did they? Her brown eyes indicated they did not, not at all. She did not compliment me on my manners, as I had hoped, neither did she argue with me on them, so, on the whole, the meeting could be counted a success. I returned triumphantly to Stegeborg to discuss the visit with Carl Gustav, to tell him, too, about seeing Chancellor Oxenstierna and the other Regents, to describe Stockholm's crowded streets and the harbors massed with foreign ships. He had been there many times, he said, but he liked to hear what I thought about it. The countryside really was better, wasn't it?

The subsequent visits were even easier, fitting into the pleasant routine that was my life. Looking back, I see how very pleasant it was, the months seeming to race by, as if it were a hare's leap from one year's end to another, until we came to the December of my twelfth birthday. The raw weather, gray, swirling in snow, of that month spread a depressed spirit through the castle, unusual for it. Aunt Katarina became ill, and, disappointingly, was not present at my birthday celebration. For a week or so afterward we dragged along, waiting for her cheering stabilizing reappearance, then she summoned us all to her chamber for the morning prayers. How buoyantly I hurried through the chilled apartments to her room!

The moment I entered she signaled for me to approach her bedside, and I did, utterly unprepared for what I was to see. She lay on the bed, emaciated, the bones of her cheeks seeming to push through a flesh that had lost interest in color. Her hair, once the glossy brown of autumn chestnuts, was dispersed wantonly in drab strands. Above the coverlet, pulled up to her chin, only her eyes seemed able to move and hold on to the shadows of their former brown brilliance, and they moved as if they carried a heavy weight within. I stared at her, and then around the room. The entire household was there, the family and the servants, most of them with their hands clasped ready for the day's devotional. Uncle Johan was at the window, fastening it against the wind, the silver winter wind. This morning the snow was not falling, banked upward in mounds of clouds above the bay and castle. I wondered if they would spill over before noon.

My aunt drew back my attention with a hoarse whisper. "Christina, will you read for us today?"

Her look toward me was an insistence. I picked up the Bible from the table, opened it where the ribbon lay at the second chapter of the Revelation of St. John the Divine, and read, slowly, the quiet of the room falling about me like a spell.

"*Unto the angel of the church of Ephesus write; These things saith he that holdeth the seven stars in his right hand, who walketh in the midst of the seven golden candlesticks; I know thy works, and thy labour, and thy patience, and how thou canst not bear them which are evil. . . .*"

The domestics pressed into the gray shadows of the walls, their heads bowed in listening.

". . . *I have somewhat against thee, because thou hast left thy first love. Remember therefore from whence thou art fallen, and repent, and do the first works; or else I will come unto thee quickly, and will remove thy candlestick out of his place, except thou repent. . . .*"

The metallic light in the room dulled. I tipped the Bible toward the window to see the words.

". . . *be thou faithful unto death, and I will give thee a crown of life. He that hath an ear, let him hear what the Spirit saith unto the churches; He that overcometh shall not be hurt of the second death. And to the angel of the church in Pergamos write; These things saith he which hath the sharp sword with two edges; I know thy works, and where thou dwellest, even where Satan's seat is. . . .*"

On the other side of the bed Adolf Johan shifted and coughed, Maria Euphrosina, hushed as a mouse, hardly seemed to breathe, Carl Gustav stood straight and calm, his eyes lowered to the carpet.

". . . *To him that overcometh will I give to eat of the hidden manna, and will give him a white stone, and in the stone a new name written, which no man knoweth saving he that receiveth it. . . .*"

At the head of the bed the form of Uncle Johan swayed very slightly, as if the support he leaned against was edging away.

"*. . . These things saith the Son of God, who hath his eyes like unto a flame of fire, and his feet are like fine brass; I know thy works, and charity, and service, and faith, and thy patience, and thy works; and the last to be more than the first. . . .*"

Small crying sounds broke out among the domestics, were smothered, and broke out again.

"*. . . But that which ye have already hold fast till I come. And he that overcometh, and keepeth my works unto the end, to him will I give power over the nations: And he shall rule them with a rod of iron; as the vessels of a potter shall they be broken to shivers: even as I received of my Father. And I will give him the morning star. He that hath an ear, let him hear what the Spirit saith unto the churches.*"

I closed the book, looked at Aunt Katarina. She half opened her eyes, trying to stretch one hand toward me.

"Christina."

I moved closer to take her hot fingers into my own cool hand. The breath through her dry lips was sour.

"Always love Him, Christina. Always be in fear of Him. You must prove your devotion to God in each duty."

"Yes, Aunt Katarina." *And he that overcometh . . . to him will I give power over the nations. . . . I will give him the morning star . . . the morning star. . . . Let him hear what the Spirit saith.*

"Obey your governors, as your father wished. Axel Baner and Gustav Horn are good men. And Johannes Matthiæ has a godly mind. Let him guide you."

A coldness swept around my neck. Aunt Katarina believed she was going to die! I watched her to see how the flame flickered. The air of the world was a thread through her body.

"Love Sweden, love your fatherland, and serve it with your whole heart. You will have great duties to perform. Be diligent, and spare no trouble to do them well. You have the mind and the strength."

She sighed. The servants were weeping openly, some quite

noisily, and Maria Euphrosina was wiping her eyes with her fists. I had no tears at all, indeed I felt as if all moisture had been absorbed out of me, my mouth was dry as if I had been chewing on a linen sheet. My words sounded hollow to me, like someone else's.

"I will perform my duties for Sweden with God's help."

My aunt turned her face on the pillow. Tears slipped down her cheeks, flowing crystals of living and leaving. Did she not want to meet *he that holdeth the seven stars in his right hand, who walketh in the midst of the seven golden candlesticks?*

"I leave behind my husband and children, Christina." Her bony fingers tightened on mine. "I beg your favor for them. I beg of you to give them your royal protection. Will you promise me this, Christina, before I go? It is all I ask of the world."

Carl Gustav raised his eyes to me, Adolf Johan, too, while their sister wept. Their father moved his lips in a private prayer. Oh, the pity of it! She, the best of all women, the only one worthy of love!

"I promise, Aunt Katarina."

Be thou faithful unto death, and I will give thee a crown of life. She relaxed, pulled my hand to her dry lips, kissed it. I felt awkward in taking it away as her hold loosened. Her gaze turned to the sobbing servants. She would console them, she would be he that overcometh, she would let them see she would not be hurt by the second death.

"Do not weep. I leave here many friends, but many others have gone before me and are expecting me now in the place to which I am hastening."

She would meet them all in time, her husband, her children, her friends, me. Wherever she was, wherever she was led to, she would be waiting for me to come, I thought, wearing my crown and holding the morning star.

Her lids sank over her eager eyes, her brow contracted in pain. Uncle Johan came to me, took my hand, and walked with me from the room. I never saw her again, for two days later she died, but my memory of our parting and of my promise did not diminish. I knew she had put the promise in my hand as one of the seven golden candlesticks. It was to illuminate our way together. On earth, in heaven, I could not fail her while I held it.

And not long afterward came another parting, just as painful, if more temporary. I was to be sent to Stockholm Castle, where the Regents were to select a new guardian for me, Carl Gustav was to travel abroad to widen his education. Our farewell was hasty, for we, pressed by the tumultuous preparations for leaving, had difficulty in finding a corner of the castle where we could be alone.

"Kiss me," I said, "kiss me." It was necessary. Lovers always kissed.

He put his hand on my pointed chin, kissed my pale little mouth.

"Will you write to me?" Why couldn't we talk? Carl never had been garrulous, but I!

He nodded. "Yes, I will write. Will you?"

"Of course." I would write every day, I would tell him the events of the castle, what I was doing, I would share my innermost thoughts. Had I really appreciated him? I would now, now that he would be away. How would I endure the months without him?

V

STOCKHOLM, Stockholm! I can see it, hear it, smell it. It was wound in among all my feelings, all my activity, and, like me, it was a youngster growing out of its own skin, pressed upward, outward, by the multitudinous affairs of men and women, of its inside and outside worlds. In the maze of narrow streets on the islands of the old city, my carriage drove among carts hauling hills of hay and stacks of wood, past horses, mules, barking dogs, soldiers, housewives shopping, arguing merchants, foreign sailors freshly in port standing in little groups, well-dressed traders, children dodging under and barely away from the noses of the coach horses, fine carriages carrying court visitors, who leaned back, burying their noses in perfumed linens against the town's stench. There was the stink of the drain from the houses, the smell of wood smoke, of dung, of spilled vegetables, of snow ground into mud. Wheels sinking and pulling out of the sticky mud streets creaked like viols out of tune, women, leaning from the low windows of timber houses, signaled to vanishing children in birdlike calls, servants shook rugs and covers from mullioned windows of the new stone houses of the wealthy, laughed and gossiped with neighbors, flirted with passers-by, the calls of workmen, the echoes of hammering, of boards dropped on boards, told of the many new palaces being raised. Forty thousand human beings are crowded into this City between the Bridges where, a hundred years ago when Gustav Vasa first marched in as

King, four hundred people had lived. Gradually the dwellings have spread to the banks on the other side of The Stream. The steeple of the Great Church is no longer alone in the sky, the spires of Riddarholm and lesser churches rising with it above the pattern of rooftops. And over the nest of the city's activity, like a Queen duck watching her ducklings preen and stretch, is the Polish tower of Stockholm Castle, its cylindrical neck topped by the Three Crowns, glistening, proud, secure in its modern magnificence, standing on the foundations of the ancient stone fort.

Beneath the tower, within the walls, beats the nervous heart of Sweden. There is the seat of government decisions, the home of the King, the monument of the people. Inside the main gate, lining the great courtyard, are the government offices, the court chapel, the kitchen, and the stairway to the entrance of the castle itself, guarded by King Johan's columned arches. The smell of cooking mingles with the odor of sanctity, the smell of horses with the perfume of countesses. The clap of feet hurrying across the stone pavement, the clank of horses' hoofs and the slam of carriage doors, high-pitched phrases of arrivals and departures punctuate the murmur of official discussions and directions. Petitioning boors and ambitious nobles flow in and out, tradesmen, clergymen, ambassadors with liveried servants, soldiers on burnished horses, seamstresses, cabinetmakers, court ladies in Parisian carriages, fussed secretaries, messengers. The hours of the day reverberate in movement.

My apartment eventually had to be moved to another part of the castle so that my windows opened onto a quiet courtyard where there was no rude noise to compete with my studies. As successor to my aunt, the Chancellor had named his sister, Beata Oxenstierna, but the appointment was only nominal. I had little to do with her, and it was the Chancellor himself who undertook to guide my personal as well as my public education. Of the two senators selected by my father to superintend my learning together with Johannes Matthiæ, one died not long after my move to Stockholm and was not replaced. He was Axel Baner, Grand

Master of the Royal House and boon companion of Gustav, particularly on his drinking-parties, gruff, headstrong, seasoned as a courtier, whose great value lay in that there was not a scrap of his being that did not roar with honesty. The other, Gustav Horn, presented a very different aspect for my edification. Book-wise and cultured, a linguist and traveled diplomat, he stimulated my speaking in foreign tongues, so, having a marvelous facility, I began to pick up languages without formal instruction. I never did have a master for French, Italian, German, or Spanish, although I have learned to speak them well. My father had declared very positively that he would not have my governors or tutor instill any feminine sentiments in me except those of honor and virtue, in all other respects he would have me a prince, instructed in all that a young prince should know. In this my inclinations seconded his designs, for I had then, as now, an invincible antipathy to all that women do or say. I was utterly unable to learn their handiwork, nor could any of the countesses who frequented the castle teach me anything of it. My talent, even then, was for problems of government and foreign politics. For this, I could not have had a better teacher than Chancellor Oxenstierna.

At the time I moved to Stockholm Castle, Axel Oxenstierna was fifty-five years old, on the side of the ancients to my eyes, but, I decided, he must have been old always, I could not imagine him young, rash, pink-cheeked. His gray hair, his grayish indoors complexion, the musty smell of his large, gaunt, black-clothed body, appearing the same, day after day, affected me like a book of theology in Latin. He was aged learning in the flesh. Nor, as far as I could see, did he vary from this in the bosom of his family. His wife—an entirely sensible woman, for what other kind would he have tolerated? —existed for his comfort and his home. To her he addressed a profound courtesy, although I never heard him ask her opinion on anything. Quite rightly. I would not have done so myself. His sons, Erik and Johan, were the golden apples of his eye. Not of mine. Both of them older than I, I could not help comparing them to Carl Gustav to their disadvantage, their eyes lacking the luster of the hunting-fields, their thick hair untousled by the wind. Moreover, they did nothing to make themselves especially agreeable to me. It was enough for them to be Oxenstiernas, dull, healthy, important. Their father had been important as long as anyone in Sweden could remember. They took it as the natural course of things that they would be, too.

Yes, I thought, Axel Oxenstierna must have been born a statesman. He must have been one of those oldish young men when my grandfather, Carl IX, chose him as guardian for his children, since he was only twelve years older than my father. He had been recognized, already, as an able senator, had won the confidence of King and Council, had shown proof of his shrewd, deliberate mind, had swayed votes by the dry measures of his eloquence. When Carl IX died, it was he who persuaded the Estates of Gustav Adolf's genius and was responsible for his being crowned King immediately, although still a minor of seventeen. Gustav promptly appointed him as his Chancellor, loved him as his friend, consulted him, let him work out the details of his schemes abroad and at home. They used to meet under an old oak tree a few miles outside of Stockholm for their discussions, the two minds, one flaming, imaginative, bold, impulsive, the other dispassionate, calculating, stepping only on stones of logic. "If we all were as cold as you, we should freeze," Gustav once exclaimed to him, to which Oxenstierna replied: "If we all were as hot as Your Majesty, we should burn up." So the two combined, a perfection in alchemy, for the development of Sweden.

After the King's death, the Chancellor continued to direct Sweden alone, as head of the Regency, for who could challenge his brain, his experience, his vast accumulation of facts? Who could challenge his prodigious memory, his mental agility, his acute sense of organization, both in himself and in everything he handled? How else could he have run the government by correspondence during the years he was out of the country, his left hand on the Riksdag, his right hand moving all over Europe in foreign diplomatics? Europe certainly realized his ability, and how could they help it? He knew the strong and weak points of every State in Europe and he was wily as Richelieu in using his knowledge. They realized, too, he could not be deterred by bribes nor won through weaknesses, Sweden was his love, work his expression of love. He was as skillful in French and German as in Swedish, but facts were his true language. He knew every nuance of their meanings, every strength of their implications. He ruled by facts, by his command of them, his use of them to bombard a meeting he wished to dominate. Many was the time we were interrupted, when studying together, by a messenger summoning him to give weight to an argument at the Council. He would be off in his red sled, to lift the reins of the argument as easily as he drove his trusty horse. A few words from Oxenstierna could change the whole vote. Indefatigable and assiduous, his relaxation being to seek more work to do, his energy could wear out everyone else, everyone, that is, except me. If he was the perfect master for me, I was the perfect pupil for Oxenstierna. Sitting with this gray, reserved man, I gulped down facts as fast as he gave them to me, I flexed my mind to follow his, I spent hours of reading in research of my own to present my view of a question. By the time I was fourteen I showed such a capacity that the Chancellor prevailed on the other members of the Council to allow my presence at their deliberations on public affairs of importance.

At these meetings I not only absorbed the political material that was mulled over, I watched the Regents, listened to them, to gauge their characters. I learned how the Chancellor turned the four other Regents to his will, even if one of them had a better solution than he. Two of them were relatives, Gabriel Oxenstierna, the High Treasurer, and Gabriel Gustav Oxenstierna, the Grand Seneschal, who could be counted on to be judicious-sounding and loud in their final support. Baron Carl Carlsson Gyllenhielm, the High Admiral, a grave, kindly Councillor, who was my father's illegitimate brother, was pushed by the Chancellor to feel he would stand in the way of Sweden's progress if he opposed him. Ships and the sea the Baron knew like the inside of his pocket, but finance, produce, copper, the intrigues of the German princes, these, to him, were a maze to be explored, gradually, as needed, and when the Chancellor turned his falcon eyes on him, reciting facts in his even tone, spreading a November air in the Council room, it was sharply borne in on the Baron that he was on land, where men invented new kinds of problems, where numbers performed different acrobatics than at sea, where he and Nature were a little behind the times, if "times" were the Chancellor's brain.

The fourth Regent, Jacob de la Gardie, the Grand Constable, was the gentleman who had won lovely Ebba Brahe for his wife. Astute as he was, victorious as he had been when a marshal in the German War with Gustav, there would be no doubt of the outcome of a clash between him and Oxenstierna if it were taken to the Estates. A lifetime of service and devotion to Sweden could not wipe out his French background. His taste, his finesse, his culture, were they not matters for suspicion rather than trust? The Constable himself had ceased worrying his heart about whether the measures he proposed were adopted or frowned upon. He was old, older than the Chancellor, his cheeks sagging with wrinkles, and, long ago, he had decided to accept, rather than fight, the prejudices and vagaries of men. Meeting him as a connoisseur of peace, of gentle qualities, of beauty in every form, it was hard to picture him as the warrior he once had been.

At first I marveled at the way Chancellor Oxenstierna seemed to forget himself and his own interests in his devotion to Sweden, at how he eradicated the sense of his personal being in his orations on "the need of the country," "the security of the people," and "the development of our beloved Sweden." Then, as I grew older and began to work out new ways to solve old problems, solutions that Oxenstierna carefully explained to me were as practical as a sieve for carrying soil, I came to see the hidden "I" in his thinking and speechmaking. What he really meant was "I am the need of the country, I am the security of the people, I am your beloved Sweden, your development lies in my brain." Nights when I lay awake I planned how to challenge that "I," how to startle him into an uneasiness that there might be something in Sweden beyond his eyesight. I tried him with facts I had learned from the bönder in their cottages, with viewpoints I had gained from my uncle, the Count Palatine, with ideas that came to me through my own omnivorous reading, but he trimmed off my talk, imperturbably, as if it had been an ungainly shoot in his green diplomatic hedge. Oh, I thought, if only Carl Gustav were here!

I missed Carl Gustav very much. There was no companion so dear to me, no person in whom I could repose such complete confidence. Oxenstierna, I soon discovered, had not rescued me from Nyköping Castle for my own sake. Not at all. I was a chess Queen that had to be moved for Sweden's sake. My mother's continuing fondness for Germany was too dangerous for young ears and impressionable minds, he told me, and, worse than that, she had become involved in an intrigue to marry me to Prince Ulrick, son of the King of Denmark, an inveterate enemy of Sweden, or, I added to myself, of Oxenstierna. He had arrived home just in time to frustrate her plan. No wonder she was furious.

I laughed contemptuously. "I would not marry Prince Ulrick!"

The Chancellor was not surprised. "Of course not. That would be a political mistake. Denmark is over-anxious to keep Sweden from occupying the shores of the Baltic."

I stared at him. He continued talking, oblivious of my rising emotion.

"Your father the King's project is more suitable. He believed a marriage with Friedrich Wilhelm, son of the Elector of Brandenburg, would be most advantageous. The two great Protestant countries would be united, and the Baltic would be a Swedish lake. When I was last in Berlin I mentioned the possibility of such a marriage to the Elector. He, naturally, cherishes the prospect." The Chancellor smiled complacently. "You may notice how much more favorable he has been to Sweden since then."

I was hot with displeasure. What about me, Christina? Did no one think to ask my opinion? I lifted my chin, spoke sharply. I would not be overlooked. "I may not choose to marry Friedrich Wilhelm, either."

"The daughter of Gustav Adolf has plenty of suitors," Oxenstierna said, in what he must have thought was a reassuring tone. Oh, yes, I had plenty of suitors, the King of Hungary, the Archduke of Austria, my three Polish cousins, sons of King Sigismund, who still called himself King of Sweden, and how many others! Oxenstierna enumerated them, with their advantages and disadvantages for Sweden and the war in Germany, while I tried to control myself, looking around my study at the parchment books, at the blue draperies, heavy and still, framing the window, at a rubbed spot on the floor, at the cold silver lines of the candlesticks. Was I to be the last to be consulted on my own destiny?

I jumped off my chair, my fists tight. "Chancellor Oxenstierna! I will not have my name handed around like a fowl at a banquet!"

"Your Majesty, that is a penalty of royal birth. Everyone knows your name, everyone uses it. Whoever can gain by it will do so. If you expect the world to be different, you will be needlessly unhappy."

"I will marry whom I choose! Perhaps I shall marry someone in Sweden, not any foreign prince at all."

Again the complacent smile. The Chancellor leaned back in his big oak chair, crossed his long legs. His eyes turned reminiscently to the past.

"Some years ago King Louis of France, or, if you will, Cardinal Richelieu, proposed a marriage between you and one of my sons. It was expedient for me to be polite, although it was impossible to consider such a thing seriously. I tell you simply that you see you are not alone in believing one of Sweden's sons would be worthy of your hand."

Erik! Johan! Those boobs! I screamed, beating my fists on the table. "I will marry the one I choose!"

The Chancellor nodded. Would nothing shake him? His voice was as calm as ever.

"Certainly, Your Majesty, no marriage agreement can be concluded without your consent."

My storm subsided suddenly. I dropped my hands, walked back to my chair. "Now," I said, "will you tell me the news from our Marshal, Johan Baner?" And we went on to less personal discussions.

Not long after this conversation Carl Gustav came back. How can I describe my elation? During the two years he had traveled abroad, he had grown into the flower of his young manhood. In his eighteenth year, neither tall nor particularly handsome, there was a sturdiness about him, an air of maturing sincerity, a direct friendliness, akin to devotion, in his attitude that meant more to me than if he had posed as an Adonis. A faint brown fuzz grew above his upper lip, the beginnings of a mustache, and his good-natured eyes, that once had mirrored for me the fields and blue lakes we both loved, had become more impenetrable, more serious. They had beheld Paris, Brussels, new people, new habits. I thought if I looked into them hard enough I could read everything he had seen. He himself was not loquacious about his journey, but, to me, his silences were permeated with excitement. The wonders of Paris, I thought, are on the edges of his mind, the speech of the sophisticated, of the great, sounds in his ears, while a wonderful affection for me swells his being so that he cannot speak, or does not wish to speak, in ordinary terms. Every word he spoke, every step I saw him take, glittered with importance. Why? He was mine. I had thrown a robe of love around his shoulders.

We were not able to see one another as frequently as we would have liked. The old days of freedom, when we lived in the same castle, rode in the same woods, bowed our heads in the same chapel, were gone. We met at court functions, where we talked as best we could under the watchfulness of my guardians. The Regents' disapproval of our friendship was easily noticed and, after my conversation with Oxenstierna, easily understood. Their ambitions for Sweden and for me did not include the son of a Palatine Count of negligible political significance compared to a choice of the crowns of Europe. There was no man in the world but would have thought himself happy if I deigned to give him my hand. I, however, was bound to choose my own destiny, and my heart was set on Carl Gustav. You will see, I said to myself, he will outshine all of you in time.

Johannes Matthiæ proved more tolerant than the others, smilingly closing his books when Carl Gustav "happened" to call at my study while I was at my lessons. "He is a nice boy," Matthiæ would say.

"A nice boy!" I was indignant. "He is a man!"

"At my age any male under thirty years seems like a boy," my teacher would reply.

Sometimes Matthiæ would talk pleasantly with us, other times he would excuse himself to move across the room to inspect books on the farther shelves, leaving my cousin and me to converse as we would. Thus, on one of these afternoons when we sat as alone as we could be at my study table, I told Carl Gustav of the Regents' marriage intentions for me, particularly of their favoritism for Friedrich Wilhelm of Brandenburg. They recently had allowed his suit to be presented formally at a meeting of the Council and had given him hope he might be accepted. Carl's reception of this news was glum, indeed he almost glowered. He turned his watery blue eyes away from me, toward the window, toward a lonely future.

"Then you are betrothed!"

"No, I am not betrothed!" I was eager to show my political acumen. "To be open to a prince's suit is not the same as accepting him. It is necessary to secure the Elector of Brandenburg's influence in the war. He is certain to favor Sweden as long as he thinks our countries may be allied by marriage. But it also is necessary to let all the other countries with marriageable princes think I might, I just *might*, choose one of them. They all have their advantages. So nothing definite will be decided until I am of age. Isn't that clever of Sweden? Everyone will want to be on our side because they might win my hand." How arch I was! "But—"

I leaned over and tapped Carl's arm—"the Regents cannot marry me to anyone without my consent."

His eyes came back to me, he grasped my hand as it touched his arm. "I thought you were going to marry me. That is what we always planned. I thought of it all the time I was away."

"Sshh!" I glanced quickly at Johannes Matthiæ. He seemed absorbed in his book. I made my voice a hissed whisper. "We cannot let anyone know."

"You must marry me, Christina!" How strong his hand was, pressing mine until it came to hurting.

"Sshh!"

He lowered his tone until his words seemed to creep across the table like sweet conspirators. "Will you promise to marry me?"

"How much do you love me?"

"Better than life. I swear it."

"I would rather marry you than anyone in the world."

"You promise?"

"Yes, of course."

"What about the Regents? I don't trust them. They will persuade you to marry some prince for the good of Sweden."

"I swear I will not let them."

"What about your mother?"

"Pooh. Not she, nor anyone else. Do you think I cannot keep a vow? Shame on you! What about you? What will you do if the Regents try to change you?"

"I? I will not be here. I must go into service in Germany."

This gave me pause. I had known he would, eventually, be sent to Germany. He was by nature, by ambition, a soldier. But now? Well, it might be just the thing. I threw love and pride into my eyes, or thought I did.

"You will cover yourself with glory. You will return a hero. By then I will be of age and we can announce our engagement."

I heard Johannes Matthiæ's footsteps behind me.

"You sound like a couple of buzzing bees. What are you talking about?"

"Riding," I said at once. "Carl Gustav does not believe I can ride as well as I used to. I have told him how I wear out all my attendants, how I tell them to go away and sleep, that I have no use for them. None of them can keep up with me." And I threw back my head to let out what I thought was a burst of boyish laughter, as my cousin dropped my hand and I unobtrusively pulled it away.

Matthiæ looked on us benignly. "We all have trouble keeping up with you, Your Majesty. But now it is you who must keep up with your schedule. And you, sir, surely have your own appointments. Even a charming young lady, even a brilliant young princess, should not hinder a man from his battle with time. It is too soon, too easily, lost."

Carl Gustav rose, bowed, kissed my hand, gazed hard at me. I smiled and nodded, childishly happy. We were engaged. I could see our promise inscribed in cloudlike letters on the door as it closed after him. How youth loves promises! How far it is from Faustus, who exacts a reward for selling his soul, this joy in promising, this lofty self-respect at having a word to give! In its rush at life, in its ignorance, youth is its own Mephistopheles.

My love is so strong that it can be overcome only by death, and if, God forbid, you should die before me, my heart shall be dead for every other, but its memory and affection shall follow you to eternity and there abide with you. How well I remember writing this to Carl Gustav to his camp in Germany! He answered in polite, loyal phrases into which I read a thousand mysteries. Why did he not write his passion plainly, as I did? Did he fear his letter might be intercepted and read by some friend of the Regents who would try to put a stop to our intimacy? What we needed, I decided, was a cipher. Suetonius relates how Julius Cæsar transposed the alphabet for his momentous epistles so that *The enemy is in great disorder, fall upon them with all expedition* came out *Xlh Hqhpb mw mq kvhdx gmwrvghv idoo ysrq xlhp zmxl doo hashgmxmrq,* a pretty little track of chicken's feet. Augustus Cæsar would not have dreamed of communicating his secret intentions without changing the powers of letters, and Pharamund, King of the Franks, devised a whole new alphabet to use when he invaded the Gauls. Clodius, Charlemagne, the line of Kings on down, invented characters, arithmetic figures, all manner of secret writing, for their purposes. This habit of Kings should be employed I thought. It would be wise to make one's meaning understood only by those for whom it was meant. It would, at the least, avoid immediate interference. Carl Gustav did not agree, straightforward writing being the kind for him, he said. Besides, he was too busy on the battlefield learning lessons of war to worry about scrambled letters, just a regular one in my handwriting being hard enough to decipher. Twice, that I heard of, he was a hair's breadth from eternity, once when a bullet tore through his hair, another time when a mischievous ball from the enemy plunged into the center of our command, carrying away the hind parts of Marshal Torstenson's horse, piercing the neck of Carl Gustav's mount and the belly of that of Captain Rabenau so that the three of them found themselves sprawled together on the ground, yet miraculously unhurt. They were on a fierce playground.

In these years at home I studied the war and its politics more than any other problem. While Carl Gustav was winning it on the battlefield, I would learn how to attend to the diplomatic side. When I was of age we would rule together, gloriously. My head was so stuffed with politics and what I intended to do that when Oxenstierna spoke to me one day in his dry voice about the necessity of having a meeting with his sister, Beata, on a matter of importance to me, I let it slip my mind. How could anything be important that he would have Beata say to me instead of himself? It was personal, he had said. Personal? What did she know about me? I scarcely ever saw her.

I almost had forgotten about it when she sought me one morning in my chamber, where I had been confined, indignantly, to my bed by the distress of my monthly feminine condition, a condition, I must say, that had filled me with indignation the first moment I heard from my Aunt Katarina I must expect it, that had infuriated me when I matured to it, that has been the source of the utmost irritation ever since, spiritually and physically, to have to submit to the same mess and discomfort as any ordinary woman. I wouldn't listen to the court doctor on its being the natural order of woman. Order, I screamed at him, I call it the great disorder of being a woman! Now leave me alone! And I would not let him talk. But I could not send Beata Oxenstierna away, in spite of how I felt, after promising the Chancellor I would meet with her, nor could I excuse myself out of the room, sitting in bed as I was with books piled around me. I pushed a tangle of hair from my eyes and answered her greeting in a surly way. Beata is a bony woman, tall like her brother, as angular and bare-looking as a tree in autumn, with a precise, chilly manner in speaking.

"I have come, Your Majesty, to speak to you about marriage."

Marriage! Had they discovered my engagement? I stiffened. I would not give in, no matter what they said. I did not answer, staring at her, until she spoke further of her mission.

"The Chancellor believes you should have a complete knowledge of the holy state of matrimony before you enter into it." She squinted at me, disgust tinging her next words. "Perhaps your ladies-in-waiting or servants have imparted their version to you?"

I shook my head. Why should I discuss marriage with them? She folded her hands in front of her, still standing inasmuch as I had not invited her to sit down, and gave her dissertation, which consisted of giving me explicit anatomical details of the human male and female and a description of the activity necessary for reproduction. I was appalled. How did this terrible thing fit into the world of love? I had seen dogs, horses, cows, and bulls coupling, but that was an animal routine. Man was a divine being.

"The holy state of matrimony!" I sneered. "What's holy about the way you speak of it?"

"God has ordained that it must be so."

"You talk as if men were animals."

"There are certain traits of animal life from which the human being has not yet risen. It may be that God has arranged this purposely so that we may realize we are not sublime, as He is. We are poor mortals. We must look to Him for the true perfection. They say—" her glance was meaningful—"that men enjoy this activity. Women must just bear it."

"Why?"

"Producing children is a woman's great gift to the world."

"Not mine! I am Queen. I have greater gifts than that for the world." I thought of my growing knowledge of government, of my plans for stopping the war.

She smiled, grimly. After all, it had not been necessary for her to marry, or to make any gift to the world that I could see.

"Sweden will need an heir, Your Majesty."

And further than this she declined to go, a woman, unchangeable in her opinions, who withdrew from arguments as if they were rain that would dampen her experience, her validity. After she left, I lay back against my pillows. How can I explain my violent inner reaction to what she had said, to facts that common girls in country cottages, unhindered by a mind, took for granted? This was not Plato's conception of man and woman, Plato, whom I read more and more, to whom I felt a kinship I never could entertain for Beata Oxenstierna, as if the centuries between us were no more than dust to be blown away by one's wit. Would the Council, the Estates, the people of Sweden expect me to produce an heir, as she said? Would they expect me to perform for them with a sire of their choice behind the gilded curtains of a State marriage bed, as she had described? I thought of the many nights I had dreamed of my cousin as a daring young officer. What did he expect of love, of marriage, of me? I would not know until he returned. It had not occurred to me before that he ever would think differently on an important subject from the way I thought. Then I mused on the religions I had studied with Johannes Matthiæ. The Catholics, I had learned, extolled celibacy, counted it as a virtue of the highest merit. What a fine thing! That was the religion for me!

When Oxenstierna came next to my study I had a nice little

speech prepared for him, which I delivered with dignity, on how I had decided I would be of more value to Sweden as a virgin Queen, that my talents were, as he had mentioned often, for politics and governmental problems, that with the princely education I had had it was not feasible to waste time being married. As an example I gave Elizabeth, the great Queen of England, who had been so clever in making hers a celebrated country. I had anticipated a stern response, such as his sister's, to which I was prepared to be adamant. To my surprise, an expression of immense kindness softened the old statesman's face.

"You are young, Your Majesty. You will have time to change your mind," was all he said as he laid the papers on the table for the day's accounting in diplomatics.

VI

WAR, war, war! How long was the war in Germany going to last? As I approached my majority and the authority it would bring, I felt it incumbent on me to learn the nature of war, of this war, that had been raging since before I was born. What was it over and above the points and lines on a map, the trade securities that Oxenstierna insisted we needed, the religious war that my father had believed in? Listen, dear friends and unknown centuries, open your patience to me, if you would learn a few truths about war, about this war. I had grown up with the principles of a crusading war, of the necessity of rescuing the German Protestants from the fangs of a Catholic Emperor, of the glory of Gustav Adolf, the Lion from Midnight who sprang from the arms of God to be the great Protestant champion, of the righteousness of the good Swedish marshals who carried on the holy battle after his death. But, if the war was purely between Protestants and Catholics, why had Gustav Adolf and Oxenstierna allied themselves with Cardinal Richelieu and France, definitely a Catholic nation, and why did Cardinal Richelieu have a secret alliance with the Pope, Urban VIII, who publicly disapproved of there being any war at all? Was it because the Pope, as some people whispered, wasn't really a Catholic? The Pope said, simply, that it wasn't a religious war, therefore he couldn't sanction it. The war-tempered Catholics, piqued at his lack of support, asserted the Pope had a weakness for the Bourbons because he was Louis XIII's godfather, and because he had enjoyed himself so thoroughly when he had visited France when still Cardinal Barberini, before the papal robes had been given him. The Jesuits, on the other hand, were active in their praise of the Emperor and the Habsburgs. They seemed to believe that God had selected the Habsburg family to re-establish Catholicism in all Germany. In this way were the Catholics secretly divided amongst themselves, French Bourbons versus Austrian and Spanish Habsburgs, each reaching for more power.

The Protestants were no better. What German prince could be relied on to do anything for the cause of Protestantism if it was not in his own immediate interest? Each had his petty ambition to pursue. Moreover, the Lutherans and the Calvinists disliked one another almost as much as they disliked the Catholics. Take, for example, Gustav Adolf's arrival at the door of his brother-in-law, the Elector of Brandenburg, a confirmed Calvinist. My father found the castle locked, the town barred against him, certainly a cold reception for a relative who had come a long way to be a savior. Not a man to be discouraged easily from making a call on a brother, he besieged the town, encircled it with his fearsome army, pointed his cannon at the castle. Now, they say the Calvinists exalt violence in the good cause and delight in bloodthirsty psalms, but, if so, the Elector ceased at this point to be a good Calvinist. He was frightened out of his wits. After a few cannon shots he sent out his trembling wife and mother-in-law to invite Gustav into the castle, suggesting the matter could be discussed better over a drink of ale. Four bumpers they drank together, then the Elector found it expedient to agree with the Golden King.

The trouble had begun in squabbles about civil and religious rights between the Habsburg Emperor, a Catholic, of course, and the German princes of the Empire, some of whom are Catholic and some Protestant, few of whom could agree. The initial passion and the later mess could have been avoided with any amount of tolerance, but no one on either side had any tolerance, and the skirmishes between the Germans grew into a great war with hidden purposes. After ten years of fighting, when the Protestant princes almost had been ruined by the rigorous Emperor, Gustav Adolf entered the war. In three years his successes changed the whole color of Germany. Richelieu called him the rising sun, the sun rising out of the arctic edge of civilization, blinding men with his brilliance. His diplomatic dealings with the German princes were bold and clever, his troops were loyal and disciplined, his genius in devising ways to baffle the enemy was unsurpassed, his good fortune in natural causes astounding. One battle was won, for instance, because the enemy could see nothing at all, the bright sun shining full in their faces, then, when the light might have dulled, a high wind arrived to blow a storm of dust in their eyes. Richelieu had expected to use Gustav Adolf for his own purposes, as an able commander to further the power of his aging King, but the rising sun kept rising. Richelieu had thought of him as a clever soldier, as a King of Snow who would melt when his season waned, but the King of Snow did not melt at all. He was a real King, a master, efficient, educated, divinely authoritative. As he won battle after battle, as he conquered, too, in his broad diplomatic campaigns, exposing to the world his relations with France which Richelieu had tried frantically to keep secret, it began to be whispered about that Europe was to have a new Emperor, that it would be the Swedish Gustav Adolf. When he was killed at the Battle of Lützen, there were those who believed it was the direct intervention of God, the word going around that *the Almighty laid his finger upon him in the critical moment at which he would have ceased to be the liberator and become the conqueror of Germany*. There were others who believed that it was not God but Richelieu who arranged his assassination, that the Cardinal could not bear to be out-generaled by a barbarian he had chosen as his pawn. It is true Gustav Adolf was hit by a bullet in the head between his eye and his ear, as if he rode into his death, but he also was shot in the back. Who knows? One's own side can be more successful in treachery than the enemy. Did not the Habsburg dynasty order the murder of their commander-in-chief, Wallenstein, two years later? It was easier to kill him than rule him.

I was six years old when Gustav Adolf died. In my seventeenth year the miserable fighting still was going on. And it truly was miserable fighting. Germans were fighting Germans, some Germans were fighting the Swedish, the French, the Danes, other Germans were fighting the Spanish, and mixed up in both sides were the professional soldiers, Poles, Italians, Bohemians, Flemish, Turks, Greeks, Scots, Irish, English, Roumanians and whatnots, soldiers flocking to be paid for a fight, soldiers, black-souled as vultures, waiting to plunder dead towns, soldiers who fought bitterly or fled or changed sides, smelling out their own advantage, soldiers that trampled down the fertility of the fields, that burned the ground black behind them, that ate up the towns' supplies. None of the generals on either side could manage their men. They pillaged, drank, raped at their will. The Imperialists used prisoners and peasants as targets in their spare-time shooting practice, the Croats had a joke of popping persons alive into their own ovens to bake them or leaving housewives to boil in their large pots, the Swedes, after the restraining hand of Gustav Adolf was gone, invented for their sport a throwing of gunpowder onto the clothing of their prisoners and setting fire to them, the Protestants tied priests like dogs beneath army wagons to jump along on their hands and knees while the wagon was driven. Tale after tale came from horrified eyewitnesses, to make one believe the nightmare painting of Hieronymus Bosch had burst into life.

Germany, these many years, was a land of fugitives, of deserted villages, of wandering rogues and robbers, of ragged burghers. Their food taken from them by the armies, the people turned into cannibals. Starving men chased dogs and starving dogs chased men. Parents, in fits of madness and wild hunger, killed their children and ate them, then, realizing what they had done, killed themselves in despair. Feasts followed the hanging of criminals, whose bodies were pulled down from the gallows for food, the dead were dug up from their graves as soon as they were buried to be sold as flesh, while the bravest men came to be nervous of walking alone through wooded parts for fear of meeting a similar fate. Dogs and cats were sold on the market, grass, acorns, goatskins were the diet of those lucky enough to find them, gluttonous women lay on the road eating dead horses along with the insects and vultures, children hid in fields and cellars where they could feed on rats. Whoever tried to share any hidden grain with a poorer soul had his stores taken away by the soldiers. Was this a religious war? Was it for this the Swedish people paid taxes that their soldiers might continue to fight for a holy cause? What holy cause? The people on the desolated grounds of Germany, blacked out from God, no longer called it a holy cause. If these were religious forces, if this was what religion accomplished, they did not want religion. This was not a war for God, it was a war with God. Only the Devil was winning.

If my father had been glorious as a just warrior, how much more glorious I would be, I thought, if I brought this senseless war to an honorable close. Would not the world thank me if I made the legend of peace a reality, if I proved Sweden a virtuous country, not a force to be hated? I burned with ambition to stop the meaningless murderous campaign, but Oxenstierna, like my father, had the illusion of complete victory, and whenever he talked of peace he made the terms impossible for anyone else to accept. During my seventeenth year came a stroke of good fortune. The army for Spain suffered a very bad defeat, and the German princes, seeing an opportunity to rid their lands of foreign powers if they acted together, whichever side they were on, decided they would have a conference to consider peace among themselves, whether the Emperor willed it or not. Accordingly, they asked Sweden and France to meet them at a congress in Westphalia to discuss terms. In December of 1644 the congress convened. It seemed to me that the stars guiding Sweden's destiny purposely had held back the opening of the congress until that time, for in December of 1644 I had my eighteenth birthday. I became Queen.

What is there to remember about the day in December of my most momentous birthday? Perhaps it was significant that the weather was neither cruel nor sweet, just ordinary, a gray bone-chilling cold, the wind compatible, neither howling nor singing as it floundered around the snow-crusted castle. The sun saw no reason to burst forth because I became Queen, to break its winter sleep. Let me be the one to shine, to open my splendor. Nor did the North Wind have to scream around corners calling for patriots in Gustav Vasa's name. I, Christina, am today's Vasa. When I speak my vows, I thought, the clarity of divine authority will ring forth in Sweden again. The people would recognize it. An impartial monarchy would reign after twelve years of the favoritisms of a nobles' Regency.

I remember that in the simple ceremony in the Great Hall, the elaborate celebrations being reserved for the coronation, I was hampered by a slight cough that kept tickling my throat so that I had to swallow repeatedly to keep my words clear. Later I was told that my slowness in speaking, together with my deep voice, was especially impressive. Certainly my thoughts weren't hampered. I walked into the hall as Queen-elect, I walked out as Queen. Now it was my hand, my mind, not the nobles', not Oxenstierna's, that would rule. Did my eyes become brighter, my voice stronger? What did the Queen of Sweden look like? Had I grown tall, beautiful, golden-haired, like the tales of Nordic princesses? No. Not at all. The Queen of Sweden was, and is, short and rather ugly. My large blue eyes almost bulge out of their sockets, my complexion is bad, as my mother foretold it would be, my blondish hair is the despair of court hairdressers, my mouth is small, and my nose an enormous beak, a true Vasa nose, aquiline and majestic. I have told how my right shoulder was injured in infancy so it is permanently humped, so I can claim no grace of figure either, although my dresses are made to partly conceal my defect. Thus the Queen of Sweden who walked from the Great Hall: so small as to be almost dwarfed by the descendants of Viking warriors who surrounded her, less beautiful than the court ladies who crowded to court her favors, but light of step, quick of mind, eager as a young hawk to secure her purpose.

Looking back, I wonder if Chancellor Oxenstierna had any suspicion that day that I considered his rule to be finished when mine began. I do not believe he did. I, however, was not blurred with any doubts at all. My gratitude to him as my teacher did not extend to adopting his old-fashioned ways when I knew of better ones. When his gray eyes gleamed and his gray lips wished me a prosperous reign, how could he know that a prosperous reign, to me, meant the retirement of his ways, his decisions, his wars?

I remember, at the banquet table following the ceremony, I looked around at the festive faces above the festive food, at the elaborate gaiety amid the elaborate dishes of venison, pig, and capon, of herring and trout, roasts and pungent sauces, puddings, spiced pottages, pastries and sweetmeats. Wine- and water-carriers leaned incessantly over the goblets. Heads turned, nodded, laughed. There was Maria Eleonora, who cared not who or what had won her triumph, even smiling, wineglass in hand, at the restrained courtesy of the Chancellor. There were the Chancellor's sons, Erik, red-faced and serious, Johan, red-faced and bawdy, the Chancellor's comfortable wife, sleepy with wine, the Chancellor's many relatives, importantly talkative and smug. There was Baron Gyllenhielm, waving his ship of bread across his giant imaginary waves, telling legends and sea tales to whomever would listen, my Uncle Johan, the Count Palatine, gesturing sage advice in a pleasant drunkenness, ignoring the flirtations of Maria Euphrosina. There were the handsome sons of Jacob de la Gardie, and the Constable himself, almost dissolved in wrinkles, beside his still beautiful wife. These and the other nobles, the bishops, the leaders of the Estates, and their ladies ate, drank, and made merry sounds until nothing else could be heard, not the musicians pantomiming within nor the winter's wind without.

For my part, I was restless. How deep did their gaiety go, I wondered. Except for a Lutheran sermon, the celebration of food and drink is the most boring thing I know. I care little what I eat, as long as it is not that stupid mud-loving animal, the pig, and I picked at my food in an impatient good humor. I would have preferred to walk straight from the ceremony to the Council table, sit down and start to rule. The wait for the morrow was a lesson in tolerance. I looked, as I say, at the banqueters, and in particular at the Councillors, at the men who, a few hours earlier, had been Regents, the rulers of Sweden, who, now, had stepped into the shadows as my aides. My mind was busy with what I would say to them. I would make it clear that I must have peace in every corner of my kingdom, that there could be no procrastinating in ending the wars.

Yes, it had become wars, not just war. To watch Oxenstierna as he broke his bread, wiped it in a brown sauce in his plate, and put it in his mouth, one would cast him as a peaceful man. I could divine nothing from his expression except satisfaction tempered with caution. That seemed his past, his present, his future. I could not hurry him into another attitude, even in my thoughts, yet martial force was the Chancellor's answer to a country that did not answer his demands. The year before, he had started a war with Denmark over trade routes, a completely unnecessary war. Tomorrow, I decided, I would bring it up at the Council table. I would begin by saying that it was suicidal to our interests in the German war to be fighting another war at the same time. Oxenstierna would reply that our soldiers were protecting our rights in Denmark, that it was routine, that no declaration of war had been made. Then why, I would ask, is the commander-in-chief of all the Swedish armies there if it isn't important, if it isn't even a war, as you say? Why is Marshal Torstenson in Denmark with our best troops fighting the Danish army? Why isn't he in Germany, where the real war, a bitter war, is being fought? Are we not serious in our purpose in Germany? Are we not, truly, assisting the Catholic armies by diverting the Danish as well as our own regiments? How can we win the terms we want at the coming peace congress if the Protestant princes accuse us of this? Such a battery of questions pounded in my mind I could not think of any response Oxenstierna and the other Councillors might give other than to agree to leave Denmark and settle the dispute at a diplomatic conference. The Danish war was terminated in my mind.

Peace in Germany was a far more complex, more subtle, problem. All the talking would have to be done at a distance through representatives, each power to send two delegates to the peace congress. How I wished I could be there myself! At that very time the Council was considering the selection of the Swedish delegates, and—heaven help us, for we would need it—they were appointing as chief delegate a man who knew nothing whatsoever about peace, not how to achieve its faintest fragrance, certainly not how to preserve it, neither for himself, his country, nor anyone else. I turned to where he was sitting at the banquet, furiously crumbling my bread in my fist, wishing it were his ugly head. Johan Oxenstierna. He could have been chosen for no other reason than to be his father's mouthpiece. His face was red as raw beef from drinking, his lips hung wet and loose in laughing, exposing his large, widely spaced teeth, his loud remarks were wet and raw as the rest of him. Did he ever discern anything but his own vulgar world out of those pale-rimmed squinting eyes, could he imagine a world of other ideas, other natures, other ambitions? His broad chest and arms meant fat, not strength, his big stature was used only as a frame for haughtiness. Worst of all, he never had given a pinpoint of evidence that he had discovered his head was for thinking. What a delegate he would make for Sweden in an assemblage of clever nations! I spat on my bread crumbs and threw them down on the table.

The second delegate must be the true one, a strong man, an intelligent diplomat, one who would be impervious to Johan. He must be reliable for me and for peace, he must be exceptional in his relations with others, he must be experienced in foreign affairs. Night after night I had pondered the choice and I had come to the conclusion that there already was such a man in Sweden's service, that it could be Alder Salvius. Salvius was, in every respect, the opposite of Johan, sober, resourceful, gray-haired, a man of the people whose career had grown out of his own earnest efforts. His humble birth was a calm fact for him. He was not ashamed of it, neither did he let it hinder his activity nor jaundice his viewpoint. King, count or burgher, French, Turk or Flemish, whomever, whatever, he spoke to with the same resolute quietness, his blue eyes steady in appraisal, his brow furrowed in sincerity. He seemed to see through the meanest deceits and devices, yet he had not soured on people, and his wonderfully amiable nature secured the liking and respect of those with whom he dealt. Gustav Adolf had found in him a most persuasive agent, and he had used him extensively to handle his affairs in foreign countries. Although he was no longer young, I was sure his energy had not diminished, and his devotion to a mission and to his King had proved itself in every flowering of his activity. He would be the right one. I found my fingers were beating the rhythm of his name on the table board, Salvius, Salvius. Would these people never stop eating and drinking, never stop talking, joking, congratulating me? Where were the wings the hours used when I was reading? Hurry, bring me tomorrow.

The banquet did end, the morrow did come, and other morrows. I was, at last, in action at the Council table. Oxenstierna was not in favor of stopping the war in Denmark, but in the end he bowed to my fervid persecution of the matter, more as if he were giving me a present on becoming Queen than as if I were correct in my reasons. And the day came when the selection of the second delegate to the peace congress was to be made. I proposed Salvius' name with assurance, then waited for the approbation of the five Councillors. The first to lean forward to speak was the Constable, Jacob de la Gardie.

"A splendid selection!" His hands carved the air to form a delicate statue of its splendidness.

Baron Gyllenhielm began, in his slow manner, to say something, but the crisp words of the Chancellor cut him off.

"It is impossible for Salvius to represent Sweden."

"Why?" I was quickly the questioner.

"You must have forgotten, Your Majesty, that our good Salvius is not an aristocrat." Oxenstierna spoke as the patient teacher, the two other Oxenstiernas nodding their agreement.

But I was not the receptive pupil now. I was Queen. I made my words as crisp as the Chancellor's.

"I desire capable men in my service. Salvius is a natural noble." I firmly stressed the *capable*. There should be no doubt that my decisions would be based on merit, not on family relationships.

Baron Gyllenhielm rolled out his comment, clear as sunned sea air. "Gustav always liked Salvius. He said he could trust him with anything."

Nor did Jacob de la Gardie desert his approval. He crossed his legs comfortably, crinkled his kind old eyes. "My dear Chancellor, consider how many years this admirable gentleman—for I, as our Queen, see him as a natural noble—yes, how many years he has been familiar with the situation. For him there will be no thin edge of ice to cut through, there will be no shell to break to comprehend that essence of intention so exquisitely concealed by our fellow diplomats. These august persons he has measured in their own cities. Have we not had evidence before this of his influence with the French? And in languages, ah, what a chameleon he is! He shall make every shift in the discussions his own property."

Gabriel Gustav Oxenstierna burst out: "But the dignity of Sweden! The man comes from a turf hut!"

"It was the men from turf huts who followed my great-grandfather, Gustav Vasa, to win back Sweden's freedom. Where would we be now if he had depended on aristocrats?" It was the aristocrats, I remembered heatedly, who had betrayed him to win the reward and their own security, from whom he had had to escape. Others would remember, too. "I am certain the Estates will approve Salvius. They will not protest that his humble birth interferes with his merit."

The Treasurer, Gabriel Oxenstierna, cleared his throat in measured irritation, but his usual precise phrases were not added to the discussion. The Chancellor had turned his palm upward in acquiescence. There was no hint of defeat in his voice.

"True. We cannot doubt his merit, and his experience should be valuable to Johan. Shall we, then, appoint him?"

I looked at the Chancellor in surprise. By his face, he felt himself, blandly, the master, by his tone he asserted that Johan was, after all, the chief delegate, that Salvius might serve him well as a kind of superior secretary. I sensed the quick turn he made to the decision to avoid an open argument in the Riksdag, where I would have the popular side. How canny he was! Perhaps he would persuade Salvius that it was he who had chosen him, that it was from him the directives should be taken for the peace congress. No, no! Salvius had to be my delegate. I had won him, I had to keep him.

I lost no time in summoning Salvius to a private conference. With the wise old fellow before me, the confidence of his physical and mental strength filling my study, my fears relaxed. He would be a faithful bloodhound after peace. It was easier than I had anticipated to put my motives to him, he understood my intentions, it seemed, before I said them. Nevertheless, he said, he wished to have everything clear, exact, between us, always. I told him that he was not to deviate for any reason in God's world from his course at the congress, that he was to speak and act as the real power of Sweden, for I, the Queen, invested him with that power. I would send my instructions privately, we would carry on a personal correspondence in addition to the royal correspondence known to the Council, and if there was any difference between the two, he would know very well which one to adhere to. He was to pay no attention to the Oxenstiernas, whose purposes differed from ours. He never was to falter in his negotiations.

In this way I started on the road to peace, in this way I began my reign, with a gift from God to assist me. As for the congress in Westphalia, it, too, was fortunate in having Salvius. It began in a mess that no one had expected. After quarreling for a year about precedence, prestige, and numerous small matters, the delegates, when they turned to the serious business of settling a peace, discovered that nobody really knew what the war was about. Why, they asked one another, was everybody fighting? What were the principles, the sides, the reasons behind it all? Before they could end the war they had to know why it had begun. How could they negotiate in a tangle of clouds? Whence came the cannons, the shouting men? What was the game about? Truly, a debate must be held to decide the purpose of the war and the subjects of the peace conference. In all this madness Salvius pursued as straight a line as was possible, and shortly he was recognized as one of the most outstanding diplomats of the hundred and thirty-five delegates assembled. Moreover, he showed great skill in not letting Johan stand in his way.

And Johan! The happy ox rocked the town with his drinking-parties and women, exuberantly vacationing, careless of how long the congress lasted. In his arrogance he believed he was representing Sweden in representing his father and that it was enough to present the grave messages sent to him rather than figure a plan for himself. When it became evident, even to him, that he was not among other oxen, that he had strayed onto a wild plain abounding in lynx, tigers, snakes, sly foxes, lions, scuttling rats, and God knows what, he was aghast. The involvements of the issues, the deceptive promises of his competitor diplomats, the subtle path-making behind his back, the cleverness that tripped him so easily were beyond his groggy understanding. They were whirling traps, the discussions, where words flew through many meanings. This was no place for a hearty man who spelled a word only one way. Johan wrote his father declining his situation. Let someone more accustomed to these foreign tricksters replace him. Hastily the Chancellor wrote back: *Are you ignorant, my son, of the small amount of ability with which this world is managed?* And Johan, faced for the first time with his own ignorance, bowed his head and stayed.

In Stockholm, meanwhile, I had found a new confidant. As Queen I had more freedom in choosing my friends, and among those who flocked around me, one seemed to exceed all the others in the qualities I liked, particularly in political alertness and ingenuity. This was Magnus de la Gardie, son of the dear old Constable. The more we were together to discuss things, the more we felt we needed to be together. While it was apparent that his father's experience was woven into the pattern of his decisions, he had an individual energy that made it exciting to go over points of policy with him. He had, too, the hope of youth. It was not long before we were sifting, daily, the news from abroad, the letters from Salvius, the idiosyncrasies of the nobles and how we could benefit by them. His sympathy for my plans was boundless.

I depended on Magnus, and Magnus, on his part, asked my opinion on everything he did. Never before had I known such a pleased listener. There is nothing you cannot understand, nothing you cannot do, Christina, you are Pallas herself, he used to say. And how charming he looked! There was no stiffness about him. He laughed easily, frowned easily, was content to sit on a stool at my knees, gazing up at me as I talked, the faint scrolls of his eyebrows slightly raised in anticipation, his flashing eyes reflecting every sparkle of meaning. As he tipped back his head the light would slide along his creamy blond hair, down its smoothness to the hint of a curl trailing his lace collar, his firmly molded mouth would be now up, now down, at the corners, whatever the mood of my story, belying the strictness of his clipped blond mustache. The dot of a whisker on his chin gave a final delicate emphasis to his elegance, for, whatever he did, however he walked, stood, or sat, Magnus was undeniably elegant. It was brushed on him like a lacquer.

Like Carl Gustav, he had traveled abroad to polish his education; unlike him, he loved to flare into talk about it, of what had delighted him, surprised him, annoyed him. What had he liked best? Paris, of course! Could I, knowing the heat of his French blood, doubt he would respond to the pride of France? Paris, he said, is a perpetual wedding. What Frenchman is not seduced by its beauty, by the perfume of its soul, by the excitement of its worldly manners? And legally, my dear, legally! He explores his bride, the lover, the hunter, and tastes her charms, one by one. Oh, my Pallas, he would exclaim, if you could see Notre Dame in the moonlight, its towers whitened, high and strong, its gargoyles leaning, their wicked lips mouthing warnings in forgotten tongues, warnings carried away by the waters of the Seine, the silent, the moonlight-dimpled waters, winding through Paris, flowing by Notre Dame, hurrying to the sea with the wasted and unwanted images of the sweet city it serves! He, Magnus, had thrown his broken wishes to the passing water, they had been caught in its moonlight net and borne away.

And the court life! At last there was a court to rival the court of Athens. Where else could such things be found to delight the eye, the ear, the mind? The antiquities, the art treasures of that magnificent palace, the Louvre! The fountains, the gardens, the sculpture of the incomparable Fontainebleau! He described Michelangelo's Hercules, his hand moving to caress the marble. Oh, to behold it, I thought! And the culture of the fashionable Parisian life, the sumptuous ballets, the Italian music, the tragedies, like unto the Greek, played out! He had sat on the stage to witness the great Corneille's *Cinna*. He would leap to his feet, remembering, declaiming.

"*It is not injustice to betray one who is treacherous!*"

"O Virtue! In the labyrinth of their minds, what threads men seize upon in the expectation of finding you!" I would shout back, waving my arms.

"That is not a proper quoting." I was rebuked.

"It should have been. Corneille should have said it. We shall bring him to Stockholm and he shall write on Virtue here." I would laugh uproariously at the thought of defrauding the French court of its talent.

Well, Corneille was not the only one. Magnus had met Balzac, Scarron, Benserade, had stood near them to catch immortal words. He had glimpsed the Italian cardinal, Mazarin, who had stepped into power when his master, Richelieu, had died. He had had long conversations with Hugo Grotius, whom my father, in admiration for his writing, had supported by giving him the post of Ambassador to Sweden at the court of France.

I stopped Magnus. "Grotius! Tell me about Grotius. He has asked to be recalled to Sweden."

Down went the corners of Magnus's mouth. He must be completely serious about this serious man.

"Grotius," he said, "was displeased with the Regents when I saw him. He complained they had no confidence in him. Whatever business they had with France, they preferred to negotiate without favoring him with the advice of their plans." His hands gestured the hopelessness of the situation. "Why, then, Monsieur Grotius wonders, is he the Ambassador? Is he to pose as the unmoving pillar, as a statue, a discus-thrower who never throws his discus?"

"His misfortune is not to have been a relative of Oxenstierna. I believe the Chancellor would like to have fifty sons to place where fifty mouths are needed to speak his directive. We shall recall Grotius. He may be of use here. I cannot think of a more opportune moment to consult with the authority on international law."

"You will find, my Pallas, that our great author is stiff in his ideas. He thinks of his philosophical principles, of their inevitable rightness. They must prevail, he thinks, because they are true as a straight line. Long afterward, long, long afterward, too long, it becomes, he is aware of men, of this little human thing called a man. He does not understand why this man does not walk happily along his straight line, once he has shown it to him." Again the gesturing hands. "What man can live, can eat and drink, by being a philosophical principle?" His lips curved upward. "We shall bring him back and you shall see. Whom will you send to replace him? Perhaps you will send me?"

"Perhaps. Not yet."

Magnus urged me. "Perhaps you will allow me the honor of spreading the fame of the Queen of the Swedish Empire. It is certain no Councillor could squeeze his politics between you and me and those we know so well, now, in France."

"I need you here," I answered.

In truth, I believed I needed him near me more than anyone else. I saw no one in Stockholm so clever, as ardent in my interests, and, I will admit it, so enjoyable as a companion. Talk as he would about responding to Paris as a Frenchman, he was a patriot when on the subject of Sweden. Was not his mother the beautiful Ebba Brahe, that rare creature who had eluded the throne, whose family was one of the oldest and proudest in the land? Except for his vivacity and the raciness of his French blood, he was very like his mother, handsome of face and of figure, with an indefinable freshness in his attitude that permeated the hours we spent together. It was no weight to be with him. I mused on the fact that at my age my father had been pursuing his mother, hot with love. What amusement of the fates was it to have Magnus looking at me with his mother's blue eyes while I spoke to him in my father's deep voice? What kind of reparation was this, to have Magnus pursuing me? I could not resist a smile.

"It is charming of you to need me." Magnus smiled, too. "It is I who need you. And, specifically, my family needs you on the coming Wednesday. You have not forgotten your promise to attend our reception?"

"No, no. I shall be at Makalös with pleasure."

Makalös, the German palace Jacob de la Gardie had built, was, probably still is, the finest private house in Stockholm. He placed it in the new section across the North Bridge from the old city on the islands, setting it on the very edge of The Stream so that on calm summer days the palace is a Narcissus contemplating its dark beauty in the water. It is a magnificent wooden structure, this palace, imaginatively decorated, broadly spaced, each corner held by a square tower, each tower flaunting a round headdress and delicate spire. The steep roof is as high again as the lower stories, the rooftop windows shining an invitation to meet the sky. Those who wish may arrive by boat, as in Venice, ascend the damp steps to a lovely portico, and enter the spacious rooms, their ceilings brightly colored in frescoes. I preferred to go by carriage. I liked to rattle across the bridge, feeling the confusion of twisting streets and the contorted ambitions of the city so like them behind me, pretending they were disposable history, that my future would be as clear as the straight roads of the modern replanning ahead. There is a plot there, as well, called the King's Garden, although few flowers have courage enough to bloom, the stiff hedges in festoons around a weak fountain being the only attempt at grace. Like the culture in Sweden, I thought. The gateway of Makalös opens directly across from the King's Garden, so short a distance from the bridge that my horses barely had time to break into a good pace before we were there, swinging sharply into the courtyard, the other carriages making way for us, and wheeling to a stop in front of the landwise portico.

On the Wednesday of the reception, a kindly weathered day in June, I signaled to Magnus to join me on the portico overlooking The Stream as soon as I reasonably could turn away from the guests crowding the palace rooms. The splendidly arrayed gentlemen and ladies of the foremost families, the Brahes, the Bondes, Wredes, Torstensons, the Oxenstiernas, Wrangels, Rosenhanes, Lillies, these and other splendid names of Sweden, brocaded, beribboned, jeweled, were growing increasingly noisy in their friendliness as the Constable's servants pressed on them glass after glass of imported French wine. Jacob de la Gardie was a confirmed believer in wine.

"Wine!" He would laugh through his genial wrinkles, holding his filled glass to the light. "The gentle deliverer! The precious jewel of liquids! It is wine that flows over the terrible dam we make of prejudice. In this fragile glass we may sail down a river of merriment. Your Majesty, I beg of you, sip of this ruby!"

"I decline your jewel for one of my own. Diamonds, if you will." And better than that, reality, the pure virtue of Nature, I would think, as I raised my glass of clear, cool water.

Wine or no wine, Chancellor Oxenstierna looked the same,

black-clothed and dignified. And Uncle Johan, stocky, astute, talked quietly as he let his eye trail Maria Euphrosina, arch in a gown of pale-green silk, as she became animated before one young gallant, then another. Magnus was with her when he caught my signal and hurried to escort me to the portico. His cheeks were pink with excitement or wine or both, his movements quicker, gayer than usual. As we walked to the railing he flung out an arm toward Stockholm.

"Your city! I lay it at your feet."

Stockholm appeared much better at a distance, across the brassy gleam of the water, its uneven outline jagged with steeples making a pretty design of yellows, browns, and grays in the slanting sunlight. Rigged ships, trading vessels, and warships were scattered in her harbor, tiny boats bobbed on the waves, marking the rhythmical breathing of the blue Stream. But I had not brought Magnus here to talk irrelevancies. I had had enough of that within. I was impatient to be on with my plans.

"They are asking about my coronation, when it will be," I said.

"They?" The yellow eyebrows shot up.

I shed his question. I spoke firmly. "I have promised them a double celebration. We shall set the day of the coronation when I have the peace treaty in my hands. I shall give them peace, as God gives me the crown. The people shall have two great causes for rejoicing."

Magnus leaned against a slender column, twirling some kind of tiny chain in his fingers. How handsome he looked in his embroidered blue suit!

"I should like to have heard our good Chancellor's comment on that."

"Why should I speak to him about it? Now I am Queen there is no longer a reason for him to tax his mind with every problem, big and small. He is old, his health is poor."

"So you are retiring him."

I stared at Magnus. What an excellent idea!

"Why not?" I was inspired further. "We shall have an impressive ceremony. I shall make him a count." I always had wondered why my father had not rewarded his best friend with an honor equaling his regard.

"And what will the new count do with the hours of his days?"

"He may read his beloved Tacitus."

"He may even finish the Roman house he has been building for years."

We giggled together in an unstatesmanlike way.

"Then you agree?"

"I agree! I applaud you! I bow to your genius! The path to peace will be thornless without Oxenstierna."

His blond hair almost swept the ground in the exaggeration of his bow.

"Be serious, Magnus. Do you agree it is wise to postpone naming the day of the coronation?"

Both arms, this time, were stretched toward the seeming repose of the city. "Stockholm will blaze its triumph through all the Northern skies! Stars will shoot from the earth to meet the stars in the heavens, bells will sound the sweet melody of peace from one end of the Empire to the other, Pallas will ride in a golden coach, Pallas the wise, the victorious, the Queen of Peace. It will be the most beautiful day in Swedish history. We shall make it so, you and I."

As Magnus's fervor increased, my smiles dimmed. The least smell of oratory, even from those I like, makes me impatient about the work to be done. What are words? I want them to be tools for achievement. It is tiring to have them played with like pretty toys.

I cut in on Magnus's exhibition. "I shall speak to the Chancellor now."

"Now?" Absolute astonishment was on his face. This was a day of wine, of pleasure, or honeyed talk. What was I going to do?

"Why not?"

"Yes, why not!" But his astonishment did not fade. He opened the door and I stepped into the crowded, stiflingly close room, almost into the arms of Maria Euphrosina.

"Christina!" She bowed slightly. "Ah, your hair has been mussed by the wind, dear Christina. Come, let me arrange it for you."

I tossed my head. How annoying she was, trying to call attention to her own brushed brown curls lying docile, which seemed a matter of pride to her. It had taken one of my ladies-in-waiting a good twenty minutes to comb out my tangles that morning in preparation for the reception, since I had had no time for such an operation for several days. It had been painful, truly.

"Fancy curls and fancy gowns are for the idle. I have no time for them," I said abruptly, and turned my back to her to whisper to Magnus: "Tell the Chancellor I would speak with him in the anteroom."

It was quiet in the anteroom, a room of few windows, heavily draped, of unmoving shadows, relieving to the eyes after the glare of water on the portico. Several pieces of dark, polished furniture, perhaps German or French, I do not remember, two or three portraits, one small Flemish scene were all the room contained. It was not used very much, I thought, but now it would be of historic use. I had known all along I wanted to be the real ruler when I came of age. Why else would I have studied so hard, so persistently? In my innocence I had not expected Oxenstierna to continue giving out directives as if he still were Regent. What had I expected, I asked myself. That he would change his nature, that he would lay the plans of his lifetime, his habits of ruling, in the hands of a Queen who had plans of her own, far different from his? Not he, who was constantly knifed by the responsibility of his position, by the necessity of carrying out his ideas according to his honor. The only solution was for him to retire honorably. I wondered that I had not thought of it before. He had had his turn. I should have mine. We need not compete.

Should I stand or should I be seated to receive him? It would be better to sit in an imposing chair. When I stood, facing him, I could not help being conscious of his height, of my own shortness, and it was easier to conceal the hump of my shoulder when I was seated. I paced a moment to work out the few twinges of nervousness I felt. When he came in, I was seated, composed and ready. By the look on his face, the Chancellor was as glad as I to escape the vexations of pretending pleasure in meaningless conversations. I did not intend to keep him long from these vexations, however, for I knew exactly what I wished to say.

"Chancellor Oxenstierna," I began, "I am sensible of the great services you have given to Sweden during my minority in acting as Regent, in serving, in fact, as the leader of the Regents, as we all know, with little regard for your personal comfort or convenience. I wish the world to realize my gratitude, my country's gratitude, therefore I am arranging a ceremony to honor you. I will tell you, now, before others have been informed, that it is my will to make you a count."

In the shadowed room, surprise seemed to silver his countenance. There could not have been more than two or three men in Sweden with the title of count, including my Uncle Johan. It is the highest a man can be, next to royalty itself. Did his veined hand shake as he raised it to adjust the broad lace-edged collar on his black coat? Was it possible he felt an emotion, this somber bearded Chancellor?

"It is not necessary to do this, Your Majesty."

I knew that. I said: "It is my pleasure to suitably reward fine services."

He came forward, kissed my hand. "I am deeply grateful."

"I suppose you will wish to retire after the ceremony."

He straightened his great frame. "I shall be happy to continue my services as long as I live."

"Your health is not good, Chancellor. You will kill yourself working. As your sovereign, I cannot allow that."

He puffed out the strength in his voice to a low boom. "No! Work always makes me feel better, not worse. I still sleep like a boy, because when I go to bed I drop my cares with my clothes. Do you know, Your Majesty, in my life I have missed just two nights' sleep, just two. The first was when news came that the great Gustav Adolf was dead and I could not quiet my sorrow. The other, when Marshal Horn was captured and I feared we had lost the war. Nothing has disturbed my sleep since." He made a rumbling sound resembling a laugh. "I would crumble away without work to do."

I must have heard the story of his two nights' sleeplessness twenty times or more. Everyone in Sweden knew it by heart. What an old man he was, to keep repeating himself! How did you acquaint a man with his age, if he refused to notice it? Oxenstierna's skin had become spotted with brown, his cheeks creased, fingered by the years, his hair and short beard a solid gray. Couldn't he see it?

I said: "Soon this war will be over. What a glorious parting gift to our country a peace would be! It would complete an auspicious service."

"The war," he mused. "I wish the news would come from Torstenson. He does not seem to realize how important a military victory is at this time for us at the conference table."

"Are we not at the conference table to urge peace, not more fighting, Chancellor?"

He smiled. "We must maintain our bargaining power, Your Majesty."

"Then the congress is to be a market place where people and lands are traded like wares!"

"There is no coin in the world equal to a military victory, no gold so bright or so persuasive. Yes, I wish Torstenson's news would come. The princes are in need of persuasion."

I lifted my chin. "Chancellor Oxenstierna, do you really want peace?"

"Peace is a blessing I pray Sweden will enjoy soon, very soon. The responsibilities of war are sad, sad particularly for me, who has borne them so long. One day we will emerge from this shadow, we will cast off our burden, we will sit in the sun, we will breathe in repose. Sweden will be recognized as one of the great nations of the earth by the peace she has won."

"Now that I am Queen I shall take the responsibilities you have borne for me during these years. It shall be my honor to win the peace for Sweden. You have been a good teacher, Chancellor, and I insist you take the rest you deserve. I believe you would find the delights of retirement richer than you anticipate."

"I cannot desert you, Your Majesty. You are Gustav Adolf's daughter."

It always came back to that. I tightened my lips.

"When you were a little girl I promised you we would work together to solve Sweden's problems. You have become Queen. Our opportunity has come. It is on my honor to serve you and Sweden."

Serve Sweden by sustaining war? What else could he mean by having the fighting continue, intensify? I could not believe he truly wanted peace. No, it wouldn't be as easy as I had thought to deprive myself of his services. He intended to cling to his authority as long as he could stand on his two feet, nay, longer. He would be issuing orders from his sickbed when his old legs could not bear his weight any more.

"You will please me by thinking further of this, Chancellor."

"I appreciate Your Majesty's kind consideration of me." He bowed.

I rose, to end our meeting, stung that I had won nothing, that there had been no exchange. Nevertheless, I determined, we shall have peace, and sooner than he expects.

I was in no mood to discuss my failure when Magnus hastened to my side in the great reception room. To his eagerly whispered questions I had only one comment to make, that Tacitus' description of the Emperor Tiberius was an apt one when he said *his physical strength was already beginning to leave him, but not the art of shamming*, that it was the perfect, the exact, the fitting description of Chancellor Oxenstierna.

VII

I SUPPOSE it was my expectation of Carl Gustav's return that kept me from being more attentive to Hugo Grotius while he was in Stockholm. After all, I was eighteen, and what was left of my mind after the grind of government affairs slipped naturally to the sweetness of a remembered sentiment, unable to resist the prospect of a dream emerging into waking hours. Carl Gustav had been gone for three years. When he had left, I had dreamed of him distinguishing himself on the battlefield as a courageous soldier. Now he had done so. I had attained my majority, and he could ask openly for my hand. Did I still want him to? How would he look, what would he say, what would we do when we were alone together? The thought of love made me nervous, as the time drew near. How extravagant young people are, wasting thoughts on what might or might not be, catching on to the edge of rosy clouds, letting themselves drift in and out of conjectures, of half-guessed possibilities, mists that never lift without experience! I would have done better to have improved my knowledge with Grotius, even to have encroached on the hours I assiduously worked at politics or plotted with Magnus, but how was I to know that my chance was a passing one, that there would be no more visits, no letters, that when Grotius left Sweden he left the world? How was I to foresee that his ship would be wrecked in a late summer storm, that by August he would be dead at Rostock?

Since Grotius is one of the truly notable men of our century, I suppose, too, I should have a keener memory of his visit. Youth, again, I plead, for retaining impressions valuable only to my own spiritual progress. I cannot describe his appearance, his conversations, his mannerisms, his philosophical advice. He himself is vague to me, overshadowed by the excitements of my new duties and my personal problems. I find, however, that I learned two important lessons from the details of his experience, lessons on which I reflected, years later, and used. The first came, very simply, from the story of his escape from prison.

When he lived in Holland, he told me, he had been outspoken in the cause of the party which unfortunately failed to achieve power, and he had been imprisoned in the fortress of Lowestein. His property had been confiscated, his future enclosed within stone walls and locked doors. He was permitted certain consolations in prison, the visits of his wife, who attended to mundane needs such as his laundry, and a perusal of classical works. That translating Greek tragedies into Latin could be dangerous did not occur to his captors, showing how they underestimated the scholarly imagination. Actually, Grotius said, it had been his wife's plan, he hadn't believed it would succeed, his opinion of other men's intelligence being higher than that of his wife, who was the realistic member of the family. Don't be silly, she had said, the guards won't notice, they are good at sitting all day, if they were more than half alive they wouldn't be able to put up with doing nothing.

The scheme concerned the large box which was taken in and out regularly, taking in the books he needed for his translating, taking out the linen to be washed and the books he had finished. In time the soldiers became so accustomed to this chest, they no longer bothered to examine it, thus, reasoned his wife, if Grotius was inside instead of the books, he would be hauled away nicely by his guards. Wouldn't they be suspicious of the extra weight, I asked, since Grotius was no feather of a man? Yes, they were, he replied. He had curled up like a fox and let out his breath to make himself light, but when the two soldiers had lifted the box one of them had groaned at the weight, complaining there must be an Armenian inside. You're right, his wife had laughed, there are Armenian books in it, can't you manage them? The soldiers had flexed their muscles and carried him out, then, to the waiting cart, and he had been driven to a friend's house and unpacked. There he was clothed like a mason, handed a hod and trowel which no one luckily asked him to use, and taken across the frontier to Antwerp. From there he traveled to Paris, where he settled down to write his books and become, eventually, our Ambassador. He had escaped to serve the world.

"Everyone," I had offered, "has a prison to escape from. Some place, some fear, someone."

The necessity of escape does not depend on the place or thing one escapes from, Grotius indicated, as much as on the freedom one escapes to. He might have borne the narrowness of his physical circuit, it was the imprisonment of his spirit he could not bear, the entombing of his ideas, his education, his usefulness. He might not have tried to escape if he had been free to write the books he wanted to write and known that some day, somewhere, they would have been printed, that they would have reached those unseen receptive readers for whom they were intended and served their ultimate purpose. Being a political prisoner, that was, pointedly, what he was to be prevented from doing. He had to escape to a place where he could sustain his reason for living in the world.

Another man, I mused, would have missed seeing the width of a landscape bathed in sunlight, realizing he could walk across it as he willed, or he would have missed his beer in his tavern, or his family around his hearth. There are many reasons for living. What would I miss if I were imprisoned? My ambition, my love, my studies? I could not say, then, for I was on a rising tide of confidence and achievement. Imprisonment, for me, seemed too impossible a joke to think about.

The other lesson was immediate, coming more from what I saw

with my own eyes than from what I heard from Grotius's lips. The hope I had had that he might be of assistance in settling the war quickly proved to be a mirage. The older nobles were cold to him, rude, refusing to invite him to their houses, avoiding speech with him in the castle. True, he was the author of the laws of war, respected by their beloved Gustav Adolf, but he had, too, dared to write a code of Christianity in which Protestant and Catholic would be reconciled by a common piety. He was indifferent to dogmatics and sects. Such tolerance, they said, was dangerous. Was not acceptance next to dominance, where Catholicism was concerned? Was not that what the whole war was about? I almost could hear the rasping in their souls.

Grotius had arrived, moreover, when the country was shaken by the vehemence of a religious argument of its own. Johannes Matthiæ had published a book, *Idea Boni Ordinis in Ecclesia Christi*, recommending changes in the orthodox rules of Lutheranism. Very sensible, I thought, to apply the development of knowledge to suit our own age. What, screamed the oldsters, deviate from the detailed instructions of the *Book of Concord?* Blasphemy, blasphemy! Who is this man who sets himself above the precepts of our prophet Luther?

Who was he indeed! Was there, in all Sweden, a man wiser or better versed in the theory and practice of religion than Johannes Matthiæ? He had been Professor of Poetry at Uppsala University, Doctor of Theology and Rector of the College at Stockholm, he had been my father's chaplain and my tutor, the religious mentor, thus, of Kings. Immediately I became Queen I raised him to be Bishop of Strängnäs, but when his book was published neither my royal approval nor his title protected him from bitter criticism. New ideas were the last things wanted in Sweden among a people so deeply in love with their prejudices. Grotius, naturally, found in Johannes Matthiæ one of the few persons with whom he wished to converse, but Matthiæ was caught in the uproar. Where could he find the quiet to spend with the great man? Later there would be time.

Later there would be time for me, too, I thought, even while Grotius turned his face away from Sweden. Where would be his later time? Not here where his eminent position, if it was known at all, was a target for sarcasm, for quips, for hate. So Grotius left Sweden, Grotius left the world, and I was left with my lonely lesson. Always I had admired greatness, revered it, aspired to it, especially that greatness of the mind which is the result of a man's own efforts, whatever his birth or station. Had not Alexander of Macedonia written Aristotle that he would rather excel mankind in a superiority of learning than in the extent of his power and dominion? Was there anything more glorious, more akin to God, than an immense understanding? Did not the fiery wings of knowledge lift a man to be a very sun, turning above the ordinary affairs of life, shedding the gifts of his light? No, I saw now, not to be a sun, but a golden bird that cannot escape the wrapping veils of the earth nor the slingshots of the stupid. The higher he flies, the clearer he becomes a target for those who would kill his brightness. He cannot take with him in his flight those who fear to leave the ground, nor can he reflect his glory on any who hide their minds in the shade. He cannot teach those who will not be taught, he cannot open the heavens to men who will not open their own eyes. A golden bird must love the flight for its own sake.

The lesson sat before me, but, at the moment, I did not attend to it. I was too busy. I wrote a letter to Mme Grotius of my sorrow at her husband's death, and I proceeded with my private agitations. Besides the hundreds of domestic problems I must study, there was my correspondence with Salvius demanding constant alertness and decisions. I could not miss an official meeting nor be unprepared on any matter to be presented. And, as Queen, I was able to recall Carl Gustav to Stockholm.

How many nights during the first year he was away I had dreamed of my cousin, his hair ruffled by the wind, charging up a black hill of battle to drive the enemy into the melting crimson of the sky! I saw his smile as he turned his horse to bring his victory to lay at my feet. Was the lightning flashing from his eyes that of triumph in war, or could it be of triumph in love? Whatever, it had thrilled me, bone, flesh, and soul, putting me in an impatience for our wait to be at an end. When had my dream begun to dim, to be crowded away with other dreams, other visions? Was it when Beata Oxenstierna had laid before me the crudity of marriage, the expectancy of the country that I submit to producing an heir? Was it when I discovered how other young men, such as Magnus, could be equally charming as companions? Was it when I began to spend my mind and energies on political affairs and on the necessity of stopping the war, when I became Queen? Would the dream revive when I saw him again before me?

When he returned I did not summon him to see me, first, alone, nor did he rush to me, lover-like. I carefully dressed my expectations in court manners and received him in audience as an officer of the nobility, my favorites and my secretaries flanking me. I would have the great room sufficiently crowded, I decided, to forestall any premature embarrassing embrace. I need not have worried. He entered the room, a soldier in drill, his sword clanking rhythmically at his exact steps. He came to me, clicked his heels together, and bowed precisely.

"Welcome home, Carl Gustav, my dear cousin."

"Your Majesty!"

He raised his eyes to mine, regarded me with a steadfast look reeking with respect, his thick lips parted to let out the steam of any passion that might creep into a frame grown to comfortable proportions. Grown, I must add, sideways, in spots, not upward. He had not added an inch to his stature, leaving him a short figure among Swedish officers, only his belly had grown in bulk so that standing straight he had the appearance of tipping backward. Had he been on the beer front or the battlefront, I wondered. No locks teased me by drooping onto his forehead, his brown hair oiled to a soldierly order, a matching brown mustache following an inverted V around his mouth. I searched his face, his expression, for signs of suffering he might have been through or might have seen in the devastated countries. In vain. There was not a line of sadness, not a glimmer of compassion apparent.

"We are glad to have you back safely, cousin. Terrible tales of the war have reached us."

"Yes, Your Majesty. Thank you."

"Is not the war horrible?"

"Yes, Your Majesty."

"Tell us about it."

He cleared his throat, cocked his head, scraped his memory.

"War is war, Your Majesty."

"Have you no special tales to relate?"

"Did you not receive my reports, Your Majesty?"

"I have read them thoroughly, cousin."

"He saves us the boredom of repetition," said Magnus, twirling an end of his mustache to cover a smile.

"Can war ever be boring?" put in young Count Tott.

"We are hoping the war will be over soon, now that the peace congress has convened. I will be pleased to have your assistance in assuring a peace." I almost posed it as a question. How much did my cousin like war?

"I am at your service, Your Majesty." Carl Gustav's expression never seemed to change. Always complacent.

"Are you sure?"

At last I had moved him. Shock knocked away the respect in his eyes.

"Your Majesty! Christina! How can you doubt my loyalty? My life is yours, my services, whatever I can do. Believe me, Your Majesty!"

Thus it was when Carl Gustav came home. *Your Majesty*, *Your Majesty*, *Your Majesty*. A sweet sound, a title, but not so constantly on the lips of one who should be a lover. He gave it a formal edge, a metallic reverberation, a grating separateness. It called across a gulf it did not, or would not, bridge. What had I expected? What did I want? A whispered *Christina*, an unfiltered flash of lovelight, an indiscreet wink? I confess I do not know.

The man before me was the image of a little burgomaster. He looked as if he wore a coat against the sensibilities of love or of any imaginative wavering in a set life.

He did not change his attitude in the weeks following, although I found him at my side at every court function, hovering about me, his Queen Protectress, as if he were an exiled son allowed home at last. He pressed me for a private meeting, which I evaded as being too busy with state affairs. What would I say to him, alone? I wanted time to think. Then he began to complain that I seemed to have plenty of time for Magnus, so why not for him, had he not an equal right, and what he had to speak of had, certainly, a direct bearing on the welfare of the State. So I acquiesced, and appointed an afternoon for him to come to the reception room in my private apartment.

He arrived, my burly cousin, armed, not with his sword, but with the letter I had written him to Germany vowing eternal love.

"But I wrote that when I was fifteen!" I exclaimed.

"I never shall lose it," he declared. "It is my most precious possession." Why, then, did his eyes remain dull at the touch of it? Why did he stand so far from me at the other end of the room, his legs planted apart, waiting, I thought, for a horse to run under him and carry him away?

"Yes." For once I was empty of words. Were the emotions of a girl of fifteen binding forever?

"What have the Councellors done about Friedrich Wilhelm's proposal?"

I answered contemptuously. Did he make no effort to keep up with court news? "I told you I would not accept him. It was renounced officially when I came of age."

Now there was a light in Carl Gustav's eyes. He folded his hands happily on his beer belly. "When shall we announce our engagement, Your Majesty?"

"You do not need to call me 'Your Majesty' when we are alone."

"Thank you, Christina." It sounded little better.

"Are we sure we want this engagement?"

"Not want it?" Why was he astonished? "We have promised one another." His tone referred to a civil promise, not to a concern between lovers.

"We cannot say anything about it at the present."

"Why?"

Words of love or not-love were cold on my tongue. This was not the time. I called on my dignity.

"Since I have become Queen I have a great many affairs to attend to. This must wait until we can think about it more carefully."

"But I am a lost soul in Sweden! People must know where I stand, what I am. And Oxenstierna." The last words were low.

"Oxenstierna?"

"He stopped me as I was coming into the castle. He told me I should realize the Queen's situation and the delicate politics of the war. He said you had to beware of the excessive ambition of German princes and that such men should not be allowed to come into any position of high consideration. He means me, I know he means me! He thinks of me solely as a German prince. He always has hated my father and the name Palatine. He thinks nothing of my mother being a Vasa or that I was born in Sweden. What does he think I have been doing on the battlefield other than fight for Sweden? I cannot stand his intrigues, his lies, his bigwig politics. I like things to be open. I like people to know how I stand. If I have an enemy, I am willing to fight him. I am not one to hide behind fancy phrases."

"You are used to soldier's ways. When you have been longer at court you will cease to be frightened of its deceits and elusive politics."

"Frightened! I am not frightened! With God's help I shall have revenge on Oxenstierna for his intrigues."

I did not need to wonder what Carl Gustav would say if I should tell him the Chancellor's design to marry me to one of his sons. Perhaps he had noticed how closely Erik Oxenstierna attached himself to my person whenever he had an opportunity, perhaps that was the cause of his outburst. For me, an alliance with Erik was impossible, not even worthy of my speaking of it.

"In what way is the Chancellor intriguing against you, cousin?"

"You must have noticed how he stops talking when I approach him, all the Oxenstiernas do, all their friends, and they will say nothing but it is a fine day, it is a dull day. You do not have to tell me it is he who keeps me from having an official position, I know it very well. I am left with nothing to do, nothing to attend to. I am told nothing, I am never consulted on the affairs of Sweden. They are kept from me. It will be so as long as our engagement is a secret."

"That does not seem to me sufficient reason to make an engagement public."

"You do not understand, Christina! Oxenstierna will do everything in his power to keep you from marrying me. Why do you suppose he is intriguing? He wants the throne for himself, for someone he can control. He knows he cannot use me for one of his run-around-the-bush lackeys. He knows I am completely loyal to you."

Loyal, yes, there was no doubt of Carl's loyalty. But where was his trust in my ability as a ruler? Hadn't he noticed how I had taken matters into my own hands since I had become Queen? Had he not heard it was I who put an end to the war with Denmark in spite of Oxenstierna's opposition?

"I am glad of your loyalty, Carl, but the time is not ripe to make known any betrothal for me. Whatever happens, it must be planned carefully so that the Estates are prepared to accept it. Then the Chancellor will be powerless to deny it. My advice to you is to ignore him as well as you are able, to conduct yourself courageously before the court and the country. Why do you attend to him? It is far better to win the love and respect of the people."

What else could I say to him? I could neither accept him nor refuse him without probing my heart and my conscience. As for my cousin, he appeared to have no suspicion that the engagement was not as plain as the day it was made. He had to be satisfied with my postponement, for he could think of no other arguments against it, and he left me without even coming close enough to press my fingers in his browned hand.

Carl Gustav was right in assuming that Oxenstierna was watching us, and with little approval, but he exaggerated in thinking he was the only young noble to be watched and discouraged. The sharp gray eyes of the Chancellor speculated on every move I made, every conversation I enlivened with young courtiers, as if he would spy out my feelings before I myself knew what they were. Magnus laughed about it, whispering to me he hoped he would not grow overly proud for having earned the distinction of being watched by the Chancellor.

Handsome, charming Magnus! He animated every room he stepped into, he polished the most ordinary discussion with the grace of his nature. Where Carl Gustav would present a problem to me as if it were a heavy log, Magnus seemed to see problems as dark cloths to be shaken out, yes, and with delight, for he shook out stars instead of dust. How would it be, I caught myself thinking, if I had made my promise to Magnus rather than Carl Gustav, would I, then, be so disinclined to marriage? The more I considered it, the more absurdly simple the answer appeared. Magnus and I obviously were better suited. In all the world would there be time enough for our talking, our planning, our pleasuring? Was his nearness not a necessity? Even when we danced together our rhythm showed a perfect pairing. He did not avoid touching me as others did, his hand a familiar warmth in mine, his arm, in moments of enthusiasm, encircling my shoulders or my waist. If he had not spoken of love, was it not because I had not led him to it? I was his Pallas, his intimate oracle, his dear Christina, this I was told day after day, yet would not some inner censor remind him I was, too, his Queen, that he could not ask my hand unless I opened the way?

As for Carl Gustav, how easy it would be to dissolve our supposed engagement since no one outside of ourselves knew of it. It needed only our mutual agreement. Would he not have to admit, when it was put to him with the bluntness he loved to embrace, that a secret promise between minors could have no validity, personal or official, that our engagement had been a childish dream from which we, as adults, had awakened? Surely it was Providence herself who had chosen to draw together Magnus and me, Providence who had cupped her hand around the flame that had leaped between Gustav Adolf and Ebba Brahe, had not let it die, had let it flare again, for us. This time it would not be denied. Not for an instant did I believe the gossip that Magnus was, in secret truth, my bastard brother, the fruit of a passion that continued after Ebba Brahe's marriage. No. That passion would be consummated now, at long last. All that remained, I thought, was to speak to Magnus, or let him speak to me.

Late one winter morning, when the air was leaden and pressed against the body like a Northern bear, while I was taking a recess from government affairs in my study, the opportunity came. I was hunched over my table fingering a report of Grotius's library, which I proposed to buy, trying to forget the chill and the tired pain in my stomach. The knock on the heavy door irritated me, one more thing, I thought crossly, to keep me from my exploration of the sphere of Virtue, until I saw who dared disturb me. Magnus was radiant in spite of the depressing day, a laughing young lion, his cheeks flushed, his hair flagrantly bright above the modesty of his brown suit.

"Come in! Come here! Look at this magnificent list of manuscripts! I shall have to have new cabinets built for them." My voice was loud in relief.

A few long strides and he was bending over me, his arm brushing against mine as his finger followed the titles down the page.

"Our friend Grotius allowed himself a goodly selection," he said, "but let us not worry about the past on a day like this."

"Why? It is a terrible day. My bones are cold."

"It is a beautiful day! The world is wrapped in silver. The castle and the houses of the town are wrought into a silent silver shape, silver reindeer may pace unseen through solid silver streets. It is a day for innocents. The wolf cannot find his little silver prey within the silver mist, the hawk knows not where to swoop into the silver depths. The water is a carpet of stillness, haunted by ships that wait like maidens for their lovers in the silver shadows."

I smiled, stretched my arms upward, my legs outward, to push out the stiffness. Lovely foolishness.

Magnus pulled a chair to the table, seated himself, leaned toward me, his eyes catching the silver light. "Through the silver fog the gods pass. It is their day for love."

Abruptly my arms came down, my toes searched the solidity of the floor. "Love!" I repeated the word.

"You speak knowingly, my Pallas."

"Are we not of an age to know what love is? It is time to escape from that web of childish dreams we used to call love, to see it as a real person, as real beauty. I must confess I have seen it rising in you, Magnus."

"You see everything, dear Christina! You make it easier for me to speak."

I waited, he hesitated.

I waved my hand in encouragement. "Speak, Magnus. I promise you to be the kindliest of audiences. Perhaps I may even assist you."

He laid his fingers flat on the table, contemplating them, then slowly laced them together. He continued to look at them, folded before him, rather than at me, as he began to speak. He sighed out his words so gently they might have been thin glass, ready to break at a harsh breath.

"Maria Euphrosina. How beautiful she is."

I did not move, in truth I could not. Something within me clicked shut. What was he saying, in what language was he speaking that I understood him so queerly? But something within him had opened. On and on he talked of a Maria Euphrosina I never had known, could not have imagined, could not, still, believe in, of her delicate character, her beauty. Her beauty. She was a dryad, he said, an escaped dryad, trailing the mysteries and fragrances of the forest. The flush of spring petals was on her skin, her eyes reflected the green of leaves and wooded pools, the brown of acorns and bark was smoothed into the curls falling to the curve of her snow-white shoulder. She is gowned in flowers and golden webs, he said, and she moves with the grace of the tall reed's plumes. The touch of her hand is moonlight, waking my soul from darkness in its long night. Yes, for she is the moon's daughter, the magic one who drives men to madness, who teases the white doe to leap through the sky like clouds, who changes the minnows of the lake into flashing swords, who pelts snowflakes at the eyes of lovers so they may not behold Medusa's snake locks intertwining the trees of the winter woods where they walk. Maria Euphrosina was this and more, he said, did I not see it, did I not agree she was the most beautiful of creatures?

And I? How, I wondered, did he see me? Not with magic, not with beauty. I am the Sun King's dark child, stubby and deformed as the denuded autumnal twilight. My pock-marked complexion never could be compared to petals unless they were ready to be thrown away. I am a faded version of the Golden King, my body small, my hair straggling into a faint brown. Faded in looks, I told myself, but not in deeds. Did that mean nothing? Evidently it did not to Magnus, caught as he was in his moonlight rapture.

"So, my dear Christina," he finished, "I beg your blessing for our marriage. Maria Euphrosina sends you her love and greetings, and asks your indulgent consent in the name of her mother, the Princess Katarina."

Aunt Katarina. How like Maria Euphrosina to remind me of my promise to her dying mother. I could hear my voice repeating I would favor her children. If I closed my eyes I would see it all again, but I could not close my eyes, for if I closed my eyes I might see, too, that the promise she thrust into my hands was one of the seven golden candlesticks. *Who walketh in the midst of the seven golden candlesticks . . . I will give him the morning star.*

Was I to walk in the midst of promises? What was the morning star? Not love, I saw. *He that hath an ear, let him hear what the Spirit saith.* Did not the Spirit say to attain Virtue, and was it not a greater Virtue to be Queen than to be wife? I found my answer, I raised a tone to speak.

"Tell Maria Euphrosina I give her one whom I may not take myself." I cleared my voice. "Now I will lose my favorite! Love will be your sovereign."

Magnus jumped up, around the table, and to my side with his old familiarity, letting his long fine hand fall onto my humped shoulder. "Why should my marriage affect our friendship? You know how devoted I am to you and to all your purposes. How much more so it should be when we become cousins."

"Cousins, yes. And you shall be brother to Carl Gustav."

It was a travesty of feelings, one Magnus did not seem to sense. He drew away, laughingly, toward the window, as if he would look out to seek his dryad. "Carl Gustav! There is a fellow for you! He is the man we should talk to about love!"

"Do you make more sport of love or of my cousin?" I tried to speak easily. "He is a little burgomaster."

"In the castle he looks so, but truly he is a Jupiter to change his demeanor when he enters a tavern. All the pretty girls in town are in pursuit of the returned hero."

"Then he must change his shape, too."

"His shape!" Magnus sniffed happily. "They say she is the most beautiful of all the merchants' daughters, with soft wheat hair and eyes of peacock blue, curved and pink-skinned. . . ."

"Who?"

"The one he took on the long sleigh ride, the one to whom he gave his finest fur robe, the fur that kept them warm."

"What are you talking about?"

"Surely you know. Everyone does. It was your talk of his shape that reminded me. In the spring there will be a new little shape in memory of his ride."

It was no use to stare, no use to do anything. I tightened my lips, let my fist fall, once, onto the velvet of the table. "You have my permission for your marriage, Magnus."

His mouth straightened from a smile into seriousness, his eyebrow arched above his question. "You are not in the mood for gossip, dear Christina?"

"I have a great deal to do."

Magnus, not a man to be banished, had several phrases of his gratitude to deliver before leaving me, alone, to a deeper chill than the Northern weather could inflict. I pressed my fists into my cheeks.

Men and beauty, beauty and men, what a terrible duet! What is there about beauty to so enslave a man, to bewitch him, blind him, so that he gladly throws himself into chains for life? The touch of moonlight! Could he not see how the delicate shaft of moonlight disappears into the bowels of an angry storm? Could he not see how transient is its sheen, no more to be crystallized than the dews of dawn? Of what use is it? Who remembers how Sappho walked or stood, whether her cheeks wore the softness of apple blossoms or were cracked as old porcelain plates? And Lucretia of the gilded locks and milk-white sides, what did she win with her beauty except the fame of a rape any tavern maid could match, given an Ovid? Look what beauty did to Dido, foolish, foolish Dido, who became so entranced with the effect of her breasts and her cherry mouth on a passing Æneas she forgot where her real power lay! Her end scarcely could have been worse. How she supplicated before the altar of her gods, holding up her golden goblet to them, that her lover might be drawn back to her charms! She might as well have hurled the goblet to the ground and let her flowered heifer stamp it to bits. It is not beauty the gods love in a Queen. Only man loves beauty, only man tries to build it into immortality. Why? What spirit has it? Can it raise a city, ferret out a spy, rein in the wild horses of time? Can it leap through the tricks of history? It is as spineless as the blush of the proverbial rose. Then, dear God, why does it have so much power?

Well, I have no beauty, but what need have I for it? There is no man in the world but would think himself happy if I deigned to give him my hand. What a parade my suitors would make! The King of Hungary! The three Princes of Poland! The King of Spain! The Prince of Denmark! The Elector of Brandenburg! Probably the Emperor of China, should he hear of me. What does it matter that their hearts burn with politics rather than love, what does it matter that it seems easier to win wars by taking me to bed than by paying for more soldiers, that my face, to them, is the picture of the territories they gain? What does it matter that they would slide away in the night, like Carl Gustav, to find a sweeter face, a fairer body, to kiss? Ah, but if I am repulsive to them, are not they repulsive to me, too? What is a man in bed? A parcel of bones and hair and flesh with a masculine smell. Who would want to kiss that? There is nothing divine about it at all.

The King of This! The Prince of That! The King! The Prince! The King! They were a glittering parade, but what were they to me in the quiet of my heart? Names. That is all. Socrates once said: *Whether you marry or refrain from marrying you will be sorry*. I should think that everyone who marries will infallibly be sorry, but I see no reason why anyone should be sorry for not having married. Particularly I, Christina. I am a Queen, and to be Queen is to be divine, to be eternal. Why should I give up any part of my divinity to one of these names, to a name that would turn into a man who would want to master my mind and my body, who would try to direct my decisions, who would expect me to accede to the animal pact of marriage? The very thought of it disgusts me. I will not belong to any man, be he King, courtier, commoner. I never will accept a master. I was born free. I shall live free, die free.

The study was cold, yet I did not want to leave. I pulled toward me some of the books on my table. Plato, Seneca, Heraclitus. Passions are a disease of the soul, said Seneca. Man is happy when he masters his passions and is independent of the external world. And Plato. When philosophers are Kings or the Kings of the world have the spirit and power of philosophy and political greatness and wisdom meet in one, then the human race will have rest from evils, he said. Nothing is real, whispered Heraclitus, only change. Nothing will stay, only change. The sun and the stars, the forest and the river, the offspring of the deer and the son of man, all are passers-by. Nothing abides, but reason. Only reason remains the same, reason, the orderly succession of things through the ever living fire of the world.

Here is the beginning of Truth, I said to myself. Here are companions, teachers, I can trust. Was not the city of philosophers better than the city of men? There I would not be left before a closed door, waiting for someone to come with a key. There I could find my own key. In this vast city of the soul I could walk freely, a student of Virtue. Truly free, for the soul has no sex. I would be warmed by greatness, I would carve my own seat in the wall of Time. And there it would be plain that Magnus, or Carl Gustav, or any wish for love was no more than a migrant bird in my garden.

VIII

IT may be easy for an ordinary woman to avoid marriage, it may be too easy, according to her lighted wishes, popular rumor running that possession of a man is the prime capture a woman can make, that it is the chalice she is to seek and adore, that it is worth more than a crown any day, all of which persuades her that marriage is the last thing to be avoided rather than the first. Having a crown, I see a different side to the picture. I would not trade my crown for any man, nor a single jewel in it. The urge to conquer is in the nature of a man, and marriage his way of conquering a woman. I shall not be conquered, of that I am determined. Marriage, however, is extremely difficult for a Queen to avoid.

Every day I was asked, directly or by allusion, whom I would marry. Friends and foes, young and old, noble or boor, man or woman, everyone was interested. They hinted, promoted, urged, joked, coaxed. Whether or not I wanted to marry was ignored. By tradition I should take a husband and bear a child, an heir for the kingdom, therefore I would do it. When I protested that if I should have a child I would be as liable to be mother to a Nero as an Augustus, my words were laughed at as a passing piece of wit. Didn't I like men that I wouldn't choose one for my consort, bantered one of my young courtiers. Oh, yes, I like men, I said, but I do not like them because they are men. I like them because they are not women.

It was natural for these persons to be interested, for they believed their own future depended on it. Would I marry from this family or that, from this political group or that, would they be on the right side when the time came? When I rejected the suit of Friedrich Wilhelm of Brandenburg it was taken for granted I would choose someone within my own country. He had been the favored, the most logical contender. Any other husband from a foreign land, be he ever so magnificent, would involve Sweden in too many political complications, since the first wedding gift his country would send would be the papers for adoption of their dearest enemies. We would gain one ally and lose, perhaps, three or four; so, it seemed, by my marrying a highborn Swedish noble, Sweden would keep clear of the foreign entanglements she hated and distrusted. Why, then, didn't I hurry up about it, the people wondered.

They buzzed questions, wonderings, suggestions into my ear. All day, every day. What a fine young fellow this count was, tall, muscular, an excellent shot, would he not be a sweet protection for me? Had I noticed how he had outgrown his early foolishness, that he no longer rolled under the table at drinking-parties, but walked away like a real Viking? He knew how to hold his beer now. And that young gallant, his silly talk did not mean anything, his true nature, deep, wise, and kind, was hidden by his shyness. Just ask his mother. How well this courtier wore his clothes! Would he not look handsome in the purple? As for family, look at the Oxenstiernas, as old as the Vasas truly, and how pleased my father would be in his grave to know I had united with a son of his most trusted friend. After all, the Oxenstiernas were the second ruling family of the land. Look at the years the Chancellor had had the reign in his own hands. I ought to realize that if it had not been for his loyalty he could have stepped into the top place easily. It was only right for me to reward him by making his son Erik my consort, only justice that the Chancellor should be able to look forward to having his grandchild sit on the throne of Sweden.

Carl Gustav had his adherents, too. If he was awkward and

slow in his speech, his eloquent supporters made up for it. They were ardent in his cause, whispering to me that Carl never would marry if it were not the Queen, his beloved Christina.

"Oh, but he will!" I exclaimed. "Love does not burn for one alone. The crown is a pretty girl."

In the early hours of the morning the courtyards were still, the gates locked, the pavements bare of people. When the castle slept, its stone halls hushed in their echoing, I found a measure of peace apart from the constant insisting. I would waken after a few hours' sleep in the night, light the candles beside my bed, lift a pile of books beside me, and, snug in a mound of covers, read. A wall rose about me, one built of luminous words that cast light instead of shade. Skies of philosophers opened above me, ideas appeared in fresh colors like trees in spring, reflections of Truth were around me. How could I catch these reflections of Truth and hold them as solid realities? Where was the great pillar from which they shone?

Or was it a pillar? Was not Truth a moving thing, eternal, exciting, brilliantly reassuring, the point from which the soul sprang, to which it ached to return? Since there is Truth in the world and beyond it, Plato said, there is an Author of Truth. Out of the chaos of matter the World-Maker fashioned the world. Out of the chaos of ideas Truth was created. Yes, I thought, but where shall I find the Author of Truth and how shall I recognize Him? I must, for I yearned to be His Bride, His Queen. Only Truth would satisfy me. As Catholic virgins gave themselves to be brides of Christ, I would be the Bride of Truth.

How old-fashioned religion was! Cicero was right when he concluded all human conceptions of religion may be wrong but that it is impossible there be more than one absolute Truth. Why was it taking man centuries to free himself to Truth, why did he clutter his mind with ragged superstitions? What a parade his religions made! Thousands of gods, each wearing a ribbon with *Truth* embroidered in gilt letters, bearded Zeus in his goatskin leading his brain-child, the blue-eyed Athene, Jupiter carrying a lightning bolt, the Salien priests of Mars in high conical hats, one-eyed Odin, a raven on either shoulder, Diana bearing the moon, Hecate waving branches of black magic, and how many others, volumes of them. Were they not inventions of man, creatures of his fantasy? Then there were the Hebrew patriarchs, Allah, Mohammed, meticulous Confucius, lists and lists of gods and prophets, names whispered from one generation to another, worshipped in cities, on war-blackened plains, by lonely mountain rocks, in hidden forest shrines, in all countries, all ages. Were they not dreams to gratify the terrors, the exasperations, the hopes of mortal living? And the Christian God! What a cloak for modern politics He was! An Imagined Giant to carry out the ambitions of a would-be giant! Was not belief in Him just a wish for eternal life, a sensuous desire to slip from the irritations of the world, yet not vanish into oblivion, to rest in peace under an immortal wing?

The dark hours of the morning were a protection as I hugged my books to me, squinting to make out the Latin and Greek by the flickering candles. The ancient poets, the classic thinkers, Marcus Aurelius, Erasmus, Tacitus, what good friends they became! I would read everything in the world, I decided, then I would know Truth.

During the affairs of the day, however, I found there is a sad discrepancy between knowing Truth and knowing how to promote it. Take, for example, the bitter experience of the publication of Johannes Matthiæ's book.

Matthiæ had cast his net into the flowing mysteries and had ensnared some shining understanding. He was a passionate man, but he wore gentleness like a white domino, letting it enfold, not hinder, the movement of his mind, a mind flecked with eternities. When I had studied with him as a girl it had seemed to me there was nothing he could not tell me. Together we had read the Greek and Roman writers, the early Christians, the scholastics, reformers, rebels. He condemned none, finding godliness in those who sought Truth, whatever their label. It was he who first revealed to me how the base of a true religion is in one's own heart and comprehension, that there was no discrepancy of spirit in my father and grandfather having been ardent Lutherans, my mother a Calvinist, my great-uncle Johan a Catholic.

"You must seek the spring of belief for yourself," he said to me, "for if you fill yourself with the unquestioned belief of another you may be poisoned. The soul exists on purity, wherever it is found."

He was interested particularly in the writings of Giacomo Aconcio, the refugee from Rome who would have no church for his metaphysics, swearing that the dogmas of Christian churches were Satan's stratagems since they created dissension, and that the Catholic confession was Satan's list of sins. Why, asked Aconcio, do not the various creeds look for what they have in common rather than what they are opposed to in one another? Why does the good fight the good, rather than the real enemy, Satan?

Then there was Jean Bodin, who accepted all churches, all temples, who reverently visited them, wishing to offend none, lest he reject the very one which might prove to be the true religion. The goodness in every god is the Almighty, he wrote, and people should unite as humane creatures to humbly pray to the Father of All Nature to ask Him to lead us to Truth. Competition among men should be in pious deeds, not in deadly wars.

"His heart is burning!" I cried when I heard this. "It ignites his garments and leaps to chariots drawn by the wind so that I see his heart's flames traveling across the sky. Why does not his heart light the world?"

Matthiæ chuckled at my naïveté. "His heart burned, and so did Aconcio's, but they alone cannot light the world. Others, such as you and I, must carry on their progress."

I answered: "I shall say to you what Alexander the Great said to his tutor, Aristotle, that my affection for you grows as great as my feelings for my father, for while he gave me the blessing of life, you give me the blessing of a good life."

Matthiæ, thus, took the next step beyond Aconcio and Bodin: he worked on a scheme of reconciling the conflicting religions.

As a girl I had thought it would stop the war we were engaged in and prevent future religious wars. As Queen, with newer knowledge, I realized religion was only the banner of the German war, but I still had great hopes for the future and what it would mean to educate the Swedish people in tolerance. When his book, *Idea Boni Ordinis in Ecclesia Christi*, was published and caused a furor I was ready to be its champion. What I had not expected was that the book would be brought up in the Riksdag as a major problem of the country. I can excuse myself for what happened only because I was unprepared for the weight of the vehemence I faced. It was the last time I ever attended a meeting of any kind without a plan of how I would win what I wanted.

As always, I sat in my royal place, the one skirted person in the assemblage in that large cold hall, when the charge against the book was made. It was charged with repudiating the Word of God. Those Lutherans, I fumed to myself. They think God spoke through the lips of Luther and no one else. Luther was just the architect of the house they were born in. They worship the walls closing in their souls. How frightened they are by the opening of a door!

"There is nothing to blame in this book," I declared. "I order that no charge be made against it since I myself have an interest in it."

Oxenstierna stepped forward, his solemn voice filled the hall, dropped onto me. "Do not take this matter upon yourself, Your Majesty. It will make things worse instead of better."

"I am not taking the case. The book defends itself."

Truth will defend itself, it must. No one can change Truth, no man, no thing is as great as Truth.

The Chancellor continued. "This book is a dangerous error. It smells of Calvinism."

Calvinism! If there was anything Lutherans hated more than Catholicism it was Calvinism. It was not a Calvinist book, but it recommended tolerance for the brotherly religion. That was more than enough for the clergy. They were enraged. One after another they rose denouncing the encroachment on their holy Lutheran ground. Aconcio was right, I thought, these are demons masked as preachers. If I defended the book further they, in the narrow path of their fury, would accuse me, too, of Calvinism, and that would be the beginning of losing my rule. Astounded, I listened as the nobles spoke, rumbling out hot opinions in deep tones. The book must be banned. No innocent eye must see it. Matthiæ must be kept from expressing any further ideas. Some poor soul might believe him. He must apologize for writing such a sacrilege. Apologize! Why not imprison him? Sweden was God's country! No enemy of God should be allowed to enjoy it.

No, no, I beat at my thoughts. Someone must see what a kind, noble purpose the book has. Then it occurred to me that no one, probably, had read the book. Everyone had leaped to the suggestion Oxenstierna had made. He had ignited their emotions, and they, accustomed to depending on him, had rushed on in the direction he had indicated without thinking of taking one of their own. Such was leadership.

The vote came. The Chancellor, in a careful attitude of serious graciousness, recommended an apology. Certainly it would not be necessary to imprison the good Bishop of Strängnäs to have him desist from further irresponsible writing. He had been the friend and chaplain of their beloved late King, the great Gustav Adolf. If he had been led astray recently, if he had succumbed to the temptation of ideas that were ungodly, if he had erred in his ways, he was wise enough to regret it, and conform.

Led astray! I bit at my lip. Did he mean me?

Ban the book! Ban the book! Ban the book! The yeas were as regular as the clapping of hands. Worst of all, with Matthiæ standing, head bowed, assenting to his defeat, I, too, had to say yea. Yea. Kill tolerance, kill thought, kill Truth, my beloved. As the voting ended, unanimous, I burst into hot, humiliating tears.

The clergy in their elation pressed on to a further victory. Someone else might be lured by the Devil to speak against God. Prevent it now. Protect Sweden. Protect the ears of their youth and weak women. Make the *Book of Concord* the law of the country.

I became cold with apprehension. If the *Book of Concord*, the terrible Paper Pope of the Lutherans, were law, all free religious thinking would be abolished. Thinking, talking, reading. Truth would be buried in a mound as high as those of the ancient Kings in Old Uppsala, would sleep with Egil, Aun, and Biorn. Until Judgment Day, I thought, then Truth will arise and the Lutherans will be shaken, surprised, humbled. Judgment Day. Every day is a little Judgment Day. Every man may be a spokesman for Truth.

"I shall not vote for this proposed law." I had spoken aloud without realizing it. My cloudburst of tears had evaporated, my words sang, loud and clear.

Oxenstierna turned his gray eyes on me, the nobles looked, the clergy, the burghers, the bönder. Matthiæ lifted his head. The vote was taken. Yea. Even Matthiæ.

"No." I repeated my refusal. Sweden should not be lost to the darkness of complete intolerance. I should not be lost. "No."

It could not be made law without my assent. I was Queen. I really was Queen, for I kept the door from closing on freedom, I alone.

When one reads a volume of memoirs one expects a beguiling confession of sins, while in the writing of memoirs it is apt to turn into a confession of virtues. I say "confession" purposely, for who with any experience in the world would dare boast of a virtue to another lest he be hated for it? And lest the virtue disappear in the telling? Or lest what is a virtue to oneself has the figure of sin to another? On the other hand, there are actions which appear sweetly virtuous to others which one knows within oneself are sins. These are the ones which are hard to admit. Who, willingly, would depose himself from the affection, the trust, the admiration of his friends and followers? Usually, as in my case, the sins are dedicated to a purpose good in itself to which no other path seems possible. God will forgive me, one says, because I am human, because I do not know what else to do.

Now, to uphold the search for Truth surely is a virtue, as it is, also, to study to be a good Queen, to work indefatigably for one's country, and to stop war, yet, in order to attain these virtues fully, I began to realize the necessity of learning the art of deception. How, one may ask, does one seek Truth by going in the opposite direction? It is a profound question. There are those who say a degree of deception is inevitable for the sustaining of life, that it is not always a sin, that it depends on who is deceived, and why. I am not sure I agree. My own nature is direct, I love directness in others. I love honesty, which is the tongue of Truth. When I am deceived, I am furious, and I am the first to cry out it is a sin. Why should it be different when I am the deceiver? As Queen, I should be even more virtuous than others. As Queen, if I must bend to deception, I positively must not be discovered, I must still appear virtuous. Thus, I could have no confidants, no fellow deceivers, who might expose me when I had achieved my noble ends. At the age of twenty I had no doubts of achieving whatever ends I chose.

It might polish my pride, I said to myself after the vote on the *Book of Concord*, to know that my voice alone has saved the country, but it takes more than pride to rule, and it takes more than one person. I could not continue to vote alone against the four Estates. Eventually they would find a way to overrule or circumvent me. Oxenstierna would see to that. I had to learn the strategy of winning people to my side. First I would sympathize, or seem to sympathize, with their demands, then I would insist on their sympathy for mine. With these thoughts I started on my path of deception, with these thoughts I approached anew the problem of my marriage.

Although I had vowed no man should have me, that I would be Truth's Bride, that I would leave the throne before I would be forced to marry, I decided I would have to show favor to one of my suitors, that it was politically necessary. Not one person was congenial to my not marrying. It would be inconvenient for the country not to extend the line of Kings, they argued, it would be dangerous. The security of Sweden depended on my producing a natural heir for the succession of the crown. I even received an address from the clergy urgently recommending that I marry. Why did I wait? The Estates would not wait. They announced the question was to be solved formally in the Riksdag.

Procrastinate, how could I procrastinate? The choice had narrowed to Carl Gustav and Erik Oxenstierna, not through my wishes but through the activity of the politics behind them. Would I share my bed with an Oxenstierna, would I have the Chancellor's falcon eyes probing my intimate secrets for his use? I shuddered. And what of Carl Gustav's plump little bastard, who had appeared—discreetly, of course—in due time? That, I told myself, need not be my affair. I shall not marry him, I shall only say I might marry him. For it was obvious to me that it would have to be Carl Gustav whom I would favor. He was Aunt Katarina's son. There was my promise to her.

It was simple to spread a rumor of my intention in order to prepare the way for a favorable vote. I hinted to Archbishop Lenæus, an energetic friend of Carl Gustav, and a few others, that my cousin was the only one I could consider marrying. The word circulated quickly and just in time, for when the Riksdag assembled I was confronted with a choice of whom I would marry. The Estates begged me to choose a husband. The names of Erik Oxenstierna and Carl Gustav were presented.

"I thank the Estates for their affectionate regard for me," I answered. "I have no inclination to marry at this time."

There was a stirring. An argument was blowing up, against me. I knew what they would say. I knew they would increase, not lessen, the pressure against me.

I went on: "If Prince Carl Gustav should be my choice, would he be entirely acceptable to the representatives of the Estates?"

The little wind of argument settled into whispering. I saw the meaningful looks thrown here and there by Archbishop Lenæus. This was his chance, this was his candidate. With the help of my hint he had done well with his persuasion. Carl Gustav might not be the cleverest fellow in the world, but he was a prince, and he was virile, wasn't he? There was no doubt of that. And he was popular as an officer. Wouldn't it be better for the Queen to choose him than no one at all? He wouldn't forget his friends.

The decision did not take as long as I had anticipated. The representative of the Estates stepped forth, smiling.

"If it please Your Majesty to choose the Prince, Sweden gladly will accept him as your husband."

The country was delighted at the prospect of a wedding. No one paid any attention to the "if" of the matter. When would it be? Not yet, I kept saying, not yet. Carl's friends seemed to have increased a thousandfold. I heard his name everywhere, in the castle, in the town streets, in the rolling fields. I shut my ears to it.

I would have liked to shut my ears to Carl Gustav, too, but that I could not do, entirely, that is. I did the best I could. I gave him two castles, Käfsnäs and Ulfsunda, and large grants of land, as befitted a prince who had the expectations of marrying the Queen, and I hoped he would occupy himself with them. He did not. He pursued me obstinately, asking that I set the date of our wedding. He wanted to see me alone, I did not want to see him. Why not? Was he not my betrothed? Who had a better right? I had to think of something for him to do, something to take him away from Stockholm, something sufficiently important for his eminent position. There was only one answer that would suit his career, I decided, which was to appoint him General of the Army in Germany. An admirable solution! I summoned him to a private audience.

Carl, of course, in his singleness of vision, completely misunderstood the reason for our interview. As soon as the door to my reception room was closed he rushed toward me like a bull. I evaded his rough arms, indignant. What had happened to cause this sudden ardor? Whom did he think I was?

"Are you having a fit, cousin?"

"Christina, my love!"

"Keep your arms in your sleeves and your sleeves at your side!"

"Dear Christina!"

"I have asked you here for a serious purpose."

"For love!"

"Sit down, you overgrown colt."

I pushed him toward a chair.

"Carl, I have decided it would be wise for you to have a prominent post in Sweden's service. What would you think if I secured your appointment as General of the Army in Germany?"

I expected a quick loud approval. With one leap he, a young man, would be at the top of his career, but he had a higher career in mind, a higher command.

He stared at me, his mouth slightly open, his hands on his knees. "Germany! That is a long way off. When is our wedding date?"

"I did not ask you here to speak of that."

"I must know. How can anything be planned until we know the day of our marriage?"

"I shall arrange this appointment first. Then we can talk about marriage."

"Putting it off! Always you put off talk of our marriage!" He jumped to his feet. "I cannot stand to stay in Sweden when you are like this. If you do not set the date, I shall go back to war. I shall leave for Germany tomorrow. Today! Then we will see who will wait!"

"Good! You may go at once, and without your general's uniform, if what you want is to join the regular ranks. I hope you have a pleasant journey."

He sat down again. "Christina."

"Are you leaving now or are you waiting for the appointment?"

"You do not show your love very well."

"My love!" And what of his?

"We have waited so long. Why will you not set the date?"

"If you keep drumming about a marriage date before I am ready to give it, I shall break off our engagement entirely. Irrevocably. Is it not enough for you that the Estates have chosen you above Erik Oxenstierna? I have secured one triumph for you. Do you want to lose it with your impatience?"

"Why, Christina?"

"I have told you. I have too much to attend to now."

"But our love! How can you put that off?"

I turned my eyes away. Where was the window? "I no longer love you as I did."

"You promised to love me eternally. You wrote it."

Damn me! Would he never stop quoting that silly letter? I looked at him as coldly as I could. "Whatever you say, whatever you do, I will not give you a more definite answer. Not now."

His mouth stiffened, he rose and bowed.

"I see you are delighted with my offer to appoint you general, Carl."

"Yes, yes."

It was curious to see melancholy settling onto his solid frame. He was not poetic, it did not become him. He had begun to sense the "if" in my promise, *if* Prince Carl should be my choice, and, for the first time, wondered whether or not I really would marry him, whether or not he would gain the crown. The court, with its feathery congratulations and questionings, became intolerable to him. He could not bear indecision, he could not hide his feelings, so he retired to the country, his melancholy for company, and his kegs of beer.

The year had turned into 1648 before I secured my cousin's appointment as General of the Swedish Army in complete command of Germany, for Oxenstierna had sternly, but vainly, opposed it. By then, Magnus had become Carl's advocate, visiting him, advising him, hurrying between his estate and Stockholm Castle with ardent messages, many of which I was sure he had invented himself. I had sent him to France as our Ambassador, as he had wished, on his return he had married his dryad, not in the enchanted wood, but within the brick walls of the Great Church, and he had then been appointed, he said, a special ambassador by the Queen of Love. I wondered how I ever could have had dreams of him for myself.

Carl also sent messages through Johannes Matthiæ, that he had to have a definite answer about the marriage so he could make the necessary household arrangements, that he would find it very difficult to be present at the coronation if he could not tell the people the date of our marriage. Since the coronation, I told Matthiæ, is to take place at the conclusion of the peace, there would be plenty of time to make up his mind about that. In the meantime, he had his opportunity to hasten the peace by going to Germany and showing the world his brilliance as a commander. Would I grant him a private audience before he left? No.

See the poor boy, urged Matthiæ, give him courage. His heart is weak with love for you. His heart is weak with love for the crown, I thought. You must bid him Godspeed, dear Pallas, said Magnus. The Queen cannot let her new general face the dangers of death for her country without her blessing. I will see the little burgomaster if you are present, was my answer to each. So Carl journeyed to Stockholm and to me.

There are pitfalls for a beginner in deception. One's own emotions are the worst, and next the emotions of one's intimates, it being perilously easy for the truth to slip out and away in shouting accusations and denials, clouded, as one is, in anger, resentment, blemished hope, or eagerness to win quickly. Thus far I had not done very much deceiving in signifying I might marry when I had vowed I would not, but it had had the pleasant result of releasing me from a pressuring, and I had a horror of meeting Carl. Somehow, stupid as he seemed to me, he was the hardest person of all to deceive.

Immediately the three men came into my apartment, Carl began petitioning me on a settlement of marriage plans. We had been engaged since we were children, he said, and were bound by long-standing ties that could not be broken. I seated myself in a chair across the room intending to hear him out, to show myself as a dignified, controlled woman, as he gave, for him, an excessively long-winded speech of the story of his devotion from childhood to the present day. When he paused, asking again for a date for the wedding, I answered him.

"It may be that I never shall wish to marry. If I should come to this determination, I could promise to arrange that you would be my successor on the throne."

There was his desire. I waited for his amazed gratitude.

"But I want to marry you for love, not for the throne. If only I could marry you, I would be content with a crust of bread and a simple life."

"Stop talking rot! You are not made for a simple life." Who had been coaching him? Did he think the sole way to the throne was by marrying me? Someone had to succeed me, if not a direct heir, then a relation.

"You say your feelings have not changed. Mine have. I no longer love you. Still, there is no reason you should not be King after my death, and if you should die before gaining your hopes, you may realize it an honor you ever have been considered worthy of such a fortune."

"God forbid that I should live to see the day of Your Majesty's death, that I should be the one to take on power! I would be subject to the whims and fancies of the nobles of this court. I never would master them. I would get into the greatest trouble. I am a soldier, I know the soldier's way of solving trouble. God forbid I should soil my hands with their blood!"

He leaned a fist upon the table next to him, clenching it in emphasis as he spoke, flinging his other hand onto his chest as if to hold in a bursting heart.

"I love you, Your Majesty! I love you, Christina! It is my highest aspiration in life to marry you. If you will not accept me I will leave Sweden, never to return. I will sell everything I own here. I will go to live in Germany, beside a little blue lake, a modest, private man. What would life be to me in Sweden, without you? All, all would be indifferent to me. Nothing would mean anything any more."

I turned my head in disgust. Had his teacher been the merchant's pretty daughter?

"Fanfaronades! Your talk is all phrases out of some silly book of romance. Have you nothing else to do but read such nonsense? Why can you not remember you were born for higher things than idling about your father's estate? It is time you prepared to apply yourself to your duty. You are no ordinary person whom God has ordained to sit at home doing nothing. God has intended you for something higher, and you should not go against God's will."

His pose crumpled into ordinary anger, into his ordinary reasoning. "And you! Evidently it does not need much honor to aspire to your hand! What about Erik Oxenstierna? You have a lot of fine words to put me off, but I know what you really mean. What a noble husband he would make!"

"You are unworthy of what I have done for you!" Dear God!

Matthiæ interrupted. "Your Majesty, Prince Carl has forgotten that the Estates have agreed it is he who would be acceptable as your husband. May I point out that they have yet to be consulted whether or not he would be accepted as your successor without a marriage?"

"He loves you, Your Majesty," put in Magnus, "and he counts on marrying you."

"You promised," said Carl.

"I will not be bound by a promise made when I was so young. How can you believe I should be held to it? I was incapable of realizing the seriousness of the promise. It was a child's act. I knew nothing of the meaning of marriage. I knew very little about the significance of being Queen. It was a dream, it was—" I stopped myself. A hastening toward love, it had been, a wish to be plural. "It was a foolish thing to do. I am surprised you pay any attention to it."

"I have set my life on it. Please marry me, Christina."

"All I can promise is that I will not marry anyone else, and that I will do all in my power to make you my successor."

"What if the Estates will not agree?"

"If the Estates will not agree to you as my successor, then, and then only, will I marry you. You are my cousin, and I count on you as my friend, but you will remember that my affection does not extend to your person. If ever we should be married, it will be in the interests of Sweden, at the request of the Estates and my subjects."

"If the Estates do not accept me as your successor, and it is, as you say, in the interest of the country that we marry, and, at the Estates' request, then when would we be married?"

"After my coronation."

"The coronation date is not set."

"After my twenty-fifth birthday."

"That is years from now!"

Of course it was. Did he believe he could corner me so easily?

"I can tell you no more."

Carl bowed his acceptance. He had worked for a date, and he had one, at last.

"I wish you good fortune in Germany, cousin. May you bring peace to Sweden, and to yourself."

He bowed. "May I write to you, Your Majesty?"

No. Nothing close. Please, nothing close.

"You may correspond with me through your father or Johannes Matthiæ."

The air seemed to have gone out of my heart. It was over. A few more words of parting and the men left me. I had three years, I told myself, in which to plan my freedom. I was on the path to conquering my promise. Why did I not feel jubilant? Why should I mind that men do not fit our dreams of them?

I remembered there was a view from the terrace of the road Carl took away from the castle. I hurried there and stood, watching him ride away, watching him fade into the dappled traffic of the town as if he were anyone, a carter, a carpenter, a visiting trader, and not my cousin, Carl Gustav, who carried with him the prospect of being King.

IX

FOR years, now, the peace congress at Westphalia had been dawdling, had been delegating, had been favoring, fettering, arguing, deferring. They had been acting as if war, the proclaimed enemy, was an invited guest they could not get rid of. And why not? Was he the secret friend of a few? Yes, I decided, that was the reason, and one of those few was Oxenstierna. Had not the house of Oxenstierna grown in power and wealth to become among the greatest in Europe during the German war? Had the Chancellor shown any tendency to stop the war as long as there were plums for the picking, plums, that is, of gold? He said they were for Sweden, but who in Sweden benefited?

The situation in Sweden, however, had changed during the years since the opening of the congress. I had changed it. From a girl Queen, a symbol of power, I had become the Queen, the power. There were no tears, now, because I dared not vote as I wished, there was no voting alone, all four Estates opposed to me. How I developed my power is a fit subject for a historian, truly, not for memoirs concerned with the travels of a heart. That I touch on it now, even lightly, is because the ending of the war had to do with the purposes of my heart, the heart being, as I see it, the *commedia dell' arte* of love, and this particular love being played out, my love of people.

The day on which I wrote my famous letter to the Swedish

delegates marked the beginning of the true race for peace. When I sat down to write the letter I had, to enhance my authority, my own political party, formed, in opposition to the Oxenstierna party, of nobles such as Jacob de la Gardie and his sons, Baron Gyllenhielm, my uncle, Count Palatine, and my cousins, Carl Gustav and Adolf Johan, of course, and men like Marshal Torstenson, the most splendid commander Sweden had had since Gustav Adolf, who had started as a page for the King and been pushed to the top because no one else could equal his courage and decision. He was no brutal, glory-hungry soldier like Marshal Wrangel, who followed him in his command when his gout forced him to resign. He was a humanist who had seen too many men slain for diminishing reasons. He had had enough of war. It was Wrangel, whose ambition seemed to be to write his name in great letters of blood across Germany, who was Oxenstierna's man. My party, soldiers or stay-at-homes, was the party for peace.

I cannot say I had many nobles in my party. They were too old, most of them, to educate, and they had become spoiled during the Regency by an overflow of power. They cared little for the bönder's ancient rights on the land and abused them constantly, they easily managed the clergy, most of whom could not even read, who were dependent on them for the upkeep of their churches, while the burghers, needing their trade, found they could not go against them too hardily. I was not beholden to them for anything and I determined Sweden would be neither their private copper mine nor their private hunting-park, for I hold the classical point of view, that the Queen, as a divine ruler, represents all of the people, not a selection of them. By the time the nobles noticed I was a political individual, the other Estates already were aware that I was of a sensible persuasion. I saw to that, naturally, having a good sense of mathematics. The nobles were only one of four Estates.

Four Estates. Nobles, clergy, burghers, bönder. I began with the bönder, to whom I already was a beloved legend, a friend who had visited them in their cottages, listened to their woes, admired their homely arts. I became their champion against domineering landlords, I spoke for them in the lofty language of which they were incapable, outscorning the aristocrats who had scorned them, until their fealty to me was unquestioned. They, moreover, were the last people to want war, their sons being hustled away willy-nilly to be soldiers, leaving the soil unworked, the cattle untended, and trees uncut.

Then the burghers. What, I asked Nils Nilson, the leader of the burghers, was the bane of their life? Taxes, always, he had answered, so I had lowered the salt tax, and, to secure the matter, I made Nils Nilson my bosom political friend. I could not have had a better one, discreet and intelligent as he was, quick to act, solid in his backing, and, beautiful trait, with a trustworthy tongue.

To win the clergy required a different sort of persuasion, my *no* on the *Book of Concord* having frozen any love they might have harbored for me. Yes, here I had to search for a way to light a temporary love for me, a love to last long enough to end the war, for they had no wish for that, kill them all, they would cry from their pulpits, all who bow not to Luther, to Luther, my god above God. Conveniently, the old Archbishop of Uppsala came to the end of his days and died, and gave me, albeit unwillingly, the advantage I needed. Who, of the clergy, did not covet this estimable, this rich, this rarely vacant chair at Uppsala? Who, of the clergy, would injure his possibility as a candidate by voting against a measure I personally pleaded for? They vied to look for grace in my eyes, so it behooved me to ponder a long time on the choice of a successor.

Thus, when I no longer could bear the hawing of the Chancellor and his war party, their confounding of my bold directives for peace, their insistence on nibbling away at the fighting, their additions and subtractions to every official letter to the delegates so it became a mess of ambiguity to be interpreted as the reader wished, and, Johan Oxenstierna being the chief delegate, would he not interpret it as his father indicated?—when I no longer could bear the pretense of a congress that mouthed peace and spun war, I took matters into my own hands. I had the power, at last, and the fury, to do so. I wrote my letter, my plain letter of threats, to the Swedish delegates.

Why did it become famous? Because I penned it with my own hand, I suppose, secretly, without resorting to a driveling, loose-speaking secretary, because I circumvented the Chancellor and the Council of the country completely, because I acted as if I, alone, had the power to tell the delegates what to do, because I dropped diplomacy and said exactly what I meant. I told Johan and Salvius they must come to a perfect understanding of my will, that they must realize that above all things, I desired a sure and honorable peace. *Without any further dawdling,* I wrote, *you must bring the negotiations to a satisfactory conclusion by securing the best condition of the Estates, satisfaction of the Crown, and contentment of the soldiery that may be possible without breaking the peace, and no longer drag out matters as at present, otherwise you will have to look to it how you will answer before God, the Estates of the realm, and me. Let not the fantasies of ambitious men turn you from your goal unless you wish to incur my extreme disgrace and displeasure and stand accountable to me, blushing and blanching. . . . No authority nor support of great families shall hinder me from showing all the world the displeasure I feel. Therefore it behooves you to look well to yourselves.*

To my loyal Salvius I wrote an additional letter, secret, of course, as a companion piece for his eyes only, writing that *from all circumstances I see how a certain person, not being able to break off the Treaty, seeks to protract the negotiations indefinitely. I will let all the world see that the C—— cannot turn everybody around his finger,* sapienti sat. *My letter herewith is addressed to both of you, give it immediately to J. O.; although I attack him and you equally in it, it is meant for him alone. If, by God's grace, you come back here after the peace, I will reward you* Senatoria dignitate. *You know it is the highest dignity to which an honest man can aspire in our country, and were there any higher* gradus honoris *I would not hesitate to confer it on you.*

Was this deceit, to write officially when no officials had knowledge of it, none, that is, except of my own choosing, Magnus and Nils Nilson, who had to be prepared to back me in case a storm broke? Those who did not like it said it was, but I find that persons are quick to call *deceit* when they have been outwitted, when something happens they would have done their utmost to prevent, had they known of it. Was it deceit to encircle my action in silence, had it been deceit to privately instruct Salvius during the long years of the congress to see this person, avoid that one, give this message to the Cardinal, do not let that count know what you are doing? I had to, silence was my protection. I could not have fought for my way without such an armor.

But now that silence was to be broken, for Johan Oxenstierna no sooner read my letter than he answered it with a typical bellow. It was not he, Sweden's chief delegate, he announced haughtily, who was to blame for the slowness of the congress. He had performed his duties meritoriously according to the wishes of the Council. It was Salvius who paid no attention to the Council's directives, who always was dodging off on some scheme of his own, it was Salvius, and those wily Frenchmen, who were obstructing the conclusion of the treaty.

It was a sight to see the Chancellor's face when Johan's reply was read in the Council. He had not calculated, he had not foreseen, even in his most wayward suspicions, that anything important could take place without his direction, that anything of an official nature could materialize without his knowing about it. His belief in his domination was ultimate.

It was a spring day, the sun, at last, daring to sweep the castle with gold, its warmth filtering through the windows of the Council chamber, tingeing the gray heads of the Councillors. It was a day for the heart to sing, for the body to stretch in pleasure at the shedding of winter. But the Chancellor held winter in his grasp and would not let it go. At the reading of the letter he leaned forward slightly. His voice was stiff and cold.

"Why has Johan Oxenstierna written this letter?"

I motioned to the secretary to read the letter I had sent to the delegates, and as he heard the decisive phrases sent without his consent, without, even, his knowledge, the Chancellor's face grew white with rage.

"Your Majesty wrote this letter!"

I smiled.

"Your Majesty sent this letter without consulting the Council!"

"Is not peace the aim of the Council? I have advised the Swedish delegates they must secure the peace or answer to God, to the Estates, and to me."

"Your Majesty has threatened my son with disgrace!"

"If either of our delegates disgraces Sweden, he deserves the odium of the country and of the whole world."

Now his rage burst forth, his suavity eaten up by passion, his tones crackling with bitterness. "It is Salvius, it is Salvius who blocks Johan's way! It is Salvius who confounds matters! You hear what he says!" His finger was shaking toward Johan's letter. "It is Salvius, that ill-born fool, trying to run things his own way. It is a nail in our eyes that this man represents Sweden! What does he know of the trust of statesmanship? What does he care for his obligation to the Council? He evades our command, he misrepresents our intentions, he entangles our directions, he invents his own offers, he plots secretly with foreign powers. He is the dirge of our diplomacy! I warned our late great King Gustav Adolf that it was dangerous to appoint a common man to handle uncommon affairs. I warned this Council not to appoint him to this important post. Disgrace Sweden! Sweden will be disgraced, Sweden is disgraced, shamed before the world, by the presumption of this stubborn intriguer! Who can constrain him? Who can check this upstart, this bogtrotter, this vulgar excuse for a noble? How can we allow him to speak for our proud country?"

I interrupted. "My Lord! I will not permit an absent man, who cannot defend himself, to be so attacked."

Gabriel Oxenstierna spoke appeasingly, as if in explanation. "Adler Salvius is only a created baron. If he were a native-born noble—"

The third Oxenstierna cut in eagerly. "Why not send a young noble to replace him? He is an old man." And he named several highly born, utterly stupid sons of his friends.

"The offices of the State are not heirlooms," I snapped. "If, My Lords, you have sons who possess the requisite knowledge and capacity, they shall have their turn, but only their turn. When advice for the good of the State is required it is useless to ask whether a man can boast of sixteen quarterings."

"Your Majesty." It was the Chancellor's frosted twang. "You realize, do you not, what the advice is that Salvius offers? You realize, do you not, that it is not for the good of the State? Salvius would give away at the conference table what we have won by shedding blood. He would give away our safety. Sweden cannot afford to stop the war until we have won Pomerania. I cannot face the people without compensation after these many sad years of fighting. We cannot sign a peace treaty until we have won."

"Won what? Carcasses and burned lands?"

"Sweden is safe now," said Baron Gyllenhielm. "The men-of-war ride before Stockholm within the Queen's view in the safest harbor in the Baltic."

"Sweden," blasted the Chancellor, "never will be safe until we are masters of Wismar and Pomerania! If the Imperialists get a footing on the coast of the Baltic we are lost! We are in danger of invasion at any time. Do you think the Imperialists will hesitate to crush us if they can? They will laugh at our weakness, massacre our citizens, capture our trade. How many times must I tell you that we must have provinces in the German Empire annexed to the Crown of Sweden? Sweden must be a member of the German Empire, not an uninformed neighbor. We must have a place to station our troops when we make levies. We must secure our trade." Trade! Now he rode his favorite text, that the prosperity of the State consisted in the promoting of trade, that the most we could do to protect it would be the least we could do for our country, that we must husband our money, raise the prices of our exports, command the Baltic so we would not be ruined by customs, that we were not a rich country to be able to fight for nothing, that we must have Pomerania. His voice, an angry wind, rose and fell, chased its own sound around the room, whipped at us in exasperation.

I waited. He listed facts, the exports, the imports, stated figures, extolled the power of the army, the sacredness of Swedish soil, the need to expand for security's sake. He warned that in order to keep the enemy from our shores we must have provinces across the Baltic. I waited. Let the wind hound its own tail. It could not change my course. When he had finished, at last, I spoke firmly.

"My Lords, we must relieve our country of the odium of ambition and show before God and all the world that we are willing to agree to reasonable terms, whether or not we gain Pomerania. Surely it is better to secure solid advantages, those we already have won, than to trust to the uncertainties of war to gain still more. The great victory we have aimed at has eluded us for almost twenty years. Our generals are growing old and ailing, and yearn for the comforts of home. Let us be content with the lands and power we have."

Jacob de la Gardie's genial dawdling voice followed mine. "It is a virtue to keep well what we have put into our pockets and not try to fill them to bursting. Too large conquests serve only to weaken the State. I am of the opinion we should not accept any territories in Germany. The keeping of them would be a great charge, and would occasion many inconveniences with the neighboring provinces. Always they would be suspicious of us, always they would resent us. They would be whispering to one another how Sweden has too sharp a sword, too big an appetite."

"Your Majesty. My Lords." The Chancellor's tone had become pure ice. "The Council neglects the true reason of the war, the holy cause. Sweden's purpose in entering the war was to free the German people. Can we desert them now, so close to victory? Can we forget the dying words of our late great King Gustav Adolf: *I am the King of Sweden who do seal the religion and liberty of the German Nation with my blood*? Can we abandon him? Is our blood more precious than his that we fear to shed it? Can we listen to the horrifying tales of Imperialist atrocities and not leap to the defense of the innocent victims? Can we, worst of all, forsake men's souls, leave them in chains to a false religion? Can we condemn them, through no fault of their own, to immortal hell, and turn our backs on their hell on earth?"

The Lutheran dragon was belching his smoke. Was anyone blinded by it?

"Chancellor Oxenstierna." I was tense but calm. "It is true we have heard the tales of Imperialist atrocities. We also have heard the tales of Protestant atrocities, not excepting the Swedes, since the death of my father, the King. Why should we substitute one hell for another? Is it better to be tortured or killed by a Protestant than by a Catholic Imperialist? What is more, we all know, whether we admit it or not, that there are Protestants and Catholics mixed among the soldiers on both sides, as well as every nationality, for every mercenary who can beg his way to Germany must be there to ply his gruesome trade. The way to tell a soldier's loyalty is to look where he collects his pay."

"The men of Sweden are the soldiers of God!"

"Anyone who studies the truth of it at all can see there never has been a more meaningless war in history. We must have a peace. I demand that the Swedish delegates let nothing stand in their way to secure a peace treaty immediately."

"You would encourage Salvius to connive with foreign powers?"

"I would encourage Salvius to do everything in his power for a peace settlement. He is a sensible man, and he has not been sent to the congress to be only an onlooker."

"If Your Majesty persists in this dangerous trust of an ignoble man against the accusations of my son, and, I will add, against my word, Your Majesty will be pleased to accept my resignation as Chancellor."

There it was. There was a dramatic moment of silence, then the protests began from the Councillors, loud, insistent, bewildered, coaxing, praising. I said nothing.

It was Jacob de la Gardie who tried to raise the Chancellor above his scratched feelings, the dear old Constable not being able to bear a rupture with the man he had worked with through years of tribulations, reminding him how many times he had differed with King Gustav without leaving his service, how necessary it was not to publish a breach in the home government that our opponents would rush to worsen, to turn to their own advantage, that no one would be disgraced for everyone, surely, would ply the best interest of Sweden and the crown. And the crown. Therein lay my power. De la Gardie's persuasion was beautiful, kind, logical, but at no point did it disallow the victory I sought.

I watched, I listened, I felt the sparkle of the spring day. I would not retreat one breath from my demands. The Chancellor might go or stay as long as the world knew I was the head of the State, as long as I held the command and the scepter shone in my hands alone. And, as I sat there quietly, it became plain that the power had passed to me. In all the arguments pressed by the Councillors, in all their prevailing upon Oxenstierna to retain his office, there was not a phrase to provoke my displeasure. There were no further slurs against Salvius, so obviously, now, my delegate, no meaningless platitudes about a patriotic victory. The champion of war had laid down his arms, I could lead the way, unhindered, to peace.

Oxenstierna, the color of the day fading across his brow, blinking his eyes against the sudden glare of the setting sun, his pride, his anger, his surprise defined in his stiffened back, in his hands gripping the sides of his oaken chair, in his heavy leaning on silence, could not be convinced. The change was too abrupt. He saw his role as the father of righteousness, as the incessant shepherd of the stormy night. He was the convincer, not the convincible, he was the speaker, not the spoken to. He was the master, the hunter of other fields, not the hare, never the hare, running away. No, it was the ground that was running away, beneath his feet.

He could not be convinced that day, nor any day until he had taken his resignation and its reasons to the Estates. The Estates were resolute. They loved him, they needed him, they were used to him, he should not resign. He was a good man, they said, a gallant, faithful, good Swedish man. He had been Chancellor as long as they could remember, let him continue to be Chancellor so long as they had a memory to hold him. But the Queen must be supported. The tears ran down the cheeks of some of the poor fellows as they urged him not to abandon them, while their hearts were ringing within them that I had become the power, their power, as I had promised. In the end the resignation was retracted, in deference to the country's wishes, Oxenstierna said, and he stayed, a mournful, muffled kind of Chancellor.

This is how a page was turned in history. This is why Johan was checked at the congress, why Salvius proceeded, under my direction, to be the most outstanding delegate there in working out a peace. It was not many months until he wrote that he would be able to return, at last, with the peace treaty in his pocket.

This is why Wrangel, the Commander of the Armies whom Carl Gustav was journeying to replace, made a brilliant surge to a military victory so the glory of ending the war would not fall to another. Like Oxenstierna, he believed in war. It was his business, his avenue to personal fame. Where would he be, he, a fighting general, with no battles to plan and fight? But if the powers above him decreed the war had to end, then, by all means, he must be the one to win it, to end it. He must be the general who was cheered in Stockholm, the great, protective, wolf-eating eagle, the classic hero of a grateful people. By the time Carl Gustav arrived at the command Wrangel had lopped off his most ambitious plans and won what he needed to tidily finish his campaign. There was nothing for my cousin to do but to demobilize the troops.

The historic page might be turned, but there were persons in Sweden besides the Chancellor who had no liking for it. I constantly received letters threatening my life, and one day while I prayed publicly in the royal chapel a man, a fanatical Lutheran teacher, came within two steps of assassinating me with his knife. Count Peter Brahe saw him rushing toward the dais where I knelt in time to shout a warning, but the fellow would not stop, breaking the lances of my guards, and was almost upon me when I rose to my feet. I would have combated him myself, seeing his angry face and his hand on his pocket for his weapon, but the honor seemed due to the Head of the Guard, an enormous Viking of a man kneeling beside me, so I tapped him on the shoulder to attend me. He sprang upon my assailant when he was so close I could see the parting of his dry lips and the dirty teeth pressed together for his effort, he threw him to the ground, and the other guards took hold of him. I had no fear. I was as whole as if Death had been a thousand miles away, rather than within the length of an arm. To the world, moreover, I was more alive, more triumphant than ever because of the attack, and I was congratulated by all Europe.

On October 24 of 1648, a little over a year after I had prevailed over Oxenstierna, the peace treaty was signed officially in Westphalia. The glorious news reached Stockholm on a windy day in November. I was ecstatic.

"You have brought me the most noble news in the world!" I shouted when I read the almost unbelievable words. For four years I had been expediting peace, now the blessed notice was in my hands. I was crowned with endeavor! What victory in war can equal the final one of peace? It is easy to get into war. But peace!

Why is it always so hard to have peace, the one thing everyone says he wants? This was the first complete peace in Sweden in eighty-seven years. I could have thrown my arms around the messenger who stood before me. I blessed him with my words.

"You who have brought me this noble news shall be a noble! By my word you shall be a noble! And the arms of your House shall be the olive branch, the dove, and Sweden's three crowns! Your family shall carry the emblem of peace always."

Fire the cannons! Sing the *Te Deum* in the churches! Rejoice! A golden chain for the courier who carried the message to Sweden! A senator's robe for Salvius! Rejoice! Peace has arrived, peace, our sister, is home!

I was so delirious with pride and delight I hardly noticed the rumbling of bitterness around me. I was so young in my jubilation I did not realize that he who climbs to the top of a mountain must be prepared to descend it, as well. I was prepared to stay there forever. Virtue had won. I had won. The people had won.

The people, of course, were jubilant with me, the bönder, the burghers, my noble friends. But the clergy complained bitterly. There were those who screamed from their pulpits that the people must not admit the peace, they must fight on, they must cherish hatred in their hearts against the Catholics who dared call them heretics. I had to issue a proclamation prohibiting the clergy from condemning the peace in public. And the older war-wishing nobles shook their heads, whispering contemptuously that I had been weak in not insisting on all of Pomerania, that Salvius had been bribed to make terms, that the peace would not be of long duration anyway. It did no good for my friends to point out that we had received substantial territorial gains as well as five million rix-dollars in cold money. We should have received more, said the old gloom-boxes. It was the Queen's fault.

Why couldn't everyone see what an unnecessary war it had been! The best the peace treaty could do was to have the secular affairs revert to the conditions of 1618, the year of the beginning of the war. The Germans had been Catholics and Protestants then, they could be Catholics and Protestants now. They had been Catholics and Protestants all along, but now they had to face it. Toleration was to be the law. Behold, I said, the Empire has been jumping up and down beating itself with a stick for thirty years. It is maimed, sore, blackened. If we saw a man doing that, we would know he was seized by a fit of madness. Why not an Empire? Thank God I am blamed for stopping the war.

X

THIS is an interlude. I am writing it because I am wearied of being accused of murdering Descartes. That he died in Sweden is not my infamy, nor was it due to my inattention, nor was it, as others claim, a strike of the hand of God. No, it was the jealousy of those ancient ferocities who still raven our land, the Northern gods, it was the fear of Thor, of Odin, of Njord, or, most probably, of Loke, the evil one, at the coming of a new god into their realm, one who knew how to dispel their magic with the ease of doubt. Their killing him was an exasperated thrust at our modern world, a spasm of an icy will terrified at its view of extinction, for the gods, above all people, desire immortal triumph. To those who do not believe what I write, who say today is the Almighty God's day, the pagan idols lost in a frozen dimness of Time, I say, look, then, at the souls of men to see what is imaged there. No god is dead who finds a man to harbor him.

It was not hard to recognize Descartes as a god. When the pilot of the ship that bore him across the Baltic came to report to me on his arrival, I questioned him about the notable I had not yet seen.

"You have brought a famous man to Stockholm. What is your opinion of your passenger?"

He replied: "It is not a man whom I have brought over to Your Majesty. It is a god. In three weeks he has taught me more about the science of the sea and the winds and about the art of navigation than I have learned in the sixty years I have been sailing the seas. I think I am capable now of undertaking the longest and most difficult voyages."

In truth, I would be the last one to want to hurt René Descartes in any way. I may be an ugly Queen to look at, but my mind is not ugly. I love Virtue, I love philosophy that seeks Virtue, and, consequently, I love philosophers. Who, thus far in the seventeenth century, has found the philosopher's stone and polished it as brightly as Descartes? When I invited him to Stockholm I considered it a brilliant honor to have him at my court. I still do. The falling of a shadow across this honor was not my fault. But I shall relate the tale exactly as I knew it.

I was introduced to Descartes by that wise and charming man Pierre Chanut. Chanut came to my court as Ambassador of France in 1646, when I had been Queen for little more than a year. Although I was precociously learned for the nineteen years I had spent on this earth, I was beginning to realize how lonely a throne can be. Love eluded me, friendship was difficult, but I liked talking to this Frenchman with a lean face and mannered hands, I liked listening to his profoundly humored conversation, to the way he let his words fall almost carelessly, as if he were relinquishing any credit or any blame, as if he were a spectator whose observation could be valued for its sharpness and its detachment, or dusted away, as the listener chose. He could discuss with equal enthusiasm the leap of a hare, the point of a treaty, or the probability of the universe, he could change from one language to another as easily as he could change his hat, from French to Latin to Greek to German to Italian to Arabic, to whichever best ornamented the occasion. Moreover, he linked me to a world for which I yearned, speaking intimately of the artists, the scientists, the literateurs whose names spell the culture of our time, Corneille, Bourdon, Poussin, Saumaise, Gassendi, Descartes.

The flexibility of his mind incited me to say things which I said to no one else, that and his venerable age, I suppose, and as the months passed I found I was telling him my dreams, my secret jokes, my wild cosmic humors. When I made an expedition to inspect the mines at Fahlun, Chanut accompanied me, and it was there, in the manor house, that he spoke particularly to me of Descartes. I had been eager to descend into the mines, to walk the dark heart of the earth, to join the men who plunder it, but Chanut had refused absolutely. He took my arm as if he had been my father and hurried me away before I felt I had finished talking to the miners. Let the official expedition party make the inspection, he said, that was what they were for. It was an unhealthy thing to do, for me as well as for him, there was no telling what chills and fever might come of it, even my youth could not protect me against the dampness, the dirt, and the terrible threat of being buried alive. And so he had hurried me off to a room in the manor house.

"Madame," he sighed, when we were safely in a sitting-room with a warm porcelain stove, "when will you learn to secure yourself from danger? I admire your courage, but when will you learn there is a scale of duties? You cannot do them all. Your pedestal is at the top. You cannot descend so frequently to labors that should belong to others. You are the Queen. More, you are Christina, the last of the great Vasas. No one could replace you."

"Am I Queen or not? What does it matter? Behold my crown!" I lifted my feathered black hat from my head and dropped it to my feet. "All men ought to devote themselves to Virtue alone, regardless of advantage or position."

"Is it not your devotion to Virtue to rule well, Madame?"

"You preach, Chanut." I turned my back impatiently.

"On the contrary. All the world is dazzled by the brilliance of the new ruler in the North."

"All the world except Sweden!" I laughed, but not easily. "Let us be honest. Simple people, like these miners, love me. Their love is about as powerful as a green reed. It makes a pretty sound, that is all. I am surrounded by hate, and of what use is this love against the careful practice of hate? You have been here long enough, My Lord, to see how most of the nobles hate me. They would be very pleased to be rid of me."

He shrugged. "Rulers always are hated by those who would replace them. If you have had an overdose of hate, you must try more of love. Why do you not marry?"

"Marriage!" I kicked at my hat. "What has marriage to do with love? Why should I tolerate a bull in a gilded coat in my chamber?"

I threw myself in a chair, pulled up a stool for my legs, and delivered a short lecture on my favorite subject, Virtue. What was Virtue? Where was it, or she, or he? Had he stone lips that I could not hear him speak? Was he a Phœnix of the South whose wings failed before ice? A moth, hiding from our winter night? This I knew: Virtue was not in Sweden, not in this vulgar country, backward and primitive, that no one wanted to change except me. No, if I wanted to see the face of Virtue I would have to leave Sweden, leave the throne. If ever he tried to visit Sweden he might be frozen for eternity in a snow hut of the Lapps, perhaps, or beneath the solid white clouds of the Northern Ocean. Where had I had to go for clues to his being? To books, to ancient classics, to Plato, Epictetus, Marcus Aurelius. Why could I not be a seeker of Truth as they had been, why could I not win a crown for my mind, rather than have that paltry metal thing for my unlovely head?

"You would leave the throne for this! You would leave the throne for the very reason you should be there! Come, Madame, come!" Chanut exclaimed. "You have a magnificent opportunity! To be ruler of a country that is awakening like a great lion to its power! To be Queen of a court, ah, not only to be Queen, but to be the supreme cultural spirit of a court where Virtue may be born anew! You are beginning your reign. The hour to complain of a supposed failure is at the end of it. But how can you fail? You have youth, intelligence, daring. Your power will grow as you grow. You are impatient, Madame, and perhaps you have set too bookish a standard. Certainly it is not something found between the covers of a book, our Virtue. It is alive, vibrant, colorful."

"Virtue is not in Plato?"

"For you? As much as the warm breath of joy touches you from these happy creatures." He waved toward the bright mythical painting on the ceiling.

"I wish Plato were here so that I could learn from his own lips."

"Why not?" Chanut smiled.

Why not! Who has not dreamed of meeting the admired men of other centuries, of embracing them as friends or lovers, of exploring their counsel on a personal problem! How much more perfect they are, we think, than those we see around us!

"Or," he continued, "if you prefer a live philosopher to a ghost, a genius who is not sitting at a banquet of one or two thousand years ago, but writing in his study, a master of sciences who opens men's minds to themselves and to the universe, then I would introduce you to René Descartes."

Chanut was trumpeter for no man, thus he surprised me with the grandeur of his praise. Tell me more, I said, for I knew little of Descartes at that time.

Descartes, he told me, lived in solitude in Egmond, in Holland. Although he was an amiable man, none kinder, none more entertaining, none more interesting as a conversationalist than he, he chose to think and write in an atmosphere solely his own with Nature his neighbor. He was a Frenchman, of course he was a Frenchman, born in Touraine, not of nobility but of an excellent family, Madame, and a product of the Jesuit school in Maine. He had been restless as a youth, volunteering to fight in Germany, first on one side, then on the other, so he had seen a piece of Europe and the customs of more than one court, and all the time he had studied. The more he read and studied, the more he felt the need to study, until the problem of human knowledge became an obsession. He felt he must know Truth. He prayed desperately for light, he was tortured because, no matter how much he read, he could not conquer knowledge, his mind, rather than seeming to advance, being desolated by moods of utter darkness.

Then he had had three dreams which had revealed the way he was to go. In the first one he dreamed he was a lame man lost in a storm. Limping, trying to run, pursued by the black wind, he had found shelter in a church. He could remember even after waking the sense of peace and safety as the door closed on the tempest. The second dream had been simpler. He had heard bursts of thunder and seen sparks of fire around him. In the third dream he had held a book of the poems of Ausonius in his hands. He had opened the book, seemingly without purpose, and there before his eyes, distinctly lettered, was the line: *Which way of life shall I follow?* The moment he awoke he knew he had to answer the question in the dream. He vowed to turn his back on scholastic learning, on the books that kept him in darkness, and to seek only the knowledge he could find within himself or could see in the book of the world. He would begin by making a pilgrimage to Our Lady of Loretto, by going humbly to Italy, a land strange to him. These vows, Madame, became the basis of his famous philosophy, a completely new philosophy that each must judge for oneself.

"Did he marry?" I asked.

Chanut's old eyes shone with amusement. "Descartes says he has not found anyone as beautiful as Truth."

How like myself, I thought, and I declared he must be a happy man, living in the richness of his quietude.

"Unfortunately for his happiness, he began to write and publish the fruits of his meditations," Chanut answered. "When I talked with him in Amsterdam a year ago he told me he was disgusted with his career, that if he had been as wise as a monkey he never would have let himself be known as a writer. Why had he labored to share his philosophy with a world that largely showed it did not care whether he wrote or not, that misunderstood him, that had no use for him or his work! I contended that the comparative few who read his books were well worth writing for and that he should not be overly depressed by careless tastes, but his response was that savages believed monkeys could speak as human beings if they wanted to and only refrained for the sake of peace and quiet. Because he had not had the same wisdom to live without words, he believes, he has not received the pleasures of repose he would have had.

"You realize I am admitting, Madame, it is the welfare of my friend Descartes that concerns me as well as your own. This great philosopher is presently suffering in a state of discouragement. It is not only that when one of his books is published it is attacked by all those academicians who are antagonistic to anything new in thought, that where he expects harmony, or, at least, serious consideration, he is given blank disavowals and petty contradictions, for these things, as a mature philosopher, he could explain and discount in other men. He himself has a loathing for glory and the mechanisms men invent to gain it for themselves. It is beyond this, it is that he has come to be fifty years of age and sees the foreshortening of his span before him, that he feels the monument of thought he has been building boldly, yet patiently, with infinite care and honesty, is worthless in the sight of the world, and will be covered with dust when he disappears, if not before. Remember, Descartes is not a priest, not a saint at all. He has a vigorous love for life, a passion for Truth, a human desire to succeed. He cannot have employed his mind and gained the results he has without realizing his own excellence. And now he is infected with the fear that all his efforts have been wasted. I wonder if any young person can understand what that can mean to a man of fifty!

"If the remarkable Queen Christina of Sweden were to evince an interest in the philosophy of Monsieur Descartes, how many others would be influenced to do so! There is not a cultured person in Europe who is not aware of your supreme taste for knowledge. One phrase of appreciation from you would be worth a thousand from ordinary people. One word might be enough to banish my friend's despair."

My curiosity was so aroused by Chanut's narration I would have liked to invite the philosopher to come immediately to my court, but I could not overlook the fevered hatred of Catholics in Sweden, particularly of Jesuit Catholics, and it would be enough to stamp Descartes that he had been to a Jesuit school when a youth. Those were war years, and although it was a war for power rather than for religion that engaged us, the popular viewpoint was that it was for religion. No, it would be too delicate a matter to initiate.

What would I do? How does one encourage a scholar other than by supporting him and circulating his work? I could not do that unless he were in Sweden. As I was considering this, I heard the rattle and chatter of the returning mining party outside, marking an end to our privacy. The activities of the day must go forward. I suppose, I thought, some sort of correspondence could be arranged. Why should he not have that one word of appreciation from me? On the other hand, how could I appreciate a work I had not read? Then suspicions began to nag me that there might be harm for me somewhere in relating myself in any way to a man I did not know. Might not the intrigue be to get a letter from me that could be misinterpreted to my disadvantage? Chanut was charming, but how could I be sure he could not be fooled or used as a tool? So I did nothing except say that I was enthusiastic to read Monsieur's writing for myself.

After some months, however, a way opened to test the thought of the man. Chanut and I argued constantly on the properties of love and hate, and we decided to ask Descartes's opinion. I gave Chanut the question: *Which produces the most evil when its use is abused, love or hate?* to send, and the philosopher's long magnificent answer exceeded every expectation I had had. It was love, he concluded, that was capable of accomplishing the most harm, for while hate has a morose character whose pleasure is that of a demon, love is a passion of greater energy and force and more liable to excesses. I was jubilant, for I had a mistrust of love. Had I not been almost suffocated by my mother's so-called love?

Was not Sweden still at war more because of an overdeveloped love of wealth and Lutheranism than because of hatred for a faraway people? Yes, love was an ungainly giant whose vehemence must be avoided.

"By what I see of his writing, Monsieur Descartes is the happiest of men," I exclaimed. "It seems to me he is deserving of envy."

"Certainly it is the effect of Madame's interest," was Chanut's reply, with a courtly bow.

Perhaps it was, for when Chanut wrote Descartes to assure him of my great esteem, Descartes replied that it caused him extreme joy, that the glorious Queen had easily understood things the most erudite men deemed obscure, that he had promised himself the thoughts in his letter would not be fruitless if I relished them since I was one of the important persons on earth. That in itself, he said, would serve to profit the public. Naturally I was pleased at this recognition, and, from then on, accorded Descartes the privilege of writing directly to me. I was through with emissaries, through with my suspicions; our friendship, I felt, was destined for greatness.

Still, until the peace treaty was signed about two years later, I was wrapped in politics at home and troubles abroad, and any moments left to me for my own pursuits seemed to vanish like snowflakes on a warm pane. I did not do more than send another question, this one on the Supreme Good, which brought another magnificent answer. Then, in the autumn of 1648, when I thought the treaty had abolished the need of seeming to publicly hate all Catholics, I sat down to read a manuscript Descartes had sent me, *The Passions of the Soul.* Need I express my excitement at the clarity of his analysis, the brilliant flow of his perception, the ease of his writing? The body and soul, separate, yet together like passing friends! Together like the tree and the lark! Oh, sweet discovery, that the beauty, the Truth, I sought, had not to be bound forever by my deformed body! Even Plato saw no beauty in deformity!

I summoned Chanut and Freinsheim, the famous Livy scholar whom I had brought from Germany to be my State librarian, and requested them to begin immediately on a report of Descartes's major writings. The philosopher was discouraged? I would show him what it was to be appreciated by a Vasa! I would turn Sweden into a Cartesian country!

To Descartes himself I sent a present of reindeer skins and an invitation in my own hand, urging him to come to Stockholm. I insisted to Chanut, who was preparing to make a trip to Paris, that he must go to Holland and bring back his friend with him. I must meet this marvelous man, I must hear his philosophy from his own lips. I would send the Swedish Admiral to meet them in Amsterdam in the spring and bring Descartes to the North in our kindest season. He was not a man, Chanut said, who cared for the cold.

Everything miscarried. The Admiral's winds were too fair for my plans, and he arrived in April, before he was due. He sought out Descartes in Egmond, but, the letter I had sent by courier not having arrived, delayed five days by God knows what muddy mishap, and the Admiral having an idea he would travel better on land disguised as a simple officer in the fleet, Descartes was taken by surprise and thought the sailor was attempting to kidnap him. What was this plot of his enemies? he wrote to Freinsheim. He turned away the Admiral, and by the time Chanut reached him, delayed, too, the fleet had sailed.

I was in a fury, but, again, what could I do? When the philosopher finally received my letter he said it was as surprising to him as if it had descended from the clouds of heaven. Would he come? I waited. Would he come? I wrote Chanut. Would he come? I could not wait forever. Yes, he would come for three months in the summer, although he believed the voyage would be dangerous to his health. He would return with Chanut. Chanut was delayed, the summer crept past. I waited, increasingly impatient. I do not like to wait for anything, even a friendship. Where was he? Yes, he would come alone, and I sent a ship. In the beginning of October, in the brown-leaved autumn of 1649, Descartes stepped onto our chilly shore. That he went to stay at the house of Mme Chanut was, again, not my fault. He was welcome to be my guest at the castle, but he said he did not feel free to refuse the apartment she had so carefully prepared. Well, whatever, however, my philosopher was in Stockholm, I could unpin my anxiety, I could prepare for new worlds. The day after his arrival we met.

There was Descartes before me, there was the great philosopher, the greatest of our time, of who knows what time, come to attend my court, my court whose jewels were snow crystals, whose halls were hung in midnight shade, whose music was the moan of the North Wind. Would he not change all that? Would not the glaring light of his knowledge compensate for the light of the sun? I tingled with joy as I welcomed him.

"Monsieur Descartes, we can understand why you, born in the gardens of Touraine, who have lived in a land flowing with milk, could not easily resolve to come to our country to reside among bears and ice. We hope our appreciation of your genius and the use we make of it will compensate for the rigorous journey you have undertaken for our sake."

He bowed and answered. What he said I do not know, his answer floating past me to whisper to the pillars behind me, historic, marvelous as it might have been, I cannot remember it. I was too earnest for the perfection of my own speech to hear what must have been a sweet sound for my ears, too intent on regarding his person. If Descartes had been in the loose white robes of Plato I would not have been surprised, or if he had had Mercury's wings on his heels, or been in the dark habit of a dedicated priest or worn the clothes of a careless townsman, spotted and rumpled, oblivious of finery for himself. I was surprised, for somehow I had not expected it, to see him attired as a very prince of courtiers.

His suit must have been in the latest Paris fashion, its pinching in here and its swaying out there so calculated, the breeches so frilled in ribbon loops, and he with his shoulders thrown back so the folds of his fine clothes would not disappoint the dreams of his tailor. Not tall, not short, he seemed to stand just so, his feet shod in almost crescent-shaped shoes of a gleaming satin. He had no sword at his side to disturb the free swing of his coat, or, I thought, of his philosophy. Then I saw his gloves, oh, his gloves were trimmed in beads of snow, spangled with white frost, a fancy of winter moonlight, a fable in pearls. The poetry of the universe would move at these fingertips. They were made to lift a superb phrase from its sleep, to describe the unspoken arc of an argument, they were fashioned for errant grace, for the glittering gesture. Thinking back, I must close my eyes to that sparkle, for was it not the sparkle, too, of icy death? How could Descartes have come to Sweden with the glaze of death already on his hands?

When I looked beyond the clothes I saw, of course, the man who could not be disguised. Although his whitening hair was curled in the French style and his meager mustache brushed to an elegant line, his large head, the prominence of his brow, and his big heavy-lidded eyes could belong only to the scholar. His whole visage was more strong than handsome, the olive complexion, the thick foreboding eyebrows, the generously sized nose, the wide mouth with the lower lip jutting out as if it were holding a pronounced judgment, all marked with a slight disdain, a disdain, I thought, not of petty social distinctions, but of falseness of any kind, from a superficial detail to a grand illusion. He obviously was a man who never sought to hide the brilliance of his mind, nor would he seek to exhibit it. He was one of the lords of creation and he knew it.

This day when he finished speaking a smile swept his countenance, settling irrepressibly into the disdain, flexing an astonishing gaiety across the deep somber lines. What can be more dazzling than a stern face giving way to joy? It is a real smile, I marveled, the first real smile I ever had seen, a smile that was a thing in itself, not like the stiff chilly curves my Swedish Councillors intend for a smile, not related at all to the silly grins of the courtiers, nor to the foolish dimpling of the ladies-in-waiting, nor to the open-mouthed gasping of children when they swallow a delight and cannot digest it. This smile was a distinguished visitor, a bearer of rapturous news, a haphazard goddess in jewels the philosopher embraced. I could have embraced him myself, so glad I was to see reality before me.

I did not hold back the fullness of my pleasure and my esteem, smiling with him, praising him, and those in attendance at court did not like it. The older nobles held back, bowed, and said no word beyond a formal greeting, watching the stranger as if at any moment he might make a dangerous move, hoping, it seemed, he would, to give them the excuse to censure him, to exclude him. The scholars, the grammarians, the scientists who should have gathered with me to hail this King of Scholars approached with gray withdrawn expressions, plagued with envy that they, for all their labor at my court, had not been so openly praised, had not been called geniuses. And, they whispered scornfully among themselves, of all men, this one, who had not a certainty but a doubt to offer as a new banner for philosophy! Even the ladies, rustling in brocades and velvets, who like to prey on a new man like silken foxes, hung back uneasily, afraid of anything to do with thought.

When the audience was over, while I was still flushed with the gratification of Descartes's appearance, the old Chancellor came to me. Axel Oxenstierna, as everyone knows, loved power, loved to rule, would have loved to rule me, but since I had defeated him in the supreme decision of whether there should be war or peace, since he had lost his scheme to continue the war, he had been, apparently, quiescent. He had pursued his official duties methodically, without the flame of his former insistence to have an order of his own making, without attempting to sway the Estates with his oratory. Now as I saw him I almost felt sorry for him. Not that I would yield to him one atom of my purposes, but that he was declining into the cracked thinness of antiquity, his tall frame beginning to lean, burdened with discomfort. I do not like to see anyone or anything die, and he was leaning toward death. Was he not, after all, a gallant old noble whose loyalty to my father had been indispensable, and who had guarded the Kingdom for me until I came of age? One can afford to expand in success, I thought, and I turned to him cheerfully to hear what he had to say.

"Your Majesty." How gloomy his tone was! "You have honored the new arrival with marks of distinction you have shown to no one else. Do you know who this man is?"

"He is René Descartes, the famous philosopher. Surely you have heard of him."

"I have heard of a French writer, Descartes. How do you know this man is he?"

"Not Descartes?"

"The Jesuits are a very clever order, and they are determined to rule the world through Catholicism. For years we have watched carefully to keep them out of Sweden. There is no trick they will not resort to, no disguise they will not assume. They are the Devil's own clan, their tongues spilling lies and seductive promises, using any artifice to steal the confidence of their victims. Is not Descartes a confirmed Catholic?"

"All the world knows he is."

"What better way could there be for a Jesuit to gain the secret attention of Your Majesty, who is known to enjoy reading philosophy, than by impersonating a philosopher you undertake to admire? There is no one here who is familiar with him. You will notice Ambassador Chanut has been detained in Paris."

"What nonsense!" I laughed.

"You would scoff at your own destruction and at that of Sweden! I urge you to heed me, Your Majesty. These Jesuits do their work like worms underground. They sneak in, hoping to remain unseen while they strike at the roots of a country. If they cannot win by war they will try to win by subversion. When I heard this writer Descartes had been invited here I took the trouble to inquire into his background. Are you aware that he was schooled by Jesuits and has been influenced by them ever since? I am told he visits his old teacher regularly in Paris for instructions. It would be natural for him to fall in with a plot to let himself be replaced on a journey he hardly could wish to make himself. The passage to the North is an arduous one. Your Monsieur Descartes is noted for his sedentary habits and his love of a warm bed. Before you pour any more praise into the ear of the person who has arrived or confide your affairs to him, which I pray you shall not do at any innocent moment, be certain Monsieur Descartes is not sitting quietly at his writing in his own house in Holland. You may be playing with a viper of a Jesuit priest."

"I know of Monsieur Descartes's former connection with the Jesuits, My Lord, and I am certain that the only teacher he has at present, and has had for many years, is Truth. He would be incapable of the deceit you suggest."

"Do not confuse fame with the practice of virtue, Your Majesty."

This is the Lutheran dragon, I thought. He will eat any Catholics he can find in the land he claims for his own. Beware of foreigners! How many times had I had that thrown at me! Beware of Catholics! As if all Lutherans were good, all Catholics evil! As if the world were not divided differently, into two kinds of people, yes, but not into Swedes and foreigners, not into Lutherans and heathen. There were just honest men and dishonest men, as I saw it, regardless of their religion or their nativity.

Oxenstierna could not impress me with his fears and suspicions, and he left me, a resolute old man in black who would watch Descartes for an unjustified action, a dubious word. He would find something wrong with his behavior if it were possible to do so, even, I thought, if it were impossible.

At Descartes's second audience with me I revealed to him my desire to have him established permanently in Sweden. A fine house would be his, a royal pension, and a dedicated appreciation of his genius, but he turned aside the suggestion with an elegant gesture and an elegant compliment, setting the span of winter for the length of his visit. Would the master, then, begin personal lessons in philosophy for Her Majesty at a quiet hour in Her Majesty's private library? What command could be more agreeable, he answered, but when I named the hour his poise could not hide his astonishment. Five o'clock, the waking hour of the morning. It was, I explained, the only hour when we could be assured of being undisturbed.

Why wouldn't Descartes stay? Were the nobles making trouble, threatening him? Was Oxenstierna telling him lies about me to persuade him to leave? I would put a stop to that. I called Freinsheim, my librarian, to my study and asked him. Why had Descartes refused my invitation? Had a whispering against our friendship reached his ears? Or was my offer not sufficiently generous? The philosopher wanted appreciation and I wanted to appreciate him. There was no place in Sweden or her territories he could not choose for his home. Every scrap of his writings would be published, now, nothing of his light should be hidden from the world. Would he take a trip of a month or six weeks to acquaint himself with the country and the people? I was sure he would love them, they were not like the rigid-minded nobles, suspicious and grasping, they were kind, willing to serve their Queen, willing to learn. If he would stay, we, as King and philosopher, could form an ideal State.

"It must be the rigorous climate," Freinsheim said, "and that he feels a winter of Your Majesty's appreciation will equal more than a lifetime of another's. He has expressed no dissatisfaction with his visit here. And, Your Majesty, Monsieur Descartes has asked me to convey this request to you, that since five o'clock in the morning is hardly the hour for ceremony, you might be pleased to dispense with the miseries courtiers affect, that in this lonely hour you may meet as two philosophers."

Was I not joyful in giving my assent? To have Descartes call me a philosopher!

I suppose there are few people, and those few must have

wooden heads, who do not look back on certain rare hours and wish they had cherished them more at the time. No matter how greatly they are valued, they were not valued enough. They are diamonds set in a dull tapestry of days, weeks, years. The distractions that surrounded them, a stomach-ache, perhaps, a worry about some affair long since forgotten, a mind tending to wander off with the wind whipping at the outer walls, fell away and cannot be recalled, while the marvelous hours continue to shine. Would we be blinded by their illumination if we saw it clearly at the time, too amazed at the strength of a delicate word, or by the penetration of an impulse that seemed, then, no more than a reaching out to pluck a violet? I would like to have known. Why are there not clocks to strike these important hours and leave the others unsung?

The dark starlit hours Descartes spent with me in my library were of this rare kind. I say starlit, although the draperies were drawn so tightly against the creeping cold we could not tell whether it was gray or black or yellowing in light outside, and a large decorated screen stood, as well, in front of the windows. I was conscious of the stars only when Descartes pulled aside the draperies to point to the heavens in illustration of some astronomical circumstance, or when I, alone, pressed against the chilled pane for the sound of Descartes's sled coming, crunching on the snow. Otherwise, we were enclosed in a room of brown shadows and gold candlelight.

My library was a disordered-looking room, overwhelmed with books, manuscripts, and papers scribbled with my notes, many more than could fit into the cabinets lining the walls, already squeezed tightly with volumes, both ancient and recent. There were books piled on the floor, books on the chairs, the bench, on my long velvet-covered table, books that were the despair of my secretaries because I would not let them change my comfortable disorder into their order, a sterile idea, I thought, of what was proper for a Queen. I liked it as it was. One's books are a map of one's mind, and no mind is really proper. There was not a book I could not find if I wanted it, yet no one else could solve the maze.

On top of the cabinets were busts of my favorite philosophers and emperors, Plato, Socrates, Alexander, and some others, waiting in marble serenity for my understanding, their white gazes fixed on distant victories, victories I would make my own. When Descartes was first conducted into the room by Freinsheim I swung my arm up toward these ancient masters.

"I must have you there, too. My shelf of philosophers will not be complete without Monsieur Descartes."

He laughed. "I prefer you to see my head on my shoulders as it is, Madame, and I am sure I shall be of better service to you on these two feet, awkward as they may look, than off them."

I looked at his feet. Gone were the crescent-shaped shoes in favor of a pair of heavy boots. Gone were all of his courtier clothes. He was wrapped in an enormous fur coat, which he insisted on keeping on throughout our discussion, shedding only his leather gauntlets and his thick cap. I might have thought I was sitting with an articulate bear if it had not been for those great questioning eyes, twinkling with intelligence and humor, and for the vivacious interest of his talk, which soon made me forget what I saw before me, forget that Freinsheim sat silently near us, in considering what I was hearing.

"These books–" his glance took in the disordered piles–"are ones you have been reading?"

They were, and I expounded on the ones that had stirred my enthusiasm.

"Have you found all you have been searching for?"

"Never, exactly. That is what I expect in your lessons in philosophy."

Again he laughed. "I cannot teach you philosophy. How do we know there is such a thing as philosophy? Because we have been told so? Because it is a word used by certain Greeks we enjoy?" He shook his head, his lower lip jutting out farther in his widening smile. "I can offer you my method of thinking, the results of my own meditations. You have read the ancients and learned of their discoveries, and I shall tell you what I can of my discoveries, but you must go on yourself from there. There comes a time in each one's life when one must put aside book learning and inherited opinions, my dear, and submit to the difficult task of self-examination." He leaned forward from his chair across the table until his breathing grew louder to me than the cry of the winter wind. "Rote knowledge is not real knowledge. Only that which is learned by oneself and through oneself is real. If you want to pierce the secrets of human conduct and science and this nebulous thing called philosophy, you must begin by questioning yourself. Only in this way can you be sure of what you know."

Only that which is learned by oneself and through oneself is real. I looked at my books. I had tried to carry a thread of reason through their labyrinth of learning. How well had I succeeded?

"Reading," I orated, "is a kind of mirror which shows us our faults and virtues. It should be part of a good man's duty. He ought to read for his instruction, his correction, and his comfort. He should hold the celestial hand that joins him with other great souls, notwithstanding the separation of centuries or of geography."

"I shall not deny the merits of the ancients, but they are in the past, behind us. We are alive, with new problems."

I smiled. "Yes. The oracle which advised to consult the dead no doubt meant books."

"And so," said my living philosopher, "we must doubt their use for us until it has been proved."

Doubt it? Now, anyone who has the courage and curiosity to read my pages certainly will have read Descartes's books and will be familiar with his way of evolving Truth and existence through doubt. For me, as he exposed it and prodded me into it, it was a startling revelation. Doubt, all my early teachers had declared, was the one thing to be avoided. To doubt the tenets of the Lutheran Church was a sin. Rebel that I had been, radical as I had believed myself, the simplicity of this approach never had occurred to me. I had been like a man roaming the forest looking for a whale, I had been like a silly woman expecting a magic tiger to pop out of her jewel box, I had looked in the wrong places, expected the wrong things. I had thought of doubt and Truth as unmatched enemies, doubt the buzzing fly perhaps, that maddens the lion, or a toad, doubt, trying to suck in the sky. With Descartes I found that doubt on the tongue brought the first taste of Truth, that one should believe nothing until after he had dared once to doubt it.

I must admit that at first I wondered if there was a purpose behind the doubt. Oxenstierna's warning sounded to me in spite of myself. Was I to doubt the Lutheran Church in order to accept another? Was Descartes such a zealous Catholic that part of his reason for being in Stockholm was to try to convert me?

"Monsieur Descartes," I said, "is doubt sanctioned by the Catholic Church of Rome?"

"In the hours you and I spend together," he answered, "we must talk in the sphere of supernatural Truth, where there are no boundaries of class or religion. We need not discuss pedantic theories, for Truth is known by its all-pervading unity."

"Then you believe, as I, that religious doctrines that make divisions among people instead of uniting them are to be condemned? It is a terrible evil that must be stamped out, this blindness in which people fight one another, each claiming the banner of righteousness. Why do we not have one magnificent Church of Truth? If that is what you are working toward, I willingly shall join my efforts to yours."

How amiable his expression! "My aim, Madame, never has gone beyond reforming my own thoughts and building them on a basis which belongs wholly to myself. I am not one of those quarrelsome and restless natures who always have some plans for reform. I like quiet. I like the growth quiet allows."

And he talked on in his soft burred voice of the immenseness of quiet, of its pleasures, its opportunities, its consolations, until he began to cough and excused himself from further speaking, saying his voice tired easily due to a lung disease he had suffered as a child.

I let him go reluctantly. Nor was there any time in our succeeding meetings when I did not hear his footsteps receding from my door without a sense of deprivation. We did not agree on everything. On love, for an instance, for I maintained the rarity of true love, that in its intense purity it could come only once in a lifetime, and that love and fidelity are inseparable, at which Descartes had smiled out of the bundling of his fur coat. When he was young, he said, he had loved a little girl who squinted, and ever since had felt an irresistible attraction to any lady who squinted. Was that fidelity to the little girl or to the squinting? Or to the boy, cherishing his first view of love? He had taught me to doubt, I answered, and I offered a doubt that it had been love at all. He shook his head, smiling, protecting the sweetness of his memory.

Then, although Monsieur Descartes escorted me through new regions of science, showing me mathematics as a crystalline world, resplendent in its order, with, of course, no wars between its resolute lords, its joys precise, its riches infinite, I could not see, as he did, that the mind could be explored like that world. The mind has shadows, I said, and unaccountable divisions, unfollowable directions. Not when we throw light on them, not when we are willing to open our eyes to ourselves, he said, for then the reality within becomes more clear than any object we can contemplate on the outside. I could not believe that.

I do not remember just when I began asking his advice on problems of state other than that it was after Freinsheim ceased to accompany him. It was a winter of pressures and difficulties, a bitter winter, moreover, of such cold the deepest lakes were as solid glass. The hills and fields beyond Stockholm lay in a long whiteness laced by trees, a world ruled by wind and snow, a land to stay away from unless one were a reindeer or a star. The city huddled within its walls, pulling its stone closer about its shoulders, puffing smoke, unable to shake off the ice and graying snow.

Voices were staccato in the sharp air, and the crack of a whip echoed a horrible cry. Yet Descartes rode the streets to the castle on a green sled painted with flowers. He never missed an appointment.

Within the houses, within the castle, certainly, the human climate was as heartless as the winter of the fields and forests. Descartes, my prize, my honored guest, was snubbed, was given no more than a chilly bow by courtiers and grammarians alike. Extraordinary merit is a crime which is seldom or never pardoned, and those who have access to Kings are equally hated by those that have it and those that have not; thus Descartes, for the very reasons for which I cherished him, became an offense to everyone else. When his scientific demonstrations were arranged for the court the pedantic scholars and scientists either scorned his theories or were monsters of silence. They never stopped criticizing him to one another, while the nobles found it expedient to ignore him as much as possible. He is a spy, their eyes said, we must beware of him. The ladies-in-waiting tittered behind his back, giggling at the wig he wore to keep his head warm, imitating the burred speech of his slightly cleft tongue. Descartes did not desert his amiable expression, whatever he felt, nor did he make any comment other than to say he never heard anything talked about at court, and did the people's thoughts as well as the water freeze here in the winter?

I was nervous and troubled in my own predicament. The incessant noise of voices in government, the Councillors, nobles, bönder, and burghers, each with their demands, ambitions, and rights, their quarrels and jealousies among themselves, was in my ears all day and echoed through my dreams at night. Food did not agree with me, my body gave in easily to fevers, but, whether I felt badly or well, I insisted on checking my reports and petitions carefully so that I could not be deceived or imposed on in state affairs.

Then my friends, it seemed to me, were as bad as my enemies, if not worse, in their pressures, outlining before me Descartes's

XI

A GREAT triumphal arch was erected for the coronation, by order of the senators, through which the procession would pass in coming to the castle. It was just across the North Stream, facing the castle, and was made of wood covered with linen painted to look like stone, so that it was guaranteed not to be permanent. The economical Swedish senators had none of the instincts of the Roman senators to buy a piece of eternity with worldly monuments. Good deeds and a pious life, they figured, were a proper payment for a house in their heaven. The arch itself, however, was a try at copying Roman magnificence, a tall bulky structure with a high central archway and two lesser ones, twelve heroic figures surmounting the columns, and, above them, twelve more on the rectangular top, posed against the sky, with flags and banners waving among them. There was hardly a particle of the entire surface that was not decorated, with praises of me, with vines trailing Latin mottoes, designs of victorious battles in Germany, fields, flowers, the rising sun, the crown, and, best of all, a lion holding a thunderbolt in his paw. It is the lion, I thought, who will decide it in the end. He will loosen his thunderbolt and the whole thing will collapse in a brilliant flash.

As I watched the arch being put together and raised, I sometimes wondered which would last the longer, its wooden columns or my reign, whether the senators would allow either to complete a natural life or would arrange a quick ending, the praises and statues demolished, the glory left to be scraps in the dust. It was a defiance of the old Nordic gods to have the coronation in Stockholm, people said, for they threw their power only behind Kings who were crowned in Uppsala, home of the ancient Kings, their home. He who was crowned in Stockholm would have a short reign. It is a silly superstition, I had said. We are living in a modern world, Stockholm is the largest city in Sweden, there is not another place big enough to accommodate all the dignitaries to be present at the coronation. Were we to put up tents around Uppsala for them all? Let us be practical. Thus, the ceremony was to take place in Stockholm.

I had promised Carl Gustav I would marry him if the Estates would not agree to naming him my successor before the coronation. That was in 1648. Then, after the peace treaty, the coronation was set for October of 1650, so I had busied myself with my purpose of promoting my cousin. In the summer of 1649, before the arrival of Descartes, I thought I had accomplished my purpose, and, literally, I had, but I found at the same time that the flowering of a purpose is not always of the color expected.

In a stormy session of the Riksdag, when the Estates were at such swords' points in politics that I was the only one who could arbitrate their differences and it became apparent that the country would be at war with itself without a ruler to hold an olive branch, that if I were taken by a sudden death there would be no one, nothing but dissension, I brought forward my candidate for a successor.

"It is our wish that Your Majesty marry him," was the answer the Estates gave when I presented Carl Gustav's name.

"I do not wish to marry at all." My announcement was firm, irrevocable. I had arranged their problems, now I exacted my price. Stunned as they may have been at the picture of a woman, a Queen, who refused to marry, they voted as I asked them to vote, and Carl Gustav became my legal successor.

I was the only one who was elated. Carl Gustav, still busy with his duties as commander in Germany, did not accept his ascent toward grandeur with the graciousness one might expect. He wrote to his friends grumbling that he wanted to marry me. And his friends! Yes, friends really are worse than enemies, using friendship, as they do, as an iron lever to force one to do what they themselves have resolved upon. Would I have listened to an enemy as I listened to old Jacob de la Gardie and my bastard uncle, Baron Gyllenhielm? Not for a moment! At state meetings, at receptions, at private meals, they lost no opportunities, nor did any of my cousin's friends, to pursue his cause.

"Your Majesty—" and the caress of Jacob de la Gardie's tone would add *my dear young lady*— "you are very kind to your cousin, very kind." He would sigh, fingering his wineglass, a glass he no longer could see, as he slowly was becoming blind, but which he had no trouble raising to his lips, so many times had the hand and the glass made the trip together. "But as an old man—" yes, what an old man he was, bent and quavering, his smiles wrinkled permanently into his jowls— "I must tell you that his election as successor brings to us more problems than it solves."

He spoke thus at a small party at Makalös, where ten or twelve of us had gathered in honor of the success of the election, as opposed to the Oxenstiernas, a success I maintained and the others doubted. The wide windows of the room where we sat had been thrown open to the summer air, and the brassy waters of The Stream outside threw a bright jerky reflection onto the ceiling. I was relaxed, it was not cold, and I thought I had achieved what I wanted.

"How," asked Adler Salvius seriously, "will it be decided who is to follow Carl Gustav? You say that can be voted on when the time comes, but supposing he dies before you do? You are both young, of course, but he is the older."

Baron Gyllenhielm leaned forward, tapped his forefinger on his knee, his balding head shining. "If each of you marries and has children, who is to inherit the crown? We must think ahead, Your Majesty. The children may not have the affection for one another you and Carl Gustav have. They will be rivals. With Your

Majesty gone, bless your soul, and the Prince, there will be fighting, believe me, as to which line is to win the crown."

I tossed my head. "I have promised you I shall not marry."

Magnus jumped from his chair, smiling, to bend over my shoulder. "Your Majesty, marriage can be the haven of unsuspected pleasures. Surely you will relent."

"There is only one answer." The Baron continued his theme. "It is more important than ever that you marry Carl Gustav so you can have your children together. Then there will be no disagreement."

"No, I shall not marry." How many times must I repeat this?

Magnus dropped his hand onto my arm. "Carl Gustav never will give up hope," he purred.

I pulled away my arm. What was happening to my pleasure in my success, to my enjoyment in the summer's day?

"Well," concluded the Baron, "you probably will marry someone, sometime. There must be an heir to the throne. So why not Carl Gustav?"

"What!" I shouted. "I am to be plowed and seeded like ordinary soil? Never! I refuse to be treated as the poorest farmer treats his furrow!"

Magnus burst into laughter. "You are too full of spirit not to marry!"

"How else can you secure the monarchy?" asked Jacob de la Gardie.

And then Salvius. "If anything should happen to Your Majesty's excellent self, do you believe the Prince ever would reach the throne? I do not trust the Oxenstierna family to stay with the agreement. Once you were gone, to whom they may feel a loyalty as a Vasa, perhaps, I am convinced they would try to establish a republic in Sweden, with themselves at the head."

The talk always went like this, and I had to admit to myself that it was true. As soon as I released my last breath, the nobles of the Oxenstierna party would brush away their agreement as quick as the switch of a rat's tail and do, as well as they could, what they pleased. They would bury with me everything I had accomplished in my reign so that it would be as if I never had been on the throne at all.

"If Carl Gustav were recognized as the hereditary prince, they would not dare to go against him," I said.

My friends, old and young, shook their heads. That was impossible, they said, the Estates never would vote for that, the setting-up of a new royal line. When I had suggested it, I had been unanimously refused. I always would be, for it was too much to ask, it was impossible, they said.

Impossible. They see it as a final term, I thought, a stone wall with no gate, something to lean against and do nothing more, but they are forgetting that I, too, am pointing out an impossibility, forgetting it purposely because they do not like it and do not wish to see it. It is impossible for me to marry. I cannot, shall not, do it. What happens when two impossibilities meet? One, naturally, must be switched into a possibility. A way must be invented. Look how man, after centuries of calling it impossible, solved a way to visit the heavens by inventing the telescope. And how he solved a way of immortalizing his thoughts by inventing printing. The impossibility I faced was small compared to those. Surely I should be clever enough to handle it.

I turned to Salvius. How solid his appearance, how solidly age sat upon him without seeming to rub away the squareness of his strength or the burnish of his reasoning.

"Perhaps you exaggerate the present power of the Oxenstiernas. The Chancellor has been very quiet since the peace treaty."

"Quiet! He has said little publicly, probably on purpose, so that his private activities would be less noticed."

"What has he been doing?"

"Your Majesty is not aware that when delegations of the people bring their problems and petitions to Stockholm the Chancellor has them sent directly to him, rather than to the proper government office, and answers them as he wishes? Usually he sends them home again without their seeing anyone else."

I was appalled. "He has reported nothing of this in the Council."

"Naturally not. The Chancellor never has liked interference."

"Why have I not been told before? Who else knew of this?"

I looked around the room. No one had known. Salvius had had word of it through his humbler friends. The affair was plain to us without detailed descriptions or discussions. The defeat I had enforced on the Chancellor had not changed him at all. He believed the aristocrats, the pure Swedish aristocrats, not those tainted with foreign blood such as the Palatines and the De la Gardies, were the only ones fit to rule the country, and if they were prevented from doing it publicly, they would do it privately. He would deliver the Oxenstierna word of law without disturbing the Council or the Riksdag.

"I shall have an explanation from the Chancellor," I promised.

When I confronted Oxenstierna with his actions in the next meeting of the Council, he arched his gray eyebrows in surprise. Was he not doing the government a favor by giving audience to these delegations? He could not permit them to go further, they were unreliable people, an offense to Her Majesty's sovereignty, as he had told them. They had no respect for their landlords, the aristocracy, any more, making accusations against them and talking as if they would make trouble if their demands were not met, demands that were, of course, impossible.

Impossible? The word had become a challenge to me.

What right had the people to complain? The Chancellor implied they had none. They had no right to mistrust their superiors, they should stay home and mind their lawful landlords. Did they think they could prescribe laws for themselves? What nonsense! He had informed them of the government's viewpoint, that the people must learn not to complain against a just rule.

"This is not the government's viewpoint, My Lord," I interposed. "These people may have a just complaint which should be heard. I will not have oppression of one class by another in Sweden. The ancient rights of the bönder cannot be denied, and their protest may be that their landlords are overriding them. I shall see the delegations myself."

"You must not indulge these people," the Chancellor warned with his old fervor. "They are troublemakers. Their flame must be quenched. If not, it looks as if the necks of many honest men will be bloody."

I should quench their flame? There we did have a bit of nonsense. I not only would be quenching the flame of the freedom of the Swedish people, I would be quenching myself. If I was the support of the people, so were they mine. We would have to stand together to keep the nobles from sliding into power as they had in the countries around us. The Swedish bönder were the only men in Europe able to own and develop their own land. Look at Denmark and Poland, where the nobles had assumed the rule, where the people had no rights and the King was a puppet. Look at the dissension in France, where the nobles opposed the Queen Regent. Look at England. After Charles I's head was chopped off, there were nights when I awoke from mad dreams of imprisonment, my hands fondling my own neck. And now Oxenstierna was promising that if he did not have his way the necks of many would be bloody. It was a threat that had to be ignored, since the threat of the alternative, of losing freedom, was the greater.

I called the bönder delegation to a private meeting and listened to their complaints. Since the end of the war, the bönder said, the nobles were trying to pull the wealth out of their estates that they formerly had taken from foreign countries. They were taking away the bönder's land, demanding work from them, imposing taxes which no one could pay. They wanted to make serfs out of free men. They were landowners and tenants, the bönder said, they were not servants for the nobility, and they would fight for their rights if they had to.

They would not have to, I told them, for they had my complete sympathy. It was Oxenstierna's idea, not mine, that they should submit to their landlords. The aristocrats may be the privileged class, they may not have to pay taxes themselves, but neither could they arbitrarily demand taxes nor, above all, were they privileged to take away the freedom of other people.

With my support the flame spread, all through the winter of 1650, the people crying their complaints, the nobles adamant. In the Riksdag the speeches were fiery.

"The privileges assumed by the nobles against the bönder threaten us all," proclaimed Nils Nilson for the burghers. "When our neighbor's walls have burned, it will be our turn next. Has not the Swedish bönder from time immemorial been free and independent of the nobles until recent years? Is not the State dependent on the well-being of the bönder and the land? If the nobles betray the trust placed in them by our late King, should not this trust be taken from them? Who are they to monopolize the offices of the State? The offices of the State are supposed to be open to all. Is Sweden to continue as a monarchy or change to a country dominated by an aristocracy? That is the question rising before us, that is the specter chilling the minds of burgher, bönder, and clergy. No! I say no! The monarchic must prevail over the aristocratic or any other form! That is the only way to preserve our ancient rights."

And Salvius spoke. "The bönder are free men and must remain so. Are there not among them many of those whom our great Queen calls 'natural nobles'? Have our titled nobles forgotten that their families, too, once lived in humble houses? Have their minds so corroded as to believe that to build oneself a new palace to live in makes one a new kind of King? If the nobles abuse the privilege conferred on them as landholders, I, My Lords, shall cast my vote with the bönder, asking that the land be taken away from the aristocracy and placed under the protection of the crown."

"Who is the author of such foolishness?" shouted the Chancellor. "The nobles only ask their legitimate privileges."

"The Oxenstiernas seem alarmed that their authority should be questioned at all. Can it be that our Chancellor seeks the domination of the country for himself and his family?"

It was my uncle, Johan Casimir, who dared to pronounce what many suspected. And the country echoed him: *Does the Chancellor seek the domination of the country for himself?* No longer would they accept him as their would-be father. Raging pamphlets appeared, bönder and burghers held meetings, preachers from their pulpits denounced the oppression of the aristocracy, the ambition of Oxenstierna. Justice was demanded for the people. Oxenstierna, they claimed, had invented a system to plunder the State for his own and the nobles' selfish interests, the moment anything happened to the Queen, God bless her, he would take over the government, he might even try it before then, and he would do anything to keep from acknowledging a hereditary prince so he could legally introduce his own government and ruin the rights of the people forever. He came to be blamed for every wrong in the country, for letting it rain so the harvest was destroyed, for causing wives to be ill-tempered, for inciting children to disobedience. The people implored heaven for vengeance, but would they wait for heaven? The flame burned into their hearts, seared their vision. Two armies were seen floating in the air over Stockholm. An omen, an omen!

The nobles shrugged their shoulders, but they grew afraid to travel in the farming regions, or to go anywhere alone.

Then the Devil woke up. The Devil is among us, the people cried. In manor houses the brocade was torn down from the walls, chests were turned over, their contents littered, tables and chairs upset while the household slept. It is the Devil, people whispered, stomping through the homes of the nobles. And everyone knew when he came to Stockholm, the Devil. It was at dawn, the whole town looked ablaze with his hellfire as he passed through, he was a long, long ghost, he was seen melting away into the rising sun.

The time for the coronation was drawing near, and I began to contemplate the streets full of rioting instead of celebrating. The triumphal arch would be a mockery. What triumph would there be? Rather than joy, there would be civil war. What would keep the classes from fighting, the nobles presumptuous, intolerant, the people hot-tongued, furiously indignant, as their bitternesses converged toward the inevitable decisive clash?

I would. Here was something better than an invention for the impossible. Here was a simple cure. The year before, I had been told that it was impossible to make Carl Gustav the hereditary prince, the Estates had been unanimously against it. Now I would show them all that what they called an impossibility was, rather, a blindness, and I would cure that blindness.

I gave some pertinent advice to the leaders of the three unprivileged Estates. Be as bold as the nobles, I said, but make your threat into a legal act. You will vote solidly together, and I shall support you. Thus, in the last Riksdag before the coronation these three Estates presented a petition asking that the aristocracy be deprived of their privileges and be forced by law to pay taxes. By what graciousness of fortune was it that Oxenstierna was ill and absent? The nobles were terrified, realizing, suddenly, that they were only one Estate, that they would be lost if the petition were allowed to come to a vote.

I hardly had reached my apartments after the adjournment when a petition from the nobles was handed to me, a hastily written paper, humbly begging my protection. They would fall down before me, they would crawl, they would lay a red carpet before me wherever I walked, they would do anything if I would protect them, if I would prevent the people from taking away their privileges, if I would save them from destruction as a class. The Council, nervous at being in a crisis without its leader, was waiting for my answer.

Within an hour my answer was delivered to them. I made no promises, I sent them my cure. A document was given them to sign to appoint Carl Gustav the Palatine Prince, to be hereditary prince to the throne of Sweden, his male children to be heirs after him, and he to marry a Lutheran princess of the Queen's choosing. Nevermore, I thought, shall a woman sit on my throne. And it shall be clear that the prince shall marry someone else. They shall sign that, too, that I never again shall be asked to marry him myself.

Their blindness fell away immediately, for they all signed and sent the paper to the house of the Chancellor. What could Oxenstierna do in his sickbed other than add his own trembling signature?

Now that I had become protector of all four Estates, as a ruler should be, I called a meeting the following day of delegations of the bönder, burghers, and clergy and told them plainly I was rejecting the demands of the petition they had presented in the Riksdag against the nobles since it would cause a rebellion if I did not. I could not allow our beloved country to be swept into civil war, nor did I believe such was their own intention. However, I assured them, we had succeeded in our campaign against an aristocratic domination, for the nobles had agreed to insure the monarchy. I had maintained the bönder's freedom, I said. Then I exempted them from certain taxes as a bounty and promised I always would win restitution for them from the nobles. Would not they, too, sign that Carl Gustav was to be hereditary prince? That was the best way to provide for a monarchy in the future, for their safety, and mine, and, although they had opposed it before, now they would realize the necessity. They were jubilant in their agreement. They felt they had saved the monarchy for me and for themselves. And they had, with my guiding hand.

It was just in time. The festivities for the coronation were to begin the 17th of October, Carl Gustav was accepted officially as Crown Prince on October 9, only eight short days before. Those competitive brothers, defeat and victory, had run a close race. The country rolled out of terror and into joy without wasting a breath between, their celebrating true and wholehearted. Their Queen had brought them out of a foreign war and rescued them from civil war, she was a Queen worth crowning. It was worth waiting the six years for this, I thought, to be exuberantly wanted, to be wildly popular, to have proved my divine right to sit on the throne, alone.

The spectacle of the coronation was of a glittering magnificence never before witnessed in Sweden, and I wonder if it ever shall be again. For three days before the ceremony and for weeks afterward wine flowed from the fountains, red Spanish wine and white French wine, fireworks diamonded the night skies, silver trumpets blew, gold-laced banners fluttered, heralds and pages in colorful velvet liveries galloped through the streets, plumed horses pulling the gilded carriages of the notables clattered at all hours, oxen were roasted whole in the square. There was an eruption of feasts, balls, tournaments, torchlight processions, pageants, all day and all night. How many times I had to leave the music and dancing of a ball in the early morning to rush to my government duties without sleep! How glorious it was!

When before had the people seen, or even imagined, blackamoors, camels, elephants, how could they have dreamed of animals and human beings so different from our own? Yet there they were, floating in splendor through the streets of Stockholm, the fantastic little blackamoors in brilliant costumes riding the camels, the enormous elephants dragging wagons of gnomes, busy Swedish gnomes, hammering and singing. There was a ship rowed by sea-witches, and a moving burning mountain dotted with musicians playing, there was old man Time with his skull, his crossbones, and winged hourglass, his scythe lifted over Youth, a scythe that never fell, as Youth sang, carelessly happy, among lilies and roses, at his feet a child blowing iridescent bubbles, and there, behind lance-bearing knights, in a gold-and-white chariot was Venus, yellow-haired as all Swedes knew her to be, holding aloft a flaming heart. In the line of royal nobilities rode Atani Tingel Bilalgium, our imported Moorish prince in exotic African robes, on his own little honey-colored horse. And more, Roman drummers, food and song, myths and dragons, more than the senses can remember.

The passing of the coronation procession, in itself, through the triumphal arch took an entire day. Carriage after ornate carriage rolled along bearing ambassadors from Europe and nobility from every corner of the Kingdom, there were whole companies of guards, halberdiers, archers, footmen, thousands of riders, there were Carl Gustav, the Queen Mother, the officers of the realm carrying the crown regalia, everyone, everything that could ornament the pomp. It was a long undulating tail of a peacock that was drawn gradually within the castle walls.

I, of course, was the most sublime device in it, riding in a black velvet carriage drawn by six white horses shaking plumes of pink and white, on their muscled backs, like giant autumn petals, red velvet cloths stitched in gold, and silver-shod, with the white fringe of their fetlocks waving at every step. My gown was so heavy with gold, pearls, and precious stones that I felt myself a little jeweled pillar set against the velvet cushions, lifting a gemmed hand in greeting, and smiling, a haunted smile I now think, to the people who lined the procession's long way from Jacobsdal to Stockholm Castle.

Behind me my favorite pet was led, a travesty of royalty, the only one decked as richly as I, even more so, for my snow-white horse was weighted in gems, his bit and bridle of diamonds, pearls, turquoise, his robe of gold braid and pearls, his saddle of gold-threaded purple velvet, his dangling empty stirrups of bright gold, golden chains rattling on his silver hoofs. Was there another beauty there so spirited, so conscious of stepping in dignity, so aware of his own magnificence? He would toss his head, flashing the large crystal stone in the crown on his brow, arch his neck, barely lifting his luxurious snowy mane from the ground, he would prance, letting his flowing tail trail in the dust. Oh, my beauty! I would like to have ridden backward to watch you! You knew how to act!

After darkness had settled and the last riders had been gathered into the city, after the last spark had melted from the vast display of fireworks that wrote the coronation excitement across the sky and mantled castle and houses in gunpowder smoke, the banqueting began, and the seemingly ceaseless ritual. There were two days when the states and towns of the Kingdom presented me with gifts, then, on the twentieth of October, the ultimate, the reason for it all, the coronation ceremony.

But when I try to recall this ceremony my memory blurs, two pictures become one, the coronation and the abdication, the colors of one mixing into the design of the other. Is it the colors that are mixed or is it my emotions? As a child I learned to count to a hundred, then, carefully, learned to count down, backward. Of which was I proudest? Is it a greater happiness to climb the mountain or to travel down again?

There, in the coronation and in the abdication four years later, were the same leading characters, the same properties, the same spectators, the same symbols. There was I, there were Carl Gustav, the Chancellor, my tutor Johannes Matthiæ as Bishop, the Councillors, the variety of bent heads that was the court. There were the sword, the orb, the key, the scepter. There was the crown. Was I walking up the aisle to accept the crown to to abandon it? Did they refuse to put the crown on my head or to take it off? Were there only four years between or four centuries? Or four blinks of an eyelash? Was there no time, was all that happened, or seemed to happen, a quick dream, the intimation of a nightmare, of another life? When I awaken shall I be saying to myself: *Today I am to be crowned?*

But I was crowned both times, yes, there were two crowns, the jeweled golden crown of the Kings of Sweden topped with the tiny star-sprinkled sphere and the Lutheran cross, wild King Erik's crown it was, and that other crown, the Crown of Truth, composed of who knows what, for who has seen it, be it of laurel, of lotus, of sprigs of rue, perhaps of eagles' eyes, of cocks' crests, of the white wings of doves, perhaps of the glimmering rim of the moon. And where was the cross on it, with it? On my tongue? In my heart? In the years ahead?

Blessed be he who cometh in the name of the Lord. My greeting, the greeting of he who is to be crowned, but who knows the true name of the Lord, or, knowing, can pronounce it? I am anointed with His balm out of the golden horn. I take the sword,

I give back the sword. I take the scepter, the orb, the key, and I give them back. I am enfolded in the violet robe of royalty, wrapped in it as in the purple twilight, and I fling it from my shoulders. I cannot bear the weight of the Nordic Kings.

There is music. *Te Deums* and the music of planets in their wheeling and the music of weeping. Was it all the same music? Which time did I hear it? Which time did I see tears on the faces about me? Neither time, I remember, were there tears on the two faces whose lines are scratched into my memory, the Chancellor's and Carl Gustav's. When have I ever escaped them? When have they not been waiting, whichever way I turned?

I can see Axel Oxenstierna, highest count in the Order of Solemnity, bowing unsmiling, as tall, as darkly vested and tacit as a church spire acknowledging the wind. When was it he came to me and said: *You are the daughter of Gustav Adolf, you do not know what you are doing. When you grow older you will find you live twice, once when you act, and again in those later years when you discover why you have acted.*

Then I was left with Carl Gustav. I always found him beside me, my plump sturdy cousin, after the coronation, after the abdication. After the coronation it was laughter, Italian music, dancing, bouquets of flowers, attempted compliments, laughter, laughter to the very last event, that gallant effort we made in imitation of the Romans in their ancient Colosseum.

We will have some Roman sport, we said, so the castle's tennis courts had been converted into an enormous ring where wild animals were to be loosed to fight to the death. A temporary stadium was built against the castle wall, and there we sat together, Carl Gustav and I, in the royal box. The merriment of the festive weeks still sang in our ears. Now, I thought, the cruelty of the animals will bring us back to the cruelty of man.

"It will be a bloody game, Your Majesty," said my cousin. "You should have a fan for your eyes."

"You think I cannot bear the sight of blood?"

"You avoid war."

"These are beasts, not men."

"Are they different when they are wounded?"

At this unexpected bit of wit from him I could only laugh and slap at his shoulder in joy. Perhaps there were corners in him where he was not asleep after all.

"We shall see. Look! I shall choose the lion."

A lion and a buffalo had been run into the ring. If the lion is King of the animals, I commented, I do not think much of the animal kingdom. He was a shaggy fellow with soiled tan fur, a thick tangled mane, a tired tail, and a bored posture. He stood, his big head drooped, watching the sleepy buffalo at the other end of the enclosure, then, crouching slightly, moved slowly toward him as if to leap. I held my breath. But suddenly the buffalo lowered his head and jumped directly at the lion, who, starting to bound into the air at the same moment, was hit full in the chest and almost knocked over. With a surprised look at his opponent he straightened himself, shook his dignity into place, turned, and padded off, to examine the rest of the ring as if the buffalo did not exist.

"Here is a King who does not strike back!" I exclaimed.

"Why should he?" asked Carl Gustav. "He knows that fat old buffalo is no enemy of his. The next one may be different."

Since the buffalo had exhausted his belligerence and persisted in smelling and peering at the spectators instead of bellowing, pawing, and charging as he was expected to do, he was led away and a great brown bear pushed into the ring. The lion twitched his tail and went over to have a look at him. The bear reared, the lion reared, snarling a warning.

Now, I begged, now! Show him you are King! Punish him!

Dear God! The lion straightened himself again after this brief expression, calmly turned tail, and found himself a comfortable spot for a nap. He lay down, his furry head snug between his forepaws. When the bear followed him, climbed on his back and bit him, he jumped to his feet, toppling the old bear, and swung his claws at him like a father beating the ears of a naughty boy.

That was all. Neither the bear nor the lion would bother about one another any more.

"What is the matter with them? Are they sick?"

Carl Gustav was stoical. "We would not fight either if we had nothing to fight about. They have been fed too well."

Well, the lion was allowed to leave, and a wild horse was let in. The stands cheered uproariously when the bear chased the horse, the two tearing around the ring in a violent race. Oh, how you love violence, you people! Why? Why? And did I? Was not my own blood beating in excitement, my own voice screaming when the bear caught the horse, and, while the horse jumped frantically up, down, sideways, fastened onto his thigh, his front claws sinking into the soft groin of the horse, his big ugly body hoisted onto the back end as if he would be on his back as rider with the next leap! But the horse pulled in his hind legs and with a tremendous *plunk* kicked into the bear's stomach. Then he let out a pile of dung, which slubbered all over the front of the bear. Carl Gustav heaved with laughter, for the bear dropped off, ran to the tub of drinking-water, and washed himself. He would not touch the horse again. Only the decorations interested him. He pulled down a sack stuffed with hay, which had been dressed like a man in a red suit, and tore off its legs, spilling the hay over the ground.

"It is a meek substitute for blood," I said.

"A good enough act. Fighting is not for women anyhow."

Then why, I wanted to ask, have you let me do your fighting in politics for you? Did that not take as much courage and strategy as the battlefield? More!

"Do you believe women have no battles to fight? I am fighting most of the time."

"That is different and you are different. And why do you not let me help you?"

"Are you not satisfied to be Crown Prince?"

"I am grateful, Your Majesty, I am not satisfied. I have nothing at all to do. Why will you not give me an active part in the Kingdom? Why will you not marry me?"

While I, I thought, am reduced to pregnancies, to producing young monsters, you would move into the rule. Could he not wait for me to die, or was he afraid he would die first, before he attained his full glory? Why must he always come back to a question of marriage, as if it had not been resolved for once and all? It was like a dream in which one cannot run away. No matter what I did, opening door after door, I arrived at the same room, the grim bridal chamber. How horrifying it would be to go through the last door, Death, and find Carl Gustav waiting to lead me into the Forever!

Why was I always left with him, with him and his stubborn wait for triumph? I had considered him as a pawn, yet he was the one who won in the end. By waiting, by not changing, almost by not thinking, he won. He is a thing on which fortune has fallen by my wish. How dangerous wishes are, and prayers! Beware of prayers! How could I have foreseen what would happen when I prayed so ardently as a girl to marry Carl Gustav? Who was there to tell me what would happen to my wish and to me?

"The Queen is mad," said Oxenstierna when I left the throne. Was I? How plainly does a madman see? Is it madness to strip naked one's desire, to reach to embrace it wholly? One does not desire that which already belongs to one, says Plato. Why, in giving up the throne, did no one realize there was something I wanted more?

I can take away the veil of those years between that triumphant October of 1650 and the June day in 1654 when I abdicated, although I do not know that I shall be thought the better for it. Obvious history, the tempers and finances of the State, I shall leave to the history books, and narrow the stage to my own drama of desire and deceit, a play of such dreams and such absurdities I am not sure, even now, whether, in it, I was a harlequin or a saint.

XII

THE Portuguese Ambassador, Don Joseph Pinto Pereira, who had arrived before the coronation and had, of course, participated in its glorious celebrations, stayed on through the winter afterward to carry on trade conversations for his country. Although his commercial arrangements were mainly delegated to the Chancellor, I met with him, too, as I did with everyone of importance who came to Sweden.

Don Joseph was not a remarkable man. He was paunchy, small, and pompous, not at all clever except in commercial figures and in the strict maintaining of his selfish concerns, the kind of man who is apt to win his point through his inability to see anyone else's point. His great love was his array of habits. He arrived at a meeting with absolute punctuality, not a moment before nor a moment after the appointed hour, his bow was made precisely at the angle to best flatter his corseted figure, then his papers were sorted in an ecstasy of exactness. Woe to the Portuguese secretary who misplaced one! Don Joseph's shout was out of all proportion to his size, and his indignation would fly out and over the courtyards for all to appreciate. At a quarter to eleven of a morning, no matter where he was, he took a tiny amber box from his waistcoat pocket, pinched a bit of snuff between his fingers, inhaled it with a self-consoling air, and sneezed in a masterpiece of crescendo. This is the wildest act I ever saw him do.

Ordinarily I would take little interest in such a man, but Don

Joseph had one attribute that drew my observation. He was a Catholic. He had to be, as representative of Portugal, a Catholic country, yet there was apparently no chaplain in his suite. I did not wonder at this apparent omission since, years before, when Pierre Chanut's open Catholic services had been severely and publicly criticized, I had banned meetings of foreign denominations to please the country. But I did wonder which gentleman in the suite was the chaplain in disguise, for a noble of the Ambassador's nature would not part, I knew, with one of his most necessary habits. I wondered, too, what it would be like to talk about Catholicism, this religion that, personified by Chanut and Descartes, showed itself so vastly different than I had been taught it was by my Lutheran preceptors. Neither Chanut nor Descartes would discuss it with me, edging away into philosophy when my questions grew pertinent, and Don Joseph, even if he had had the intelligence and imagination for it, was beyond my asking since he spoke no language but his own Portuguese.

When the weather moved into the relentless cold of the winter months, Don Joseph's secretary, a man who hopped about to his master's orders like a wooden bird on a string, became ill, and a younger man with large dark eyes took his place as interpreter. The new secretary had exceptional qualities for his position, no wooden bird he, rather the holder of a live intellect that plied his duties and its excitements quite heedless of his body. His body in fact seemed in a perpetual hurry to catch up with his thoughts, so that his movements were jerky and his eyes almost popped out of his head in eagerness. When he listened to Don Joseph's statements he fastened his energy onto one enormous point of quiet, concentrating on the words as if he would extract the meaning like a physicist, then, turning to me, released a flood of translation in unhesitating Latin. Nor did Don Joseph shout at his new interpreter, treating him with a familiar courtesy, disguising his impatience with an imperial smile if the young man had to hunt for a needed paper.

Who was this earnest fellow, I inquired. The younger son of an impecunious noble Portuguese family, I was told, by name Antonio Macedo. An educated young buck, I declared, and I decided to participate in his learning. At Don Joseph's next audience with me I interpolated questions on classical writings with those on shipments of copper, and Senhor Macedo, alight with enthusiasm, showed himself a spirited and discriminating scholar. I was delighted, and, in my delight, quite forgot about the Ambassador and the business at hand, urging the young man into further discussion, enjoying my own opportunity to talk on a favorite subject to such an aware listener. When Don Joseph poked at his secretary to ask the reason for the unnecessary length of his interpreting, Senhor Macedo turned to him with a startled look, then back to me with a smile.

"Your Majesty," he said, "I have admitted to the Ambassador the indulgence in literary topics and he begs me to tell you he is not displeased you should find one of his countrymen sufficiently instructed to be worthy of your interest."

"He said no more than that?"

"That was all that was given for your ears."

"And what am I not to hear?"

"Nothing that Your Majesty would not have guessed already—that the Ambassador believes a friendliness between us will advance his business with more favor. I am authorized to be at the pleasure of Your Majesty when you wish to digress from the trade conversation."

"Must you report on these little digressions?"

"His Excellency's interests lie in other directions. He has no taste for the classics."

"Then you shall not bore him. Supposing we speak of other things, shall the Ambassador be spared a report on those, too?"

Senhor Macedo's alertness at this amused me. Did he think I intended to bribe him? Or to seduce him? His response was respectfully prim.

"It is necessary to tell His Excellency the least detail referring to the Portuguese-Swedish trade. The rest shall be left to my discretion."

"Then this, Sir, is for your discretion. I do not believe you are a secretary at all. Although you do not wear the usual habit, it is my guess you are a priest—further, that, by your learning, you have been to Rome and are a Jesuit."

"It is true, Your Majesty. I am the Ambassador's chaplain. When his secretary became ill, I was the only one capable in languages to take his place."

"Are you not afraid to be in Sweden as a Jesuit? Is there any place in the world where your order is more hated?"

"It is the charge of the Jesuits to undertake dangerous missions. There is no place in the world we will not go for the glory of God. In my case, however, I have come to accompany the Ambassador, to be his confessor. I was not sent to Sweden to spread the blessings of the Holy Church."

"But you would not turn aside from sustaining those who need you?"

He hesitated, as if sensing a trap.

"My instructions," he began, when I interrupted him, laughing.

"You need not worry, Father Macedo. I shall not betray you. I ask because I, myself, have questions about the Catholic Church I would like to have honestly answered. Will you answer them for me?"

"Your Majesty!" He glowed, he was fervent. "That you should so honor me!"

He would have gone on, but Don Joseph was clearing his throat, tapping his foot on the floor, deferentially, yes, but not to be misunderstood. He had no intention of being a silent observer for long when there was business to be attended to. There should be a limit even to the literary enthusiasms of royalty.

As I lay awake nights, putting off the hour of sleep, trying to protect myself from dreams, I called up the questions I would ask the Jesuit. What were the views and requirements of the

Church on a beneficent immortality? How did it paint its Elysian fields, and where were they? More important, how did it answer the needs of mortality? How could one live? Was Truth a chained bear in its courtyard? Or was it the risen phœnix, eternally youthful, eternally golden, whose magic each could seek in his own way? If I could once put my hand on this bird, I thought, if I could feel something warm, lasting, believable, something to temper the immense loneliness of being in the world!

What did the Roman Church think of marriage? Was it necessary? Were all women alike in its eyes, born to be purveyors of the generations? Could one escape from being a woman? Could one escape from dreams? How I dreaded the passages of the night, how I feared, yet felt drawn to them, as a quivering iron needle to its magnetic mountain! When sleep came, the gates of my mind went down, anyone could walk in. Carl Gustav came, his hair blowing, kissed me again and again, not delicately as he had brushed my pale lips as a child, but with such strength my lips burned, my whole body burned, pressed against his. And unknown men came, walked with me, holding my arm close to them, sat with me, whispered in my ear. Look, your lap has dust on it, they would say, let me brush it away, and they would brush, brush, brush on the skirt until I threw the skirt away. In the wild exercises of the night the body was King, no other throne could hold me.

When I awakened, my heart still racing, my mouth still hot with desire, Virtue was a cold star to contemplate. Where was the power I saw in it in the daylight? Was it froth to be blown away so handily, was it no more than a china cup to be broken in the fall of sleep? The passionate revulsions of the day flowed over me in the night in a dark sweet river, I was carried along, mad, erotic, intoxicated. Where was the iron order of my mind? Waking, I would shout to call it back, I would shout to the bedposts: *I want to be a man!* I had my father's masculine voice, I had his sharp mind, I had his throne. What cruelty of fate was it to give me a weak womanly body?

Emotion is a sin, said the Lutherans, emotion is a stain on the soul. Passion is natural in the blood, wrote Descartes, it can be used and controlled. Dear Descartes, come back from the dead and tell me, teach me! I am compelled to see, while the Lutherans try to bandage my eyes so I see nothing, feel nothing.

There was the instance of the Correggio painting, that glorious depiction of the nude Danaë receiving Jupiter disguised as golden rain, that was hidden from me. I was a virgin Queen, they said, I should not behold such a wicked painting. The painting was among the Emperor's treasures which had been taken by the Swedish when Hradshin Palace in Prague was captured during the war. All of the treasures had been sent to me, together with a list by General Königsmark, and I myself was overseer of the unpacking when the boxes arrived in Stockholm. Day after day wonders were unwrapped, books, paintings, jewels, sculptures of bronze, of marble, of pure alabaster. Thousands and thousands of diamonds and emeralds glittered at me, with bowls to hold them of gold, of silver, of crystal. There were chests of rare books and ancient manuscripts, the famous Gothic Silver Bible of the Four Gospels and the equally famous Devil's Bible, there were hundreds of magnificent paintings, masterpieces from all Europe, from Titian, Veronese, Carracci of the South to Dürer and Brueghel of the North. In my own hands I held a drawing by Michelangelo. These are the appurtenances of royalty, I thought, these accumulations of genius. And there were banners and embroideries, pearls, mirrors, clocks, a glove made of human skin, the head of a mermaid. But the Correggio painting was missing.

The castle was searched with no result, and I had given up hope when, through the vine of castle gossip, came a hint of where it might be. There is an old cleric, I was told, who lives in an obscure corner of the castle in an unused, unfurnished room, who wanders about picking up discarded objects for his quarters. The painting may be in his room. The Correggio was not discarded, I objected. The cleric, my informant insisted, believes himself divinely appointed to guard the spiritual well-being of Your

Majesty. Since only a smile answered my query of what that had to do with it, I ordered that I be guided to the place.

The painting was there. It was propped in front of a broken window as a screen against the cold. The old cleric, small, gaunt, large-jawed, and narrow-eyed, stood resentfully while it was taken down and carried away.

"Why did you take the painting?" I asked.

It had been abandoned, he mumbled, and it was the right size to cover the hole and keep out the snow.

"Where did you find it?"

"In a hall, among broken-up boxes and torn papers."

"Could you not see what a fine painting it is? It is a treasure that cannot be replaced. It was painted by the great Italian artist Correggio."

He screamed hoarsely: "It was painted by the Devil! It is unfit for the eyes of our Queen. I had a right to take it. It should never be seen."

"You fool!" I screamed back at him. "Who are you to say what is fit for the Queen? You stay away from my paintings!"

"God says it is unfit!"

His words rang in my ears as I left. It was the only way, I decided, the old man could get a nude woman into his room. Fix his window, I commanded, that there should be no further excuse for his plundering forbidden fruit.

The cleric had hinted the picture was obscene. Why? I had it hung in my apartment and studied it. Danaë, an exquisite girlish Danaë, lay naked on her bed, reclining against white pillows, her legs stretched apart. A curly-headed Cupid held an end of the bed-sheet between her limbs to catch the golden drops falling from a green and gold blob above, presumably Jupiter as a golden cloud. Cupid watched the Jupiter-cloud as if for a signal, Danaë regarded the golden rain in the sheet, mild and felicitous, on the edge of a smile, a smile of kindness. She might have been watching her favorite spaniel lap up his supper. Beside the bed two cherubs played with one of Cupid's darts, scratching with it on a piece of dark wood, a piece of the bed, perhaps, absorbed in their writing, whether it be their initials or Danaë's name or the date of the godly occasion or symbols of love or whatever it is cherubs write, perhaps nothing at all. The intimacy of the scene was pleasant as a summer's day, everyone comfortably naked, each one beautiful in nakedness, the flesh healthy and warmly colored, smoothly, graciously covering the bones, as blushing, as luscious around the skeleton as the peach flesh around its stone.

Correggio has painted the flesh of life, I thought, where Dürer painted the whitening flesh of death, flesh dominated by the skeleton, flesh pulled at by the bone as if it were being devoured, life being eaten away by death. It is flesh that is life, the skeleton that is death. If this picture was obscene, life was obscene, life and its dreams of charm.

If I could marry Jupiter and receive him thus, I thought on, then marriage would be a happy valley to live in. There were no bestiality, no coarse passions, no politics, no masked ambitions. I like politics everywhere except in a bedroom. And that is where the Lutherans would put it for me, politics, in the shape of a crude man, in a State bed. I would give every energy I had to the State and all the power of my mind, the depth of my loyalties and the stature of my imagination, but I would not have my body violated. I would not be raped by the State. Not while I was awake.

Was there no religion to assure peace in life as well as in death? Was there any religion that was true? Many great minds had concluded there must be one, that there was one, and no more than one, but I had not seen it. I had been raised in a war where religion was dressed as a soldier and sent out to kill for gain. Was there no religion that itself practiced Virtue as well as mouthed it? Was it only the individual who found Truth for himself? I held in my hands the precious Silver Bible of the Four Gospels. I traced with my finger the design of the fading Gothic letters across the purple pages. What devotion had inspired the lonely bishop who had made these letters over a thousand years ago, how enduring it was, this devotion, to be carried on through the centuries by the monks who guarded the pages, who almost wore them through with use, still preserving them. And the delicate decorations in the margins, the brushed gold of the columns twined with lilies, how many souls had gone through them to security, to God? Could I? Or was God lost in the past? Was God's word only a beautiful book?

If little Father Macedo was a carefully trained Jesuit he ought to be able to answer my questions, Jesuits having the reputation of being the most rigorously instructed men in the world. So I began putting my questions to him, mixing them into the trade conversations while the Ambassador sat beside us, nodding and smiling while we imposed on his ignorance. The time never was long enough for all I wanted to know, particularly since the priest was wont to answer what he wished to tell me in addition to what I asked and expected, but what I did learn made me curious for more. I was surprised when he said his Church sanctioned the free choice of a person in his seeking Truth, that, in fact, the Jesuits considered any teaching poisonous that dispensed with free will.

"That is what I believe!" I exclaimed. "I thought I was alone in it, alone, that is, with Descartes and the Greek philosophers."

"One never is as alone as one thinks," said Father Macedo.

"And love," I pushed at him. "What is your view of free will in love?"

"Do you speak of sacred love or profane love?"

There it was. I had not divided it, never.

"I speak of love itself. Are not 'sacred' and 'profane' only two of its faces? And is it true when it becomes profane?"

Father Macedo tilted his head toward the rumbling impatience of Don Joseph. "I shall give you a book that may answer your question better than I, a book on people who have spelled out love with their lives."

The book he brought to me was *The Lives of the Saints*, and it was, fortunately, of a small size so that I could carry it in my pocket and insert it within the pages of a large volume of Latin poetry to read. A Lutheran Queen could not be seen reading a Catholic book. Moreover, I found it a fascinating book. I began to see what a comfort it could be to be a Roman Catholic, to believe what so many noble minds had believed for sixteen hundred years, to belong to a religion that had been confirmed by millions of miracles and millions of martyrs, which, finally, had produced so many wonderful virgins who had surmounted the weaknesses of their sex and devoted themselves to God. That, I decided, was a good use for love, if God and Truth could be proved as one.

My dreams at night began to change. I found myself walking the seashore, searching for a lost bird, a bird not mine, but worthy of being found and cared for. There were people swimming through the calm light of the waters, whether it was moonlight or the summer night's sun I do not know, but it sparkled in soft crystal waves, and, although I never have been a swimmer, I dipped in, clothes and all, and swam easily, pleasantly. The bird would come to me, we would find one another. I did not mind that Carl Gustav was there and others I knew, for he, his body bare, boasting of his strength, swam into the shadows, away from from me. It was a dream I could waken from in peace.

Father Macedo was not the only one I questioned, for I invited many foreigners to my court, writers, artists, musicians, that culture might flow into Sweden with them. Those from the South were Catholics as a matter of course, but I did not feel I could speak openly of religion with them. I had to guard the fact of my curiosity and, garrulous with me, they might be garrulous with others about me. I asked about Rome, marvelous Rome. What was life like in this Eternal City of the Catholics?

The answers varied. Nicolas Cordier, the sculptor whom I had brought from Rome to work on the Swedish Marble Dream for the royal palace, maintained that Stockholm was a worthier place than Rome for an artist, that in Rome such jealousy and intrigue existed it was impossible to get anywhere by talent, it was a matter of relatives and connivance, and there had not been a fine sculptor anyway since Michelangelo. Now, in Stockholm he felt he was appreciated, he could work as he wished at my court, his work was praised, and I was a wonderful Queen with a wonderful court. My Cordier, I decided, is afraid he will lose his commission if he places Rome above Stockholm. How could it be better in this raw country?

Not so with the dapper Marquis du Fresne, editor of the works of the great Leonardo da Vinci, who had come from Paris to catalogue the collection of paintings I had inherited from the Emperor.

"Rome!" He would close his eyes as if to see the exalted city, inhaling slowly through his thin nostrils, breathing in the memory, then as slowly exhale, unable to contain so much beauty, his eyes opening, still focused on Rome. "Rome! The heaven of art!"

Tell me, I would urge, what is there and who is interested in it.

"Who is interested!" His pointed fingers would be lifted in amazement. "Who could not be interested? Rome is art, and art is Rome. The great families vie with one another in their collections, the Barberinis, the Farnese, the Dorias, the Borghese, ah, how pleasant it is to walk in the gardens of Prince Borghese arguing the virtues of the painters! And to converse in the exquisite Carracci gallery of the Farnese Palace, so exquisite, so inspiring, one cannot speak without believing oneself a philosopher!

"And the Vatican Palace! One does not live until one has seen it. There art brings us the glorification of Virtue in life, there in 'The Last Judgment,' where the rocks of Time are strewn with souls, we may see ourselves, in joy or in horror, as we have been or may be, we may see a path through eternity made by the hands of Michelangelo. Michelangelo, the Master's rival! We may wonder what Leonardo would have done if he had gained such an opportunity to probe his profundity. Botticelli, Perugino, Pintoricchio, Rosselli, Della Gatta, Ghirlandaio, what visions they have carried to the walls of that Sistine Chapel! What is there in the world to equal it?

"Yet, for me, the preference in all Rome is for the *Stanze* of Raphael. He is an artist of life, of the live man, not the dead soul. For Raphael, Time is a stage on whose steps geniuses gather. The very lips of his Petrarch bespeak poetry, the weariness of creation is in his seated Michelangelo. Who can say, seeing this figure, that life is not serious beyond the walls of thought, that it is not weary? His laureled Dante has no feature that does not admit his mastery of tragedy, the stern sad mouth, the thin nose, the cheeks sucked to the bone, the dark, penetrating eyes. There is not a weak line, not a gay one. He is a man looking at the cold structure of tragedy. Behold, he seems to say, the sadness of Truth, the tragedy of love. If we do not master it, we die, we die although we live.

"And his other figures, their activity! One hurrying this way, another turning that way, seated, rising, pointing, talking, judging, filling space as it never has been filled before. His Popes, his soldiers, his maidens, his saints, they are alive, they are lyrical. They swell our picture of life so we may begin to recognize what it is and what we ourselves feel. Ah, my dear Majesty, when one walks from those rooms into the common light of the streets, men and women take on new sizes, new colors, new meanings, for our eyes have been painted by the genius of this man."

Did he not exaggerate, I once asked.

The Marquis seemed to shiver in surprise. "How can one exaggerate life?" he protested.

Best of all my guides for Rome, however, was Tomasso, Tomasso of the golden tenor voice and the magical guitar. Tomasso was one of the most engaging gossips I ever knew. Neither malicious nor purposely scandalous, he had a sharp eye and an absolute delight in everything concerning people. People and Rome, those were his subjects. His Italianate gestures made his hands as voluble as his speech as he described the arguments on the dome of St. Peter's Cathedral, the musical doors of St. John's Baptistery, what the Pope ate for breakfast, how Bernini won the commissions of his fountains, why the prostitutes wore yellow, how many race horses one of the cardinals kept, the cost of an entertainment at the Barberini Palace, how, in the early days of the Church, there had been a woman Pope.

"A woman Pope!" This, I thought, was a more extraordinary religion than I had supposed.

"Pope Joan. But she could not remain so. Not after she had a baby in the papal procession."

"Why did she have a baby?" The fool, I was thinking.

Tomasso's brown eyes were gentle. "Because she was a woman." Which seemed a sufficient answer to him.

Yes, Tomasso had been everywhere in Rome, he had seen everybody, heard everything. Better than being a political prince, a priest, or even a valet for secrets, he said, was to be a musician. People talk to you or in front of you or about you, almost believing you are part of the music. To be a musician was to be in demand everywhere, from the greatest palace to the humblest tavern. The Pope himself had a papal musician to compose oratorios, cantatas, all kinds of music, not only sacred. If ours is the age for music, Rome is the heart of the age.

"Everyone in Rome loves music," he said. "The carriers sing as they push their carts through the streets, the cooks trill as they mix their pasta, out of the open windows float those sweet little notes of the lute, sometimes of the deep viol, or the *ping ping* of the harpsichord. Anyone who is clever may study free at Mazzocchi's school, to sing, to play, to read poetry. And the composers!"

He would list them, Marrazoli, Abbatini, Carissimi, many more I had not heard of, and of how places were turned inside out to produce their musical entertainments, while, in the churches, when the chorals were sung, the angels joined in to swell the glorious sound.

How could I, with a passion for art and for music, not burn to visit Rome?

"It almost is worth turning Catholic to live in Rome!" I exclaimed, but I laughed as I spoke. Such a remark could not be taken seriously.

Tomasso plucked at the strings of his guitar. "One day I shall be going back to Rome. Not long, not too long from now. I long for the sun. I shall be playing again at the festivals and the banquets, I shall be singing with my brothers in the chorus of my little church on saints' days, I shall be drinking wine with my friends and giving them the tale of my adventures in the North. And I shall tell them about Your Majesty, about the wonderful Queen of this snow country and how she loves Rome from afar."

"No," I cautioned. We were not alone, of course, but among a group of my young favorites at an informal display at the castle. "Tell them that the Queen of Sweden has the aim of making Stockholm the cradle of learning and art in the North as Rome is in the South. Perhaps I shall not let you return!"

But Tomasso would return, I knew. He was one of a group of Italian musicians that traveled from court to court, a year here, a year there, but always back to Rome.

"Come near me, Tomasso, and sing from Monteverdi's *Orfeo*," I commanded.

As he settled his chair and tested the tune of his guitar, I leaned toward him and spoke in a low voice for him alone.

"Be careful what you say of me, here or in Rome, Tomasso. But inquire discreetly when you return to Rome and select some learned man with whom I may correspond, some high dignitary of the Church, perhaps, of my tastes. I shall make it worth your effort, your quiet effort."

Tomasso nodded and smiled as he let his perfect voice soar into a shepherd's song. When the time came for his troupe's departure he would need no further reminding. I was sure he had a fancy for secret messages, that many intrigues before this had been woven into his pleasure of living.

It was almost a year after the coronation when an announcement cut into the enjoyment of my self-arranged instruction on Rome and its Church. Don Joseph decided to leave for Portugal with his suite. I had prolonged the conversations as much as I could, but I could not keep him indefinitely in Stockholm. What would I do without Father Macedo? Instead of satisfying my curiosity in our private snatches of talk under the Ambassador's nose, he had intensified it, and my mind is one that cannot rest when it has set out on a search, not until the object, the understanding, is attained. I could not stop, I would not.

If I could not keep Father Macedo, I would have to have another Jesuit, and two would be better, to continue my inquiry. We had not even finished our comparison of Greek philosophers and Catholic scholastics. Macedo had provoked me by asserting that Plato was by nature a Catholic, that if he lived now he might have been Pope, because his mind had reached toward the Supreme Good, which, he said, we now know is God. As his authority he quoted Justin Martyr's conclusion: *Whatever things were rightly said among all men are the property of us Christians.* I remembered that Plato had defined political science as the science of the soul, and declared that the ideal State could exist within the soul of a just man. Was this the aim of the Catholic Church in seeking its territory of souls, to create the ideal State? Macedo did not have time to answer.

Thus, the day I received the news of the intended departure of the Portuguese party, I sent for the earnest Father to attend me in my library, saying I had a business of consequence to tell him. The month was August, a warm indolent August whose usual rains had held back, a happy season when everything was blue and green and golden, when hope was easy and fear a crumb one threw to the birds. The windows of my library were opened wide to the world, letting in lazy city noises and the salty accent of The Stream. Ships at anchor bobbed on the blue water, their masts a drama of sticks in the sky. With all my hate of the sea I would have liked, at that moment, to be embarking to sail to Rome. Where were they going, and when? There was a list among my papers. I found it and laid it on my table and was scanning it, humming a tune, when Macedo, his brow damp from hurrying, was shown into the room. I motioned to my secretary to leave us alone as I greeted him.

"The sun is too much for you, Senhor. You have stayed too frequently in the shade of your books."

I indicated a chair across from me at the table, and, immediately the door was safely closed, began to reveal my plan.

"Father Macedo, you are the first Jesuit I have known, and, by the practice and revelation I have had of your virtue, I suppose I may be confident of your faithfulness and prudence. Now, since you are to depart, I desire by all means that you will procure me two Italians of your Society, who are expert in all knowledge, to be sent here. I would like to have them stay at my court under the color of gentlemen who desire to see the world, that I may make use of them without suspicion."

An expression of joy enlivened the priest's face. He clasped his hands, whether in prayer or thankfulness I do not know.

"Has Your Majesty—?"

"No."

He beseeched me. "Why does not Your Majesty consummate your holy aspirations?"

I waved away his enthusiasm. "If I were convinced the Roman religion was best, I would embrace it. I can say no more than that I wish to have two Jesuit Fathers sent to me with whom I may converse freely and in such a way that there can be no suspicion of who they are. If their identity is discovered, I will be ruined as well as they."

"Yes, Your Majesty, yes. I shall go to Rome and deliver your request to the General of our Company. I am sure he will send two Fathers to you. Thank you, thank you, for your confidence in me! I swear you can depend on my faithfulness in serving you."

"When can you leave?"

"The Ambassador has set our departure for the middle of September, in a month's time."

"I cannot wait so long. You must leave tomorrow."

"Tomorrow?" He barely hesitated. "I shall go immediately to Don Joseph to request his permission."

"Not for Rome! He might suspect some unusual affair."

"For Hamburg, then, which is on the way." His eyes were popping in eagerness. "I shall ask permission to visit the city for my own curiosity, implying I have friends there whom I would like to see before traveling back to Portugal. I shall, then, hasten directly to Rome with your message and be in Lisbon by the time the Ambassador arrives."

"Your secrecy must be absolute."

"You need not doubt me, Your Majesty."

I sighed and relaxed. I felt the sun again. "In two hours I will have a letter ready for your General, and a ship chosen for your journey. Come back then."

He left me, almost tripping in his gratitude, while I turned to compose my letter. It had to be worded carefully lest it be lost and read by an unsympathetic person. I said nothing of the two Jesuits I wanted, but, after asking the General's friendship and favor, begged him to comply with the proposal I had entrusted to Father Macedo. It was a simple letter. I might have been requesting some learned or musical manuscript, some small example of Church sculpture, something to be found only in Rome.

In two hours Father Macedo returned to my library, his face lined in dejection. The Ambassador had refused him permission to leave, had screamed at him in irritation that he knew very well how necessary his services were in concluding his business at court, and that he could make his Hamburg visit later as the party traveled south.

"Then you cannot assist me," I said.

"I am resolved to serve you, Your Majesty. What can I do?"

"You may leave without saying anything to anyone."

"Leave, saying nothing," he whispered. "Yes, if you wish it."

"There is a vessel at Balen, thirty-five miles away, ready to set sail for Lübeck in Holstein. From Holstein you will be able to proceed quickly to Rome at this season. You must make your way to Balen alone, tonight. I will give you papers to board the ship."

He looked at me in astonishment. "In which direction is Balen?"

I pulled a map from my German chest, unfolded it on the table, and laid my finger on the port. He examined it, and copied a part of the plan while I explained the roads, the fields, the villages he might pass through. He would find it, he vowed, he would find it and be on the ship when she set out to sea.

"If anyone stops you, you must declare you are a free man and not subject to Swedish law. Above all, you must not mention my name."

"You may depend on me, Your Majesty. God bless you and keep you safe," he said, signing the cross.

Then, with my letter and his ship papers secreted within his shirt, he was gone.

XIII

THE next day the court rocked with excitement. Macedo had disappeared, no one knew why or whence. A frantic Don Joseph arrived at the door of my reception room on the heels of the chamberlain sent to request an audience. He was babbling in Portuguese, his old wooden secretary, whose illness had thawed out in the summer heat, behind him, trying to catch his words and pass them to me.

When the Ambassador was able to control his storming sufficiently for me to hear the translation, I gathered that Macedo was a despicable fellow who had betrayed him, that Jesuits had no loyalty except to their own order, that he could not be allowed to escape to sell his secrets to some other power the Church angled to catch in its political net. I was petitioned to send after him immediately and bring him back to Stockholm by force. He should be put in prison where he could be kept quiet. Let him pray for his own salvation. He was the last person Don Joseph needed to assist him with his.

"This man was a Jesuit! Why did you not tell me before?" I put incredulity into my question.

"I was afraid Your Majesty would not accept him as an interpreter, and he was the only one I had."

"How do you know he has betrayed you?"

"Why else would he flee?"

"Then you have discovered some documents are missing?"

"We are searching to see what he has taken, but even if he has taken none, his head is full of diplomatic business and God knows what he will do with it!"

"What a wretch he must be!"

Don Joseph bowed. "I most earnestly request that Your Majesty and Your Majesty's government assume the responsibility for his return."

I drew a long breath. "We will do so."

"He must have fled to the sea. Where else would he go? Or he might be hiding now on one of those ships." He shook an accusing finger at the men-of-war in the harbor, his voice rising. "They must be searched!"

I became cold. "I have assumed the responsibility, Your Excellency."

Don Joseph, in the act of taking out his amber snuffbox for his morning sneeze, stopped, remembered his position, his representative dignity. Hastily he pocketed the box, mumbled his uncertain gratitude, and left, nursing his fury.

My next visitor, before I had an opportunity to act officially on the flight, was Chancellor Oxenstierna. Where Don Joseph had been explosive Oxenstierna was constrained in his anger, but he was as pressured, if not more so. Had I heard of the disappearance? I had. What did the man know of Sweden's affairs that could damage us? What a fool the Ambassador was to have such a slippery fellow with him! Why did he not have the sense to check on the members of his suite before he left Portugal! That was the trouble with foreigners, particularly the southern ones, always procrastinating, always open to bribes, always overlooking loopholes to danger. Only the Swedes could be trusted.

"Senhor Macedo seemed more interested in poetry than in politics," I said. "He did not appear a dangerous man."

"Looks cannot be trusted. Particularly in young men." The Chancellor was grim. "We must find him and take him into custody at once."

"I already have issued orders to do so," I lied. "I have told His

Excellency I would assume the responsibility for his return. And I am determined not to receive any more of these wicked Jesuits at court."

Oxenstierna glanced at me sharply. "A Jesuit! How do you know he is a Jesuit?"

"Don Joseph admitted it this morning."

"No, there must not be another Jesuit in Sweden. Not one. We shall take steps to prevent it this afternoon. Your Majesty, I have taken the liberty of calling a meeting of the Council for this afternoon. May we expect your gracious presence?"

Yes, I would be there, I told him, and begged the Chancellor not to be so deeply disturbed about the flight, that it might not be anything at all, the man might be lying drunk in an obscure tavern or fallen ill on a walk in the woods, that he had no wings with which to fly away, no magical way to vanish in a land we knew so much better than he. The old man listened, rightfully skeptical, then bowed his leave.

As soon as he had gone I summoned an officer to pursue Macedo. I handed him the order for his arrest, told him it was believed the chaplain had fled to some seaport, that if he found him he was to bring him back to Stockholm and put him in prison, that such was my royal command.

The officer turned to go, to hasten to his horse, when I stopped him.

"Wait. That is not all, Sir. I have private orders for you that are even more important. Come closer that I do not need to shout. These orders you must follow exactly. Exactly! I cannot have you fail. I have been speaking in a friendly manner with this man as the Ambassador's interpreter and it is impossible for me to turn about and be responsible for his death. The Ambassador is so angry I am sure he means to have him killed when the man may not have done anything at all beyond a love tryst. If you find the chaplain, you must use every argument to persuade him to return with you willingly. You may promise him that if he does so, we will pacify the Ambassador for his conduct. If, however, he is so obstinate as to refuse, then you must order him to leave the country at once as I have no wish to stain my hands with his blood. If this happens, and he leaves Sweden, you will have to pretend to the Ambassador on your return that you have been unable to seize him. Do you understand?"

The officer assured me he did, grabbed my hand to kiss it as if in gratitude for my mercy and my understanding of the weaknesses of poor common men, and left.

I had done all I could. If each one did as he had been directed, everything should be all right. Yet I worried, the rest of the morning, the noontime, the early afternoon hours. Had I been too impulsive in sending Macedo now? Should I have curbed my curiosity, stilled the demands of my soul, practiced patience, let Macedo wait until after he had left Sweden with the Portuguese party before leaving them to go to Rome? Then I would not be so involved, so in danger. What would the Council have discovered, what would they have to say?

Oxenstierna had been responsible for the religious statute of 1617, established years before I was born, which he would not hesitate to invoke, nor would the others. It reads: *Whomsoever from this day onward, of whatever class of society he may be, falls away from our true Christian faith and evangelical doctrine, shall have neither house nor home, nor enjoy any inheritance, right, or privilege within the boundaries of Sweden, but shall be regarded and considered in matters of inheritance and other rights as dead, and be outlawed in Sweden.* The words were black and white in meaning. I would not be spared because I was Queen. I would be deprived of my crown, have my revenues taken away. I would be a ghost, a pauper without a country. Would it not be better to give up the crown voluntarily, to ask for a sustaining income, to live in some other more kindly capital of the world? That is, if I were not condemned already in their minds.

When the Councillors gathered in their chamber I searched their faces for clues. They were solemn, foreboding, except for old Jacob de la Gardie, still genial although he had grown fully blind, his head tipped back to smell the life around him, his sensitive fingers rarely quiet. It was he who tried to brush aside the importance of Macedo's flight, speaking in his quavering voice.

"Magnus says he could not resist the ladies. He says the Portuguese are like the Italians, they go quite mad at the sight of blue eyes and flaxen hair. These poor Catholic priests! Once let them out of their barn and they run like wild colts. I would like to see the pretty girl who made this one into a Lutheran!"

But no one laughed with him. It was a precarious time for Sweden, Oxenstierna said. Our finances were in a shockingly low condition, depleted by the expenses of the coronation, by the slowness of the payments coming in from our conquered territories, by the fact that we had less from the war than we had deserved, and that Her Majesty had seen fit to excuse certain towns from any payments at all.

"They were historic towns, ancient seats of culture," I countered, "and they had been devastated by the war. They had not the means to pay anyway. We need not be slave-drivers because we have won."

And because, the Chancellor continued, Her Majesty also had excused the bönder from certain taxes, so that the nobles, the officers of the land, had not the money to preserve the State. The importance of the chaplain's disappearance was in what he could tell other powers about us, his flight showed him to be unreliable, and it was most unfortunate that Sweden was in such a low condition that she could be taken advantage of by an unfriendly power who was given the facts. Was it not common knowledge that the Jesuits were devoted to the Emperor? We must be ready for an emergency. The Jesuit might have copied secret papers, might have eavesdropped, might have learned anything. Who knows with whom he connived?

My hands seemed to be frozen in spite of the warmth of the day. I brought them carefully to the table top to steady myself.

"My Lords. I cannot believe Sweden is in such danger as the Chancellor claims, but I have something to say to you. I am resolved to give up the crown. It is not a meet position for a woman. I am convinced that a man with strength to fight and to lead soldiers should be the ruler of Sweden. I assure you, my concern is for the good of the State."

No. The word was echoed vigorously by each Councillor.

The Chancellor leaned forward. "This announcement has come on me unawares, Your Majesty, and it is one that brings tears to my old eyes. Men are born for toil and troubles, especially Kings and sovereigns. If Your Majesty finds the burden too heavy, we will assist you. Councillors, we must join together to persuade the Queen to abandon her intention."

His eyes were moist, and I felt the tears spring to my own eyes in relief and surprise. I realized I had not expected to be safe, certainly I had not expected the unanimous support of the Council to keep me on the throne. I answered that I would be pleased to accept their assistance, particularly that of the Chancellor in the State finances. I had been blamed for their low condition, but I inherited the lack of funds, I had not made them. Were not countries always complaining of being impoverished? I would appreciate the Chancellor's experience in carrying this responsibility.

It was somewhat of a shock to have the Chancellor's friendship again, as I had had it as a child, the years of contention suddenly over. It is not I, it is the State he values, I thought, so we have that in common, and not another person in Sweden could handle finances as cleverly as he. He would be a rock to depend on, unless—always there was that *unless*—he discovered my intrigue.

Sometimes I believe Macedo's flight succeeded because it was August, because it was a sleepy summer, because in the fragrance of foliage and late flowers, with the dry taste of dust and the languid amusements of birds around, a sense of pleasantness breeds. How could a man's word be untrue any more than the flashing waters of Lake Mälaren were untrue? Sunlight melts anger and fear soundlessly, faultlessly, unreservedly disposing of shadows, turning suspicion into the simplicity of yellow leaves.

Who could doubt a man going to Balen to be free? Doubt is for dark winter months, and for castles whose gray halls and brocaded rooms hold on to winter all the year. Who would not flee a stone sepulcher for the open warmth of August?

When the pursuing officer returned to report, he said he had been unable to uncover the hiding-place of the Jesuit, that he might have fled north to Dalarna with the aid of friends, in which case it would be impractical, in fact, impossible, to find him in the immense stretches of forest and mountains. And he gave back to me the order for his arrest.

Confidentially he told me he had come upon Macedo in Balen and had talked to him. He urged him to return to his duties in Stockholm to avoid a scandal, but Macedo answered he was a free man, that he had committed no crime and he would not return to Stockholm to possible imprisonment. The officer then declared that the government in Sweden had the right to decide who could be in the country and who could not, that if he would not return to Stockholm, he must take his departure on the first ship. This Macedo peaceably agreed to do. So, Your Majesty, the officer concluded, we are rid of him.

Yes, we were rid of him, but not of the scandal. The Ambassador spread his fury all over Europe, writing to everyone he knew how his chaplain had turned out to be a knave, how he was a traitor to his sovereign and a deserter of his faith. He had met Satan in Sweden and fled in his company, or in her company. The court was convinced he was too young, too brown-eyed, too romantic, for were not all Southerners romantic, to have escaped the enterprising Swedish girls. That was the real reason, they said, there was nothing to do but to laugh about it.

The winter of waiting had little to recommend it. Oxenstierna proved a wizard at finance, while my solid friend Adler Salvius grew sickly, and, some months later, died. Tomasso and his musical troupe left for the South, some of the scholars left, other scholars arrived, among them the notable, the consciously notable, Claude de Saumaise. His patron, the exiled English King,

Charles II, proposed marriage and was refused, and his rival, the English writer John Milton, wrote a challenging account called *A Defense of the People of England* wherein he claimed the people of a land had a right to put on trial a man as a tyrant, whether or not he was a King, and that a King, above any others, should love Virtue and follow it. I heartily agreed with this point, both privately and publicly, thus winning the annoyance of my guest Monsieur de Saumaise, who, nevertheless, did not leave, and the unstinting praise of the unknown Mr. Milton.

One day I thought my Jesuit had arrived when a priest was blown by a tempest onto the shores of Sweden, but he was not destined for me. He made no secret of being a Jesuit, returning to Spain from his post with the Spanish Ambassador in Denmark, and he left as soon as the weather became more temperate. It seemed to me I was sitting on a vast iceberg waiting to receive, to read, a Great Book whose pages would be wings for me.

It was Carl Gustav, who had retired to prepare for his future by drinking beer at his country estate, who sent me the disturbing message of the winter. He wrote me an uneasy letter that he feared all was not well in Sweden, attaching an anonymous pamphlet accusing the Queen of ruining the Kingdom, of being the pawn of the Chancellor and the De la Gardies, whose main aim, it declared in flaming language, was to keep Carl Gustav out of the government, preferably by a timely poisoning. Carl Gustav, therefore, was summoned to the defense of his country, awaiting his word to arise, he was to take arms for its sake and murder the Queen and her Councillors, to ascend the throne himself.

The letter and the pamphlet reached me late in the evening. It was in December, I remember, for I was sitting next to the stove in my bedchamber, a candelabrum pulled close so I could read the poorly written message, and I was startled when my chamberlain hurried in to say my officer Governor Fleming had intelligence of the utmost importance for me. I had him brought in, a big, red-cheeked man, well whiskered, to hear, again, the story I had just read. Someone had betrayed the conspirators and the officer had hastened to me to get an order for their arrest. They must be apprehended immediately, he said. I regarded him for a few minutes, quietly, then decided to be outspoken.

"What you say, My Lord, is well judged, but what do you say of the hereditary prince? I may know more than you, for I know they have communicated their damnable project to Prince Carl Gustav. You are in his confidence. What do you think of it?"

He had no hesitation in answering. "It is very possible. But what I know for certain is that His Royal Highness does not bite the hook."

"Then, in order to get an exact knowledge of the conspirators, we must let the matter come to a rising and have them all together on the stage before we drop the curtain and catch them all in a trap. We may have a battle in it, but I fear the issue not a jot. Not with my people."

For some reason the officer was horrified, either at the idea of bloodshed or of taking such a daring attitude, when all that need be done was to make certain arrests. Everything would be known in good time, he assured me, and the matter would be taken care of with no noise made. That was the best way.

I allowed his counsel to prevail, but, in as many days as it took an express rider to go to my cousin's estate and back, I had another letter from Carl Gustav informing me of the author of the pamphlet, and, thus, of the conspirators. He had traced the pamphlet to a page in his service whose father had sworn my downfall. Arnold Messen. I rubbed my finger across his name. There was a man to whom I had tried to do good. Long before I had been on the throne he had been imprisoned with his father, a hot-minded scholar and politician who had died in prison, and all because they had been implicated in a plot to smuggle a Jesuit into Sweden. I had released Arnold Messen when I became Queen, appointed him my historiographer, given him a pension, and raised him to the nobility. He could not have fared better, if as well, if he had not been in prison those years. But because I compelled him to make restitution to a sister he had mistreated, his gratitude turned to hate. Sometimes I believe gratitude is hate. Now he wished to murder me.

Messen was arrested and confessed readily—worse, he boasted that the finest men in the Kingdom were co-conspirators and named them, men such as Nils Nilson, one of my close advisers, the leader of the burghers. He even hinted that Carl Gustav had been open to listening to his scheme. Suddenly I found I did not want to know it all, and, after the necessary trial, I ordered the records destroyed. They were lies, they had to be lies. It could not be these men who had worked with me, planned with me. They were acquitted, all but the Messens, who had to be executed.

Natures like theirs, Oxenstierna told me, should be treated like a fire which we must furnish with the right material to feed upon, to prevent them from doing evil. And who is going to be the nursemaid of the fire, I asked, I? As Queen I am the mother of the country, not of each man. Had he no responsibility of his own, he, a scholar, for Virtue?

It is well to remember from this, all ladies who would like to be Queen, that there is no one to be trusted absolutely, that there is no time when, with a sharp true look, you may not find yourself in a web of lies.

I still was adjusting my mind to the outcome of the plot when the Jesuits arrived, so clever in their disguise I did not recognize them. Perhaps it was because I was close to giving up hope. Seven months had gone by with no word, enough time for as many journeys, I thought, for anyone who was serious in his hurrying. The whole project must have failed. No one was interested. Or perhaps it was because they were presented to me as distinguished Italian friends of Baron Rosenhane, a conservative noble of Oxenstierna's party, friends who had traveled north with him from France whom he had persuaded to attend the Swedish court, insisting his Queen would be delighted with their remarkable knowledge of history and literature.

His Queen was not at all delighted at first. I had presented to me a Roman-nosed Signor Casati, who breathed heavily through his mouth as he rolled off courteous trivialities and vague allusions to historic figures. Every date he gave was wrong, every description trite. Just what the Baron would choose for me, I thought, a helpless hapless person who calls himself a scholar. The second gentleman, Signor Malines, was old and elegant and plump, with round eyes, a round mouth, a soft voice. His favorite position was in a chair pulled close to a green porcelain stove, where he would sit, yawning, buttoning and unbuttoning his brocaded waistcoat for exercise, on his knee an open volume of Corneille, whose pages he never was seen to turn.

It was only because they were Italians that I decided to ask them if they had brought any word to me from Rome. One evening, as we were leaving a banquet in the castle where they had been included as guests, I motioned that they precede me in passing through a door. When they were near, I tilted my head forward and whispered in French.

"Perhaps you have letters for me."

The Italians walked on as if they had not heard. Neither head turned. But a low "yes" came back to me.

"Do not mention them to anyone," I ordered, as quietly.

There is a flavor, a spicy tang, to the triumph of an intrigue that rarely is equaled. One has outwitted the world, one has passed, invisible, among one's opponents. Any deceit has been absolved by success. It is the brilliant performance of a drama in which one is both playwright and chief actor. What does it matter that one is the audience, too? When I opened the letters identifying the Italians as the Jesuits sent by the Company in Rome, my ears rang with my own applause. Now Baron Rosenhane would be praised for his protégés, he would be complimented on breaking the dullness of the winter by bringing to his Queen two gentlemen with whom she could be entertained with conversations on history. He need never know it was the history of the soul.

In my library, the day after the discovery, I greeted Father

Paolo Casati, Professor of Mathematics in Rome, and Father Francesco Malines, Professor of Theology in Turin, ready, sensible scholars who shed any pretense of vacuity once the door was closed behind them. What had taken so long, I asked, what had happened to Father Macedo?

"Your Majesty's letter created a dilemma in Rome." Father Malines sighed, remembering. "When Father Macedo arrived after six weeks of painful travel, for he was alone and poor, he found the General of our Company, Father Piccolomini, to whom your letter was addressed, was dead. He tendered the letter to the Vicar-General, Father Goswin Nikel, but he refused to do anything about it. He is a German, he had been in the war, and he could not forget what the Jesuits suffered because of the Swedish soldiers. And it was too delicate a negotiation for him. He does not know how to manage such things. The letter was a nettle in his hands.

"Finally he confided in a friend, Cardinal Chigi. You will recall Cardinal Chigi was the Pope's delegate at the peace congress, so he is versed in Your Majesty's reputation. The Cardinal was in great joy at the news. He welcomed the task, and invites your confidence. It is he who has made all the arrangements, who chose Father Casati and me, and sent us on our way. Father Macedo remains in Rome for the present. He does not dare to return to Portugal until the exquisite reason for his flight can be made known. He implored us all to secrecy. I assure you, Your Majesty, no one in Rome, besides the few persons I have named, has heard of your letter or the purpose of our journey, which was given out to be to France."

"The Pope was informed, of course."

"Cardinal Chigi judged it best not to speak of it to His Holiness."

I frowned at this. "Why not?"

Father Casati answered in his quick, rather sharp voice. "It is his sister, Olimpia. She is not to be trusted. She might not like the prospect of a great Queen becoming a Catholic. She loves importance for herself. Your Majesty is too brilliant a woman for her to like you."

"I have not said I intended to become a Catholic, Father."

The two men blinked, as if wondering why they had come.

"Your journey was pleasant, I trust."

"No, unfortunately no," said Father Malines. "I am too old and fat for these arduous trips. I have spent as many days on my back as on my feet since we left. I am not used to the cold, and I do not like the ice. In our eagerness to hurry here we pressed our horses too hard, my beast slipped and fell, carrying me down with him. I was in bed for days. Such weather!"

He looked at the window, crusted with snow. There was no view through it, only a pattern of frozen flakes.

"We are not familiar with snow in Rome. In northern Italy it lies silently on the ground where it belongs, but in the North the snow rises and swirls, slapping at the face like white demons, blinding the eyes, finding the least opening in clothes to slide, wet and cold, against the skin. We rode through white fields among black trees week after week, mile after mile, until we could not tell the weeks from the miles, for they seemed frozen together. It was a blessing to meet your Baron Rosenhane and win his friendship and his carriage."

"Your laborious journey will not have been in vain if I can feel satisfied," I said.

What was it I wished to know, they asked, they were eager to answer any questions. Did I wish to read holy literature? They had brought books, carefully bound and titled as profane histories. They had with them the great Bellarmine, who had answered, once and for all, the controversies between the Christians and the heretics, who clearly demonstrated the falseness of Luther's divergence.

It was not the dispute between churches that concerned me, I told them, it was the dispute within my own soul. My questions could not be answered by books, for I wanted answers as direct as my questions. How could I identify evil? What was the mark whereby I could tell the difference between evil and good? Was it utility? Was it the beneficence of the end? How could it seem to change colors like a chameleon? Would they bring me the answer in two days?

The Fathers shifted uneasily in their chairs. Father Malines pursed his round lips, lifted his eyebrows. Father Casati sniffed noisily up his big nose, smiled thinly. Yes, they would speak to me of evil, they would come to me at any time I appointed, they would do their best to satisfy me.

They came, for two months they came to me in my library and talked, Father Malines in his slow dreaming voice, Father Casati in his sharp nasal accents. They worked diligently, but rarely pleased me. I had to have answers I could use, I said, my life and my soul were separated, I needed to know how to bring them together. I was a Queen constantly faced with critical decisions, millions of people depended on what I said and did, I realized what a fearful reckoning I would owe to God if I did not perform my duties rightly, the realization haunted me at night, and I had to have a measure of rightness that would not fail, that I would not fall in the trap of believing I was doing good and finding I had evil results. I could not have peace until I knew, I had to have peace, I had to know Virtue, I had to know evil, I had to know evil's form, and the smell of its breath as it approached.

Evil is known by his serpent's tail, they would say, and the touch of evil is sharp and disturbing, like a drop of water hitting a rock. When the soul is evil Satan can enter softly and silently through open doors as into his own house. Saint Ignatius teaches how the Creator alone has the right to go in and out of the soul, how His touch, the touch of good, is light and sweet to the soul, like a drop of water falling into a sponge, but the wicked angel pretends to this touch, the wicked angel, the false dove, enters the soul disguised as the angel of light and turns the soul about, turns the holy thought to the perverse, and comes out undisguised, his depraved purpose bared as the wings of light unfold as wings of darkness. The dove seems to become a serpent, but it always has been a serpent.

Reason, I must have reason, I would say, I must have something I can see. Since Truth is the triumph of reason, there must be steps leading to it.

And they would say that the revelation of Truth was beyond reason, that the pillars of faith rose above any vision of numbers. All the numbers in the world and the infinite numbers of the universe, piled like sticks, could not reach the cloud of unknowing. Reason walks in her sleep, they would say, reason lifts up her hand to strike, but what will she strike? How high does her hand go?

Oh, I told them, they might as well return to Rome, they were wasting their heads on me, for I never could become a Catholic with a whole heart. They spoke of their abstract faith, yet they worshipped little pieces of wood and stone, images and idols. They had not departed from the pagans.

Images mean what those who use them wish them to mean, they would argue, and in a picture those who have learned no letters, who cannot spell out the Holy Word of the Bible, may behold what they shall adore. Paintings are the books of the ignorant.

Paintings, I would exclaim, paintings of God's family, of saints, of angels bearing souls to heaven! How can you prove it? How can you prove the soul of man is immortal?

Faith, faith, they would whisper.

How can you prove God cares anything at all about the creatures in this terrifying world? How can you prove He has any design to protect a good man? When I am strong, I win, when I am weak, I lose. I ask you, how can you prove Providence exists?

Faith, they would insist. The revelation of Truth is beyond reason.

The Fathers persisted and pursued, akin to the birds that patiently rebuild their nest whenever it is torn away from them, but they began to show their worry, for while their answers satisfied themselves, they did not satisfy me. Was I not an alien hawk's child?

Alone, I would ask myself if I ever could have faith without reason. Had I ever had a revelation without realizing what it was? Suppose I were to cease thinking of God as the end of a theological discussion and approach the idea of Him without prejudice, in their way, as a Pure Spirit, as the Spirit whose touch I had felt whenever I had sensed joy and goodness. When had that been?

A vivid memory arose of the furious rides I had taken as a girl, sometimes racing through the pine woods with my cousin, sometimes alone, galloping across the fields near Lake Mälaren, I felt again those intoxicating hours when I was a creature of the sun, its shining liquid flowing through my veins, as I plunged through the dappled light tinged with green. I was the winged rider dispersing phantasms of evil, I was Bellerophon on Pegasus, half flying through enchanted woods to slay the monster, with the lion's head and the dragon's tail, that vomited flame. I was Mercury, with the wind in my eyes. In the thoughtlessness, the breathlessness, the scampering emotions of those rides, was there a touch of God? Could I fly again through forests of hours with the sun and wind combing my hair?

Was it true the Catholics trusted emotions, as the Lutherans distrusted them? Could it be so that the emotions were not wicked, that they were not stallions to be hooded and checked with an iron bit?

And the moments when I thrilled to the words of Plato. Were those touched by God, too? The power to see the light exists in the soul, Plato said. As the eye turns with the whole body from darkness to light, so the mind turns with the movement of the whole soul, from a becoming to the brightest of being, life in goodness. The soul turns. My mind jumped. That was a conversion, the turning of the soul!

Perhaps the Fathers were trying to tell me in their stumbling earnestness that passion has eyes we know not of, that we see God with other eyes than those blind sockets given to tabulating the furniture of the world, that in passion, rising, we behold God. But to sense God, I thought, to be able to whisper in His ear, need not mean choosing a Church, the dividing of souls into churches being the work of man, not of God. Still, my reason nudged me, God is not a tyrant. He would not have instilled in man the feelings of wanting religious support without having provided a means of satisfaction. He stirs a soul to a question that He may give the answer. A vagrant notion rose of God as a prism, each side, each religion, reflecting a color of the same pure light, falling effusively, indiscriminately, in rainbows. No, as Cicero had decided there must be only one true religion, so I believed there could be only one true vessel for His Authority on earth, even as I was the only divine instrument for rule in Sweden. God is The Authority, I said to myself, and because I am Queen and closer to Him than common minds, I should be one of the foremost in recognizing His will, I should be able to judge the true religion, I knew His word by heart, I had read of His saints and virgins.

Virgins. I remembered my first reaction to Roman Catholicism, when I was nine years old and heard that celibacy was celebrated in that Church. "How beautiful!" I had exclaimed. "I want to profess this religion!" Perhaps I had begun to be a Catholic then, perhaps I was just arousing to a decision that had been made long ago, perhaps it was decision itself that was peace.

On a cool May morning when Father Malines and Father Casati came to my library for our regular discussion, I pointed to the windows, clear and free of frost, although snow still spotted the ground outside.

"The sun comes to melt the snow in time. Even Sweden cannot deny the power of warmth and light," I said. Then, as they seated themselves: "What would you say if I were nearer to becoming a Catholic than you supposed?"

The Jesuits looked like men raised from the dead. Father Casati ventured his first wide smile, Father Malines stirred in a soft excitement.

"If I were a Catholic, would it not be more advisable to live privately according to the precepts of Rome and to follow externally the religion of my own country? Could not the Pope give me a dispensation to practice my faith secretly and take communion publicly according to the Lutheran rites once a year?"

They were motionless. Father Casati stopped smiling, his face was drawn into the shadow of his seriousness. His voice, not loud but distinct, vibrated my world like a clap of thunder.

"No. The simulation of a false cult is an act fundamentally insulting to God."

I had a moment of dizziness as if I stood on the edge of a precipice. What Swedish King had defied the religion of the people and been allowed to live? The ancient Kings crowded around me, pressed at me, the bloody, the burned, the poisoned. The first Christian King had been burned, King Johan had been smothered by his dream. The Swedes had not changed. The law of the land was inflexible against a conversion in religion, I would be outlawed as if I were dead. No, if I were a Catholic I could not be Queen.

Yet, how could I give it up? It was my life, the one I had been trained to act in, and I liked it. I like the play of politics, the planning, the studying, the exercise of authority. How could I have known that in seeking Truth I would find it lay in another direction, that Truth and the crown were separate goals? They were separate and I must choose. I could not be, like Buridan's ass, starved to death because I was unable to choose between two desirables.

I took a deep breath. Descartes had taught that when one elects to go in one direction one must not give it up because of temporary doubts, one must proceed to the conclusion to be free. I had sought Virtue, now I believed I saw it. I must have the heroism to follow it to the end. My throat was dry and my words seemed to stick in it as I spoke.

"Then there is no help for it. I must resign the crown."

XIV

PULL apart the draperies. Let in the sun. Come on, you bat, no need to tear the silk. Pull gently."

Cool fingers on my wrist, on my brow, pinching my cheeks.

"You see? A little pinkness. She is not dead. She will not die for an elephant's years. If those German doctors will stop bleeding her."

I was riding comfortably. I did not know if I wanted to get out of my carriage. I knew it was the carriage of the dead, I heard the lapping against the wheels, I knew it was sinking into the sound of the endless ocean.

"Breathe. Breathe like the ocean. Slowly, deeply."

We had passed the Greek temples, I had kicked at the stone heads of the judges lying in the ruins, I had seen myself come from behind an Ionic column. I was a spider spinning a web across eternity, an Orion breaking into stars. And I will give him the morning star. I wore it in my forehead. That was the secret.

"The secret."

"She is speaking. What? Damn the dust in these bedcurtains. Who cleans this room? Brush it off my coat."

Someone was humming a tune, it jiggled around me on yellow threads. I knew that tune. Tomasso. Tomasso had sung it. I pushed up my lids to look at it.

"Your Majesty."

It was too much trouble. Who was he? I lay on a cloud, I hid the star. Next time, I would listen to the star next time. I opened my eyes again. The sun slanted across the floor of my room.

"Who are you?"

A head of dark curly hair was almost touching my coverlet. It jerked up from a bow, laughed at me from deep-set eyes. A hand caressed an impudent pointed beard.

"Your Majesty. The Doctor Bourdelot, at your absolute service."

He took a spoon and a bottle of strawberry-colored liquid from an attendant.

"Taste this. I assure you it is delicious. Are you a gourmet of medicines? Yes? No? The medicine should have a slight taste of sweetness, not so sweet as to cling to the roof of the mouth, and it should bring a mysterious remembrance of fruit, the grape, the apple, the wild berry, sometimes a hint of spice, a taste to set the patient to wondering. Do you not agree? Only when the patient has no wish to recover must the medicine be bitter."

"Are you a friend of Tomasso?"

"Swallow. There. Soon you will feel like the lark in spring. Tomasso? Who is he?"

I could not raise my voice. Where was my strength? He bent to my pillow to catch my words.

"Rome," I whispered.

"Rome? Tomasso is a Roman? I have not been to Rome since I refused the Cardinal's hat. It was the late great Barberini Pope, Urban VIII, not the present fellow. It was his wish to keep me in Rome to take care of his health. I am much better than the Italian doctors. But the summer!" He shook his head.

"How did you get here?"

He straightened, and folded his hands, or what could be seen of his hands beneath the dripping lace of his cuffs, over his scarlet waistcoat.

"I flew to you, Madame, on Mercury's feet as soon as I received your command. And just in time. You were in a faint. I have waited six hours for you. Six hours! That shall not happen again, now you have the Doctor Bourdelot. Your Swedish doctors, those German doctors! They would bleed you to death! Blood is what you need, not what you should lose. Fortunately for you, I had brought your order with me, *Attend me at once, Christina*, and I put them out. 'Gentlemen,' I told them, 'Monsieur de Saumaise has sent me to Sweden to cure the Queen, and I am ready to begin.' Fortunately, also, for you, these gentlemen do not like me, so they will not hamper me with advice. Now."

His fingers were on my brow again. The French doctor, the friend of Claude de Saumaise. What had he said of him? That his methods were unique, and marvelously curative, that he was in constant demand by the crowned heads of the world, that it was he who had treated the son of the Prince of Condé when everyone else was baffled because the boy kept jumping onto tables in the belief he was a rabbit. But my sickness was invisible. Oh, there were the visible occurrences, the fainting, the fevers, the pains in my organs. No doctoring, no medicines had been able to cure them, and I knew why. One cannot cure a person who is not there. The sickness was in the root, the invisible, bitter root, and where was the root? Where was I? I was suspended between the person I had been and the person I was to be, I was two persons, I was no person at all. Was I lost or found? Which was my own face? Was I taking off a mask or putting one on?

"Still a fever. Very well. A light diet, mineral water to drink, and baths. A warm bath each afternoon."

"Baths!"

"And my elixir, of course." He held up the strawberry liquid. "The doctor must feed the expectation, Madame. I may seat myself? I am grateful. Madame, a few questions. It is better that we talk alone. I have your permission?"

He signaled the ladies-in-waiting and chamberlain to leave. His questions were tempting, some on my pains, more on my habits and interests and duties, what I thought about them, what I did about them, what I dreamed about them.

"The illness is clear." He stretched, crossed one leg over the other, smiled, more like a companion than a doctor. "It is the digestion."

"My food could not be plainer. I eat little and I drink no wine at all."

"It is your duties you cannot digest. And those volumes." He shook a finger at the pile on the table beside my bed. "Why do you read so much when you already know more than all of Sweden and half of Europe put together? Why worry about competing with Minerva? You are Minerva. Why do you fuss with those quacking geese who call themselves doctors and professors? Professors of what? Of how to play dead while alive? Propounders of the meaningless, the dull, the oversufficient! Professors of the printed fact. What about the facts of living? They are not dull. Let us look at them. That is the food you need, Madame. That is what you have to digest, the delights of living."

I turned my head away from him. Life, that was what I wanted. A horrible tear rolled off my cheek onto the pillow. I had been waiting for a long time. Father Casati had left for Rome with my letter of credence to the new General of his Company, and, unlike Father Macedo, no one had remarked his departure, no one had seemed to care when the elegant Signor, intimating he was bored with the North and preferred to see the rare tulips of Holland, had been driven off in a gilded carriage. I had committed myself to become a Roman Catholic. My decision, now, to give up the throne had to be irrevocable, not like the half-hearted talk I had indulged in previously.

And, as Grotius had said, there must be a freedom to escape to. I had to have a protector, a sponsor. I had wanted Father Malines to accept me as a Catholic, but the priest had demurred, he, he said, not being adequate to approach the Pope, although he would be pleased to bear a letter to Cardinal Chigi, who had demonstrated his enthusiasm in my situation, whenever I wished. But who other than the Pope could receive absolute royalty? I had to enter the Catholic world as a Queen. Surely he understood that. What freedom was there in becoming a beggar? How could I ride away on a tiger in the hope it would be kind?

"You are restless, Madame. Life, I assure you, is not as bad as you may think it is." His hand was on my arm.

I shifted to look at him. He is skillful, I thought, a quick figure of a man who can digest anything, utterly without spleen, sympathetic, experienced. There was a fresh, spiced odor about him that cut into the staleness of the room, and, while he never seemed to be still, lifting his eyebrows or stroking his little dark beard, bending, gesturing, swinging a leg, curving down to pick up a book and flutter its pages or plucking at the gold fringe on the table, there was a pleasantness in his energy that was soothing. He had the balance of a fine ballet.

"Do you know the King of Spain?" I asked.

It was the King of Spain, Philip IV, whom I had selected to be my sponsor, although His Most Catholic Majesty was not yet aware of it. I was waiting for that, too, waiting for the Ambassador the court of Madrid had promised to send, praying he would be clever and amenable to my plans. I had arranged for him by sending a Swedish Ambassador to Madrid to discuss possible trade, carefully choosing, in deference to the Council, a stanch conservative with no ideas beyond commerce. Is there anything worse than waiting, weeks, months, with a secret whose pregnancy insists on growing? Had I talked in my sleep as I tossed in my feverish illness? If my chemise had learned my secret I would have burned it.

"Impossible. I cannot stand the Spanish food. They say he is a great connoisseur of art. Look at the artist he found, Velázquez. Is there a painter in Italy today to equal him? But for literature, for drama, yes, all in all, I shall take, and, Madame, I would give you, the court of France. Mazarin is a true patron of the arts. And the young Louis! What a will of his own! What unconfined appreciation! Have you heard the story of how he laughed so hard at the mime Scaramucci that he wet his little royal pants?"

He was off in a cloud of stories and anecdotes. I found myself listening in spite of my worries, I found myself laughing in spite of the pain in my stomach. Something unlocked within me, something dark and hard slid away. The world was wide and various. Perhaps I could go to the court of France and live a new life. Would God let me live, would He permit me to leave Sweden? Had I not worked hard? Was I not worthy of it? Did not everyone want, at some time, to change his life, to walk away leaving old duties, old habits, old fears and irritations behind, discarding them like worn-out clothes, letting friends and enemies fall away together in a jumble of memories? It is a way of temporarily conquering death, of living twice, an expedient to outwit that judge before whom one always stands as a possible prisoner. It could be the cutting away, at last, of the parental net.

For in the dreams of my fever my father was not dead, my mother not remote. The yellow-haired Gustav Adolf walked with me, counseled me, lovingly trusted me, enfolded me in the comfort of his arms, his flesh so warm, his voice so vibrant, I could not believe the black curtain that fell on him when I awoke, alone and forgotten. Why do the dead forget the living so quickly? It is they who forget us, while we cannot forget them. And while my father walked with me Maria Eleonora beat the air with a stick, calling: *Fix your hair, Christina, lower your voice, wear the purple skirt, not the gray, see that your crown is polished and set straight, and my dew, remember to have my dew brought to me, daughter.* Or she was lost in a world afire and I could not find her, still I heard her calling through the flames, calling to save her for she was wearing her new blue satin gown. I could not escape her voice although I flew with the eagles over the snow mountains.

"I would like to live twice."

"Ah! The appetite begins to return already! Soon you will be like one of Scarron's giant heroes, so hungry you will chew up oxen without bothering to pluck off their plows. But you yawn, Madame. Now you will sleep naturally."

"You may visit me tomorrow, Dr. Bourdelot."

"Tomorrow! Madame, I shall be here this evening and again tomorrow morning. I must watch that you do not wilt, and I myself must administer the doses of my most important prescription." He pointed his forefinger upward in a mock Biblical sign. "A gay life!"

"Dr. Bourdelot."

He jerked up from a deep leave-taking bow.

"I shall not receive the Queen Mother Maria Eleonora while I am indisposed."

"Certainly not, Madame. Your visitors must comply with your cure."

I was able to bear with my mother any time except when I was ill. I could listen, on my perfunctory visits, to her prattle on the morals of a servant, on the puff of a sleeve or the treatment of pimples, on the rose gleam of a pearl or the sweep of a skirt in a curtsy, I could nod my head at her newborn enthusiasm for architecture, bend over her plans of rooms frescoed in the victories of Gustav Adolf, glittering with Venetian chandeliers, floors inlaid with lions and crowns, columns shaped like Kings and angels, beautiful rooms with no doors, carefully guarded by watchtowers with no staircases. Where did the corridors lead to? Why need they go anywhere as long as they were beautiful, more beautiful than the flowering of Eden? I even had persuaded her to return from her flight, when she had slipped away from the gray walls of Gripsholm Castle on a moonless night to a waiting ship sent by the King of Denmark, when she almost had precipitated a war with that jealous country. But when my weaknesses bore into me I could not suffer her pecking, to make her servants respect her, to make the Councillors adopt her plans, to buy her new silk underclothes because her old woolens were a house and garden for lice. She would order her carriage at the first news of my illness and ride to Stockholm Castle to entertain me with her troubles, to hover about my bed in her rustling black gown, and, when I grew faint and fevered, to pray beside me for the dying Queen, to tell me how the people in the streets hid their faces not to see the phantom funeral galloping by, and how the thieves in the King's Garden were fleeing in terror from the specters dancing in the hedges. She would pray for my soul, that these evil specters would not capture it, that I would be saved in spite of my sins. No one had been able to keep her away, to deny her tearful demand to be with her daughter, perhaps for the last time.

Could this smiling Bourdelot keep her out? Easily. He had a thousand excuses ready on his tongue, nor did he hesitate to use my name for any order he wished to give. Why do you weep, he would say, this is not your last visit, the Queen is not going to die, and he would turn away Maria Eleonora or anyone who came in gloom. Gloom and business, both were excluded, secretaries with papers to sign, with petitions to be read, with estimates for State buildings and new roads and statistics on foreign trade, with recommendations to impose taxes or forgive taxes, were turned away. Indigestible, he would exclaim, a pinch of it later would suffice.

The "later" was pushed further and further into the future. There is a great deal to catch up on, a great deal to undo, he would say, when one lets knots and tangles form it takes time to untie them. I did not question his rightness, for he had saved my life, there was no doubt I would have died if he had not arrived at my side, and, for the first time since I was a girl, I felt the flexing of health in my body and the sweetness of sleep for my mind. Somehow it began not to matter who I was or what I was or where I was, it would be a huge joke to be two persons, to be swung between them as between a before and after.

Young people, laughter, music, games, we must have all the healing vanities, and, above all, Truth, Truth in the delight of its deeds, not in the talk about it. Test it, test the talk, Bourdelot urged, and you shall see. So the Dutch envoy Van Breunigen, who claimed he had read every treatise on horses and riding from Xenophon to the present day and argued that, although he never had sat on a horse's back, no horse could resist his knowledge, was

robes he had sent me, to join him at Hanau. What a conquerer he was! Everyone knew it, everyone gathered around to admire him, and the camp behind was full of prisoners, and when I arrived they all were there, the officers, the soldiers, and he in front of them like a god, tall and golden, and for a moment I felt dreadfully sad I could not meet him alone in his tent, to kiss him, it had been so long. Then I stepped forward to him, I was resolved I would possess my own anyway, and I put my arms around his neck before them all. 'Now you are my prisoner,' I said. Yes, that is what I said, 'Now you are my prisoner.' And he laughed and kissed me. Kissed me, as my husband, before them all."

He is not her prisoner now, I thought, and he never was. He is buried safely in Riddarholm, you cannot have his heart, he never gave it to you.

When I did not speak aloud, only staring at her, my mother spoke on a little more nervously.

"Dear Christina, we should speak more of your father. We are the ones who remember him. We are the ones to carry on his beautiful principles."

We should speak of him! The ears of your ladies-in-waiting are worn thin with your ranting, I thought. But I kept silent.

"You remember how wonderful he was about religion, always reading his Bible, always performing his pious duties in dignity. How humble he was before God, our glorious King, how gentle he was, he, the Lion of the North, kneeling down before the divine Lamb of God. Can we do otherwise, Christina? We must be humble before God's Word, we must accept His path for us without thinking of ourselves, we must show our respect for Him and His ministers on earth in every way we can."

I watched her steadily, waiting. The tone of her voice rose, ringing out, thin as a handbell of weak metal.

"You always are talking about reason, why do you not listen to God's reason? Why do you not listen to the preacher? Taking your dog to church! Wearing that old gray skirt! What an example for a Queen to set! Leaning over the back of your chair, twiddling with that silly spaniel's floppy ears when the preacher is giving you the Word of God! What will the preacher think? What does God think? Oh, I knew nothing good would come of all that studying you did as a child! Why would you never listen to me then? And now! You think you know everything, you are sick of what you have done, you must go to the opposite extreme. You think of nothing but of having a good time. But—" she softened to a cooing—"I realize it is not your fault, Christina. It is that cheap barber Bourdelot. Why do you allow him at court? Why do you listen to him? You ought to know what everyone is saying. Everyone says it is an outrage. He is a horrible quack. An ambitious Frenchman. Melons and ices! What decent doctor ever prescribed such things for a delicate stomach! He will kill you! What hold does this man have over you? How can he make you forget your royal responsibilities? Christina, listen to me, you are too innocent to recognize these things. This Bourdelot is a vulgar seducer. He will ruin you, and he will ruin Sweden, too."

She had my complete, cold attention. Her voice rose again.

"Christina, you must attend to me. You must! I am going to die. I know I am going to die."

The pale thread of her mouth wavered. Her gold rings made a scratching sound on the arms of her chair as her hands slid along them, gripping them as if she could hold herself back from Death, as if Death were there, trying to pull her away. Her eyes widened, the darknesses of the night streaming into them.

"I have seen the White Lady. She came into my bedchamber in the hours before dawn, her gown as white as her marble face, her hair blowing in a silver wind that moved with her, her feet walking insensibly on the cold snow. The candles flickered out as she parted my curtains. She raised her hand high above her, her fingers outspread, and they blackened out the moon. Oh, do not push away the moon, not yet, I wanted to cry, but my speech caught in my throat and would not sound. Then, from without, came the plaint of an unnatural bird circling the castle. What is it, what is it, I asked of my heart, is it an eagle lost, a pigeon in the talons of an owl, a great nighthawk? No, no, my heart answered, it is Death winging around me, Death that will fly through my window regardless of bolts and shutters, to bear me away, helpless, Death, of whom the White Lady has come to give warning. Go away, I begged her, go away! I threw my jewels at her, but she did not pick them up, they rolled away on the floor. She did not speak, but I knew her answer, that I was the only jewel she came for, that I was to be Death's jewel."

She paused. The draperies at the window behind her stirred as the wind found its way through some crack in the frame.

"Why do you not speak, Christina? Why do you look at me with eyes of blue ice? Your eyes are as blue and as cold as the White Lady's– Oh!"

Her words dropped away from her. Did she believe I was the White Lady? She looked around the room, as if to see that it still was there, cleared her throat of the whisper of Death.

"Listen, Christina, listen. I am going to die, but what you are doing is worse than dying. You must not ruin yourself with this terrible man. You must send him away, you must not let him take you from God. You must obey God. You must listen to Him. You must listen to His words in church, you must remember the preacher is not your servant, he is the messenger of God, his serman is the message of God for your good. What will you do when the Day of Judgment comes–"

I interrupted her.

"Leave these matters to the clergy, my dear mother. I know very well who has sent you, and I will give them good reason to regret their interference."

Her breath seemed to stop, her eyes glazed with an uncomprehending astonishment. Understanding is impossible for her, I thought. When breath flooded again into her body it came as a long sob shuddering up through her bones, rushed on by the lavish tears that surged out and streaked down her cheeks. She put her palms against her eyes as if to catch the precious pain that should not be loosened to the world. Now she acts the child, I mused, the beseeching child, while I am the parent, the sovereign. I waited for her to control herself, but she had no spirit to do so, her sobs swelling, her weeping growing more and more fluent, spilling through her fingers onto the stiff silk of her dress. I had listened to her, I had humored her. I rose, turned my back, and walked from the room.

I was more shaken than I could admit. I sat in my library, my elbows on the table, my chin in my fists. A book lay open before me. I did not see the pages, I did not know what it was. The ones who had sent my mother as their emissary, the clergy and the nobles who backed them, would not stop with this attempted scolding. I recognized the threat of a campaign against Bourdelot, perhaps against me. They would shave away any Catholic, any non-Lutheran, who had the audacity to be near me. Yet it was not this that deeply disturbed me, for I had beaten the nobles before and I could do so again, if, that is, my Catholic sympathies were not discovered. Only that would keep the people from being wholeheartedly on my side.

The bafflement, the irritation I could not rid myself of, seemed to stem from something Bourdelot had said. How could he imply, even jokingly, that I could be jealous of my mother, of the silly weak weeping woman I had just seen? She hated me, she always had hated me, but one is not jealous of hate. How would it have been different if she had loved me? Of what value is the love of a foolish person? Does a fool know how to love? That was not love, that chattering emotion, that dripping talk of kisses and prisoners. Love is profound, shy, common, yes, but rare in announcing. It is seen as wild marigolds among importunities, felt as the spoon bringing life to one's lips, heard as the cathedral bell bursting one's heart with its ringing. She could not yoke the glorious Gustav Adolf with her flimsy tinsel. Her tale of love was a fantasy, it was not the Truth. I knew, for I was his seed, the heiress of his being. The seed being placed, by chance, in her womb had not precluded our being strangers. He had to put it somewhere.

The shadows of the room were lengthening, engulfing me. A knocking on the door and the man who came in wakened me from my lethargy, Poissonnet, with a taper to light the candelabra, his sharp nose catching the patina of the yellow flame. Bourdelot, he said, was waiting to attend me. Bourdelot. I had forgotten the appointment. I stretched to throw off my mood. Let him come in.

Bourdelot flurried in, his eyes alight, his mouth in its usual curve of a smile. What had been the importance that had pressed my mother to see me?

"You," I said.

He did not lose his smile. Rather, it widened.

"Then she is alert to the delicious difference in the court! I hope, Madame, you have converted her to the necessity of pleasure?"

"My pleasures never could be her pleasures, nor hers mine. Moreover, she did not come for herself. She was an emissary. From the clergy."

"A weathervane! And how does the wind blow?"

"They say it is from heaven. But where is heaven? They point to the North. I know, like you, Bourdelot, that heaven's winds blow from the South."

He looked at me, his head cocked like a bird, not certain of my meaning.

"I mean, Sir, that I intend to become a Catholic."

Bourdelot burst out that it was a marvelous thing, and how had it happened, as he could not remember talking much of religion, having come to Sweden to cure me of my physical ills, not my spiritual, although, as the great Descartes had said, the health of the body follows the mind. He was astonished when I told him I had made my decision before his arrival, that I, a woman, had been able to keep such a secret.

"Marvelous! Marvelous!" he kept repeating. "For thirty years the Church sought to win the North by war. Now, in one stroke of peace, Sweden is hers!"

I corrected him. "Not Sweden. Sweden never will be a Catholic country. Not in our lifetimes, as least. It is I, alone. And if it were known, I would lose my crown, my revenues, perhaps my life."

"Ah!" He laughed, seemingly in spite of himself. "The Church came to conquer a country, and she has conquered a woman."

"I was not conquered. I converted myself."

"So you must believe," he said. "So you must believe."

And now, I told him, I must find a place, a country, a city, a palace, to which I could retire when the time came for me to leave Sweden. Implicit in my decision to be a Catholic was the compulsion to abdicate, and I could not ride away without a destination. I did not intend to be a martyr. Between us we agreed that France was the obvious home for an intelligent person, that Paris was the hub of the cultural universe, and that Bourdelot should proceed there to make inquiries on my establishing residence. I promised to satisfy his curiosity as to how such a remarkable conversion had come about when the time was more fitting, when there were no suspicions to allay, no walls that might be listening for my doom.

Not long afterward Bourdelot left the country, while I, true to my word to my mother, severely reprimanded her clerical friends that they should discriminate against a doctor who had saved my life and done them no harm. Reluctantly they offered the apologies I demanded, even while they could not suppress their gratification that he was gone.

I did not care, for my plans, at last, began to fill into the shape I had cast for them. A letter, of interest more than of aid, had come from Rome from a Lucas Holstenius, librarian of the famous Vatican Library, who, he related, had the inspiration to initiate a correspondence with the renowned Queen of Sweden because of a musician in Rome, one Tomasso, with whom he had had some conversation one day in St. Peter's Cathedral. And, most important, the Ambassador from Spain had arrived in Stockholm.

His Majesty Philip IV sent as his representative a distinguished nobleman from León, Don Antonio Pimentel, an experienced soldier rather than a diplomat, who, nonetheless, conveyed a charm in his bearing and in his language that had not been matched by any diplomat I knew. On the day he was presented to me he bowed deeply and retreated without uttering a word in answer to my greeting, explaining later that he had been too impressed, too overcome, on beholding the great Queen of the North, the brilliant Queen Christina in person, to control his speech, that his tongue had turned to jelly.

I, for my part, regarded closely the man whom I had chosen unseen to be my deliverer. He was darker, more olive-skinned than the Italians, and taller, a noble figure, his eyes assessing and intelligent, his full mouth molded with pride, his curling mustache carefully brushed. In clothes his taste was French, and the Swedish courtiers stared to see his bountifully ribboned breeches, his low shoes with red heels and bright butterfly bows, and his beaver hat waving orange plumes. His age I could not guess, not young, but not old, his years masked behind his courtliness, and he had that peculiar restraint which is fascinating to women. If I had not been Queen, I promptly would have fallen in love with him.

I knew better than to think of love in connection with myself, and during the more than a year that Pimentel graced my court, I took care not to misinterpret his compliments. I must admit there were difficult moments, for he is the kind of man who conveys a feeling of intimacy, not so much through his conversation, which is lively and civil, as in the brooding sympathy of his black eyes, in the measured understanding of his touch, and, when I shared the secret of my conversion with him, in his passionate interest in the path my spirit had to follow. As a soldier accustomed to activity, he saw no reason I should dawdle on the road to Rome, and he went vigorously to work with me on my scheme. That it took so long was not due to any lack of effort on our part. It was fortune, tripped, as usual, by circumstance.

First we dispatched the patient Father Malines to Rome with a sheaf of letters: one for Cardinal Chigi, who had sent him; one, on the advice of Pimentel that the Pontifical nephew always is the door to the Pope, to the nephew of His Holiness, Cardinal Panfilo; and one to Father Nikel, who had succeeded as General of the Jesuits. After Rome, Father Malines was to go to Spain with a letter for Philip IV asking his protection, and another for an influential friend of Pimentel, Don Lewes de Aro, to make certain of the King's good reading of the letter. Then, after months of nervous waiting, we decided Pimentel in person would be my strongest support at the court of Madrid to give credit to the letters and solicit the effecting of their contents, so he sailed for Spain.

He was back in Stockholm in an incredibly short time. A leak in the ship, and the captain had sailed straight back to his home harbor. By another ship from Germany came a message from Father Malines. He had delivered my letter to Cardinal Chigi, had gone to Madrid and waited in vain for Pimentel until his superiors had recalled him to Rome. He had, however, he assured me, faithfully seen that the letters we had entrusted to him reached the hands for which they were intended. By the same ship came an answer to those letters, a shocking answer. It was written to Pimentel. If the Queen of Sweden, argued the King of Spain, has the wish to be a convert to the Roman Catholic faith, why has she not the sense to stay on her throne? How else could she add advantage and glory to the Church? And remember, he added, that she is a woman and apt to change her mind. All women are inconstant. He did not want to sponsor such a risk.

Inconstant! My fury need not be described. Pimentel rewrote his letter to His Majesty, stressing the masculine and determined quality of my mind and detailing the laws of Sweden making it impossible for me to retain the throne, and sent them off with a Dominican priest, a Father Guemes, who, as chaplain to the Spanish Ambassador to Denmark, had been by a lucky accident on the same leaky ship as Pimentel, and had been waiting in Sweden for a new passage to Spain.

Pimentel stayed at my side to assist me in another unexpected blow. Cardinal Chigi wrote to him advising that the Queen not

PS 2954 .O5 1987

Stowe, Harriet Beecher, 1811-1896.

Oldtown Folks

visit Rome at the present, that Her Majesty had best wait for better times, until, specifically, such a woman of greed and ambition as Olimpia was no longer in power. The Pope's sister, unfortunately, would set too bad an example to the new royal convert.

"He means I must wait until the Pope dies!" I was aghast.

Yes, that was what he probably meant, Pimentel agreed. But I could find comfort in that the Pope was an aging man, he could not last very long.

"How do we know he will not be a Methuselah with all the doctors in Rome striving to keep him alive?"

Well, said Pimentel, Cardinal Chigi was not the only one able to notify the Pope. He was certain that His Majesty Philip IV would be favorably disposed to approach His Holiness as my sponsor after receiving his new letters. We only had to wait.

That winter of waiting moved with exasperating slowness, when it moved at all, along its frozen path. I wondered if the sun ever would break out of its ice horizon and rise for me. Whips were useless in my hands, for one cannot strike at the sun, nor at a King of whom one asks a bounty, and what else, who else, was there? I went through my duties heartlessly, but adequately, attending meetings, reading and signing papers, appearing at holiday functions and ceremonies of orphan homes and whatnot, everything as regularly as possible, and every day and night I seemed to hear iron shutters clanging, open, shut, open, shut. The situation could not last forever. Some day the shutters would clang shut and I would be inside, never to escape.

Still, apprehensive as I was, I hardly was prepared for the tidbit Poissonnet brought me one day toward the opening of spring. He rather relished it as a joke, and told it as one, that the fine, the elegant, the high-talking Italian gentlemen who had visited my court were not gentlemen at all. They were Jesuit priests. I was horrified. Why was such a thing believed, I asked. Why, he said, a letter between them had been intercepted, from a Father Casati in Rome to a Father Malines in Stockholm. Probably they had been trying to catch that other one who had fled in Sweden, perhaps they thought he was in this cold country yet, although he himself could not think it. Probably, perhaps, I said, and I sent him for Pimentel. How long had this been known and nothing said? What trap was being prepared for me?

Pimentel had to leave at once, he had, for the sake of God, to go to Madrid and arrange matters with the King. I could wait no longer, I, too, would have to leave as soon and as best I could.

He did go, and Poissonnet, as well, I sent off, with my books and paintings, to Flanders, saying the books had to be rebound and the paintings to be framed. Then I prepared my own way.

This time I could not fail. The Council must accept my abdication, they must arrange an income for my lifetime, not much to ask for a successful Queen. I planned the reasons I would give: that a man should rule Sweden and produce the heirs they wanted, that I never would marry, and, in case they worried that I would relent, I absolutely did not wish to have children, that my desire was to retire to a private life to study, and that certain feminine illnesses from which I suffered made it necessary to go at once to the baths at the Spa in the Low Countries. I would be firm about it, and, to make sure of its acceptance, I would preface the meeting with a private interview with Axel Oxenstierna so that he would not surprise me with a protest as he had before.

The Council, when I met with them and announced I was not asking permission for this act, that a decision had been made that would not be retracted, did not mistake my solid intention. They accepted, in the quietude of a May morning, the fact of my abdication, almost silently. Oxenstierna, in our private meeting, had not been so silent.

Oxenstierna was an old man. For the past year I had expected him, daily, to send word that he could work no more. Gaunt, blue-veined, white-haired, refusing to wear a wig or give in to any move in fashion, his black velvet cap and simple black coat advertised as telling a contrast to Pimentel's colorful fashions as his changeless character. It was almost pain to watch him rise from a chair, to complete the feat of calling his bones to order and testing their steadiness. He had participated in three reigns, two of them from beginning to end, and now I was to tell him he would witness a fourth.

I sat with my back to the window in the reception room of my apartment and waited until the Chancellor had seated himself in an oaken armchair, facing the light, before opening the conversation. I began with the condition of the State finances, a subject dear to his heart and, at the moment, to mine, listened to his habitual declaration that the coffers were depleted and the inference that I gave away money out of all proportion to what there was to give, and I answered, as was my custom, that a Queen had to be liberal, that one might give reindeer antlers to a foreigner as a curiosity, but land, golden chains and medals, or the coin of the realm were the only presents worthy of royalty, that the wealthy owe their money to the poor, as the poor owed their labor to the rich. Then I said that, since the treasury was low, it would be better not to take a large sum of money but to arrange for the income of various territories for my settlement.

"Settlement?" His gray eyes, I saw, had not lost their keenness.

"Certainly I do not wish to ask the new King for an income after my abdication."

He gazed at me in the pause. I hurried on.

"We must set the date of the ceremony for as soon as possible. I am not well. I need a rest. I shall go to the Spa in the Low Countries for the spring cure."

"Your Majesty, I will not deny that I have heard some talk of this. I shall repeat to you a story the English Ambassador, Mr. Whitelock, told to me, about an old man who decided to retire from duty and give his properties to his oldest son. When he did so, and the son asked him to sit in the kitchen during the celebration because of his vulgar habits, he revoked his decision, saying he was resolved to spit in the parlor as long as he lived. And so, Your Majesty, will a wise young lady."

"Not this time, My Lord."

He spoke then with a hue of his former eloquence, of the glory and achievements of my father, of the large and mighty Kingdom Sweden had become, of the Vasas whom Almighty God had chosen to rule, of the fidelity of the nobles who had preserved the State while I was in tender years, of the necessity of sacrifices for Kings, of the oath of allegiance the people had taken to me and the one I had given them.

"I shall release them from this oath, and they must release me. I shall ask them to give their allegiance to Carl Gustav, as I ask you."

He sighed. "I always shall give my allegiance to the King of Sweden. Your Majesty, will nothing make you change your mind?"

I stubbornly listed my reasons. He leaned back in his chair, closing his eyes. When I had finished he lifted their grayness to me again.

"I shall have nothing to do with it."

I hurried on. I would settle my residence when I returned from the Spa and had the health to consider where to live privately for my studying. My choice was the castle on the Island of Öland, a pretty place, with a large park for deer.

"And the Jesuits?"

I stopped, appalled. I had relaxed my anticipation of discovery, and my heart beat maddeningly.

"What Jesuits?"

"The Italian gentlemen who accompanied Baron Rosenhane to Stockholm. Your clever little French valet must have told you that a letter we intercepted from Rome clearly proved the two to be Jesuit priests with a mission here."

"Perhaps they came to find the Portuguese Jesuit who disappeared."

"A Jesuit in a foreign country could have no purpose other than intended conversions. Can Your Majesty tell me if it was disclosed during the conversations with these men whether or not their mission was successful?"

I looked straight at him. "No, I cannot, nor can I understand,

My Lord, why you propose the subject at this time. My necessity now is to hear that you will support my abdication and my settlement."

"I shall have nothing to do with it, Your Majesty," he repeated, "but I shall not stand in your way."

With his consent came an inexplicable sense that Oxenstierna knew everything. Worse, that with his knowledge of my character, it was he who had tipped my thinking in the direction of abdicating. In spite of the stiffness of his exterior bearing, there was no more subtle mind, no more persistent schemer in the world I knew. Had it been he who planned I should leave the throne, or had it been I? He had not once inquired why I wished to abdicate, it was I who rushed my reasons at him. Why had he not come to me immediately on learning of the Jesuits' identity?

Ten years, I had reigned ten years, without a blemish. But what would be done to my reputation when I was gone, when I was not here to deny rumors and accusations? I would be hated thoroughly when it was known I had left the Lutheran courtyard. Nor could I comfort myself that the religion to which I pledged my soul would give me a complete love. Are converts ever fully trusted?

I managed some words to express a gratitude for his years of service as Chancellor during my reign. Then, as I rose, Oxenstierna, laboriously, like a tree leaning on its bent branches after a storm, rose with me, to leave. There were no questions in his eyes. He pulled up his frame and faced me as for a final farewell, his voice heavy.

"You are Gustav Adolf's daughter. You will regret this."

And he turned away.

There was the abdication ceremony to be gone through, so like the coronation, then I found myself sitting, again, with my tenacious cousin. The end of the picture had come. We were in the Great Hall of the Vasa Castle in Uppsala, seated at our banquet table, facing the banqueters, the feasting nobles and ladies of the court, the candelabra on the tables curiously lighting their chewing, their leaning, and their talking, dazzling the silver of their wine cups. And I was acutely aware of Carl Gustav beside me.

He could not conceal his happiness, drinking goblet after goblet of wine, his mustache greasy from the fowl he had enjoyed, his hair mussed as he nervously ran his hand through it, some of the brown locks dripping onto his forehead as in his lost boyhood. A few wine spots already blurred the elegance of his embroidered suit, and how the gilded buttons shone and shook as he laughed, stepping up and over the hill of his belly. Why should he not be happy? For me it was an abdication, for him a coronation. Two hours after my abdication ceremony in that ancient red Vasa Castle, he was crowned, very quietly, in Uppsala Cathedral. The gods would not be tempted this time by a crowning in Stockholm.

I sat, carefully boisterous in my manner, beside the new King of Sweden. I had discarded my state gown of gold and jewels, I had thrown off my majestic robe of purple, and wore an unadorned garment of white silk. I drank no wine, I had no taste for the meat and pasty dishes, only for the fruit brought from the South. The hall was unbearably stuffy, reeking with wine and perfume and the body sweat of the crowding celebrators, all the windows closed because of a dismal blowing rain. It was early June, the fourth day, now the night, to be exact, in 1654.

In talking to me Carl Gustav was so seriously polite he bordered on being obsequious, but when his head was turned to a friend or pretty lady I noticed he could not resist a smile or a rumble of a laugh. Now he was telling me about the twelve ships he was having outfitted for me for a passage to Wismar. I had announced I would take a holiday in Holland at the Spa to recuperate my health, and it seemed a decided pleasure for him to arrange for my leaving. He described the apartments, the furnishings and decorations he had ordered for me on the vessel, he spoke of the riggings and fittings, of the masts and sails, he lingered over the details he loved, the mahogany rails, the teakwood decks, the cut of the prow, the angle of lean in the wind. It made him yearn for the sea to talk of it, he said, until he wished he were going with me.

I hate the sea. It is the land that is beginning to flower with man's reason, the beautiful land, and the jealous sea, the hungry sea that would swallow the world if it could, never ceases gnawing at it, biting away its rocks and sand. The sea is just one gray splash after another, a meaningless width moving, rolling, sighing, a gigantic, uneasily dreaming stone. I cannot comprehend how the seamen endure it day after day, month after month. When they come back from a voyage, salt in their hair and in their glance, they are more sea-trolls than men, they have cut their affinity with the earth, they have been to nowhere and back.

I remember when I first was shown a compass and watched the needle trembling because it could not point away from the magnetic mountain far in the North, trembling because it was a bit of iron, I was told, and the magnetic mountain drew all iron toward it, even big ships, yes, the ships had to be careful not to be drawn too close else they would fall into pieces as their nails and ironwork pulled away to speed northward to the unseen mountain. Never shall I sail on a ship, I swore! And those seas in the North, I was told, were the haunt of sea monsters with heads as large as the ship itself, monsters that vaulted out of the water and onto a vessel to drag it down to archaic depths, they were the haunt of sea owls, half fish, half bird, that raised their enormous beaks to hack at the deck and destroy it. Who wants the sea may have it, not I! I like something I can strike at, something I can take hold of, with hand or mind. The sea is unknown, it is evil, deceptive, sickeningly unsolid and cold, it is a vaporous floor frothing in fantails and ferns and feathered foam.

"Christina!" The quality of Carl Gustav's voice rasped as if he had been speaking the name again and again. He was holding toward me a cloth to dry my fingers. I had been dipping them insensibly in the bowl of water at my place, the bowl with its miniature ocean.

"The venison was sticky, but how delicious!" He bared his teeth in a grin of polite delight. "May I give you this?"

I looked at him, I looked at the cloth, and suddenly I began to laugh, throwing back my head, letting the sound come out in deep rolls. Was this what he had to give me, was this all, this scrap of linen, this menial smirk, when I had given him a Kingdom, when I had bestowed eternal divinity on him? But as I laughed I felt tears smarting at the rims of my eyes. These laden tables, this high-beamed hall, this ancient castle were mine no longer. Carl Gustav was King, was host, I was the guest, I who had been born to own it all.

I pushed my chair from the table, rose, and, without looking again at the new King, I hurried from the banquet hall. I ran through the anteroom, down the stone stairs, out of the castle. I could not stay there, oh, I could not! My horse, where was my horse? I commanded the guard. He gave me a startled, utterly stupid look. My horse! My horse! My voice burst into a fury. The rain? he stuttered. Bother the rain, you idiot! Then somehow I was in my saddle, riding out of King Johan's gates.

I took the road to Stockholm, my horse plunging through a heavy curtain of rain that neither lifted nor receded, slopping through mud, sliding, pulling up in a jerk as thunder snapped at us or lightning crashed branches across the road. The Lapps have uncorked their witchcraft tonight, I thought, but I defy them, I defy them all to stop me! I passed the familiar farm buildings, the churches and bell towers, that now were only darker blots in the darkness around me, pricked my horse past the emptiness of fields and whistling bending trees. If we had not known this road so well, my horse and I, we could not have found our way through that driving rain.

When my horse began to pant in his constant effort and the froth of his sweat mingled with the matting of the rain, I slowed him to a walk, patted his neck, and bent forward to reward him with friendly words, for he, at least, was left to obey me in a world of shifting waters. He half turned his head around and perked his ears. He heard more than my voice. I listened, too. Behind us, pounding against the rushing sound of the rain, were horses' hoofs, many horses. I could not think who or what it might be, but we were off again in a gallop. My horse's freshness was worn, and my pursuers, for pursuers they proved to be, gained on me until I heard their cries of wait, wait, stop, stop!

I reined in beside a humble stone church where there was a flat clearing and waited. A wind rising from the North began to push away the storm clouds and scatter the ferocity of the rain, letting a silvery evening light emerge, and I could recognize the riders as they caught up to me. The first was Carl Gustav, and, close on him, many of the young nobles who had been my friends.

"Go back! Go back! Why do you follow me?" I implored.

More men came up, the hardier of the older nobles, and young and old dismounted, approached me, formed a circle around my horse.

Carl Gustav stretched out his hand. "Christina, why must you leave like this?"

As he spoke, carriages rattled up, doors creaked open, and the brocaded ladies of the court stepped out and hurried to the circle, murmuring to one another, sending their anxious glances toward me. Why, the sweets had not even been served, I heard one say, while a pucker-mouthed old countess admonished that I would be ill of the rain. What is it, they asked, what is it?

Had all of the banquet migrated to me? What would I say to them? What was there to say? They had to go back, they had to leave me alone.

One of the men came forward, Per Brahe, he to whom I had handed the crown when I had lifted it from my head.

"Do not hurry away thus from Uppsala, Your Majesty, from your friends, your countrymen. We beg the honor of your presence with us."

I could not stop the tears from streaming down my face. What did they know, what did they understand of me? From my mount I looked down at the bewildered faces surrounding me. I had to say something, yet the tears flowed faster, try as I would to check them. When the words came they were unplanned pressured words, sharply true, words that came of their own and flew off my tongue.

"I have governed here for many years. Would you have me stay to see another in possession of the power which so lately belonged to me?"

What answer could be made? Everyone there had felt the troubles and the glory of my ten-year reign. I was looked at in silence.

"It is you who must go back, you who must finish your banqueting. You have a coronation to celebrate. I do not. I go to Stockholm. When your celebrating is over we shall meet there."

Carl Gustav walked toward me, raising his arms as if he would assist me from my horse in spite of what I had said.

"No! No!" I turned my horse's head to move through the crowd and be off, on my way to Stockholm. I could not risk what he might say. Emboldened by his crown, he might humiliate me by proposing marriage, once more, at this emotional moment, in front of everyone. At the hint that I regretted losing my place on the throne, he might offer to share it with me. And so I repulsed him, hardly glancing in his direction.

He dropped his arms, said no more, only gazed wonderingly, his hat in his hand, his hair dripping drops of water onto his fine suit.

I wish I could say that I galloped off then amid a hushed reverence, that not another word was spoken except by the wind, that my horse lifted his silver hoofs and flew off with me in a poetry of flight. But Truth, deep and dramatic as it is in its secret places, seldom allows for a clear heroic instance on the surface, becoming spattered with a multitude of banalities so that one cannot do what one would like to be seen to do.

It was the women. The men became properly abashed by my manner, but the women refused. Other things were more important than heroics—my wet clothes, my rain-soaked hair, the possibility of pleurisy, the night air, my tired horse, my aloneness, a hundred confoundingly practical details were pleaded, insisted upon. Led by that beautiful and determined young countess Ebba Sparre, who placed herself in front of my horse in a low curtsy as I would have passed through my pursuers, they presented such arguments that I found myself persuaded to dismount and continue in a carriage, wrapped in a dry cloak. I did, however, go on to Stockholm while they all returned to their banqueting in Uppsala, and, save for the driver and footmen, I went alone.

XV

AND so I freed myself, or was freed, from the throne of Sweden. What more is there to say? Very little.

After the abdication I was in a rage to leave the country. It had become too late to go to the Spa in the Low Countries for the spring cure, so I pretended my destination was the restful confines of the castle on the Island of Öland, the retreat which, it was agreed, was to belong to me. Five days after I lifted my crown from my head at Uppsala, I left Stockholm. Many of my young friends accompanied me, nor did I stop the rush of nobles who felt their presence was necessary to honor the departing Queen. At three hours after sunset, cloaked by nightfall, not to see the affection and tears of the simple people who stood, immovable and mute, from the castle wall to the gates of the city, who, of all in Sweden, perhaps in the world, loved me with their hearts and not their ambitions, I rode out of the clumsily sculptured portals of Stockholm Castle and across the bridge, followed by a long line of carriages. The clatter of wheels and hoofs on the planks were muted by the cannons at the fort and the warships in the harbor, discharging the royal salute, so that we seemed a ghostly procession. I did not look back to see the City between the Bridges, the towers, the roof peaks, the spires reaching above the crude timber into the starlight, the cold Viking starlight.

That night we rode without stopping, and the next day, as well, until in the evening we pulled into the courtyard of Nyköping Castle, where I paused long enough to say good-by to my weeping mother. Then on, for I would not stay the night, I could not rest. For days I hardly slept, driving past fir trees, white birches, hardy oaks, and turfed huts, driving west and south, ostensibly toward Öland, my object, of course, the Danish border. I had a terrible feeling of being pursued, almost the sense of panic of the dream where, run as one may, one cannot outdistance the arms of a lumbering bear.

I was punished for my haste by a stitch in my breast, which turned out to be pleurisy, and we were forced to stop some miles beyond Jonköping at the manor of a private Swedish gentleman named Giornonotte, where I was eight days in recovering. Here my pursuers, for pursuers there certainly were, dispatched by the new King, caught up with me. He had sent the officers of the realm and a Lutheran cleric, named Brodin, to wait on me to the castle in Öland, to see, I thought, that I would be properly installed in my island prison. Baron Lind, Councillor of State for Carl Gustav, brought me the royal message that His Majesty repeated the offer of his hand, and that the twelve gala ships he had prepared for me were waiting at Kalmar to take me to Öland.

My reply was tart. If I had been inclined to marry, I said, I would have done so while I was Queen. His Majesty wished to avail himself of my experience and wisdom, persisted the Baron. You may tell him I know he is prudent enough not to need my counsel, I said, and, as to the ships, the winds were not favorable, so I preferred a pleasurable trip by land. In truth, I went on, the time was opportune to journey to Hamburg to find a princess for the King, I had given him a Kingdom, now I would give him a wife. The Baron pushed his suit no further.

For two days' travel beyond Giornonotte's manor I bore with my splendid entourage, then, on arriving at Halmstad, I dismissed them, all but five young nobles and three grooms, directing about fifty of the suite to meet us in Hamburg in six weeks' time. The rest, the officers and the Lutheran cleric included, rode back into the heart of Sweden, leaving me within walking distance of the border.

The border! All preparation is for this, I mused, that one comes to a border and crosses it. A man may become another man, may become a deer, a laurel, a snail, he may become a god, if he learns how to cross the border and does it, if he crosses it, although it seems invisible. A border is the signal for change, of transfiguration, it is the meeting of limits. A border is an absolute. Yes, the idea of a border interests me, for men always are making borders which God overrides.

At this border I would be free, completely free, I decided. I would be out of my cage, I would be on the road to Rome. I would go to the Pope myself, if no one else would, to receive a grant of residence. And, not to be pursued again on the trip to Hamburg, moreover, not to be flustered by bandits, I would travel in disguise. At Laolm Castle, outside Halmstad, where our party of nine rested our last night in Sweden, I ordered my old chamberlain Johan to get out his scissors and rid me of my thick womanly curls. At first he refused, as if my power, like Samson's, lay there.

"Cut my hair close, Johan," I urged. "Why should I, who have forgone a throne, sorrow at the loss of my hair?"

And he did, his foolish tears falling with my locks. But he was an old man and knew no better. In the morning, wearing a black wig, I dressed in boy's clothing, in boots and breeches and jacket, slung a carbine over one shoulder, and threw a red scarf around my neck in the Spanish style. I would travel as the young Count Donoau. As I practiced pacing up and down in my hunting-boots, which were somewhat too wide for me, the carbine slapping against my side, liking the dramatic swing of masculine attire, I thought how well it fitted my deep voice, my ugly face, my impatient shouts. If only I had been a man instead of a woman like a man!

The moment we reached the Danish border I jumped out of my carriage, joyously stepping on to the fresh ground, prickly with June's green growth, and shouted: "Free at last, and out of a country which I hope never to see again!"

There it was, the border, my border, a silver line, a small stream which had been easily bridged for the road. I saw a hare carelessly dash from one country into another, the sun, for him, shining equally on both sides. I saw how an oak on one side of the line was at the same stage of unfolding its notched leaves as an oak on the other side, how a windmill on the rise ahead looked very much like the windmill we had passed a few minutes before, the dust, the stones, the same, yet I felt the sweet change I could not see.

But was I free, am I free? Perhaps I was during those weeks I swaggered in breeches, when my castle was a commodious wagon and the future a day's sightseeing visit to Frederiksborg or an evening of joking in a hostelry. No past, no future, no present duties. Is that freedom?

Now, in Innsbruck, as I sit at the ebony desk trying to shake from my mind these old dreams of living, I can hear the rain drumming softly at the stones of the palace, brushing plaintively the windowpanes. Yesterday's wind has continued rising until it has torn apart the clouds, pulling them over the mountain peaks, smearing them with gray and spreading them around the city. Everything outside looks gray and cold, the mountains not visible, the view closed in to the trees in the palace park, shaking their damp leaves, and the street beneath, its mud glittering in the beginning shower.

The days have hurried by since I began these pages, crowded with people and entertainments. Mornings Poissonnet comes in with the news from his fellow servants and that from his favorite tavern, The Golden Rose, how the Jesuits and the Franciscans have resolved their claims on my soul by having the ceremony, due today, in the court's Franciscan chapel and the sermon by a Jesuit priest, his text to be: *Give heed, oh my daughter, and incline thine ear, forget thy people and thy father's house*, and he tells me, too, Poissonnet, what the Archduke is fussing about and how the Archduchess will dress on the day's excursion, what Pimentel is doing, and the Pope's Nuncio, Lucas Holstenius. He will not tell me, however, whether the court taster died of poison or apoplexy, whether his soul was snatched by the Devil or gathered by God. I pray in the oratorio of the chapel, and I am entertained, and I am given sumptuous meals, and I watch, in the Great Hall, as viols and lutes and violas da gamba play an enchanting music, pages dance, holding their candles high, while other dancers float down from the ceiling and back again, while Mars and Adonis contend for the love of Venus, Mars in his shining armor, Adonis in his shining flesh. Is this the way Virtue lives in the world, in this mixing of the theater of comedy with the theater of Truth?

It is the nights that have walked slowly on furred feet while I could not sleep, surrounded by the past. Still I am trying to cross the border, still I am waiting, and I wonder that my soul pauses on the threshold. What has happened to my sense of victory, to the elation of my escape?

It could not be because I have lacked homage, for ever since Hamburg, where I became again a skirted Queen, there has been such a continuation of celebrations as would weary the most avid of glory. I can see, even now, the fireworks exploding as I was borne into Brussels on a gilded barge pulled by twelve immense horses, I can see the two angels in burning lights over the city gates holding up the flaming letters of *Christina.* I can hear the cheers and the musket volleys along the way, and the astonished attention to the Lutheran Queen, the Queen of Sweden who had left her throne.

At Brussels, where Pimentel finally arrived with the coveted letter from Philip IV sponsoring my advent into the Roman Church, I professed my new faith in a private ceremony this last Christmas Eve, but in January, when Pope Innocent X gave up his soul to God at the age of eighty-one years, he died unaware of the famous convert, and I was left waiting, waiting, while the Conclave in Rome debated the choice of a new Pope. It was April before the fortuitous selection was made. Cardinal Chigi, he who had sent the Jesuit fathers to me in Sweden, who felt personally the pride for my conversion, became Alexander VII. My future in Rome was assured.

Why, then, this disturbing wonder on my part? Is it because he has insisted that, to live in Rome, I must declare publicly my faith, while I have preferred to worship privately? Today my soul, so long hid, will be a banner before the world, the markings on it plain for all to see. Tomorrow I must write to Carl Gustav to announce my faith, for he, who guarantees my funds, must hear the truth from me.

There is no need to write Oxenstierna, for, two months after my leaving, he, too, left, never to return. He is dead. He died predicting I would repent of what I had done, that I was, none the less, the daughter of the great Gustav. And Carl Gustav as King, who, when only my cousin and a prince, had hated the Oxenstiernas, has taken as his boon adviser his former rival Erik, the Chancellor's son. So does the press of circumstance change a man's prejudices. He is married, now, to the princess I recommended to him, a daughter of the Duke of Holstein-Gottorp, and Sweden has the breeding Queen it wants.

You, Maria Eleonora, whose nervous whispers have harassed me, must be quiet. You are dead, you must stay in your ill-loved Swedish grave. I am going to leave you behind, as I leave behind the faith my father fought and died for, as I abandon Sweden and all its Nordic Kings. Today I shall walk between the Catholic chapel's iron Kings and Queens, I shall become a new Queen among Clovis, King of the Franks, Joan the Mad and Albrecht the Wise, Charles the Bold and Arthur, King of England, Philipp the Benevolent and Frederic the Penniless, Mary of Burgundy, Elizabeth of Hungary, Leopold the Pious, Theoderic, King of Goths. I shall pass by their iron piety, their smoothly combed iron locks, their iron beards and braids and wrinkles, their graceful iron skirts and drooping iron sleeves, their iron eternity. I shall not hesitate, seeing the turbulence of a life left in one iron gesture. I shall profess their faith, I shall join their eternity.

And the words of the Church shall be in my ears, the words, this morning, of the gentle Abbot Dominic Loer, Prelate of Wilten, Order of St. Norbet in Innsbruck, who will be before me at the altar: *O fortunate and most pleasant light radiating Tyrol, today comes a Queen, not from the South but from the North, not to Solomon but to the true light which is Christ. Amazement fills the place.*

The hour has come for me to pray and to prepare for the chapel, to put on my simple black dress and to pin on it, over my heart, the diamond cross. Yet my pilgrimage is not finished. I shall go to Rome, but first, as Descartes in starting his life anew left the books of his past behind by traveling to Loretto, so I, too, shall travel to Loretto to leave my crown on the altar. Then I may find Virtue, as he did.

I lay down my pen this third day of November, 1655.